PRAISE FOR MATT

"Farrell has done it again! A crime thriller that grabs you from page one. Engrossing, haunting, and compelling, *Don't Ever Forget* is his best yet."

—Liv Constantine, internationally bestselling author of *The Last Mrs. Parrish*

"Matthew Farrell has done it again. A tense and twisty thriller, *Don't Ever Forget* grabs you by the throat from the first page and does not let go. The result is an edge-of-your-seat, up-all-night read that packs a final punch you won't soon forget. Fantastic!"

—Danielle Girard, *USA Today* bestselling author

"Take a deep breath now, because once you start, you won't get another chance. *Don't Ever Forget* is a twisty, pulse-pounding read from a writer who has quickly established himself as a can't-miss master of thrills."

—Brad Parks, international bestselling author of *Interference*

"Fans of fast-paced thrillers will be engrossed in this propulsive page-turner that expertly delves into memory, crimes of the past, and terrors that haunt us our whole lives."

—Vanessa Lillie, bestselling author of *Little Voices*

"Matthew Farrell's delicious new thriller is definitive crime fiction: propulsive, compulsive, unputdownable, and, oh yes, unforgettable. Get it now."

—Bryan Gruley, author of *Bleak Harbor*

"Matthew Farrell does it again. He's intricately woven together a diabolical and propulsive story of deception with betrayal and madness. *Don't Ever Forget* is engrossing, jarring, and unpredictable. It kept me on my toes as I journeyed with investigator Susan Adler through a wild maze, stopping at nothing to find the truth. An absolutely thrilling adventure."

—A. F. Brady, author of *The Blind* and *Once a Liar*

"An exciting police procedural . . . The high-energy narrative swerves into surprising and terrifying territory before slamming into its truly chilling finale. Farrell takes the reader down some dark and twisting paths."

—*Publishers Weekly*

"This sinister novel is perfect for suspense junkies who love *Dirty John*."

—Women.com

"Matthew Farrell's skill as a storyteller is evident from the first pages of this novel. He draws readers in, assures them the story will be a typical murder mystery following the usual pattern, then tears up the outline and throws it away."

—New York Journal of Books

"*I Know Everything* takes off like a shot, with a shot, and the pulse-pounding pace never lets up. Fans of John Sandford and Lawrence Block will flock to Matthew Farrell!"

—Wendy Corsi Staub, *New York Times* bestselling author

"Dark and constantly surprising, this is a must-read for fans of twisted, intelligent thrillers."

—Mark Edwards, bestselling author of *The Magpies*

"A page-turner from beginning to end. Take a deep breath and hang on—this relentless thriller will keep you guessing until the very last masterful twist."

—Jennifer Hillier, author of *Jar of Hearts*

"Seriously haunting."

—Betches

"A young crime writer with real talent is a joy to discover, and Matthew Farrell proves he's the real deal in his terrific debut, *What Have You Done*. He explores the dark side of family bonds in this raw, gripping page-turner, with suspense from start to finish. You won't be able to put it down."

—Lisa Scottoline, *New York Times* bestselling author

"A must-read thriller! Intense, suspenseful, and fast paced—I was on the edge of my seat."

—Robert Dugoni, *New York Times* bestselling author

"One hell of a debut thriller. With breakneck pacing and a twisting plot, *What Have You Done* will keep you guessing until its stunning end."

—Eric Rickstad, *New York Times* bestselling author

DON'T EVER FORGET

OTHER TITLES BY MATTHEW FARRELL

What Have You Done

I Know Everything

DON'T EVER FORGET

MATTHEW FARRELL

THOMAS & MERCER

Text copyright © 2020 by Matthew Farrell
All rights reserved.

Published by Thomas & Mercer, Seattle

www.apub.com

Amazon, the Amazon logo, and Thomas & Mercer are trademarks of Amazon.com, Inc., or its affiliates.

ISBN-13: 9781542019767
ISBN-10: 1542019761

Cover design by Rex Bonomelli

Printed in the United States of America

For Mom and Dad:
You're the strongest people I know. I love you.

AUTHOR'S NOTE

Although this book is considered the first in the Adler and Dwyer series, the origins of both main characters can be found in my previous novels. Liam Dwyer is first introduced in *What Have You Done*, and Susan Adler is first introduced in *I Know Everything*. You don't have to have read those books to enjoy this one, but if you find a line or two referencing something from their pasts, chances are it can be found in the books mentioned above.

—MF

1

Her high beams were the only lights guiding Cindy Garland along the Taconic State Parkway. Tree branches hung low over the roadway, and fallen leaves, wet from an earlier rain, made the pavement slick. The clouds hid the moon, plunging her into a darkness so thick it was impossible to see past the first line of elms that flanked both sides of the northbound lane. She was alone on the road, out in the middle of nowhere, the only vehicle in either direction.

Where was he?

Her trembling hands gripped the steering wheel at ten and two. In the glow of her dashboard lights, she could see the blood spatter on her wrists and knuckles. The same knuckles that had knocked on the door. A knock that had been followed by an innocent smile. But then the shouting began. And the crying. And the violence. Nothing had gone like she'd thought it would. Like they'd planned. How could she have been so wrong?

A set of headlights appeared in her rearview mirror, quickly gaining until she had to flip the mirror up to dull the glare. It was him. He'd finally caught up. She stepped on the accelerator and listened as the engine revved, the sudden momentum pushing her back into her seat. The headlights kept pace. She could feel her heart beating in her chest as she rounded a curve in the road and teetered on the brink of losing control.

How fast did he want her to go?

The headlights were only about a car length behind her. She checked the speedometer. Seventy-eight. She couldn't risk going any faster on the twisting mountain roads. Not with the darkness and the slippery leaves and her nerves that still seemed frayed. Why was he going so fast?

Red lights suddenly popped on behind her, and the headlights that had been closing in began flashing strobes. It wasn't him. It was much worse. It was the police.

No.

Cindy pulled off to the shoulder and watched in the rearview mirror as the cruiser stopped inches from her bumper, illuminating the interior of her car with splashes of red and white. There was a moment when she thought about taking off and hoping for the best, but she knew she'd be caught. She didn't know these roads like the cops did, and in her current state, she probably wouldn't get more than a few miles before she ended up in a ditch or wrapped around a tree. She'd just have to play it cool, take ownership of her speeding, and move on. Whatever happened, she'd have to avoid drawing any kind of suspicion. Not with the kind of night she'd had. Not with everything that had gone wrong.

Not with a body in the trunk.

A dark figure exited the cruiser and made his way toward her. Cindy rolled down her window and hid her shaking hands in her lap. The state trooper ducked down and shined a flashlight in her face, then around the interior of the car. He was clean shaven, smooth skin. Couldn't have been more than thirty years old. She could see his name badge on the breast pocket of his uniform.

Kincaid.

"Good evening, ma'am," the trooper said.

Don't panic.

"Hello."

"You know why I pulled you over?"

"Speeding?"

The trooper nodded and pulled the flashlight away. "You can't go eighty on these roads. You'll end up hitching a ride in the back of an ambulance. Or worse. Speed limit's forty-five on this stretch for a reason."

2

"I'm sorry. I didn't know."

"I need to see your license and registration."

Don't panic.

Cindy exhaled slowly. "I can give you my license," she said. "But this is my friend's car. I don't know where the registration is."

"Who does the car belong to?"

"Rebecca Hill. She let me borrow it. I had a date back in Peekskill, and I needed to borrow her car."

"Where are you heading now?"

"Nowhere really. Just driving around. The date didn't go so well."

The trooper turned his flashlight back on and used the beam to point toward the glove compartment. "Check the glove box. I bet the registration's in there. Usually is."

Cindy nodded and unclipped her seat belt. She leaned over to open the glove compartment.

"Ma'am," the trooper said suddenly. "Stop what you're doing."

Cindy froze.

"I'm going to need you to sit back and put your hands on the steering wheel."

"What's the problem?"

"Put your hands on the steering wheel."

The trooper's tone had changed. He was serious now. Anxious. Cindy had done the one thing she'd told herself not to do. For whatever reason, she'd drawn suspicion.

Don't panic.

She slowly placed her hands on the wheel and looked straight ahead.

"Why do you have blood on your hands and pants?"

Tears started to well in Cindy's eyes. The silence stretched between them, raw and unsteady. Nothing had worked like they'd thought it would, and now she was sitting on the side of the road with a cop who was asking about blood on her hands. In a matter of hours, months of meticulous planning had gone to shit.

Don't panic.

She opened her mouth, but nothing emerged. Her hands gripped the wheel tighter as her breath came in short bursts.

"I'm going to need you to step out of the car."

Trooper Kincaid opened Cindy's door and backed away. He kept his flashlight on her until she was out and leaning against the back quarter panel by the gas tank.

"I'm going to ask you again," the trooper said. His voice was stern now. "Why is there blood on your hands and clothes?"

"I—I—"

"Where were you tonight?"

"I told you. On a date. In Peekskill."

"What was your date's name?"

"I don't—"

"Tell me what happened. Was there an accident? Is someone hurt? Did someone try to hurt you?"

Don't panic.

The questions were coming too quickly. Cindy held on to the one she thought she might be able to play with. *Did someone try to hurt you?* Yes, she could tell a convincing story about that. She could blame her date. She could get the trooper on her side and maybe get out of this. She'd fill out a form and leave a fake number and get back on the road. *Did someone try to hurt you? Why, yes. Yes, they did.*

The trooper shined his flashlight down the rear of the car toward the bumper. "Ma'am, you have more spatter on the back of this car. Tell me what's going on right now."

And just like that, her story was useless. There was blood on her hands, on her clothes, and now he'd found some on the car. Too much blood to explain away. It wouldn't be long before he'd discover the body in the trunk, and that would be it. The truth that she'd sought for so long and was so close to obtaining would stay hidden forever.

Don't panic.

The trooper brought his flashlight around and shined it in her face. He grabbed the radio that was fastened to his shoulder. "Ma'am, I'm going to ask you one last time. I need you to focus. What is—"

There was movement in the darkness, away from the flashlight and the pulsing red and white. Before Cindy could register what it was, the flashlight left her face, and the trooper fell to the ground.

He'd caught up to her.

The wet thump of crunching bone and blood echoed in the night as he hunched above the trooper, beating him with something she couldn't make out. The sound made her want to vomit. She watched his arm come up once, twice, three times, then a sickening fourth. It was over in a matter of seconds, and the roadway was, once again, brought to a deafening silence.

He straightened and looked at her, his chest heaving as breath smoked from his lips. She could see now that he was holding a tire iron, the curved end covered in the trooper's blood. She knew there would be bits of skull and brain matter on it if she looked, so she kept her focus up and away, watching as he rushed toward the police cruiser.

The cruiser's engine died, and all the lights went out. As soon as they did, she could see his car parked behind the trooper's, the lights off so they hadn't seen him approaching. He ran back toward her and, without stopping, bent down and dragged the body until it was hidden from the road, next to the patrol car.

Cindy watched it all, frozen in place, unable to move. How could so much go wrong with such a simple plan? Things had spun so completely out of control, and they hadn't even had a chance to get started. They'd murdered two people in one night. How could they ever turn back from what they'd done?

Trevor Foster had saved her from arrest, and at the same time, he'd punched her ticket to hell.

Okay. Panic.

———

She rode with him, but neither of them had spoken since they'd ditched the car with the body in the trunk. Tears streamed down her cheeks as she cried silently in the passenger's seat.

"It's going to be dawn in a few hours," Trevor said, looking out at the road as the radio played quietly in the background. "We should've been back at the house by now. Hagen's going to be contacting us."

"I know."

"Listen." His voice was calm, serious. "If we're going to get through this, you have to be smart. Why were you speeding when you had a stolen car and a body in your trunk?"

"I didn't realize I was going so fast," Cindy choked out through her tears. "When I saw the trooper's headlights, I thought they were yours. I thought you were telling me to hurry up."

"That could've been bad. Real bad." He ran a shaking hand through his hair. "All I want is for us to do what we have to do in order to get out of this mess. I didn't ask to be dragged into a kidnapping, and I sure as hell didn't ask to be part of two murders. I just want my life back, and I can't have you screwing up that chance."

"I'm sorry."

"My wife and my kid are the only priority here. I don't care about the old man or any of this garbage. I want my family returned to me safe, and I want to forget this ever happened. If you get in the way of that, I'll kill you too."

Cindy nodded and looked out the window. She knew he wasn't kidding. No hyperbole. He'd kill her and the rest of them to save his family without a second thought. She would too. If she had any family left.

They were back on the highway now, blending in with a few other cars getting an early start on the day. The sky was beginning to lighten. They'd be at the house by sunrise.

"He saw the blood on my hands and pants," she said. "The car too. I was just going to take the ticket and get moving, but he kept asking me what happened."

"I told you to wash that off."

"I tried. It's not like I could take a shower. We had to get out of there."

"Did he get a look at your license or anything?"

"No, we never got that far."

Trevor nodded. "No doubt he called in his position and your license plate, though. That's standard procedure."

"It doesn't matter," Cindy said. "They won't find the car."

"Doesn't mean they'll stop looking. He had a dashcam. We're on video. Let's just hope there wasn't a clear angle on your face, or this'll be over before it begins."

"A camera?"

"And a cop was killed. They'll hunt like dogs to find us. They'll trace the plate to Rebecca, so they'll start looking for her right away. When they can't find her, they'll start pulling apart her life, and when they come to the old man, they'll know something's wrong. We didn't leave things in the best shape back at his house."

Cindy turned away from the window and stared at him, her eyes wet and swollen. "Then we have to stay hidden until it's done. We can't risk getting caught. If they know who I am, fine. But they'll never find me until it's over. We'll just have to make adjustments on the fly until then."

Trevor sighed, looking out ahead of them. "Okay, but know this: I won't allow any more screwups. We get this done, and we move on. The faster this is over, the better. We stay hidden until we know what the cops know."

"I'm sorry I got you involved."

He nodded slowly, his lips curling back to reveal his oversized, jagged teeth. "Yeah, me too."

2

Officer down.

All hands on deck.

State Police Investigator Susan Adler hopped from her car and made her way over to the crime scene. The mass of emergency vehicles filled both lanes of the northbound Taconic and one lane southbound, closing the parkway until further notice. The morning traffic was being diverted onto local roads and eventually onto Route 9. Normally they'd be looking to clear the scene and get things opened again as soon as possible. But this was a different circumstance, and the investigators involved would take as much time as they needed.

State police, EMT, Fire and Rescue, and uniforms from a few local departments milled about, trying to find something to do to be useful in a situation that was still too new to have a direction to go in. Susan crossed the road and walked toward her boss for an update.

The call had come in about an hour before her alarm was set. Ever since her mother had moved in full-time, it had become an unmentioned tradition for Beatrice to cook the morning meal, but with the twins at their father's, Susan had been planning to sleep in. Instead, she'd grabbed a coffee to go and gotten to the scene as soon as she could. Everything else was put on hold.

Senior Investigator Jasper Crosby, a former college football player and respected supervisor throughout the state, was her mentor as well as one of her best friends. He gave her a quick nod when he saw her and broke away from the crowd he was speaking with.

"Thanks for coming."

Susan looked past her boss and saw a covered body lying next to a patrol car. The forensics team was working on both.

"What happened?"

"Trooper Kincaid called in a routine 10-38. He reported the plate number and proceeded to investigate. No follow-up report after that, and after two location check-ins passed without dispatch hearing from him, they sent another car out. He appears to have been bludgeoned to death in the roadway, then dragged over there. No shots fired from the trooper and no indication that any firearms were used by the perp."

"How long ago was the 10-38 called in?"

"About three hours." Crosby walked her closer to the scene. "The car was registered to a Rebecca Hill. We got her address, and I need you to pay a visit. White Plains PD will be waiting for you when you get there. You go in and grab her. If she's not there, see what you can find. A warrant has already been issued, and a BOLO is being circulated to all area departments."

Crosby handed her a piece of paper with the address on it.

"Be careful."

"I always am."

"I'm serious," Crosby said. "I don't know what this woman is capable of or if she's working with someone, but she's already demonstrated her willingness to kill. Watch your back."

Susan pulled away from the crowd. "Always do, boss. Don't worry."

"You need a partner on this one. Let me see what Chris and Bill are up to."

Susan shook her head. "I said I got it."

Before he could respond, she was jogging toward her car. It looked as though a new homicide investigation had begun.

3

Susan pulled up in front of Rebecca Hill's apartment and saw the two White Plains police officers standing out front with the facilities manager. All three had their backs turned to the cold November wind screaming from west to east.

The apartment building was on Lake Street, just north of downtown. It was a ten-story brick structure that blended in with all the other brick apartment complexes that filled that section of the city. Rebecca lived on the fourth floor. Susan, the two officers, and the super took the elevator.

"We checked the parking lot, the garage, and a five-block radius in all directions," one of the officers said. "No Civic."

"Okay," Susan said. "I'll knock and announce. If she doesn't answer, we go in. Are you guys ready?"

The officers nodded.

They stepped off the elevator and walked down the hall. The facilities manager—Juan, according to the name badge sewn onto his jacket—stayed back by the elevators. Susan stopped in front of a door that was identical to all the others and knocked.

"Rebecca Hill! This is the police. Open the door!"

They waited about ten seconds. Susan put her ear against the door and listened. Nothing. She motioned Juan over, and he pulled a set of keys from his jacket pocket. He slid the key into the lock, opened the door, and moved aside.

The apartment was a one bedroom, neat and decorated simply. White walls, beige carpet, beige tiles in the hallway and kitchen, furniture from IKEA. Nothing that screamed originality or wealth, but it held a warmth, nonetheless.

Susan and her backup quickly swept the place, moving from room to room, weapons drawn, focused.

It was empty.

"Glove up," Susan said. "Let's see what we can find."

"Ten-four."

Juan remained in the hall while the two officers retreated toward the entryway, allowing Susan to walk around. She put on her latex gloves as she looked at the pictures displayed throughout the space: friends, family, no sign of a husband or significant other. No kids. She picked up a framed photograph of an older woman, frail and thin, and figured it to be the mother or an aunt. Another frame held a photo of the same woman featured in other pictures around the place. Susan figured that was Rebecca. She was with a younger man, sitting together on a picnic table bench, arms around each other, smiling. The engraving on the frame read *Brothers & Sisters: A Special Bond.*

"Looks like she has a brother," Susan called out. "Let's get on that."

"Okay," an officer replied from behind her.

There was a small stack of books on the coffee table. Most of them were medical journals; a few romance thrillers poked out from the middle. Nothing appeared to be out of place. Cabinets were closed, doors were shut, as were drawers and cubbies. A small pile of mail sat unopened on the kitchen counter, and a closed laptop had been left on the couch. Susan pointed to the computer.

"Need this wrapped," she said.

One of the officers nodded as he pulled a plastic evidence bag out of his pocket. "Yes, ma'am."

She walked into the bedroom, and it was more of the same. White walls, queen bed with a white comforter, distressed white dresser and nightstand, a few scattered pictures. The bed was made.

Susan began opening the drawers and giving them a cursory search, but there were only clothes folded neatly, one kind of clothing for each drawer. She made her way to the nightstand. Inside, there was a book of crossword puzzles, a small notebook, and a black leather address book. The notebook appeared to contain names along with a schedule of specific medications and dates. The address book was an address book. Names, addresses, phone numbers, and emails.

"Let's get these bagged too."

Susan peeked into the closet, but there was nothing there that would tell her where Rebecca Hill was or how she could be involved in a trooper's death. She retreated from the bedroom to go talk to the super, who was still out in the hall.

Juan looked to be in his forties. He had a thick black mustache that covered his upper lip and stubble where his beard would be if he let it grow in. His uniform seemed one size too big.

"Hi, Juan," Susan said as she stepped out into the hall and held up her shield. "We haven't properly met. I'm Investigator Susan Adler from the state police. I appreciate you helping us out today."

Juan shrugged and smiled. "No problem. Police say open, I open. I don't want no trouble."

"How long have you been taking care of this building?"

"Fifteen years."

"Wow, that's a long time. Good for you."

Juan's chest puffed just a little. "Fifteen years, and we never had no major problems. No leaks, no heat problems in the winter, everybody got working AC in the summer. I keep the walkways clear from ice. Never a problem."

"That's great. How long has Rebecca Hill been living here?"

"I'd say about five years."

"She a good tenant?"

"Sí. Never a problem. Always pay her rent on time. Never complain about anything. Nice lady. She give me a good tip for Christmas."

"Do you know what she does for a living?"

"She's a nurse."

That would explain the medical books in the living room and the names and meds list she'd found with the address book.

"Does Rebecca live here with anyone?" Susan asked.

"No. She lives by herself."

"Any boyfriends come and go?"

"Not that I noticed. Her mother and her brother come to visit on Sundays. Not every Sunday, but they come a lot and stay for the day."

"Do you know their names?"

"The brother is David, but I don't know the mother's name. I just hear Miss Rebecca call the woman Mom. I think she's sick. Cancer or something."

Susan lowered her voice when a couple came out of an apartment down the hall and made their way toward the elevators. "We have reason to believe Rebecca might be in trouble. We're thinking maybe she ran off. Do you know where she might go if she was in trouble?"

"I don't know her like that," Juan replied, wide eyed. "I just take care of the building, and we say hello when we see each other. That's it."

"I thought maybe you heard something over the years while you were working."

"I don't hear nothing."

"You're sure."

He held up his right hand. "Hand to God. I swear."

Susan dug into her pocket and came away with her business card. "Take my number. If you hear anything or she comes home, I need you to call me. Don't tell her we were here. Just call me. It's very important."

"Okay."

As Susan turned to make her way back into the apartment, her cell phone rang.

"This is Adler."

"Susan, it's Mel."

The sergeant's voice sounded gruff so early in the morning.

"Yeah, what's up?"

"Crosby told me to call you. Dispatch just got a call from a physical therapy center about an elderly patient of theirs who they think might be missing. Asked us to take a look. He lives in Verplanck, so I sent a unit over. The place looks fishy."

"How so?"

"According to my guys, it looks tossed."

"What's the patient's name?"

"James Darville."

"Never heard of him," she replied. "And I'm working the Trooper Kincaid homicide right now."

"Rebecca Hill is your suspect."

"That's right."

"Well, she's the visiting nurse who's assigned to our missing guy."

Susan squeezed the phone. "Give me Darville's address. I'll meet you there."

TRANSCRIPT

I'm recording this today because the fog has lifted and my mind is clear. It won't be long before this disease takes complete control of me, and once that happens, I can't trust myself to tell the truth about the children. They're starting to ask too many questions, and when the fog is thick, I know I won't be able to guarantee what my answers might be, so getting it out while I can recall the details seems the most logical thing to do.

At least the safest thing.

I guess I can think of my condition as both a blessing and a curse. It's a blessing in that one day I'll forget what I've done and the people I've hurt. I won't remember anything about the lives I've altered, nor will I be able to recall the names, faces, or scenes that haunt me every moment, asleep or awake.

I can rest easy knowing that soon I won't remember the sound a shovel makes when it first pierces the earth. I won't remember the noise a skull makes when it cracks open. I won't remember the innocence in a child's voice or the look in their eyes when they know something's wrong. These are things I look forward to forgetting.

And most gratefully, I won't remember *her*.

So that's why I'm making this recording. I want to ensure that whoever finds this and listens will know what I've done and why. The more they ask their questions, the more I realize I've been speaking out of school and I can't trust that what I say is always accurate. These recordings will document everything as it actually happened with dates and names and places and the truth. No more lies. No more misremembering or jumbled thoughts. I'm going to speak of my sins while my mind is clear enough to offer the details they want to know. I've done some truly awful things, and this is my confession . . .

4

Cindy walked into the kitchen and stood in the doorway. Her hair was still wet from the shower, and it chilled her neck and shoulders. Trevor was leaning against the counter next to the stove, the burner phone in his hand.

"Did he text?" she asked.

"Yup."

"What did he say?"

"He asked if we got James. I told him we did."

"Did you tell him about the girl and the trooper?"

"Not in so many words. I told him we had a few hiccups that would need to blow over in the next few days."

"And what'd he say about that?"

Trevor held up the phone, and she could see the picture of his wife and son. It was a close-up, so she wasn't able to make out where the picture was taken. Smart. They were smiling, but there was something off about it. They were scared. She could see it in their eyes.

"They look okay," she said, trying to be reassuring.

"No, they don't. They look terrified." He flipped the phone shut and stuffed it back in his pocket. "Hagen's response to me telling him we screwed some things up was to remind me that he has my family. I don't need to be reminded."

Cindy pulled nervously on her wet hair. "I'll start working on James. Maybe if we can show Hagen that we're making progress right off the bat, he'll forgive us for the trooper and the girl. I'll see what I can get out of him. Like you said before, the faster we get what we need, the faster this can all be over."

Trevor nodded as he stared at the phone in his hand. "Okay. And we gotta keep doing what we normally do as best we can from here. Basic day-to-day things. The people around us can't think anything's different. Make calls if you have to. Tell them you got a new number. Things need to appear normal."

"I'm going to have to record some more episodes for the podcast. I only had three preloaded. I didn't think we'd be stuck up here."

"Then get going. And get your confession so we can get our lives back. Hagen gave you two days before he comes up here and kills the old man. I suggest you take every second he's giving you."

"We can fix this."

"Hagen doesn't care about James's story or the truth about what happened to your sister. He just wants him dead." Trevor leaned forward, and she could see the hate in his eyes. "And know that if anything happens to my family, you all die. Hagen too. That's a promise."

5

Susan snapped on a new pair of gloves and walked through the back door of James Darville's house. It opened to an ancient kitchen. Linoleum-tiled floor, pink Formica countertops, brown oak cabinets. She made her way into a small dining room that held a cheap folding table, four chairs, and nothing more. Dated wallpaper surrounded the living room, and a worn carpet, stained with seasons of weather being tracked in, stretched from end to end. The place hadn't been remodeled for decades. Even the television was from an era that had passed long ago.

In the hallway she took notice of a cluster of photos nailed next to the closet, each one no larger than a five by seven, stored in cheap plastic frames. The photos were black-and-white pictures of nature. Trees, fields, flowers, a cloud-filled sky. No people. No family.

The single-story house was empty, but it was apparent it had been rummaged through. Her trained eye could see the furniture that had been moved and not quite put back in its original spot. She could see that the drawers of the secretary desk in the living room had been left open just a touch. The cabinets in the kitchen had been rifled through, and judging from the splinters of porcelain on the floor, a few cups or plates must have shattered. The coat closet had been torn apart. The drawers in the ancient china cabinet that doubled as a linen closet had been gone through. Someone had been looking for something.

Sergeant Melvin Triston was in the living room with two other uniformed troopers. Mel was an older man, gray haired and slightly overweight, a few years away from a retirement he talked about end-lessly. Fishing in Key Largo. He was counting the days. He looked worn, his face an Irish pink, his tired eyes projecting a kind of resignation with life on the job.

"What are we looking at?" Susan asked.

"Not sure yet. Definitely more than a B and E. There's evidence of a struggle." Triston took his notepad from his breast pocket and flipped it open. "According to the neighbors, Darville's lived here for about fifteen years. Sixty-eight years old. Suffering from Alzheimer's. A pretty tough case of it, according to the physical therapy center who called this in. They said James comes in to see them Tuesday through Friday each week and has been doing it that way for the last two years. He was in this past Tuesday with his visiting nurse, Rebecca Hill, and everything seemed fine. Then he was a no-show on Wednesday with no call to cancel. They rang his house and got no answer. Same with the nurse. They called her cell, and it rolled to voice mail. Same deal on Thursday. Didn't show for the appointment, no call, and when the therapy center called him, no one picked up. Happened again this morning. He had an eight o'clock appointment, same day and time as the last two years, and he didn't show. No call. No answer from James or the nurse."

"So this is the third day he's MIA, but everything goes down with the trooper last night? If the nurse and the old man are connected with Kincaid's homicide, then where was the old man for the two days prior to last night?"

Triston folded his notepad. "No idea."

Susan looked back at the house. "Show me the evidence of a struggle."

"Looks like it started in the bedroom. We have traces of blood that someone tried to wipe up. Still tacky, so pretty fresh. Come on."

She stepped aside and followed Triston down the hall into the bed-room that was back past the kitchen.

"Dr. Trammel, the guy who runs the physical therapy, had his staff call some area hospitals thinking maybe Darville had an episode or something," Triston said as they walked through the house. "But no one had a James Darville on their patient list. Trammel said he didn't know what else to do, so he called 911 and asked if we'd come over to take a look. My guys gained access through the front door, which was unlocked. They saw that the place had been turned, and called it in. We didn't even know it was connected to the trooper until the nurse's name came over the wire."

The bedroom was like the rest of the house, old and unkempt. The bed was large, the frame a thick dark oak that appeared to weigh a ton. There were no sheets or blankets on the mattress. An old gray armchair with a ripped seat was in the corner, with clothes draped over it. Dresser drawers had been left open, as had the closet. The items on top of and inside the nightstand were scattered about and toppled over.

"We contacted Rebecca Hill's employer," Triston continued. "A place called Traveling Healthcare of New York. They're out of Mount Kisco. Woman there said she talked to Rebecca on Monday and that everything seemed fine."

Susan walked around the perimeter of the bedroom. "What does the old man have to do with our trooper shooting?"

"That's why you're here."

"The locks weren't broken. Knobs are all intact. Hinges are good, and no windows are open or busted. You think she did this?"

"Makes sense," Triston said. "And after tossing the place, maybe she found what she was looking for and took off with the old man in her car. Did Kincaid mention a passenger when he called in the 10-38?"

"No, but that doesn't mean there wasn't one."

He knelt down next to an old radiator that had been painted silver and pointed to a piece of flooring that had been removed. "This wasn't put back exactly like it should've been, and it caught my eye." He ran his fingers over the grooves that had been carved out. "Opens up to a pretty large storage area under the floor. I think whatever was in there was what Rebecca might've been looking for." He lifted the panel of flooring to reveal a hole about a foot long, a foot and a half wide, and a foot deep.

Susan bent down next to the sergeant and shined her flashlight inside the hole. It was empty, dust balls in the corners.

Triston took Susan's hand and aimed the beam at the bottom of the bed. "You see where the bed frame used to be?" he asked. "Where there's no dust?"

"Yeah, I see."

"I'm guessing there was a struggle in here. This bed is solid oak and really friggin' heavy. Would take a lot to move it halfway across the room like that."

"Then maybe she had help," Susan replied. "From what I saw in the pictures at her apartment, Rebecca Hill is five feet tall and one hundred and ten pounds. No way she has an encounter with the old man that's fierce enough to move this bed like that. She has a brother, though. He looked like he was in good shape."

Triston moved her hand holding the flashlight from the bed to the opposite side of the nightstand, by the closet. "There's the blood we found. You see the droplets there? Maybe half a dozen?"

"Yup."

He stood up and walked to the closet, pulling the door away from the wall. "Got some more here that they tried to wipe up."

The smear of blood on the wall was fairly sizable and ran down to the floor. Someone had attempted to clean it, but the walls were too dirty, and all it did was leave streaks of pink stain.

"So maybe Rebecca is already here with Darville, and her accomplice comes knocking and she opens the door to let him in. Maybe Darville falls asleep, and while he's sleeping, Rebecca and whoever she's with toss the house. But she can't leave everything messy, so she does a half-ass job putting things back the way they were so the old man wouldn't notice."

Triston nodded. "That would lead you to believe the old man wasn't part of the plan. If they were always planning to take him, they wouldn't care about cleaning up."

Susan walked to the wall and studied the blood. "Right. But they woke him up when they were pulling apart the floor. That's when the struggle started. That's when the plan fell apart."

"Sounds plausible to me."

"What was in the floor? What did they find that was worth taking the old man and killing a cop over?"

"Gotta be a bunch of cash, right? What else would you keep in a hidden compartment in the floor? Could've been enough cash in that hole to start a new life somewhere else. Who knows?"

Susan turned away from the wall, and the beam of her flashlight caught something in the corner, next to the bed. She walked over, bent down, and grabbed it. It was a small gold locket, half-rusted and beat up with time. She could faintly see the initials *SG* engraved on one side. She shined her light farther along the baseboard and under the radiator.

"Got more evidence of a struggle," she said over her shoulder as she reached under the dusty radiator and pulled another object out. "Let's get forensics in here to do their thing."

"What'd you find?" Triston asked, watching her.

She turned the object over in her hand, studying it. "First I found a locket," she said. "Then I found this tooth."

6

Even before his vision had a chance to clear, the old man knew the ghosts were standing at the far end of the room. They were gray corpses, hand in hand, just inside the line of shadow near a small corridor that led to a set of hurricane doors. A boy and a girl. Tattered clothes, frail frames, overgrown and matted hair. Their skin was too damaged from the decades of decay to determine exactly how old they were, but they were young. He'd seen them before. He'd seen the others come too. As his vision sharpened, he locked in on their eyes. Fresh. Focused. Very much alive. It was too dark to make out the details of their faces, but he could feel them staring. At him. *Through* him. From across the room.

"Go away!" he barked. His throat was dry and sore. He coughed and bent over, covering his face until the hacking stopped and the spasms in his chest ceased. When he sat up, he could feel the pain in the back of his head. The boy and girl were gone. He was alone again.

"Hello?"

He waited for a few beats to see if they would return, but no one came. He let out a thin breath and relaxed, realizing just then that he was sitting in a wheelchair. Both of his legs were in braces, positioned up and out from the chair so he couldn't bend his knees. He tried to recall where he was and how he'd ended up there, but nothing came except the increasingly familiar sensation of walking through a thick fog. He knew his name was James. And he knew he didn't like being called Jim. He also knew beyond a shadow of a doubt that he'd run out of detergent and would have to get another bottle before a new load of wash could be done.

He looked around and saw that he was in a basement. Finished. Nice enough. There was a distant familiarity to it, but no way of knowing if he'd been there before. The space was one large area with tiled floors. A sofa, television, and coffee table created a living room, while a bed, dresser, nightstand, and full-length mirror made up the bedroom portion on the opposite side. A small refrigerator had been placed up on a crate next to the television, perhaps to make it easy for him to access while in the wheelchair. It was the right height.

James wheeled himself past the couch and stopped at the base of three windows lined side by side near the top of the wall, directly across from a step up that continued down a corridor that he knew led to a set of hurricane doors, then outside. The height of the windows made it impossible for him to see out, but he could hear the hustle and bustle of the city and knew he was on Manhattan. The horns. The traffic. The shouting. The sirens in the distance. That noise was unique, like a particular song that could never be replicated and couldn't be mistaken for anything else. He loved the city. It felt good to be there again.

A single flight of stairs sat in the middle of the room, reaching up to what must have been the rest of the house. His house? Someone else's house? He couldn't recall. Detergent. He needed to get detergent. He couldn't wash the clothes without it.

James slowly spun around in the chair when he heard the door open at the top of the stairs. He saw boots first, small and clean. Then jeans, a red sweater, and finally a face he thought he recognized but couldn't be sure.

The woman looked to be in her forties. She was pretty, with pale skin and brown hair that held tight curls. He could see her blue eyes from across the room and took notice of her full lips. No makeup. She smiled when she saw him.

"I know you," James whispered, more to himself than her. "I know your face. I've seen it before."

The woman was carrying a tray of food and placed it on the coffee table. She stood straight and looked at him, her smile never fading. "How are you feeling?" she asked.

"We need detergent. I can't do the laundry without detergent."

"You don't do the laundry. That's my job."

"No," he replied, head shaking. Why couldn't she understand? "I'm not asking you to do the laundry. I'm telling you we need detergent."

"Okay, I'll get some."

"Good."

The woman waited. "Can you tell me where you are?"

He thought for a moment, looking around the room. "I'm in the city."

"But what is this place?"

"A basement. My room."

"Very good. And where is that?"

The fog was thick. He tried to work his way through it, following her questions, then losing them in the white blanket of nothingness. "I need detergent."

The woman nodded, the smile fading just a bit. "Look at me."

He did.

"What's my name?"

"I don't know."

"Think. Try and remember."

"I can't do the laundry with just water."

"Okay. Can you tell me *your* name?"

He gripped the armrests on his chair, looking away from the woman, embarrassed, ashamed. "Why are you making me do this?"

"Come on, tell me your name."

"James," he grumbled. He could feel his face flush.

"Good. And what's my name?"

"I don't know! Bitch! How about your name is Bitch? I need to wash the clothes!"

The quick outburst brought the room to a silence. The woman walked past the coffee table and placed her hand on his. "It's okay," she said softly. "I'm not here to make you angry. I just need to know where you are today."

"What do you mean where I am? I'm right here! In this . . . basement."

"I need to know how thick the fog is."

He stared at a woman who was both a stranger and someone he was certain understood him in a way others couldn't. "You know about the fog?"

"Sure."

He sat helpless as she pushed him over to the edge of the coffee table and sat on the couch. Dammit, he knew that face. Knew the smile and the voice. He just couldn't remember her name.

"We're going to eat now," the woman said. She unrolled a fork and spoon from a napkin and placed them next to his plate of chicken and rice. "My name is Cindy."

"Are you my daughter?"

"I heard you talking down here."

"We ran out of detergent. Will you get me some?"

"I will, but first you need to tell me who you were talking to."

"No one."

"I think I know who it was." The woman leaned in. "Did the ghosts come back?"

"How do you know about the ghosts?" James asked.

The woman scooped a forkful of rice and fed him. "You've told me about them. They come around whenever you're having an episode."

"When the fog is thick."

"That's right." She placed the fork down on the plate. "Who were they? The ghosts."

27

"A boy and a girl."

"You said sometimes they come to scare you. Why would the ghosts want to scare you?"

"I don't know."

"Are you sure about that? Think for a minute. Why would they want to scare you?"

"The detergent. We need some."

Cindy sighed and took two pills that were sitting on the edge of the tray. She handed them over.

"What are these?"

"Donepezil. It's for the Alzheimer's."

The word hung in the air between them. Alzheimer's. He wondered how many times she'd had to tell him about it. He was confused, the fog thick, his general recognition of things cloudy, like a rambling story without any real detail.

"How long?"

The woman looked away. "Too long. A few years now. Started with little things. Misplacing your keys. Forgetting where you put your phone. Not being able to follow your shows on TV. It got worse over time. You'd leave the house and forget where you were going. Then you started forgetting how to get home."

The old man scanned the room again. It was as if he were looking at it for the first time. "My name is James."

"That's right. James Darville. And I'm Cindy."

"How many times have you had to tell me that?"

"Enough."

"I'm sorry."

"Don't be. It's not your fault. Come on now, eat."

James leaned his head forward as Cindy brought the fork up to him again. He took a bite and fell back against the wheelchair. "Am I married?"

"No."

"So how did I get you?"

Cindy smiled and pushed the chicken into a pile on the plate.

"I need to get to the store," he added. "I'm trying to do the laundry, but we're out of detergent."

"I'll get you your detergent."

James nodded and chewed his food. He took a sip of water from the bottle the woman had given him. "Those ghosts are real," he said. "They watch me, and I don't like it."

"They're just hallucinations. Part of the disease. If you see them, I know you're having a flare-up, so it's important to tell me, and we can talk about them. That's how we work with it. I heard you yelling at something. Figured it was them."

"No, I'm telling you, they're real."

"Okay."

James finished his meal in relative silence. His mind tried to absorb all the new information he'd been given, but by the time he was done with his plate, a lot of the particulars had already been lost. He knew he had an incurable disease. He knew he was living with this woman instead of in a nursing home, and he knew she'd told him her name, but he couldn't quite remember what it was. Cathy? Christy? The rest of it was lost in the fog.

"That noise," he said, pointing toward the high windows. "That's Manhattan."

"West Village," the woman replied. "Christopher Street."

"Can we go outside?"

"Maybe tomorrow. It's raining pretty hard out right now."

James watched as the woman packed up the tray, rose from the couch, and made her way toward the stairs. She stopped and turned back to him.

"I'll get you that detergent."

"We're all out."

"Okay."

29

"I can't do the laundry without it."

"I know."

After the door to the main floor closed and returned him to the silence of his surroundings, James spun the chair around and backed himself into the corner next to the television so he could scan the room beyond the stairs that held darkness and shadow. That was where the ghosts would be, watching him, reminding him of things that even his disease wouldn't allow him to forget. Things he wanted to forget.

Things any person would beg to forget.

7

Two patrol cars were parked in front of Maxine Hill's small bungalow on the corner of Grove Street in Mount Vernon. They were empty, which meant the troopers were already inside. Susan climbed the four brick steps and knocked on the front door.

A younger man, late thirties perhaps, answered. He was dressed in a black turtleneck sweater and jeans. Susan recognized him from the photograph in Rebecca's apartment.

"I'm Investigator Adler from the state police," she said, holding up the shield that was hanging around her neck. "I need to see Mrs. Hill."

"I'm her son, David," the man replied, opening the door wider. "Come in. The other officers said you were coming by."

Susan followed David into a small living room that held a tattered love seat, an armchair, and a coffee table. Maxine was sitting in the armchair. Her frame was pretty much skin and bones. She looked sick.

The two troopers were monitoring Maxine and David and fielding any phone calls that came in. News of Rebecca's involvement in the police shooting earlier that morning hadn't been released to the press yet, so the activity in and around the home was minimal. Just a few nosy neighbors who'd stopped by when they saw the patrol cars out front.

Susan introduced herself and said she was there to talk about Rebecca.

Maxine let her head fall back on the chair as she looked toward the ceiling. "My baby didn't kill no cop," she said. "She doesn't have it in her. Rebecca's a good girl. She's a nurse. She helps people. No way she would ever do something like that. Her job is saving lives, not taking them."

"We're just trying to figure out what happened at this point. We need to find her."

"Yes, you do."

Susan took out her notepad and pen. "When was the last time you spoke to her?"

"Two days ago," Maxine replied. "Called to check up on me like she always does. She's a good girl."

"How did she sound?"

"Normal. We talked about my cirrhosis and how I was feeling. Had a bout in the hospital, so she wanted to make sure I was okay. We talked about our Netflix shows. She said she was going to stop by and see me this weekend."

"How was she doing at work?" Susan asked. "Everything okay there?"

Maxine shrugged. "Don't know. She didn't say anything particular, and I didn't ask. I don't pry. If my kids wanna talk, they know where to find me. Otherwise, we just enjoy each other's company."

Susan nodded as she wrote. "I understand you and David meet with Rebecca frequently. For dinner and visits?"

"That's right. Try to do it every week, but with this liver of mine, sometimes we can't make it happen. But we always make it a point to spend time together. After my husband died, we realized how little we saw of each other. Rebecca wanted to change that, and she did. We reconnected after Earl passed, and it was the best thing to come of his death. Get to see my children on the regular again."

"Does she discuss her patients?"

"Not really," Maxine replied. "Like I said, I don't pry. Sometimes she tells us little stories about the man she's taking care of, Mr. James. She talks about helping him get about or tells us how she takes him food shopping or something mundane like that. I can't think of anything she's told me that would help you find her. You should ask Mr. James. See what he knows."

Susan pointed to David. "How about you? Rebecca ever tell you anything more about James Darville?"

"No," David replied, shaking his head. "Like Mom said, just little stories here and there. I know she likes him. They get along."

Susan turned her attention back to Maxine. "Do you know if Rebecca is seeing anyone romantically?"

The old woman chuckled and shook her head. "Just Mr. James. Of course, I'm being facetious, but my daughter only has time for that man and no other. I should be up to my neck in grandbabies by now, but neither of my children are much in the romance department. My Rebecca is married to her patients, and this one is married to his writing career. What can I say?"

"You're a writer?" Susan asked David.

"I write for an online magazine, and I'm working on a book."

"Working on that book for a decade," Maxine quipped. "Never quite finished."

Susan turned back to Maxine. "How about close friends? Rebecca have any?"

"Not that I know of," Maxine said. "She's always been a shy girl. Never knew her to have friends like you and I might think of it." She looked up at her son. "You know any of Rebecca's friends?"

"No," David replied. "Sorry."

Susan closed her notepad and leaned forward. "Mrs. Hill, a state trooper was bludgeoned to death on the side of the road this morning. He had a wife who was four months pregnant and a little boy who's three years old. He was a son, a grandson, a husband, a father, a brother, a cousin, and a friend to more people than I can count. His life was stolen, and all he was trying to do was his job. I need to know anything and everything you can think of that might help us find your daughter and find out what happened on the side of that road. Please. Think."

Maxine looked at her as her thin lips pursed and her brow furrowed. "My baby's no killer. You can keep your men here to listen to every phone call that comes in, and they can answer my door every time someone comes knocking, but you'll never find an explanation that involves my Rebecca because there isn't one. My baby's a good soul. She wouldn't hurt nobody, and she certainly wouldn't kill nobody. I want you to find her as much as you do because I believe she's in trouble. We need to get to the bottom of what happened. Rebecca is innocent. I just pray to God she's still alive. Now go find her. Go."

8

The Cortlandt State Police barracks was empty for the most part. There was a trooper working the dispatch desk in the front of the building and a few others milling about by the break room, but none of the other investigators were on the unit floor, and the building itself was quiet. Susan walked inside from the rear parking lot and made her way over to her desk. The serenity was a welcome surprise. She needed to think.

The flat-screen television that hung on the brown paneled wall next to the rotation schedule and whiteboard was on, but the sound had been muted. Local news was replaying the scene on the Taconic, complete with footage of the closed road and an interview with the senior investigator who was in charge. It wouldn't be long before they'd start running footage of family members and friends. By the end of the day they'd have information on Rebecca too.

She put her bag down on her desk and sat in her chair. The empty desk across the way reminded her of her old partner who'd come and gone, and the chaos he'd left in his wake. Every time she looked at the empty seat, all she could think about was the trust she'd put in him and the betrayal that had cut so deep. Trooper Kincaid had fallen for that same kind of betrayal the moment he had pulled Rebecca Hill's car over in the middle of the night. Trust that turned to carnage. The only difference was Susan had lived.

The news on the flat screen changed over to the local weather, and Susan's stomach rumbled. She realized she hadn't really eaten anything before she'd gotten the call that morning and turned on her laptop. She was about to head over to the vending machine when Crosby walked onto the unit.

"Adler, you're back."

"I am."

"Fill me in. What are we looking at?"

She waited until he'd reached her desk and sat in her partner's old seat.

"I'm not entirely sure yet. The old man Rebecca was caring for is missing, and his place was definitely tossed. We found some blood on the wall that forensics will try to match with Darville or Rebecca. I also found a small locket, which may or may not be something. And I found a tooth, which would further confirm there was a struggle. If there was money in the hole we found hidden in the floor, that could point to motive for Rebecca."

"How so?"

"Her mom has liver disease. Cirrhosis. She could've taken it to help her mom. Maybe there was enough to split with whoever she was with."

"You think there's a partner?"

"Had to be. She's too small to cause the type of struggle we saw, and her brother has the type of build who could overtake the old man and get him out of the house."

"Type of build to beat a cop to death."

"Possibly. I have two troopers on him at the mother's house. I don't want to show my hand just yet."

Crosby leaned back in the chair. "Next steps?"

"I got some units doing door to doors in Verplanck and through Rebecca's apartment building in White Plains. See if anyone saw or heard anything the last few nights. Also hoping one of Darville's neighbors has a security camera on their property that might catch something. We have no traffic cams in that area, so we're blind. Forensics is going through the house picking up samples and pulling prints. Another team is taking samples from Rebecca's apartment. I sent the tooth for DNA testing to see who it belongs to. Got hairs from brushes at Darville's house and Rebecca's apartment for the possible match. I'll follow up with secondary interviews with Rebecca's work and the places Darville went for his treatments."

"Sounds good."

"Anything on your end?"

Crosby sighed and shook his head. "Not much. Waiting on the dashcam video to come back to see exactly what we're dealing with. Hopefully we can catch a clear image of Rebecca or her brother or whoever is responsible for what happened out there. We have a BOLO out for the old man. Details about Darville and Rebecca are being given to the press and surrounding departments in a fifty-mile radius. Maybe somebody saw something."

"Let's hope."

Crosby got up from his seat. "You want some help with this? I got other investigators clamoring to assist. All hands on deck and whatnot. I can call Hawthorne or Manhattan and have them send us someone. Or, like I said before, I can pull Chris or Bill if you want to keep it local."

"No," Susan replied quickly. "I'm good. Mel's helping."

"Mel's got his own troop to worry about. He's a sergeant, not an investigator."

"I know, but it's all hands, right?"

"You're going to need to take on a partner with these tougher cases. We all know what happened, and I've been trying to give you space, but on things like this, you need backup."

Susan looked at the empty desk across from her. She knew she was being foolish for refusing a partner, but she just wasn't ready to trust anyone yet. Not after everything that went so horrifically wrong. Not after so many lives had been changed. It wasn't time.

"I'm good right now," she said. "Seriously. If things ramp up and I need help, I'll raise my hand. And after this case is done, we'll talk about taking on a partner on the next one. Just let me run with this."

Crosby walked across the unit and stopped when he reached his office. He looked back at her and pointed, his large frame taking up the entire doorway. "This is the last big one you're running solo on. Got it?"

"Got it."

"You need help, you tell me. Mel has enough to worry about, and if I have to pay him overtime, the captain's gonna get pissed."

"If I need help, I'll tell you. I promise."

"Find these people."

Susan nodded. "You know I will."

9

Trevor was sitting at the dining room table, huddled over his laptop, his back to her.

"How is she?" he asked when he heard her come in.

"Not great. I gave her a Valium."

"She better learn to relax. She's making me nervous."

Cindy walked farther into the room. "What're you looking at?"

"The trooper story," he replied. "It's all over the news. All the major New York outlets are running with it. A few national websites picked it up too. Associated Press has a small article, but by tomorrow this is going to be all over the place."

"Do they know anything?"

"They released Rebecca's name and picture. That's it so far."

"Nothing on James?"

"No."

"No mention of the dashcam?"

"Not yet."

Cindy sat down in a chair next to Trevor and looked at the screen. Patrick Kincaid. She had a mental image of his young face appearing in her window, explaining that the roads were too slick to be driving so fast and suggesting she look in the glove compartment for Rebecca's registration. Fractured images kaleidoscoped in her mind. The blood on her hands. The sound the car door made when Trooper Kincaid opened it and instructed her to get out. The wet slop of the tire iron crushing that poor man's skull. She looked away from the screen, afraid to read on, not wanting to know what loved ones he'd left behind because she already knew what being a loved one who was left behind meant. She knew what it felt like. The shock. The pain. The hurt. Her sister had left her behind. Then her mother. She knew what the trooper's family would be going through in the days, weeks, and months to come. She'd lived it.

"I got a text from Hagen."

Trevor stopped reading and looked at her. "What'd it say?"

"He's following the news like you are, and he's not happy. It's going to be more than two days before he can make it up here. He doesn't want to draw attention by leaving when so much is going on. He told us to stay put and told me to work fast to get the truth from James. He's not going to wait any longer than he has to. I told him I already started."

"I wouldn't call feeding him chicken and talking about laundry detergent working on getting the truth."

"You can't just go in with a bunch of questions. He'll end up confused, and the dementia will kick in. This is a slow process. That's why we're here and not back in Verplanck, where everything would be a distraction. If Hagen just wanted him dead, he could've walked into the house and shot him or strangled him while he was sleeping. He's giving me the opportunity to finally learn why James killed my sister and the other kids. I think he wants to know the truth too."

"So get it."

"I need to build trust, and then I need to extract the real stories carefully. I've been waiting a lifetime to learn why my sister disappeared. I can't get this close and screw it up. It's gonna take time."

Trevor fell back in his seat and covered his face with his hands. "I don't know how long I can last. I need to know my wife and son are okay. I need to know where they're being kept. What's happening to them? Are they in danger? Are they being taken care of? Is my son going to be okay after this? It's driving me nuts. I need to help them."

"You help them by doing what we need to do. Once this is all done, you'll see them again."

He didn't reply.

"What are their names?" Cindy asked. "We can talk about them. Maybe that'll help."

Trevor pulled his hands away from his face. "You don't need to know their names," he snapped. "The less you know about me, the better. All you need to know is that I'll stop at nothing to get them back. That son of a bitch took my family to force me to join this sick game, and now I've already done things that I can never go back and fix. He made me *kill* people. He broke me; he broke the man that I was. The husband and father that I was. He's breaking my family as we speak. But I killed those people because my end game is getting my family back. That's all it is, and they're all that matter. Got it?"

"Got it."

Cindy wanted to comfort him, but she knew it would do no good. Having been the left-behind loved one, there was no real comfort she could offer when someone's family was in danger. All she could do was follow Hagen's instructions and extract the truth she'd needed to hear for almost forty years. What Trevor was being forced to endure seemed unfair compared to what the rest of them had been promised. But he hadn't needed anything, so it had come down to exploiting his love for his wife and son. The others *needed* something, and promises were made in order to get them to join the team. She felt guilty getting what she wanted while he was suffering with worry.

"Did you upload the new podcast?" he asked.

"Goes live at eight. Just a retread of some old news, but at least it's posting."

"Make any calls?"

"None to make. Besides, no one's going to recognize the burner phone's caller ID. They'd roll me to voice mail anyway."

"What about the old man?"

"Almost time for bed. I'll see where his head is at when I go down. I'll press him if there's an opportunity."

"I'll go," he said. "I want to get a better look at him now that we don't have all the other distractions. I want to see what makes him so important." Trevor turned back to the laptop and clicked to another news story. "And I want to see how easy he'll be to kill, if it comes to that. I'm guessing it'll be easier than the cop."

10

Icy droplets of rain tapped the windshield as Susan tilted her head back on the driver's-side headrest. The engine of her car hummed in the background, heat streaming through the vents. Her mind churned. By now the trooper's wife had been informed of what happened. She'd been brought down to the morgue to officially identify her husband's body and was probably hosting well-wishers who would line the block offering support and a shoulder should she need it. His son was still too young to understand exactly what had happened, and the baby she was pregnant with would never know its father. Tomorrow Mrs. Kincaid would be brought to the funeral home to make arrangements for a service with every honor one could think of. That was standard protocol when a fellow officer went down in the line of duty. Susan wished she could be there but knew finding his killer was much more important than being the hundredth person to offer condolences. There wasn't a minute to waste.

From what she'd learned so far, she knew there had to have been a link between what happened to the trooper and what happened at James Darville's place, and Rebecca Hill was that link. But if Rebecca had found what she was looking for in that hole in the floor, why did she take Darville? He was suffering from Alzheimer's and would be a hindrance if she were on the run. Experience told Susan that he had to still be alive. If he'd been killed in the house, Rebecca and her accomplice would've most likely left the body. He'd be tricky to move without being noticed, and there would be no real point in risking transporting a body when the scene they left behind already pointed to foul play. So why take Darville? And what had been in that hole? Too many questions, and the top brass wanted answers.

She shifted her body and listened as the sleet picked up outside. It appeared the old man had no family. No real friends other than some neighbors who looked after him every now and again. He'd arrived in town a decade earlier, but no one in the neighborhood knew where he'd come from. Google searches came up with 459,000 name matches. A needle in a haystack if there ever was one.

She hit the wipers and put the car in gear, carefully pulling out of the parking lot and onto the Post Road. The temperature was still dropping, and the sleet made the pavement slick and navigation tricky in the dark. As Susan drove, she could see the orange halo of salt trucks working just beyond the horizon. It was going to be a long night for those guys, but the overtime would be sweet just before the holidays.

Susan passed the on-ramp for Route 9 that would've taken her home, deciding instead to take a ride to Darville's house. She wanted to walk through it again, alone, without the distraction of a crime scene investigation going on around her or Triston talking in her ear. She wanted to see if anything popped out that they might've missed before. She doubted she'd discover anything substantial after the forensics team had done a sweep, but sometimes just feeling the vibe of the place where a crime had happened helped reset her mind.

Traffic was heavy on the back roads of Verplanck. Headlights blinded her as cars passed by in the opposite lane, most of them coming home from the city or picking up passengers who'd just gotten off the train. No one dared drive above twenty-five miles an hour for fear of sliding off the road or rear-ending the person in front of them. Susan took her place in the long line of traffic and listened to the radio until her turnoff came. She pulled away from the commuters and headed toward the outskirts of town, toward the Hudson River and the old man's house.

She was the only one on 9th Street. The tires crunched the sleet that was beginning to accumulate on the road. No salt trucks or plows bothered to work on dead ends while the main roads still needed tending to. She pulled up along the curb and shut her headlights off just before rolling to a stop one house down from Darville's place.

The street was quiet. No traffic. No one outside walking pets. No one salting their driveways or shoveling their stoops. Even the streetlight at the end of the block wasn't working. It was as if life had ceased to exist on this dead-end road. Nothing was moving.

Except for the light that was on in James Darville's house.

Susan grabbed her phone and dialed.

"Cortlandt SP. This is Trooper Carson."

"This is Adler. I need you to roll a unit to 356 9th Street. That address is an active crime scene in an open investigation associated with this morning's 10-38 upstate. There are lights on inside the house. Could be nothing, but I'm going to check it out and would rather have a unit rolling in case I need it."

"Ten-four," the trooper replied. "Unit rolling."

"No lights. No sirens. Come in quiet. I don't want to spook them."

"You got it."

She hung up the phone, shut off the engine, and quietly stepped out of the car. The wind coming off the river was biting. She unclipped the snap on her holster and hurried toward the house, extracting her Beretta and holding it down toward the ground.

Susan peeked through the window next to the porch, but her vision was blocked by dirty blinds. If she remembered correctly, she was looking into the living room, which would make it the kitchen light that was on. She listened for a moment, trying to hear footsteps or talking or movement of any kind, but there was just the quiet of the street and the wind howling off the Hudson.

The ground was soft and muddy from the rain, but it was beginning to freeze, making her footsteps crunch as she worked her way toward the back of the house. In the silence, each step sounded like a small explosion. The kitchen was in the rear, and as she turned the corner into the backyard, she could see two windows fully illuminated as well as a shadow of movement beyond the shades that had been drawn.

Someone was definitely inside.

She carefully climbed the back stairs and studied the back door. Glass had been punched out of the pane closest to the knob and dead bolt. She held her Beretta up at her chest now, poised and ready if the situation warranted such force. She held her breath, turned the filthy brass knob, and pushed.

The lights went out.

Blackness.

Before Susan's eyes could adjust or she could pull back from her position, the door she was leaning on slammed shut, knocking into her and sending her down the three steps she'd just climbed. The ground was cold and wet as she scrambled to her feet, ran back up the stairs, and burst into the house, gun drawn and ready.

"State police!" she cried. "Stop right there!"

She saw a shadow slip through the kitchen doorway and immediately pursued. What had been a quiet, serene setting only moments before was now chaos and mayhem. The person was running, tripping over furniture, and grunting.

"I said stop!"

The figure burst through the front door, hopped down the steps, and ran across the street. Susan followed, pushing the front door open in time to see movement disappearing along the shadows of the house on the opposite side of the road. She scurried down the steps as the trooper unit was pulling onto the street.

"This way!" she cried.

The unit sped up and came to a stop next to her.

"We have one suspect on foot. Just ran behind that house. I'll go around on the north side, and you flank him on the south."

"Ten-four."

The trooper jumped out and ran around the dark house on the south side. Susan crept around the north end with her back against the siding, her coat sliding along, making too much noise.

The neighbor's yard had no light. Susan got into her shooting position and scanned the area as best she could, trying to pick out something, anything, but it was too difficult to see. The wind was all she could hear.

Movement.

Running.

Out of the corner of her eye, she saw a bush sway, and as she turned in that direction, she caught a glimpse of her suspect hurdling a small fence and running into an open area that led to the banks of the Hudson River.

"He's heading toward the river!" she yelled.

She could see him now; the lights along this section of the Hudson were lit as part of the perimeter grounds of the Indian Point nuclear power plant. They'd soon be at the restricted area, and Susan knew that if the suspect kept running, he'd trip sensors. Once he did that, she'd no longer have to worry about pursuing. The highly trained plant guards would take him down in a matter of seconds. And inside the perimeter of the plant, the use of deadly force was always authorized.

"State police!" she screamed as loud as she could over the wind coming off the water. "Last warning. Stop running or I will open fire!"

She slowed down and got into a shooting position. Behind her, she could hear the trooper approaching, his breath heavy as the cold air stabbed at his lungs. When he reached her, he got down on one knee and aimed his weapon as well.

"Stop!"

Spotlights suddenly came on, and Susan pulled her head away before she was blinded by their intensity. She held up her hand and squinted enough to see the side of a building that had been hidden in the darkness. It was the power plant's warehouse structure.

The suspect stopped running, caught in the light, confused and panicked.

"Put your hands up!" Susan instructed as she and the trooper approached.

The suspect put his hands up.

"Keep your hands up, and get on your knees!"

The suspect fell to his knees.

Susan holstered her weapon while the trooper kept his aimed and ready. She pulled cuffs from her back pocket and opened them.

"No sudden moves," she said.

"Okay."

She could hear guards from the plant approaching and pulled her shield out from beneath her coat.

"What's going on down there?" a voice asked from behind the lights.

"State police!" Susan shouted in return. "Suspect in custody. We're good!"

She took the man's wrist and twisted it around, placing it behind his back while fastening the first cuff. She did the same with the second. When he was secure, she frisked him. He was clean. No weapons. Nothing from the house. No ID. But as she turned him around and saw his face, she knew she didn't need his ID. She recognized him from earlier that day.

It was David Hill.

Rebecca's brother.

11

Susan walked David back to her car, a tight grip on his arm, pushing him forward. As was procedure, the trooper walked behind them in case assistance was needed. It was always easier to step up and run forward or draw your weapon at a target in front of you. His position was as much tactical as it was practical.

They got to the trooper's patrol car, and she opened the back door, then pushed David inside and immediately shut it.

"I'm going to need a minute with him," she said to the trooper. "You can wait out here or go sit in my car if you get cold."

The trooper pulled keys from his coat. "I'll wait here in case you need something. Start the car and run the heat. It gets chilly in there."

She nodded, opened the driver's-side door, and climbed behind the wheel.

David was in the back seat, his head leaning against the window, a fresh set of tears streaming down his cheeks over the frozen ones that were beginning to thaw. He'd been crying since they caught him, saying nothing more than "I'm sorry" over and over again. He was doing it now, mumbling the words as he looked out toward the house he'd just run from. James Darville's house. Susan watched him in the rearview mirror, wondering what he was so remorseful for and if this would be the first break in the case.

"I need you to stop crying so we can talk. Can you do that?"

David lifted his head off the window and nodded once, short breaths coming sharp as he tried to stop sobbing.

"I have to read you your Miranda rights so we get this off on the right foot." She pulled out her phone and began recording as she read David his rights and he acknowledged that he understood them. When she was done, she paused, allowing them to ease into an awkward silence with only the sound of the engine acting as a backdrop.

"I'm sorry," David whimpered.

"You keep saying that. Sorry for what?"

"I'm sorry I went into his house. I know I wasn't supposed to, but I couldn't help it. I had to."

"Why?" Susan asked. She repositioned herself so she was facing him instead of watching him in the mirror. "Why were you in there? Why did you have to go?"

"I need to find my sister. There's no way she killed that cop, and if she didn't do it and no one can find her, that means something's happened to her, and I was getting freaked out. I've been calling her. My mom's been calling. After you left, I went to her job and the physical therapy place she takes Mr. James to. I went by her apartment, but the cops wouldn't let me in. Something's up. You don't know her, and I'm telling you, Rebecca is a good person. There's just no way she would hurt someone. Something's happened."

"You went into a crime scene without permission. That's serious."

David nodded as new tears fell from his eyes. "I'm sorry. I didn't know Mr. James's house was a crime scene. I came here to see if he'd seen her, and when I showed up, I saw police tape and I panicked. I wasn't thinking straight."

"Then why did you run? I identified myself as state police. Why did you keep running?"

"Because of this!" David turned to show his cuffed hands. "A black man breaking into a crime scene after his black sister is suspected of killing a cop? You think I should've hung around and talked through it once you came in? I got scared and bolted."

"Unlawful entry into a building with the intent to commit a crime is bad, but when it's a residence, it's considered a felony. Did you know that?"

"I wasn't doing no unlawful acts. I didn't touch nothing. And I had on gloves anyway. I didn't screw up any evidence."

"You broke the back door window to unlock the dead bolt."

"I'm sorry. It was stupid."

Susan nodded at him. "Take off those gloves."

She rolled down the passenger's-side window and motioned for the trooper.

"Take his gloves and put them in an evidence bag."

"Yes, ma'am."

The trooper opened the back door, and David turned around so he could take the gloves off his hands. As quickly as the door was opened, it was shut again.

"Why is Mr. James's house a crime scene?" David asked. "Did he do something to my sister? Is he connected to what happened to her? Please, I need answers."

Susan shut off her recorder, stuffed her phone in her pocket, and stepped out of the car. "Okay, we're done for now. We're going to take you to the barracks to talk some more. Sit tight, and we'll straighten all this out."

"Did Mr. James do something to Rebecca?"

Susan shut the door. It wasn't that she didn't want to answer David's question. It's just that she couldn't. She really didn't know.

TRANSCRIPT

Screaming, yelling, feet stomping the floor, chairs being moved aside, papers and folders falling off the desk. Then, in a matter of seconds, the room went from complete chaos to utter silence. And there was nothing but Noreen's deep, ragged breaths, in and out.

The girl's body was lying on the classroom floor, facedown, her dark hair tangled and flailing out in every direction. I remember her left leg being folded under her right in an awkward angle, and for some reason that's always haunted me. She didn't move. Not a twitch or a spasm or a muscle contraction or a jolt. It had become so quiet. A heavy kind of quiet that was trying to crush us under the weight of what Noreen had just done.

Noreen was staring at the girl, my paperweight still in her right hand. Her breathing was beginning to slow down, but she couldn't take her eyes away from the body. I watched her, waiting for her to say or do something. Anything. A few minutes earlier we'd been in each other's arms, kissing, touching, caught in the throes of a forbidden affair that was exhilarating and passionate. I swore I'd locked the classroom door, but the knob and lock were old, and sometimes the bolt didn't properly catch the frame that had warped and been painted over too many times to even guess.

That one mistake had cost us everything.

Blood was beginning to pool onto the floor around the girl's face. Her body was lying between the classroom door and my desk. I forced myself to take one step, then another, until I'd finally worked my way over to the room's entrance and peeked out into the hall to make sure we were alone. Most of the other staff had left about an hour earlier, which was what allowed Noreen and me to meet up like that at the school. No one other than the maintenance staff should have been around.

"She was going to tell," Noreen mumbled as I gently closed the door and locked it, checking that it was really locked this time. "I had to get her to shut up. I didn't mean to hurt her. I just needed her to stop yelling."

I pushed myself off the door and knelt down beside the body. My trembling hands felt for a pulse on her neck and wrists. There was nothing. She hadn't been more than thirteen.

Noreen started to cry. "Is she dead?"

"Lower your voice," I whispered.

"Is she dead?"

"Yes."

Noreen fell to the floor, dropping the paperweight. It hit with a heavy thud, and I winced, remembering the sound it had made when it hit Tiffany's skull. It was an iron sculpture of the Headless Horseman, one of my favorite literary tales. I'd found it at an antiques shop in Vermont and thought it would make for an excellent conversation piece in my classroom.

"She wouldn't stop," Noreen mumbled as I stood back up. Her eyes were glassy, her mascara beginning to run, making her look like a cartoonish version of herself. A bit off. "She was going to tell her parents and my husband and my friends and the people I work with. She was going to ruin me. And you. The school board would run you out of town. Ruin your career. She was going to enjoy ruining our lives. That smile. That stupid grin on her face when she told me she was going to tell Sonia. I had to make her stop."

"You didn't have to kill her."

Noreen held her breath for a moment and stopped crying. She looked at me, and I saw a different woman. Furious. Rageful. "I didn't mean to kill her," she said slowly, each word dripping from her mouth like acid. "I just needed her to quiet down."

"Well, she did."

"And now what?"

"I don't know." I turned in a circle, and that's when I spotted something. It was a small tooth in the corner by the blackboard. Noreen must've knocked it out when she hit Tiffany. I don't know why, but I picked it up and stuffed it in my pocket. "We have to call the police."

"No!" Noreen reached out for me, her eyes wide with terror. "We can't call the police. We can't let anyone know what happened. It'll ruin us. They'll put me in jail and take my family away. Jackson will take the girls and I'll never see them again."

"It was an accident."

"The police won't see it that way. They'll put us both behind bars, and we'll rot there for the rest of our lives. No, we can't let that happen. I won't let that happen."

Noreen scrambled to her feet and went to my desk. She grabbed my jacket from the back of my chair and was moving before I knew what she was doing. She was in survival mode.

"I love you, and I'm not going to hang us out to dry," she mumbled. "I know this isn't right or ethical or even halfway sane, but I need you to just trust me here. Can you do that?"

I looked at her, but I didn't know what to say. Maybe shock was taking hold.

She held up my jacket. "I'm going to wrap this around her head to stop the bleeding from getting all over the place. We're going to put her body in the coat closet in the back of the room, clean up this mess, and you come back later tonight when the janitorial crew is gone. Take her somewhere and bury her. When she doesn't come home, we'll act as shocked as everyone else in town, and we'll volunteer to help look for her. Day and night. As long as it takes. After enough time goes by, the police will stop searching and we can all go about our lives."

I couldn't believe what I was hearing. "Are you serious?"

She shrugged and smiled as if we were arguing about who was going to do the dishes.

"Do you have a better idea?" she asked. "Because I don't. Do you want to confess?"

"I want to call the police. There's nothing to confess. It was an accident."

"They won't see it that way. A little girl is dead at the hands of two adults who were having an affair. How do you think that looks? How do you think the police and the judge and the jury and the rest of the town will see it? You can't kill a child and get off on a misunderstanding. Her parents will want to see justice. They'll ask for the death penalty." Noreen started crying again. "I was just trying to make her stop."

It was my first step into the abyss. Love, fear, guilt, confusion overwhelmed me, and so I simply handed my freedom over as if we were trading baseball cards. "Okay, I'll do it. You go home and act normal. No hysterics. Be yourself."

"I'll try," Noreen replied. She was shaking all over. "Do you love me?"

"Of course."

"Then we have no choice. We have to do this."

I got my arms under the little girl's body and lifted her off the floor.

"Wait," Noreen said as she fumbled through my desk. She came away with a pair of scissors. "I want a piece of her hair to remind me of what I've done. I don't ever want to forget. I don't ever want to give myself the satisfaction of moving on. I want to remember what we did and what we're doing. Always."

We didn't know we were passing the point of no return on that sunny afternoon, but we should have. We should've realized you can't do something like that and go back to the way things used to be.

That's not how fate works.

12

James sat in the middle of the basement, his arthritic hands gently caressing the rubber treads of his wheelchair. He looked at the digital clock that had been set up next to the television. It was flashing 12:00 over and over. What good was a clock that didn't tell the time? At least he had the windows to tell him if it was day or night. He couldn't see out of them, but he could see that it was night outside. The woman whose name he couldn't quite reach in the fog had told him it was raining, but he had no proof of such news. His room might as well have been on Mars. He couldn't see anything but light and dark. There were no other details beyond the concrete walls that surrounded him, dressed in drywall and painted a calming yellow to try and make him feel like he was living in an apartment. But the reality was, he was trapped in that room, in his chair, and within his failing mind. He was a prisoner in every sense of the word.

James spun around and wheeled himself to the landing when a different set of legs started down the stairs. These legs were thicker. Longer. Brown leather boots and khaki pants.

"You look familiar," James said as he backed away and let the man come all the way down. "We've met, I think. I can't remember what you told me your name was."

"Not important," the man replied. "It's time for bed."

"Where's Bonnie?"

"Who?"

"Bonnie? Where is she? I need to see her. I think something might've happened. I think Noreen got ahold of her."

The man ignored him and walked behind the wheelchair before grabbing the two handles and pushing James toward the bedroom portion of the space.

"I think she might be hiding," he continued. "I can't find her, and if I can't find her, then that means something might've happened. Have you seen her?"

"You're not making sense," the man said without any inflection in his voice. "No one knows who Bonnie is, and it doesn't matter if you think she's hiding or whatever. You won't remember any of this come tomorrow."

"Well, that's a hell of a thing to say."

The man remained quiet as he pushed the wheelchair to the edge of the bed, engaged the brake, then came around to face James. He unhooked each leg from the chair but left them in the braces, easing them to the floor.

"How long have I been here? I don't remember ever doing this before. Please."

The man bent down, laced his arms under James's, and lifted him out of his seat, spinning him quickly and dropping him onto the bed. Before James could move himself, the man straightened his legs, positioned his torso so it aligned with the rest of his body, gently placed his head on the pillow, and pulled the covers up to his chest.

"Am I going to bed?"

"Yes."

"I need to change into my pajamas."

The man pulled the covers back. "You already did before."

James looked down and saw he was wearing blue-and-white-striped pajamas. He had no memory of putting them on. "I . . . I . . ."

"I'm sure you'll tell me you don't remember doing this tomorrow night too. That's why it doesn't matter what my name is or where

Bonnie is or whether Noreen has her or whatever else you have on your mind. None of it will matter because you'll wake up with the same questions tomorrow and the next day and the day after that, and to be honest, I have enough to worry about. When we get to the end of all of this, we can take a breath, but for now, I just don't have the patience or the time."

Even in the dim light, James could see the man's eyes were almost vacant.

"I think something might've happened to Bonnie."

The man took James's hand and dumped two pills into his palm. "Take these."

"What is it?"

"They'll help you sleep."

"Do I usually take these?"

"Yes. Every night."

"Is Bonnie doing the laundry? Maybe that's where she is."

"Take the pills."

James popped the pills in his mouth, and the man helped him sip from a glass of water that was on his nightstand.

"You need the bedpan?"

"No."

"Okay then. Go to sleep."

"Is Bonnie up there?"

The man didn't answer. He crossed the room, his boots thumping on the tiled floor. When he got to the landing, he shut off the lights and plunged the room into a thick darkness.

"Please tell me your name. Even if I'm going to ask again tomorrow, just tell me anyway."

A sigh. "Trevor."

"Thank you."

The only reply was the sound of the man's boots stomping up the stairs and the basement door quietly closing.

13

Cindy was waiting in the kitchen when Trevor came up from the basement. He closed the door, and they looked at each other as the noise in the house settled.

"How is he?"

"Physically, he's doing fine. I don't think the bump he got is affecting him. As for his mental state, he's a mess, but we knew that going in. Has no recollection of what happened, which is definitely a good thing. He kind of knows he hadn't gone to bed down there before, but I played it like he's been here for a while. He kept asking about someone named Bonnie."

Cindy pushed off the counter she was leaning on. Her eyes grew wide. "That's a good thing," she said. "He's remembering. Bonnie was one of his victims. I knew he'd start to remember. I knew it."

"I don't know if you'd call it remembering," Trevor replied. "More like random thoughts popping into his mind. He just thinks of something, and it comes out of his mouth."

"No, he's remembering. Same with the ghosts he's seeing. They're the kids he abducted. He's remembering."

"Okay, whatever." Trevor made his way over to the table and sat down. "Just work on the old man so you can get your answers. If you think Hagen wants to hear his confession, then get it before he comes up, because once he's here, it's over."

"I know. I'll push a little harder tomorrow."

"How's our girl doing?"

"She's fine. She's in bed. I gave her a couple more Valiums."

"She's getting pretty amped up."

"Yeah, well, this isn't something that people do every day," Cindy said. "Of course she's gonna be a little freaked out. We killed two people, and now we're stuck up here. The original plan crumbled the second those red lights started flashing."

"No, the plan crumbled the second you decided to go twenty miles over the speed limit."

Cindy ignored the jab.

"I'm sorry," Trevor said. "I know you didn't mean to do it. I'm just saying she's making me nervous. If she wants to help her mom, she better learn to calm down."

Cindy sat down at the kitchen table across from him. "She'll be fine. I'll watch her. Help her through it."

"Okay," he said. "You're the boss."

14

Susan followed the trooper back to the barracks, and they put David Hill in one of the two small interview rooms. He was seated at the far end of a tiny table that looked like it would be more appropriate for a poker game than an interrogation. The room itself was no bigger than a walk-in closet. A camera mounted in one corner recorded the interview and fed a live feed to the flat screen hanging in the investigators' unit. There was no large two-way mirror or separate viewing room. There simply wasn't enough space.

Susan opened the door and slipped inside. She dropped a file and her notebook onto the table and then made her way toward the camera. "We have to record this. For your sake as well as ours."

David nodded.

"You ready?"

"Am I going to need a lawyer?"

"Eventually," Susan replied. "You're going to be charged with trespassing, breaking and entering, and disrupting a crime scene. You can ask for a lawyer at any point, but if you cooperate here and talk to me, I won't file charges for running from the scene. I just want to know what you can tell me about your sister and James Darville."

David fell back in his chair. He wasn't crying anymore, but his eyes were red and swollen. "The quicker I tell you what I know, the quicker you can find Rebecca. Ask me what you want. I'm good."

Susan nodded. She ran through the details of who was in the interview for the benefit of the video record, asked David to confirm that he was aware he was being recorded, then opened her file.

"When we spoke with you and your mother earlier, your mother indicated she last talked to Rebecca two days ago. When was the last time you spoke to her?"

David thought for a moment. "I'd say about two days ago also. My mother had been in the hospital for a couple days, which is why Rebecca called."

"She wasn't there when your mother was discharged?"

"No, she couldn't leave Mr. James. I took care of it."

"Is that unusual? Your sister, a nurse, not being there after your mom was sent home from the hospital?"

"I don't think it was that unusual," David replied. "Sometimes her patients have to come first. We get it. It happens."

Susan made a few notes. "When you spoke to Rebecca two days ago, did you notice anything different about her tone or her mood? Was she worried or stressed or nervous? Anything like that?"

David nodded. "She was worried about my mom. My mom needs a liver transplant, and time's running out. She's older, so she's always at the bottom of the donor list. We thought this might be the end, so we were both freaking out a little."

"Could she have been worried or stressed for another reason?"

"I have no idea. She didn't say anything."

More notes. "Did you ever meet James Darville? Rebecca ever introduce you?"

"No. Like my mom said before, we knew about him, but we never met him."

"Did Rebecca ever tell you about what's going on in his life? Friends? Relatives?"

"No."

"Enemies he might've had?"

"No. Nothing like that. Just that he had dementia and she was taking care of him. That's all she ever told us other than a funny story here or there." David leaned forward. "We've already been through this. Why is Mr. James's house a crime scene? What happened to him?"

Susan ignored the questions. "Did Rebecca ever come across as nervous or uncomfortable talking about James?"

"No." David sat back and looked up at the ceiling. A fresh set of tears ran down his face. "Where is my sister?"

"Believe me, everyone's looking for her."

"She would never kill anyone."

"Yet her car was used in a state trooper's murder."

"No way she did that!" David yelled. "You have to believe me."

He began to cry again, his shoulders shaking as he buried his face in his hands. Susan leaned forward and spoke softly.

"Where were you last night?"

David looked at her. "Me?"

"Yeah. Where were you?"

"Home. Why? You think I had something to do with this?"

Susan shook her head. "Just trying to figure out where everybody was. Anybody at your house who can verify you were home?"

"No. I live alone."

David gently slapped the table with his hands. "I know breaking into Mr. James's house was stupid, and I'm willing to accept whatever charges are filed against me because of it, but I refuse to waste time being some kind of suspect here. What makes you think I had anything to do with my sister missing and that cop's murder?"

Susan flipped a few pages in her file and looked up at David. "James Darville is missing too. That's why there was tape on his door and his house was a crime scene. There are signs of struggle inside, and from the looks of your sister, I don't think she's strong enough to overtake

Mr. Darville without some help. You, on the other hand, look like you're in pretty good shape."

David buried his head in his hands. "You're wasting time."

"Maybe."

"I guess I'll take that lawyer now. Didn't think I'd have to fight for my innocence, but if you wanna go down that road, I guess we'll go."

———

"So?" Crosby stood up from his desk and stretched.

Susan leaned against his office door. She was tired, and her back hurt from sitting in a metal chair in the interview room.

"I think he's telling the truth, but he sure looks strong enough to move the heavy furniture at Darville's place. I don't know."

"There are a thousand people who could move that furniture."

"But how many are directly connected to Rebecca Hill?" She paused for a moment, thinking. "I don't have anything to hold him on, and, for the record, I think what he did was more anguish and desperation than breaking and entering. He was scared for his sister and did something dumb. We're booking him now for the B and E, and his lawyer's on the way. We'll get him in front of a judge tomorrow morning with a notice to reappear."

"DA okay with that?"

"Yeah. Just got off the phone with him. We'll keep an eye out, but I'm pretty certain he's clean."

"Okay then."

Susan rolled off the door and stopped. "I'm going to set up a couple of our minicams at the old man's house and at the nurse's place. I can't have friends and family disrupting these places with the case still active. If someone tries to break in, I want them on camera."

Crosby nodded and snatched a mug of coffee from his desk. "Sounds good."

Susan made her way back out through the investigators' unit and into the hall. She was beat and wanted to hit the road to try and make it home before Eric dropped off the kids and her mother put them to bed. A hot meal, a cold beer, and a set of hugs from the twins would set her straight. It would take about another twenty minutes to officially charge David Hill. If he kept his mouth shut and didn't ask any questions, she could get it done in fifteen. Maybe even ten.

15

It was strange walking into the house without hearing the patter of feet running down the hall or the shouts of excitement welcoming her home. There was no television blaring or music pumping. No crunching of plastic toys being played with or the high-pitched laughter of children having fun. When Susan walked through her front door and placed her bag down at the base of the coatrack, there was only a curtain of silence to greet her, and in that brief moment, she realized how much she missed her kids.

She made her way into the living room while reading an email that had come in on her phone. Triston had been able to get a list of Darville's doctors from the physical therapist who'd called 911. She'd make some calls after the kids got home to try and line up interviews starting in the morning.

Her mother was lying on the couch, eyes closed, a thin rumble of a snore rising from her throat. Beatrice looked peaceful and pain-free, which were two adjectives that had recently been stolen from their vernacular. A year earlier she'd suffered a pierced liver, nicked intestine, and collapsed lung as a result of being attacked while trying to protect her grandchildren. But she was a fighter, and although the physical therapy and general recovery had taken their toll, she refused to give in. Beatrice always liked to say living fine and free was the best revenge. Susan couldn't have agreed more.

She sat on the edge of the couch and rubbed her mother's leg. "Ma, get up. If you sleep now, you'll never get to sleep tonight."

The old woman opened her eyes and looked around. Perhaps she, too, was confused by the silence. This had been the first time the twins had been gone overnight since she'd moved into the house full-time.

"I was reading. Must've dozed off."

"Did you eat?"

"I had a bowl of cereal earlier."

"Cereal isn't dinner. I'll cook us something quick."

Her mother swung her legs onto the floor to sit up. Susan kicked her shoes off and walked into the kitchen.

"What'd you do all day?" Susan asked.

"I had my shows. Did some reading. Did my exercises."

"Strange with the kids not here, right?"

"Very strange. I miss them."

"Eric should be by any second to drop them off. I talked to him before. He said they did great."

"Good. He needs to spend more time with his children. They're going to be off to college before he knows it, and he can't miss out on them growing up. Not like he's been."

Susan could hear her mother coming to join her in the kitchen as she pulled a pan from the lower cabinet next to the sink and spun around to snatch the butter and cheese from the refrigerator. "He's been better. I think after what happened, he started reassessing his role as Tim and Casey's dad."

Beatrice huffed and sat down at the kitchen table. "Too bad it takes attempted murder to get him to play a part in his children's lives."

"Relax, Ma. Put the claws away."

Susan opened the bread box and took four slices from the bag. She buttered each side, then tossed them onto the pan. She and Eric had been divorced for two years and separated for three. He was still dating his much younger coworker, which in its own twisted way made her feel better about the divorce in general. If Eric's new relationship had only lasted long enough for him to get his rocks off or for the younger executive to get that promotion she so clearly wanted, Susan would've felt as if the separation and the heartache would've been for naught. But the happy couple were still together, hanging in despite their slightly ridiculous age difference, and that made her feel as if her ex really had moved on to something he perceived as better. But having said all that, screw him. He was an asshole for leaving her the way he did, and despite learning to coexist with him for the sake of the twins, Susan knew she could never really forgive him. That wasn't going to happen. Ever.

"So how was your day?" Beatrice asked, breaking her from her thoughts.

Susan flipped the sandwiches. "A trooper was killed during a traffic stop this morning. The entire troop is on full alert."

"I saw that on the news. You're involved in the investigation?"

"Kind of. Our suspect lives in White Plains, but there are some ties to Verplanck, which is our jurisdiction, so I'm checking it out."

The doorbell rang.

Susan looked at her mother as a smile crept upon her face. Beatrice was smiling too.

The twins were home.

"Give me that spatula," Beatrice said, standing from the table. "I'll finish the sandwiches. Go."

Susan handed her mother the spatula and raced down the hall. She took a moment to compose herself and opened the door to Casey falling into her legs.

"Mommy!"

"Hi, honey!" Susan rubbed her daughter's back and couldn't help but laugh. "How was your sleepover?"

"It was great! We went to Chuck E. Cheese and watched Netflix shows and played dance games. It was the best!"

"That's terrific!" She looked up and saw Eric standing in front of her. He was tired, which made her happy. His eyes were two slits. "They wear you out?"

"Oh, yes, they did. We had fun, though." He smiled, and for a flash, it made her knees weak. That smile always did, although its power over her had been diminishing with time. "I looked for an off switch but couldn't find one on either of them."

"I've been looking for that switch for six years. Believe me, if it was there, I would've gotten to it by now."

"My babies are home!"

Susan turned to see her mother standing just inside the kitchen, arms outstretched, a look of pure joy on her face.

"Grandma!"

Casey broke away from Susan and ran down the hall. Susan watched the six-year-old jump into her grandmother's arms; then she turned back around to find Tim hugging Eric's leg.

"How you doing, bud?" She bent down and brushed the hair out of her little boy's eyes. "Did you have fun too?"

Tim nodded. "Yeah. We had lots of fun. I didn't want to leave."

"I know, but Daddy's gotta get on a plane in the morning for his work, and from the looks of him, I think he needs a good night's sleep. Can I have a hug?"

Tim slowly let go of his father's leg and hugged Susan. It wasn't as tight or as full of the same vigor as Casey's, but that's how his hugs had been since his innocence had been stolen inside his own house. The trauma was still with him, and although he'd been making progress with his therapist in Philadelphia, he still wasn't—and might never again be—the Tim she'd known up until that night her work had invaded her home.

Susan stood back up and gently guided Tim inside. "Go say hi to Grandma. I think she missed you more than I did."

The little boy nodded and snaked his way through the living room, through the dining room, and into the back of the kitchen so as to avoid that certain spot in the hallway. This was how he'd walked into the kitchen every day since that night, always refusing to step across the spot where the bad man had held a knife to his throat. He never once mistakenly crossed the area out of habit or distraction. Never.

"How was he?" Susan asked as Eric walked inside and shut the door.

"He was great. They both were. I think getting him out of this house was really helpful. He was more like his old self at my place."

"Well, that makes me feel *so* much better. Thanks."

"I'm not saying it to be an ass," Eric replied quickly. "I'm telling you the truth, though. This house, it has a history now. For whatever reason, Casey wasn't affected by what happened, but Tim's traumatized. And every time he walks in here, and every time he looks at that spot in the hall, he's reminded of what happened. It can't be good for his well-being."

"It's not like I can pull up stakes and move," Susan snapped. "I changed the carpet in the living room. I pulled up all the flooring in the hallway. There isn't a trace of what happened left here. Everything's been cleared out."

"Except there's the spot," Eric said, pointing. "Might not have the same floor, and it might be cleaner than any other area in the house, but there's the spot." He took her hands in his. "If you want Tim to heal, I mean really heal, I think you need to consider selling this place. It might be exactly what he needs to put everything behind him. Move on, you know?"

She could hear her mother in the kitchen with the kids. The house was back to its regular volume of activity and chaos. Footsteps, laughter, conversation, the television, the radio, the family.

Her family.

Her home.

Her new life.

"You think we should move?"

Eric nodded. "I do. But that's not up to me. That decision is entirely—one hundred percent—up to you."

16

Trevor and Cindy sat in the living room. The windows were black, the night having taken full hold. The house was quiet. Trevor was scouring the internet for updates about the trooper's death, and Cindy was paging through a magazine she couldn't concentrate on.

"You ever think you'd be in a mess like this?" she asked, her voice cutting through the silence.

"Not in a million years."

"When I was younger, I took my childhood for granted like every other kid does. I figured there would always be friends and school and sports and memories of summers that I'd cherish. I'd daydream about boyfriends and what things might be like in college. I'd fantasize about my future husband and a house full of children. But nothing turned out like that. It was all just a fantasy because my sister went missing one day after school, and everything changed. It started as a normal day in a normal family, and by the end of it, we were all different."

Trevor looked up from the laptop. Cindy closed the magazine.

"I keep asking myself how I ended up here, and the only answer I keep getting is fate. It was fate that Hagen found Rebecca, right? And that Rebecca found me? I need this. I need to hear the truth about what happened to my sister from that man down in the basement because I need closure. That's all I want. Just the closure. The peace to live the rest of my life like a normal person."

"We don't even know who Hagen is."

"I don't care who he is. If he can give me this one gift, I'll be grateful."

"I hope you get what you're after."

She closed her eyes. "I can still see everything like it was yesterday. Everything's still so vivid. The town swooping in to try and help find her. The people we'd known all our lives joining search parties. I can still smell the wet fur of the dogs that were used to track her scent. These are the things that haunt me every day. I figure if I can find out what really happened to Sonia, some of those images and memories can finally start to fade. Maybe the nightmares will stop too."

She opened her eyes back up and looked at him.

"The police were always hovering around the house, asking us questions. Even the television news stations out of Pittsburgh did a story about it. But then everything started dying down, and that's when I could see things for what they were. All of a sudden friends weren't allowed to come over and play with me anymore. Teachers would look at me funny. Grown-ups at the supermarket would go out of their way to avoid us. There was this cloud of suspicion hanging over me and my parents, like we did something wrong. That's a tough thing for a child to wrap their head around, and that's what I think ultimately made my mom kill herself. It wasn't just the grief. It was the grief and the suspicions others in town had of us. My mother could never get over that. It was too much."

"How did Hagen find you?" Trevor asked.

"According to Rebecca, it was the podcast. She said he listened and always heard me talking about how Sonia had been my best friend even more than she'd been my big sister, and when she disappeared, the girl I was disappeared right along with her. The girl who replaced her was lonely and sad and troubled. This girl didn't bother with boys or school dances or friend groups. She didn't care about making memories. There was only the obsession of finding out what happened to her big sister. Apparently, he thought he could use the truth to leverage my willingness to help capture James, and he was right. He had Rebecca contact me, and then I contacted you."

"You ever ask Rebecca how she was connected to Hagen?"

"She said she got a call. Just like us."

Trevor shook his head. "Maybe."

"What do you mean?"

"Rebecca was the only one contacted directly by Hagen. She got in touch with you, and you reached out to me. Rebecca was the only one to talk to this guy herself. I think she knows who he is."

"I never really thought about that."

"Maybe you should," Trevor replied. "Maybe we all should. And maybe we should ask her about it when she wakes up."

17

Dr. Phillip Calib was sitting at a bistro table in a coffee shop across from his office in Croton. He looked to be in his late forties, with dark hair, a thick beard, blue eyes, and olive skin. He was fit, but not overly so, and dressed in a simple pair of tan corduroys and a blue shirt, he could've been anything from a student to a professor to an engineer to an attorney. He was the type of man who was seen without being seen, always part of the backdrop in someone else's situation, never a person to stand out in a crowd.

Susan dodged the line that stretched out the door and dropped her bag on the table before taking her seat. Dr. Calib smiled and pointed toward the counter. "Can I get you a coffee or a muffin or something?"

"No, I'm good."

"They make the best croissants in Westchester."

"I ate before I left the house." She looked around, scanning the room. "Cute place."

"You should see it during the week. Twice as busy. I come here every morning before the office opens. It's my one chance to take a breath before the waiting room fills up and we're off and running. Once I step through those doors across the street, I won't see the outside until I'm leaving for the day, and by then the sun will be down and the town will be deserted."

"Sounds a little depressing."

"It is what it is."

Susan took out her notepad and placed it on the table. "As we discussed on the phone, we're conducting an investigation regarding the state trooper who was killed yesterday morning, and Rebecca Hill is a person of interest. James Darville is also missing, and we know she was his nurse. I just need to confirm some information about your relationship with them. I know you can't disclose doctor-patient stuff. I'm just trying to paint a larger picture for the case."

Dr. Calib took a sip of his coffee as he gazed out the window. "I understand." He paused for a moment. "That poor man and his family. The wife was pregnant, right?"

"That's correct."

"So tragic."

Susan took the cap off her pen. "How long has Mr. Darville been a patient of yours?"

Dr. Calib turned away from the window. "He's been with the practice for a little over ten years. I looked it up after I got off the phone with you last night. He started with Dr. Solanso, who retired six months ago. I came on board, and all of Dr. Solanso's patients were transferred to me at that time, including James."

"Where were you prior?"

"I worked in a large office with a conglomerate out of Cherry Hill. South Jersey. I came up this way looking for a smaller practice in a smaller town. Suits me better. I met Dr. Solanso through a mutual friend and learned he was retiring. It was like it was meant to be. We're still part of the larger conglomerate here—that's just the way the industry is these days—but our office *feels* small. I like that."

"Did Dr. Solanso's notes say where James was prior to him coming in ten years ago?"

"It said Pennsylvania, but it wasn't more specific than that. Dr. Solanso never got medical files transferred. He just treated James as a new patient and did initial workups and tests in the first few visits to establish the baseline."

Susan wrote the information down. "How many times have you seen James since you took over?"

"I can't give you specifics as to why he was in to see me, as that would be a HIPAA violation, but I'm his general physician, so you can draw your own conclusions. I've seen him twice since taking over. You already know about the dementia, so no violations there. He spends more time with the specialists in that field than with me. As it should be."

"Dr. Sara Phines is his neurologist out of Phelps, right?"

"That's right."

"Do you ever recall him coming in with someone other than Rebecca Hill? We're trying to track down any family or friends he might have."

"No," Dr. Calib replied. "He was always with Rebecca."

"Do you work with any of Rebecca's other patients?"

"No. I've only ever seen her with James."

Susan scribbled her notes. "Are you familiar with Dr. Trammel?" she asked.

"Yes," Dr. Calib replied. "We're all in the same network. I believe Dr. Phines referred James to Dr. Trammel for physical therapy."

"Have you talked to any of them lately? Do you get updates on Mr. Darville's condition?"

Dr. Calib took another sip of his coffee and shook his head. "No. All of our notes are in the system, so we have access to shared files and get our updates that way. That's one of the benefits of being in the network together. If James was scheduled for a visit, I'd read up on his progress through the system. The other doctors would do the same to go over my notes. That's how it works."

"Susan!"

Susan looked up when the barista shouted her name. A younger girl bounced through the crowd and grabbed her coffee. False alarm.

"Last question," she said, turning back to Dr. Calib. "Is there anything you can tell me about Rebecca Hill that might help us in our investigation? Might help us figure out where she is?"

Dr. Calib shrugged. "Not really. Always seemed like a nice woman. We didn't really speak much, but I wouldn't peg her for the type of person to kill a state trooper in cold blood, that's for sure."

Susan closed her notepad and slid off her seat. "Thanks, that's all I have."

"If I hear anything from James, you'll be the first one I call."

"I appreciate that," Susan replied. She got up and swung her bag over her shoulder. "Enjoy the daylight while you can. Those office hours start soon."

18

"Hey, time to wake up."

It took a moment for James to open his eyes, but when he did, a bolt of pain shot down his right shoulder. He tried to roll onto his side, but the braces on his legs kept him from moving. He reached up and massaged his neck as best he could, his breaths short and quick until he felt things loosen a bit.

"You with me? You okay?"

The voice came from his left side, and he turned, straining to see the woman who was sitting on the arm of the couch, a tray of cereal and a steaming mug of coffee on the table behind her. He knew this woman. Knew her face. Her hair. Her frame. But her name escaped him.

"I think I hurt my neck."

She walked over to him and bent down to examine the area he was rubbing. "Let me see." Nimble fingers brushed his hand away and began gently caressing his shoulder, pushing into the muscles and tendons. "Does that hurt?"

"Yes."

"How about here?"

"Yes."

"Getting better?"

"A little."

She patted him on the chest and stood straight. "You probably slept on it wrong. You're fine."

"I can't sit up. I think my legs are caught under a boulder. I must've slipped in the cave. So clumsy."

"No cave. You have braces on your legs."

"Can you help me?"

"First things first."

The woman pulled back the covers and, with one motion, yanked his pants down to his knees and slipped the bedpan underneath him.

"Go."

"Now?"

"Yes. Go."

"You're here. I can't."

The woman sighed and turned around so she couldn't see anything. He felt his face flush as he relieved himself. When he was done, she took the pan, set it on the floor, and pulled his pants back up. She looked disinterested, as if she'd done this a thousand times. She probably had.

"You ready to get out of bed?"

"I guess so."

The woman swung his legs out and got him into a sitting position. When he was upright, she brought the wheelchair over and helped him fall into it. The pain in his neck and shoulder was beginning to dissipate now that he was in the chair. She was right. He'd probably just slept wrong.

"You want some breakfast?"

"I want Rebecca," James said without really understanding what he was saying. The request and the name just slipped from his lips. "Where is she?"

The woman got behind him and began pushing him toward the living room. "Who's Rebecca?"

"My nurse. Where is she? Did she call out sick today? Are you my nurse today?"

"No. I'm Cindy."

"Where's Rebecca?"

"There's no Rebecca. Just you and me."

"Cindy."

"That's right. Do you remember me from yesterday? And the day before that? And the day before that?"

When she said her name, bits of memory began to show themselves, a half scene here, a quarter of a scene there. But nothing he could string together with any cohesion.

"I'm sorry," he whispered. "I do remember. I do. You're Cindy."

"That's right."

"You brought me here to take care of me instead of putting me in a hospital."

"Right again."

"They were beating me at the hospital. They threw me onto the floor."

"If you say so."

"No, it's true. They threw me down. Two men. I hit my head."

"Okay."

He closed his eyes to steady his thoughts. "I'm in this wheelchair . . . because of a car accident?"

Cindy stopped pushing and bent down in front of him. She looked him in his eyes, her gaze deep and focused. "Can you tell me your name?"

"My name?"

"Yeah. What's your name?"

And just like that, it was gone.

"My name . . ."

He struggled to remember, but the fog moved in quickly, thick and gray, overtaking the slivers of memory he'd held only seconds ago.

"My name . . ."

He fought to hold on. The car accident. The basement. Cindy. But those details, too, began to fade, and only a single question surfaced.

"Where's Rebecca? Did she call out sick today? Are you her backup?"

The woman's chin dropped to her chest as she stood and gently took the coffee from the table, handing it to him. "We were almost there."

"Where? Where are we?"

She dug into her pocket, came away with a pill bottle, and opened it, shaking two pills in his hand.

"What's this?"

"Tylenol. For your neck. It'll make you feel better."

He took the pills and sipped the coffee. "I want to go outside. I need some fresh air."

"We will. Gotta stop raining first."

"And can we fix that clock? I never know what time it is. It's hard to tell what's up and what's down. I need to go outside or upstairs or something. I need to get with people. Interact."

"You do. You've been up and out and in group sessions and to physical therapy. You've interacted with doctors and volunteers, and you have friends at the community center. You just don't remember any of it."

James closed his eyes, frustrated and sad. He tried to force the fog to part for just a moment so he could grab on to something. "You're . . . Rebecca."

"No."

"Cindy! You're Cindy."

The woman smiled. "That's right."

"I'm . . . James. James Darville. Don't call me Jim because I hate that. Just James."

Cindy clapped her hands. "Yes. Very good." She parked the wheelchair at the edge of the couch and sat in front of him. "The man from last night who came down to help you into bed. Do you remember him?"

"Yes. Nasty fella. Tried to talk to him, but he had nothing to say."

"He told me you were asking for Bonnie."

"Who's Bonnie? Why was I asking for her?"

"Think. Try and remember."

"I am," James said. "I don't know who Bonnie is. I'm sorry."

The woman nodded and sat back against the couch cushions. "Let's try this. Tell me about yourself. Where did you grow up? What did you do for a living?"

He closed his eyes again, searching for the answers he knew were in his head, his heart aching for reasons he couldn't quite understand. The fog had rolled in like a giant wave over a jetty in high tide. There was nothing. He looked at the woman, who looked somewhat familiar.

"Where's Rebecca?" he asked. "Did she call out sick? Are you her replacement?"

Then he was gone.

19

The next office on the list Triston had made for her was Traveling Healthcare of New York. It was tucked away in a nondescript brick building in Mount Kisco, about a mile east of Northern Westchester Medical Center, on the border of Bedford Hills. The building's tenants covered almost every kind of medical treatment that might come to mind: podiatry, cardiology, ENT, joint replacement, obstetrics, rheumatology. The directory itself stretched from floor to ceiling. Susan found the staffing agency on the third floor and took the elevator up.

Beth Ruelle was a short woman, maybe four feet, with cropped silver hair that hung just below her ears. A white lab coat covered a black dress that fell past her knees. Black-rimmed glasses took up most of her face and magnified her brown eyes. Susan watched as she made her way around several cubicles and out to the waiting area, a tiny hand extended in greeting.

"Beth Ruelle," the woman said as they shook.

"Susan Adler. Sorry to call you in on a Saturday."

"No worries at all. This is important. Please, follow me."

Susan retraced Beth's steps around the cubicles to the back of the spacious office and followed the older woman into a conference room. Beth sat on one side of the long table while Susan sat opposite her, her back to the glass wall looking out onto the rest of the floor.

"I can't believe this happened," Beth said, her gaze fixed elsewhere as the words floated out of her mouth. "As soon as I saw it on the news, I started getting calls. Still no sign of Rebecca or Mr. Darville?"

Susan took out her notepad and slid her chair forward so she could write on the table. "Nothing yet."

"Such a shame."

"As I mentioned on the phone, I just wanted to get a sense of Rebecca Hill's history with your firm."

Beth waved a hand. "Ask anything you want."

"How long has she been employed here?"

"Twelve years. She's been assigned to Mr. Darville for two. Mr. Darville came to us through Medicaid as a referral. His disease had progressed to the point of him needing care more often than not."

"Alzheimer's."

"That's right. He hasn't reached the point of needing full-time care in a facility just yet, but that's, unfortunately, inevitable. Perhaps in another few years."

"Any relatives?"

"None that we've ever known of. No visitors. No calls. I know Rebecca herself tried to do some digging but came up empty."

"So why not just roll him into a nursing home or specialized facility, rather than having him live on his own, if he has no family around?"

"It's all about the budget," Beth said quickly. This wasn't the first time she'd needed to explain this. "Right now Mr. Darville is in a house that's paid off in a town where property taxes are relatively cheap, and his social security covers them. As far as Medicaid is concerned, one of our nurses, a home food-delivery program, and his current household expenses were less expensive than a skilled nursing facility. They're going to save every penny until full-time care is mandatory. That's how these things work."

Susan jotted a few notes. "You said Rebecca kept files?"

"Yes. All my nurses have to keep daily patient files so we know what's going on day to day. We share these updates with the patient's primary or secondary care doctors so everyone's in the loop. It also helps if a nurse leaves us or calls in sick. The files can make those transitions seamless."

"I'd like a copy of her files as they pertain to Mr. Darville."

"I'll see what I can do," Beth said. "You know, HIPAA and all."

"Do you know anything about Rebecca's personal life? Any idea why she might've been driving north on the Taconic at two in the morning?"

Beth shrugged. "None of that is my business. My focus is on the medical side of my nurses' lives. What they do off shift is not something I care to know."

"Was James Darville Rebecca's only patient?"

"Yes. Rebecca requested Mr. Darville when he came up in our queue and had seen him Monday through Friday for the past two years. Never had a problem. Never called in sick. She was a good nurse. That's why this is such a shock."

Susan stopped writing and looked up. "Wait, she *requested* Mr. Darville? Is that the normal process?"

"No, but he came through, and Rebecca had the availability, so she raised her hand. I think she knew it would be a long-term assignment, and long-term assignments bring steady paychecks."

More notes. "Who looked after him on the weekends? Or if he needed something overnight?"

"From what I understand, he had neighbors look in on him on the weekend. We never had an episode with him at night, but if he did need us, we have a direct dial on his phone that he knows how to use. And, of course, there's always 911."

"Do you know which neighbor looked in on him? Because we've been through the neighborhood and everyone said they knew of James, but didn't interact with him."

"I don't. I'm sorry."

Susan dug into her bag and came away with several sheets of paper. She laid them out on the table side by side and pushed them closer to Beth.

"I found a notebook in Rebecca's apartment. These are copies of its contents. As you can see, there are names and lists of drugs and dosages next to each one. Do you know these names?"

Beth took the papers and read through them, nodding as she went, her crooked fingers tracing the names and drugs across the page to the dosage. "Yes, the names listed here are Rebecca's old patients. Can't be certain that every single name was with our firm, but I do recognize most of them. My guess is she kept this with her so as not to forget who gets what when it comes to administering their medications."

"Is that normal?"

"It's good practice, if you ask me. We obviously provide a full charting of each of our care patients, and most of it is digital now, but if this was a backup to what we gave her, I'd say she was being prudent. Smart."

"Do you know if any of these people live up toward where she was driving?"

"I wouldn't know without looking at each patient file."

"And HIPAA."

"Exactly."

Susan took the papers back. "Last question. Would you say Rebecca is a good employee? A good nurse?"

Beth took her glasses off and leaned forward, her eyes locking on Susan's without blinking. "Investigator Adler, I've owned this company for twenty-two years, and in those twenty-two years, I've had countless nurses come work for me. Some stay. Some move on to more permanent positions in hospitals and nursing homes. Some get fired. During a few rough years, I've even had to lay some off. But all that being said, I've never had a better nurse than Rebecca Hill. She's smart, caring, efficient, and one hell of a good healthcare provider. There's no way she did what you all think she did to that poor trooper. And if she didn't do it, then someone had her car, which begs the question, where *is* Rebecca? And if something's happened to her, it will impact those she never had a chance to care for, and our world will suffer because of it. I pray that Rebecca and Mr. Darville are okay and that you find them soon. And with that same prayer, I ask God that you find the person who's really responsible. I pray you find the person and that he or she pays for what they've done. That is my only wish. My only prayer. Find the real murderer, because my Rebecca wouldn't hurt a soul."

20

It was normally a thirty-minute drive from Mount Kisco to Tarrytown, but traffic was light and Susan made it to Phelps Hospital in twenty. She pulled in from the side entrance, drove down past the ER and the outpatient surgery center, and parked around back where the endoscopy center and therapy wing were. She'd checked in with the barracks after her meeting with Beth Ruelle to see if there had been any developments, and Crosby let her know they were expecting the dashcam footage from Kincaid's cruiser at any moment. There was nothing more to report.

Dr. Alfred Trammel was a tall man in his late thirties with a full head of dirty-blond hair. His skin was pocked with old acne scars, but what drew more attention were his sparkling green eyes. He stood on one side of a long counter, leaning on the surface as if he were about to take a drink order. Susan sat on one of the stools opposite him. Behind them, a handful of patients and therapists worked on exercises and stretching among weights, treadmills, Smith machines, mats, and an array of other materials.

"We appreciate you calling this in," Susan began. "A lot of people might've ignored the change in routine and not gotten involved. We were able to connect Mr. Darville's disappearance with the shooting quickly. I'm glad you gave us a heads-up."

Trammel nodded. "I knew James's absence wasn't normal. They were always on time on each day he was scheduled. Rebecca made sure of it."

"Tell me about Mr. Darville. How long has he been coming to see you? What do you know about his condition?"

"James has been coming to us for almost two years now. We started with some basic exercises twice a week after he was first assigned a full-time nurse. I guess at that point he'd been diagnosed for about a year, and things were starting to take a turn for the worse. As the disease intensified, we increased his visits to three days, and finally the Tuesday through Friday schedule he has with us now. He's been on the current schedule for three months."

"And then all of a sudden he stopped coming."

"That's right. We saw him, as usual, on Tuesday, and then nothing. I really didn't think anything of it at first, but after the third day of no show and no call, I started to think something might be wrong. We checked with the agency Rebecca works for, and they hadn't heard from her, either, so I called a few area hospitals and then you guys. Next thing I know, I'm watching the news about the trooper and see that Rebecca is a suspect. Crazy."

"How was Rebecca with James?"

"Those two had quite the relationship," Dr. Trammel replied. "He trusted her, and she was so kind to him. I think, even when he was having a particularly bad flare-up, that he somehow knew she was by his side. From what I could tell, she cared for him deeply. There's no way that woman killed anyone, let alone a state trooper. I can't wrap my head around that."

Susan made a few notes in her pad. "What would a session look like for a patient with Alzheimer's?"

Trammel gestured to the others who were working around them. "Not that much different from our other patients here. We give them the cardiovascular fitness, the endurance, and strength they need from a physical standpoint to be able to get around. Maintaining a semblance of physical fitness can increase motor skills and, in some cases, reduce the rate of mental decline. It's a mandatory part of treating the disease, as far as I'm concerned, and James was doing great."

"Any staff here different or new in the last few months?"

"No. We run lean and mean here. There's me, Dr. Ramis—who's been my partner since I got out of medical school—and Jason and Audrey, who've been our assistants for six or seven years now. No new staff."

"What about new patients?"

"Well, sure. We're always getting new patients."

"Can I get a list of who they are?"

"Not without a warrant. I'd love to help you, but we have HIPAA laws to abide by."

"Of course." Susan got up out of her chair and shook the doctor's hand. "Thank you for your time. I appreciate you seeing me."

"I wish I could help more. If I think of anything, I'll call you. And, of course, if I hear from either James or Rebecca."

"Thank you."

Dr. Trammel walked Susan past the exercise machines and the patients grunting their way toward rehabilitation. He stopped when they reached the door.

"We heard James's house was bad," he said. "Is that true?"

"Can't talk about it," Susan replied, opening the door. "You got HIPAA, and I got an open investigation. Sorry."

21

James didn't know how long he was sleeping, but when he woke up, he was in his wheelchair, sitting in front of the television. The TV was on, and Alfred Hitchcock's *The Birds* was playing. It was just at the part when Tippi Hedren was meeting Rod Taylor at the pet shop where she would buy the two lovebirds. Chaos would ensue soon after. He knew the scene—and the entire film—as well as he knew his legs were in braces, but he had no recollection of starting the movie or watching it up to that point. The remote sat on his lap, yet he couldn't recall a single moment when the woman or the man helped him start the movie. He aimed the remote at the screen and turned it off.

The basement was quiet, and from what he could hear, the rest of the house was as well. There were no footsteps walking above him or muffled voices having conversations he couldn't make out. The hairs on his arms stood up. He had no reason to feel frightened, but the atmosphere made him uneasy. Something wasn't right.

James spun his wheelchair around and made his way to the landing of the stairs. He looked up and saw the basement door was closed. He counted fifteen steps to the top. In his condition, it might as well have been one hundred and fifteen.

"Hello!" he shouted, his voice hoarse from sleeping. "Is there anyone up there?"

No answer.

"Hello! I can't find my lesson planner, and I need it for class! Can you hear me?"

Nothing.

He waited a few minutes, listening for movement. The house appeared to be empty. His class was due to start soon. Without his lesson planner, he'd be lost. The students would laugh at him. They could be so cruel sometimes.

James wheeled himself into the bedroom area, huffing as he went. How could they leave him down here like some animal when he had a class to teach? And what if he fell? What if he needed to use the bathroom? He couldn't ask a student. That would be inappropriate. He was in no condition to be left alone. He needed care. He needed someone to be with him in case something went wrong. What if there was a fire? Who would save him if he needed saving? Did his students know first aid? Were they equipped to handle a teacher who was handicapped? What would the school think of all of this?

He stopped in front of his dresser and pulled the top drawer open, searching for his lesson planner. He wasn't sure the last time he'd had it, but it couldn't have been that long ago. It had to be close by.

The drawer was empty. No clothing, no lesson planner. He closed the top drawer and opened the second. It, too, was empty. He tried the third with the same result. The fourth and final drawer, empty.

Where were his clothes?

James backed out of the bedroom area and wheeled himself around the perimeter of the basement, searching for storage bins or a closet or another room that might have his clothes. There was nothing. The room was just one big space except for the single step up to the tiny hallway that led to the hurricane doors. He made his way to the edge of the step, where the shadows met the light, and stopped. He knew the ghosts were down there, waiting. The step looked to be about six inches high. Too high for his chair to roll over. He reversed himself away and returned to the light.

James spun the chair around so he could see the entire basement laid out in front of him. For the first time, he noticed that nothing in the room appeared to be his, other than the pajamas he was wearing and the robe on his bed. There were no books or magazines or newspapers or music. He couldn't see any of his nature photos that should've been framed and displayed. No keepsakes or knickknacks. The space he saw was cold and heartless. Completely anonymous.

"Rebecca!" he cried. He needed Rebecca. She would know how to make him feel better. She would help him get ready for class and find his planner.

"Rebecca! Where are you?"

The fog began to grow thicker. How could he be living down there without his belongings? It didn't make sense. Where was his nurse? Why were his drawers empty? Where were his books and pictures? Where was his life?

What was happening?

22

Dr. Sara Phines was James Darville's neurologist, and the last doctor on Susan's list. Dr. Phines was a tall woman, towering well over six feet, thin, her hair short and gray with barrettes pinning back her bangs. A pair of bifocals hung around her neck and tangled in the collar of her oversized lab coat. She smiled when she saw Susan and extended a rather large hand with bone-thin fingers, no nail polish. Susan watched her own hand disappear when they shook.

"I appreciate you seeing me."

"Anything I can do to help. I can't believe James is *missing*. And I saw the thing about his nurse on the news. So terrible."

They walked into an empty break room and sat on plastic chairs at a round table.

"I spoke with Dr. Calib and Dr. Trammel earlier today. I understand you're in the same network."

"That's right," Dr. Phines replied. "I first met James about three years ago when he was presenting with Alzheimer's stage three, which is considered a mild decline. He was initially brought into the ER after he collapsed at a supermarket. The people there thought he was having a stroke. James was having trouble finding his words when he was speaking and was quite disoriented. The staff neurologist made the diagnosis, then passed him to me. Two years ago, we requested full-time care when he slipped into stage four. He was having short-term memory loss. Couldn't pay his bills or do the math required for balancing a checkbook. His disease has progressed to stage five now. Unawareness of his surroundings. Inability to remember people, sometimes even himself. Inability to remember anyone's history. It's not a pretty disease."

Susan made a few notes in her pad. "Do you know if Mr. Darville has any family?"

"I looked through his file when he first came to me, and it never mentioned family or next of kin. He always came and left with Rebecca."

"What can you tell me about her?"

"I've only known her through James. She seems nice. Cares for James a great deal. You can see it in the way they interact."

"Ever see her outside of your practice?"

Dr. Phines shook her head. "No, sorry."

A woman came into the break room and stopped when she saw Susan and Dr. Phines at the table. She quickly grabbed an apple from the refrigerator and left.

"Did James ever talk about friends?" Susan asked. "Any acquaintances we should be made aware of?"

"I literally never saw him with anyone other than Rebecca," Dr. Phines replied. "And he never talked about friends. He rambled about things, as patients do in their decline, but nothing I could definitively point you to."

"Give me an example of something he would ramble about."

Dr. Phines looked up at the ceiling, thinking. "I gather he used to be a teacher because he's always talking about his students, and he often went on and on about losing his lesson planner. All typical behavior. His mind is confusing the past and the present."

"Anything else?"

"Every once in a while he talks about a specific set of kids. Bonnie and Sonia. There are a couple more, but I can't think of them right now."

"Any chance you took notes?" Susan asked. "The names could point us in some kind of direction."

Dr. Phines shook her head. "I stopped taking notes after stage three. His thoughts are too incoherent to make heads or tails of anything."

"But the names he mentions and losing his lesson planner are consistent things he talks about?"

"Nothing's ever too consistent, but he brings them up every now and again."

Susan took a business card out of her jacket pocket and slid it across the table. She stood from her seat, say goodbye to Dr. Phines, and left. Rebecca had no real friends, no boyfriend, and no social life other than hanging out with her mother and brother on Sundays. James also had no friends and no family. They had each other, and they were both missing, and there was no question Rebecca had been with someone else that night in Darville's house.

So who was her accomplice?

23

Susan walked onto the investigators' floor to find Crosby waving her into his office. She placed her bag down on her chair and went to see what he needed.

"Still here on a Saturday?" she said.

Crosby pointed to the news on the flat screen. They were doing another story on the trooper's death. "All hands until we catch our guy."

"Right."

"Any luck?"

She sat down in one of the two chairs in front of her boss's desk. "Not really. Just trying to get a background from friends and family, but neither Rebecca nor Darville has friends and the old man has no family. I got nothing from Rebecca's mom and brother yesterday, so I've been talking to the old man's doctors. Not much there, either, but the general picture everyone has painted is that Rebecca was an excellent nurse and cared very deeply for James. I'm starting to think there might be a twist in this we're not seeing."

Crosby turned his computer screen toward her. "There is a twist, and I'm about to show you. We got the dashcam footage. Check it out."

He clicked his mouse, and Susan was suddenly looking through the lens of the trooper's dashcam. There was no sound. She watched as the trooper's car caught up with Rebecca's Honda. He hit the bar lights, and the Honda immediately complied, signaling and pulling off to the shoulder. The trooper walked to the driver's side, and the window rolled down. He was talking and shining his flashlight from the front of the car to the back. Everything appeared routine. Then he pointed at something.

"What's he see?" Susan asked.

"No idea."

The driver nodded and leaned toward the passenger side. The trooper stiffened up and yelled something. The driver stopped moving as the trooper shined the flashlight back down on the driver's lap. A few more words were exchanged; then the trooper opened the door.

"He spotted something. He's making the driver get out of the car."

A woman emerged from the driver's side, tall and well built. The wind blew, and her curly hair fell in front of her face.

"That's not Rebecca Hill," Susan said immediately. "This driver's too tall."

"And she's white," Crosby replied. "Keep watching."

There was a blur as someone stepped in front of the dashcam, and by the time Susan could see the next frame, the trooper was falling backward, and a figure wearing dark pants and a black hoodie was beating him with a tire iron. A few hits. It didn't take much. The attack was over in seconds. When the figure stood back up, it appeared to be a man.

"Who the hell is that?"

Crosby points. "White male. Look at his hands."

Indeed, she could see his wrists between his gloves and shirtsleeves. He was white. The male came back toward the trooper's car. His face was covered and his hood was up.

"He knew the dashcam would be on."

"Yup."

The video terminated a few seconds later.

Crosby stood from his chair and turned the monitor back toward him. "He cut the power to the patrol car. That's all we got."

"And no sign of Rebecca. Or the old man."

"Could've been in the car the male came from. No way to know."

Susan's mind was spinning. "This fits within the time frame of when Darville went missing from his house, for sure. Could be the same night. Forensics is testing the blood we found in the bedroom, which will confirm how old it is. But according to Darville's physical therapist, they hadn't been able to reach him for three days. Not sure what the gap in time might be."

"Maybe this couple spent a few days searching the house until they found whatever was in that hole in the floor."

"Yeah, that's what I'm thinking." She got up from her seat. "Are we getting these images out to the media?"

Crosby shook his head as he shut off the video. "Not yet. We want to keep this in house for now. Your new suspects are both Caucasian, a woman taller than Rebecca and a man younger than James Darville. Rebecca may still be involved, or she might be dead and her car stolen. We just don't know. Keep digging and see what you come up with. Play it safe."

"Copy that."

"You need anything from me at this point?"

Susan turned to leave the office. "I need a copy of that footage so I can study the tape. I could also use a few more hours in the day."

TRANSCRIPT

I sat in my car across from Tiffany Greene's house for about an hour, willing myself to have the courage to walk up to her parents and tell them what had happened. I watched as Mr. Greene opened his door and looked up and down the street. I knew he was looking for Tiffany. I knew he was starting to get concerned that she still wasn't home yet. I wanted so badly to call him over and confess, but I was a coward. All the things Noreen warned me about—jail, the death penalty, losing everything—were overwhelming. We'd made a mistake, and I was too weak to cop to it. I drove away, crying.

Choosing Pifer Mountain, West Virginia, was nothing more than figuring out a destination far enough away from West Finley, Pennsylvania, where the authorities wouldn't bother looking, but would also be close enough to allow for a round trip in one night and a buried body in between. I recalled some coworkers discussing hunting in the Pifer Mountain area and knew it was popular as a rugged hike and a hell of a climb. I figured there would have to be some remote area at the base that would work, so I made my way back into the school at midnight, wrapped Tiffany's body in a sheet I'd brought from home, and took her out the back way by the gym that was hidden from both the street and the surrounding neighborhood. No one would see me come in, and no one would see me leave. Tiffany was in my trunk, and I was on the road in under thirty minutes.

The drive took a little over two hours, but I can't recall much of the trip. At that point the mechanics of the body had taken control, and my brain was on autopilot. I know I hiked about a half mile off a trail at the southern end, picked a spot I thought would work, and started digging. Flashes of that afternoon entered my consciousness from time to time as I worked, but for the most part, my logic had shut down and my survival instincts had kicked in. I remember the earth being rocky and the digging being harder than I thought it'd be, but I got a hole big enough and deep enough to bury my student. The next time anything really registered was when I was back on Interstate 79, alone on a dark highway in the early-morning hours.

I remember a semi passing me on the other side of the road. Its headlights lit up the interior of my car, and I looked at my soiled hands gripping the steering wheel. It was at that moment the reality of what I'd done hit me. The truck was gone as quickly as it had come, and my car was dark again, but I kept staring at my hands and could suddenly feel the callus on my palms from where I'd held the shovel and swung the pickax. I could feel the grit of soil in between my fingers and the earth caught in my nails. I looked down and knew my clothes were stained with dirt and mud and probably some blood. I'd buried a body. I'd taken a little girl from her family and hidden her so they would never find her. They'd never have the closure they'd need and would forever wonder what had happened. Or worse, they'd wonder if she was still alive and suffering. That uncertainty would hurt more than knowing their daughter was dead. I was aware of that, but I had to stick with the plan. I started crying again, and through the tears and the sobbing and the sorrow that scarred my heart, I kept telling myself that what happened was an accident, but my carelessness was what put it all in motion. If only I'd checked the door.

If only.

It was my responsibility to make things right, and if that meant Mr. and Mrs. Greene would never know what happened to their daughter, so be it. Sometimes life only hands you one option, and you have to take it, whether you like it or not.

I told myself I was doing this for love. Noreen and I met years earlier when I was teaching in Ohio, and we'd spent so much time together since that point. Back when she'd first started her job and had a little piece of Ohio to cover, we met at a coffee shop, and that was the beginning of everything for us. I moved to West Finley to be closer to her, and we eventually decided we were going to get married as soon as her kids were old enough. She was going to leave her husband, and we were going to finally be together without having to sneak around. In saving Noreen, I told myself, I was saving us. For love. Instead, I'd damned us.

Forever.

24

"Where were you?" James growled at the woman who was squatting down in front of the DVD player, pressing buttons as the credits from the movie rolled on the screen.

"I'm right here."

"I mean before! Where were you? I called and no one answered. I was down here alone. The house was empty. I needed you. I needed you to help me."

"With what?"

"Never mind now! Why was I left alone? Where's Rebecca, dammit? She should be with me."

The woman stood up in front of the television. "I've been home the entire time. I came down and fed you lunch, but you were confused again."

"That's crap! I was calling for help!"

"You didn't know who I was or where you were. You never called for me. I've been here the whole time."

"No!" James pounded on the arms of his wheelchair. "That's not right. No one fed me lunch. No one was home. I was shouting until I was hoarse, and no one came!" He took a deep breath, his mind scrambling to try and remember if she'd been down to feed him. "And where is all my stuff? You said I live down here."

"You do."

"Then where are my pictures and my keepsakes and things from my old house that I would've taken with me? I don't even have clothes in those drawers!"

The woman walked over and sat on the couch in front of him, taking his hand. "You remember we talked about you living here?"

"Sure."

She smiled. "Good. Maybe you're having some clarity now. The fog was bad before."

"Why was I down here alone with no food, none of my stuff, and no clothes?"

Cindy grew quiet. "I'm telling you, we were here the entire time. I fed you lunch, and you got changed. Look at your shirt."

James looked down, and his world turned on its side. His blue-and-white-striped pajama top had been replaced by a bright-red golf shirt.

"When did I . . . ?"

"I don't know. I came down, and you were already in it."

He searched his memory to find the exact second when he'd put it on, but there was nothing. "Where did it come from?"

"I assume your dresser."

"I don't have any clothes in my dresser."

"You do."

James wheeled himself over to the bedroom area, his stomach tying itself in knots. He pulled open drawer after drawer. In each one, a full wardrobe. Underwear, undershirts, pants, shirts, sweaters, socks.

"I . . . I don't understand."

Cindy stood from the couch. "When you agreed to come live with us, you said you didn't want any of your old pictures or belongings to come with you. We brought them anyway and stored them in the attic. That's why none of your stuff is down here. You didn't want it here. You said it reminded you of too much sadness. I can bring you some pictures."

"Would you?"

"Of course."

He could hear her approaching, faint footsteps on the tiled floor. Thin arms wrapped themselves around his chest and neck, and when

104

she leaned in to hug him, he could smell the strawberry from her shampoo. His mind had become a dangerous thing, showing him a reality that he couldn't trust, tricking him into an alternate universe he had no control over. What was he supposed to do when his mind showed him lies that looked and felt so real?

"Where's Rebecca?" he asked quietly.

"There is no Rebecca," Cindy replied, her voice muffled in his neck.

He began to cry. "My name is James. Don't call me Jim."

25

Trevor got up from the desk in the corner of the dining room that the baby monitor sat atop of. James was on the screen in black and white, sitting in the living room area, unmoving. "The hug was a nice touch."

Cindy pulled the refrigerator open and grabbed a can of iced tea. Her hands were shaking and her head throbbed. Touching that man with any sense of affection was one of the hardest things she'd ever had to do. Playing the role of daughter, or whatever that bastard thought she was to him, was starting to get to her. She could taste blood in her mouth from biting the inside of her cheek. She took a sip of the tea.

"The hug was a necessity. All part of showing him I care. That's how I gain his trust. If he trusts me, he'll start to talk. I can move on to the pictures in the album now. He's the one who's asking for his things, so that'll be the excuse to show him. If I just came down and shoved pictures in his face as soon as we got here, he'd never learn to trust us and we'd never get anywhere. This is how it has to happen."

"I don't know how you can stay so calm after knowing what he did to your sister. It's impressive. You're like a professional actress. If it were me, I'd want to slit his throat or choke him or beat the crap out of him."

Cindy chuckled. "Believe me, I want to do all of those things, but I know I can't. I have to get the truth. That's all I want before Hagen comes to kill him. I just need to know what happened from his own lips."

Trevor stopped inside the doorway between the kitchen and the dining room. "You got his mind all squirrelly when he saw those clothes in the drawers. That worked good."

"I'm not trying to confuse him more, but now he knows he can't trust his own thoughts. That was a big step, even though we never planned it."

"Whatever. I just hope he doesn't start trying them on. I don't think too many of my granddad's things will fit him."

Cindy took another sip of her tea and let out a sigh. "Still no word from Hagen today?"

"Not yet."

"I'm sure he'll text."

"That's what I'm afraid of." Trevor walked in and hoisted himself up on the counter near the stove. "The cops gave a picture of James to the news to go along with Rebecca and the trooper thing. They made the connection. Knew they would. It's been leading the hour on all the channels."

"That doesn't matter," Cindy said quickly. "James Darville was never supposed to see life outside that basement again anyway. Hagen's going to kill him. That was the plan all along."

"Yeah, but I'm starting to wonder if we've become too much of a liability."

"What do you mean?"

Trevor lowered his voice. "We've screwed this up from jump street. At some point we'll be hurting Hagen more than helping. We have three different police forces out looking for Rebecca, and now they're looking for James too. That's too much attention, and if the heat gets turned up too much, Hagen will have to eliminate all the loose ends. That means us. If he needs to clean house in order to get away, we all die."

Cindy turned away from him and looked out the window above the sink. The sun was shining. It was a beautiful day. The kind of day that made her second-guess what she was doing. Was her need for the truth that strong?

"I hate to keep bringing this up, but we're going to have to do something about your friend."

"I know. She's getting worse."

"She wants to see him. Won't stop crying. Keeps begging me to let her out of the room so she can go down and make sure he's okay."

"We can't do that. Not when she's hysterical like this. It'll just upset him, and we'll have to start this all over."

"I know. That's what I keep telling her."

"I'll handle it."

"I hope so," Trevor said as he looked behind him and pointed to the baby monitor. "Cause if not, I'll have to handle it. For the sake of all of us."

26

Most of the time, a case was solved through good police work, an attention to detail, and the small things like knocking on doors, interviewing witnesses, and scouring a suspect's background to find evidence that was never meant to be discovered. But every once in a while, a little piece of luck came along to make things easier. When that happened, it was like Christmas, New Year's, and your birthday all rolled into one. This was one of those times.

They found Rebecca Hill's silver Honda Civic submerged in a shallow section of Candlewood Lake near Brookfield, Connecticut. One of the men who worked on a dock in the town of Sherman had come down to retrieve a party boat that was being sealed and stored late in the season. As he was towing the boat away from its summer mooring, it ran over something and got stuck. That something ended up being the back end of Rebecca's Civic. The dockhand called the police, and the match to the BOLO was made.

By the time Susan arrived on scene, an ambulance, four Brookfield police units, a forensics van from the Connecticut State Police, and a command sergeant were already there. Yellow police tape had been stretched from the road leading to the boat launch, to the tree line that surrounded the back of the parking lot, and around the cluster of emergency vehicles. Candlewood Lake Road had been closed between the Down the Hatch restaurant and Indian Trail.

Three members of the forensics team milled about the Civic, which had been towed from the water and left on the boat ramp. They worked inside and out, taking samples and bagging everything they could find before they would have the car sent back to their lab for further analysis. It would be hard to pull anything solid with the entire vehicle having been underwater. There would be no prints, no DNA. It was a mess.

Susan noticed how gray the sky had turned on her ride up from Cortlandt. The chill in the air held the promise of snow, but she couldn't recall anything being forecast on the news. She climbed out of her sedan and pulled the collar of her jacket closed as Sergeant Triston approached.

"Hey, Mel," she said. "Thanks for meeting me."

"No problem."

"What do we have so far?"

"The nurse was in the trunk," Triston replied. "ID was in her purse, which was also in the trunk. Body's a bit bloated. The forensics team will take prints and a hair sample when she dries off to confirm, but it's her. Fits the description. She was wrapped in a blanket. Could be from Darville's bed. All his blankets and sheets were missing. Also looked like she took a bit of a beating."

"Might be her blood we found on the wall and floor."

"Yeah, probably."

Susan snapped on her gloves as she made her way over to the car. All four doors were open, as were the trunk and hood.

"Now we know why they panicked and attacked the trooper," Susan said. "They had a body in the trunk."

"Brookfield PD checked around," Triston replied. "None of the dockhands or harbormasters saw anything. No one heard a crash. Same with the bars and restaurants in the area. Most of them are already closed for the season."

"The parking lot or marinas have any security cameras?"

"Already requested. The marina has cameras, and so does the dock at the edge of Cadigan Park. We'll get something."

Rebecca Hill had been stuffed into the Civic's tiny trunk with force. Her body was in a tight fetal position among a workout bag, patient files, and the spare tire, which was not in its proper compartment underneath the trunk mat. Her neck alignment seemed off.

"The team said they need about ten more minutes, and then the EMTs can extract the body and bring it in for examination and autopsy. Connecticut agreed to let us have her and the car as long as we give them a copy of our reports."

"Sounds like a plan."

One of the members of the forensics team moved Susan out of the way and began taking pictures. She and Mel hung back by the tree line. The surface of the expansive lake was as calm as glass, reflecting the cloudy sky.

"So either Rebecca wasn't in on what happened at James Darville's house," she said, "or she was in deep enough to let someone she thought she could trust double-cross her."

"Sounds about right."

"I saw the trooper's dashcam. We have a male and female, both white, both fairly young, from what I could tell. No sign of Darville."

"Okay, so that's two or three people, depending on whether Rebecca Hill was in on this, all working together to get into the old man's house and take whatever he was hiding in the floor."

"I figured it was money," Susan said. "But now I'm thinking it might've been something more. This is a lot of carnage for a few bucks."

"Could be way more than a few. Could've been enough to make it all worthwhile." Triston pointed to the car. "I want to know where the old man is. I mean, if they killed the trooper and the nurse, they probably killed Darville too. So why not dump his body with the nurse?"

Susan began pacing as she talked. "Maybe because they didn't want to kill him. From what we could see on the dashcam footage, Darville wasn't with the woman in Rebecca's car."

"You think the old man was alive in the other car."

"Either that or the divers who're in the lake are about to discover another body." Susan stopped pacing and looked at Triston. "Did we ever find out if Darville had a car?"

"We're still looking into it with the DMV, but it doesn't look like he did."

"Got something!"

They turned to find the forensic tech who was taking the pictures raising his hand and backing away from the trunk. They went over.

"What's up?" Susan asked.

The tech pointed. "I was taking interior trunk shots and noticed something in the victim's hand. Take a look."

Susan craned her neck to peek inside. Rebecca's hands were balled into fists and tucked under her chin as if she was praying. Susan took her phone out of her pocket and engaged the flashlight so she could see better. The edge of the object was stuck between her index and middle fingers, too small and hard to see its details, but Susan knew what it was right away.

"I'll be damned," she muttered.

"What is it?" Triston asked.

"We got another tooth."

27

The Hitchcock movie was on again. Kids running out of the school. Seagulls attacking. Screams. Blood. James sat with his hands folded on his lap, trying to focus, but was distracted by the digital clock that was next to the television, flashing 12:00 over and over. He wanted to fix the time but had no idea what time it was. The more he tried to ignore it, the more his eyes found their way back to it. He was certain he could hear a ticking noise every time the numbers flashed.

Tick . . . tick . . . tick . . .

The basement door opened, and the woman came down carrying a book tucked under her arm.

"You," he said.

The woman waved.

"I know you."

"Yes, you do. Think. What's my name?"

"Rebecca."

"No."

"Where's Rebecca? She needs to fix my clock. Something's wrong with it. I can hear it ticking, and it won't tell me the time."

"There's no Rebecca," the woman replied. "And that's a digital clock. It doesn't tick."

"I can hear it."

"Okay."

Cindy plopped down on the couch and waited until James wheeled himself over to where she was sitting.

"Do you remember when you were saying you wanted to see some pictures of your life? You said it was too plain down here."

"I think so."

Tick . . . tick . . . tick . . .

"I thought you'd like to look at these."

She opened the album and flipped to the first page. She pulled a picture from its pocket. The photo looked old. Not ancient, but not as crisp and clear as a new one would be. The picture was of a young girl with large brown eyes, straight brown hair, and an oval face. Her pink cheeks looked like blush that was too heavy on her pale skin. She was beautiful.

"Do you recognize this person?" Cindy asked.

James studied the picture, then slowly shook his head. "No. Who is she?"

"Think."

"I don't know."

"Her name is Tiffany."

"Tiffany," James repeated. "How are we related?"

Cindy ignored the question, put the picture back in its pocket, and turned the page.

Tick . . . tick . . . tick.

The next picture was of another young girl, this one a little older, maybe high school age. James was certain he knew those angelic brown eyes and that wavy red hair.

"I think I know this one," he muttered.

"Good. Take a good look. Who is she?"

The freckles on her cheeks, her thin lips, the tiny round birthmark just under the right side of her chin. It all seemed so familiar, but he couldn't find the name.

"I'm sorry."

"No guess?"

He shook his head.

"You said you knew her."

"I think I do, but I don't know her name."

"Her name is Bonnie."

"Were we married?"

Cindy chuckled as she put the photo back. "No, you were not married."

"How is she part of the family?"

She flipped to another page, pulled the photo out, and held it up for him to see. "How about this one?"

The picture was of a young boy. He had a darker complexion, with brown eyes and an afro. He looked sharp in a dark suit, white shirt, and fluorescent-pink tie.

"Does he look familiar?"

"Maybe."

James studied his face, his skinny neck, his puffy cheeks, and his pointy chin.

"What's his name?"

"How is he related?"

"What's his name?"

"I have no idea."

Tick . . . tick . . . tick.

Cindy dropped the picture. "This is Marcus. Look again." She held the photo up. "Marcus Ruley? You don't recognize him?"

"No."

Cindy grunted as she stuffed the photo back in the pocket and quickly turned the page. James could feel the tension growing between them and could hear the incessant ticking of the digital clock. He was making her angry. She pulled the next picture out and held it up.

Tick . . . tick . . . tick.

"Take your time with this one and look closely. You can do it. Focus and try to remember her name."

115

James reached for the picture, but Cindy pulled it away. He studied it, leaning in, almost willing his mind to come up with a name. This face was even more familiar than the others. It was a girl. Maybe ten? Blonde hair in pigtails, a bright-red ribbon tying off each one. She was smiling with all her might, her crooked teeth showing gaps that braces might be able to fix sometime down the road. She had brown eyes, and her skin was tanned from a summer of playing outside. Like the other pictures, this print seemed to have aged. It was clearly a school picture. The nondescript mottled backdrop was a dead giveaway.

"Is it you?" he asked, looking from the picture to the woman sitting across from him on the couch. "When you were younger? A school picture?"

Cindy shook her head. "It's not me. Look again. Try to remember."

Tick . . . tick . . . tick.

It was a headshot, but he could see the top of her blouse, white with tiny blue flowers scattered about on a butterfly collar. She was beautiful in her innocence. He was certain he knew the girl. He knew she loved that blouse with the tiny blue flowers. Her name was on the tip of his tongue.

"Think."

"I am."

"What's her name?"

"I can't remember."

"What's my name?"

Tick . . . tick . . . tick.

"Cindy."

"Good. What's your name?"

"James. My name is James."

She squeezed the photo between her thumb and index fingers, shaking it in front of him. "What . . . is . . . her . . . name?"

Tick . . . tick . . . tick.

116

It was there, but the fog was keeping him from seeing it. He pounded his fists on his thighs. "I don't know. I'm sorry."

Cindy sighed. "Look at the picture."

"I am!"

"Try and remember."

Tick . . . tick . . . tick.

"I can't think with that clock!" he screamed, pulling away from the couch and wheeling toward the television. He let the wheelchair crash into the TV stand as he grabbed the clock with fumbling hands.

"What are you doing?"

He ignored the woman, instead focusing all his rage and frustration on the clock that he held above his head.

Tick . . . tick . . . tick.

James yanked until the cord released from the wall and watched as the display went blank.

"I'll kill it!"

He threw the clock against the tiled floor as hard as he could, listening as it shattered into tiny plastic pieces. The room fell silent but for the movie that continued to play on the television. James glared at the woman who was watching him, her mouth agape, the picture still in her hand.

"Her name is Sonia," she said calmly. "Does that ring a bell? Sonia?"

"No," James snapped, his chest rising and falling, his breath heavy. "It doesn't ring a goddamned bell."

Cindy put Sonia's picture back in its pocket and closed the book. "It's okay," she said. "It's this disease. It's taking your life away from you, piece by piece. I'm just trying to trigger something you can recognize from your past. I didn't mean to upset you."

"I know."

She got up and left the book behind. "I'm going to leave this here. Look through it and see if anything sparks a memory. You wanted a piece of your past with you. Now you have something."

"Thank you."

"I'll be down later, and we'll clean that up. If you need anything in the meantime, just holler."

"Can we go outside? I need some air."

"We can't. It's raining."

"I love you."

He didn't know where those words came from. He'd meant to say goodbye. She smiled and tapped her heart with her hand, then turned to leave. When he heard the basement door close and her footsteps cross the floor above him, he wheeled over to the table and picked up the photo album. He paged through it, the names she'd told him already fading as he asked himself the same question over and over.

Who are these people?

28

Susan stumbled through the front door feeling the weight of the day on her shoulders. The rest of the afternoon had been spent extracting Rebecca's body from the trunk of her car and transporting it back to the medical examiner's office in New York. They put the car on a flatbed and towed it to the forensics lab to be further analyzed with the proper equipment. Statements had been taken, and a general canvassing of the area around that section of the lake had been executed until it got too dark to work. It was the break in the case she'd been hoping for, but at this point, there were still more questions than answers.

Susan dropped her bag and kicked off her shoes, leaving both items at the foot of the coatrack. The house was quiet. No kids. Just the TV in the living room playing to an audience of empty chairs and an abandoned couch.

Beatrice was at the kitchen table, a bottle of beer in front of her. Susan leaned against the wall near the refrigerator.

"Looks like you might've had a worse day than I did. Where are the twins?"

"In their rooms. I sent Tim up right after dinner. Casey decided to follow. We had an incident today."

Susan joined her mother at the table. "What happened?"

"I took them to the park," her mother began. "It was chilly, but the sun was shining, and I figured it would be good to get them some fresh air for a few hours. When we got to the playground, everything was fine. Casey was with a group of kids they know from school, and

Tim was off by himself going up and down on the slide. I start reading my book, and the next thing I know, I hear screaming. I look up and I see Tim on top of another boy, and he's hitting him over and over. Me and another mom rush over and pull Tim off, but Tim has this look in his eyes. This blank look like he doesn't even know where he is. I finally snap him out of it, and he collapses into me and starts crying."

"Oh my god," Susan muttered. Her heart was shattering with every word her mother said.

This is your fault.

"I smoothed things over with the other boy's mom, and I called just before dinner to make sure everything was still okay. Luckily, they're only six, so Tim couldn't do much damage. Turns out the other boy, I forget his name, was more scared than anything else, and by the time I called, it sounded like the entire thing had been forgotten. I thought the mom might be upset, but apparently she has three older kids and had been down this road a few times already."

Tears welled in Susan's eyes. "Did Tim say why he attacked the other kid?"

"He said the other boy was going to hurt Casey, but when I asked Casey about it, she said they were just playing tag. Maybe Tim saw him chasing her, and he reacted?" Beatrice took a sip of her beer. "I told him that's not the way we react to things, but to be honest, I think he already realized that on his own. He kept saying how sorry he was for the rest of the day. I made him go to bed after dinner. I felt like we needed to set some boundaries when it comes to fighting and the like. Hope I wasn't overstepping."

"Not at all," Susan replied. "You did the right thing. I wish you'd called."

"What good would that have done?" Beatrice asked, her voice no more than a resigned whisper. "I had it handled, and you were working. No need to bother you."

"Still, these kids are my responsibility. Things could've gone sideways if the other parent wasn't so understanding."

"These kids are *our* responsibility. I got your back, lady."

Susan climbed out of her chair and kissed her mother on the top of her head.

"Dinner's in the microwave."

"I'm going to go see Tim first. I think we need to talk."

———

For a moment she thought her son was asleep. He was lying in his bed, the covers pulled up to his chin, the lights out, no noise. But as soon as Susan started to close the door, he sat up.

"Mommy?"

"Hey, buddy," she said as she stepped into the room, leaving the light off. "I didn't realize you were awake."

"I heard you come home, but Grandma made me stay up here."

"I know. She told me about what happened at the park today. You wanna talk about it?"

"No."

"I think we have to."

"I don't want to talk about it. It makes me feel bad."

"Because you were hurting that boy?"

Tim nodded in the darkness. "I thought he was going to hurt Casey. I didn't know they were playing tag. I just wanted him to stop chasing her. I'll tell him I'm sorry in school, I promise. I feel bad that I made him cry."

Susan didn't know what to say. She sat on the edge of her son's bed and hugged him, running her fingers through his thick mop of hair.

You did this. All of it. You're away from your kids for hours at a time right at the age they need you the most. You should be guiding them and building their sense of self, but instead you're inviting evil into your home

121

and putting their lives in danger. What kind of mother are you? What kind of protector?

"We'll get you all better," Susan whispered, not knowing what else to say.

"I'm glad you're home."

"Me too." She pulled away and looked at Tim. "Do you like it here?" she asked. "Do you like our house?"

Tim shrugged. "I guess."

She was afraid to push him with more pointed questions. She wanted to ask if he thought about what happened the night the bad man came for them. She wanted to ask what he thought about every time he came downstairs and saw the spot where the bad man died. She wanted to ask him if he cowered under the covers at night for fear the bad man would be standing in his bedroom doorway, silhouetted by the hallway light, watching him sleep, ready to take him. She wanted to ask all of that but knew she couldn't. She couldn't trigger the memories again. She had to let the psychiatrist do what he was trained to do, not interfere. She had to tread lightly.

Susan kissed Tim on the forehead and helped him get back under his covers. "We don't hit others, okay? Promise?"

"I promise."

"Good. Go to bed, and I'll see you in the morning. When you wake up, we'll forget this happened, but we won't forget our rule."

"No hitting others."

"That's right." She stood up, wanting so badly to curl up next to him and listen as he fell asleep. "I'm going to go kiss your sister. I'll see you later."

"I love you, Mommy."

"I love you, too, honey. More than you can ever know."

29

The man came down the basement stairs holding a six-pack of beer in one hand and a bag of chips in another. James watched as he made his way to the bottom landing.

"I brought you something to snack on," the man said, walking into the living room area and placing the chips on the table. "Pabst Blue Ribbon and Utz potato chips. Your favorites."

"They are?"

"They are."

The man snapped a can from the pack and placed the beer down next to the chips. He took the remaining five cans and put them in the refrigerator by the television. When he turned back around, he saw that the pictures from the photo album were scattered on the couch. The album itself was on the floor by the table.

"You messed up all the pictures?"

James looked at the photos on the couch but said nothing.

The man smiled and shrugged. "I'll tell you the truth: I really don't care, but *she* gets pretty sensitive when it comes to these. The last thing you wanna do is start tossing them on the floor and taking them out of the album. She's been known to have a bit of a temper, and you don't want in on her bad side."

James watched as the man bent down and snatched the album from the floor. He sat on the couch and began gathering the pictures. James rolled over next to him.

"I didn't make that mess."

"Okay. Whatever."

"I'm serious."

"I believe you."

The man stopped when he got to the photograph of the little girl in blonde pigtails. The two red ribbons seemed to shine right through despite the age of the photo. James looked, too, focusing on the girl's blouse, the tiny blue flowers scattered against the white fabric. The butterfly collar.

"Sonia."

He said the name softly, without really thinking about it. It just came.

The man looked at him. "What did you say?"

"Sonia. Her name is Sonia."

"That's right." He tapped the picture with his finger. "You remembered."

"I guess I did."

The man got up out of his seat and walked to the bottom landing. "Cindy! Hey, Cindy! Come down here a sec. Hurry up!"

James listened as footsteps thumped above him, then came down the stairs. The woman—Cindy—looked uneasy.

"What's up?" she asked.

The man handed her the picture of the girl in blonde pigtails. "Our boy here remembered Sonia's name."

Cindy took the picture and walked over to James. She sat on the couch and held up the photograph. "You remember her?"

"Her name is Sonia."

"That's right. What can you tell me about her?"

James shrugged. "I just know her name. You told me her name was Sonia, and I remembered."

"But what do you remember *about* her?"

"Nothing."

"Think. Look at the picture and think."

124

He wanted to make something up just to satisfy them. They were both looking on with such anticipation, but he knew Cindy would recognize a lie. His mind began to cloud, just a thin line of smoke for now, but the fog was forming. "I don't know her. You told me her name, and I remembered."

"Look at her face. You knew her. She knew you. Come on—you can do it. You can remember."

"I can't. You told me her name so—"

"Just do it!"

It was the first time Cindy had raised her voice to him. Or maybe it wasn't. They sat in the strained silence, the man standing in the background watching them both.

"I'm sorry," James whispered. Fear crept up the back of his neck. "I'm sorry."

"It's okay," the man replied.

Cindy got up from the couch and snatched the photo album off the couch. She stuffed the picture back inside, and for reasons James didn't fully understand, he closed his eyes and braced for her to hit him.

"You said yourself that you can't force it," he heard the man say.

"I know," Cindy replied. "But we need to start making progress at some point. We're running out of time." The photo album hit the coffee table with a thud. Footsteps pounded up the stairs. James opened his eyes when the basement door slammed shut. The man was still standing there.

"I told you she could get pretty sensitive," he said. "You remember me telling you that?"

"Yes."

The man lowered his voice. "Good. Don't ever forget that."

30

Dr. Emily Nestor led the way down the long corridor that connected the lobby of the medical examiner's office to the autopsy rooms. Susan followed behind her, a trip she'd taken more times than she could count. When they opened the door, the familiar scent of pine air freshener met her, always trying to mask the smell of blood and always unsuccessful in doing so. The very essence of what they did here—the autopsies and examinations—had seeped into the walls over time, becoming as much a part of the building as the mortar in between each brick or the wiring that snaked from floor to floor. Nothing would ever truly hide the scent. Nothing ever could.

Rebecca Hill's body had been placed on one of the two stainless steel tables that were bolted to the floor in the center of the room. She was faceup, a blue sheet covering her. It was easier to see the details of her features now that she was out of the trunk and somewhat dry. Her face was swollen and bruised. One eye was larger than the other, and her lips were double the size they should've been. There were a few large lumps on her forehead as well as one just below the left cheek. Dr. Nestor grabbed a file from her desk and stood on the opposite side of the table.

"Autopsy is scheduled for either later today or first thing tomorrow," she said, opening the file. "I'm still finishing with the report on the trooper."

"They tapped you for that?"

"They did."

Susan pointed to Rebecca's body. "Did you do a once-over?"

"Yeah, when she came in. As you can see, she took a pretty good beating, but she was strangled to death. Dead prior to being placed in the trunk."

"You got a TOD?"

"Hard to be super exact with her body having been submerged, but judging from what I see, and the state of rigor, I'd say she was killed about two days ago. Coincides with her body being in the trunk when the trooper pulled her car over. Once I get a look at the organs and see how the blood settled, I can confirm."

"But you're sure about the strangulation."

Dr. Nestor nodded. "It's the only COD I can find. No stab wounds. No bullet wounds. She has bruising on her neck that coincides with fingers exerting intense pressure. There's also evidence of petechial hemorrhages, which is another sign of strangulation. Plus, we have the bloodshot eyes, and from what I can feel superficially, it appears her hyoid bone has been fractured. But again, I'll confirm everything during the autopsy."

Susan pulled the sheet down Rebecca's body. "Any other signs of trauma besides the face?"

"Lump on the back of her head matches up with what I read in the report about the blood you found on the wall at James Darville's house. She's type A, which also matches, so our perp probably slammed her against the wall hard enough to leave the lump and cut. He beat her up and strangled her. I'd say he gained control quickly. No defensive wounds. It doesn't look like she put up much of a fight. Maybe caught her by surprise. Knocked her unconscious."

"Any skin in the fingernails? Did she scratch him?"

"Not that I could see."

Susan covered Rebecca's body. "Anything with the two teeth we found?"

"Sent them both up for a DNA screen and general analysis. They're not our victim's here. I can tell you that for sure. She has all her teeth intact, and no prosthetics."

"Maybe James Darville's?"

"Sure. Why not?"

Dr. Nestor walked back over to her desk. She closed the file and placed it in the cabinet that held her examination reports and then picked up a plastic bag. "I did as much as I could with this locket," she said. "Tried to pull some prints, but it was ugly. No clean sets of anything. I'll have the partials run to see if we get anything, but don't get your hopes up. This thing is old. Rusted. Scratched up. Long shot on an ID for sure."

Susan took the bag and stuffed it in her pocket. "I'm heading back to the barracks to get Crosby caught up. I'll place this in evidence."

"Thanks."

"Anything else I should know?"

Dr. Nestor shook her head. "Not at this point. You'll get my full report after we open her up and see what we can find."

"Thanks, Emily."

"No problem."

31

Wilson Woods Park was on the east side of Mount Vernon, almost on the Pelham town border. Susan drove down the road past the wave pool and water slides, then turned right at the large fountain, all of which had already been shut down for the season. She stopped in a small parking lot facing a pond she didn't know the name of and killed the engine.

Maxine Hill and her son, David, sat on a bench facing the pond, their backs to her. A wool coat shielded her frail body, while a matching knit hat and gloves covered her head and hands. She leaned on David, who sat pin straight.

Susan stepped over a guardrail and went to meet them.

David got up from the bench and extended his hand. "Thank you for coming, Investigator Adler," he said. His eyes were pleading. "It's nice to see you again, although I wish it was under different circumstances."

It was obvious David hadn't told his mother about his arrest. Susan shook David's hand and played along. "Hello. Nice to see you too."

David's shoulders relaxed.

"Is it true?" Maxine asked, her gaze fixed on the placid body of water in front of her. "I know it's a stupid question. You wouldn't be here if it wasn't true, and the police wouldn't have come to my house if it wasn't true, but they won't let me see her yet, so I need to hear it from you. Is it true? Is my Rebecca dead?"

Susan nodded. "It's true."

"They stuck her in the trunk of her own car?"

"I can't really talk about particulars."

"I understand." The elderly woman looked out across the lake. "That's what the young officer who showed up with the news told me too. But I got a little off-the-record information. A mother needs that kind of thing sometimes." Maxine closed her eyes for a moment, then opened them and wiped a tear. "My baby used to love to come to this park. Of course, back then they didn't have all these fancy slides and wave pools. It was just a park with a community pool, and that was enough. I'd bring her here to go swimming. Her father taught her how to fish just off this very spot. She'd play and we'd have picnics. Now she's gone. Just like that. But at least now you know that she didn't have nothing to do with that trooper man's murder. Now you know for sure."

Susan watched a hawk circling in the sky above the water. It looked so graceful. "I realize we went over my questions when we first met," she said. "But James Darville is still missing. His body wasn't found with Rebecca. Any idea where he could be?"

"We didn't know the man," Maxine replied. "I told you that."

Susan looked at David. He shrugged and shook his head. "I have no idea. All we know about him is what my sister told us, and it wasn't much. She was his primary caregiver and had been his only friend since she had him as a patient at the hospital."

Susan took a step forward. "I didn't know Rebecca worked at a hospital. Which one?"

"Phelps. In Sleepy Hollow."

"She was on staff?"

"Worked per diem in the med-surg unit. That's where she met Mr. James."

Susan stared at David, furious that he hadn't brought this up the last few times they'd talked. "How long was she employed by the hospital?"

"About fifteen years. Had the home care job for a little less than that. Once Mr. James's condition got worse, she spent more time with him and less at the hospital. I think she was only down to one shift a month on the weekends. Something along those lines."

Susan let the information process. Rebecca had met James Darville as a patient at Phelps Hospital prior to her becoming his full-time nursing aide. Rebecca had requested Darville, and now Susan knew why. Phelps Hospital was the connection.

Susan motioned toward David. "Walk me to my car."

"Yes, ma'am."

She extended her hand toward Rebecca's mother. "I appreciate your help, and I'm sorry for your loss."

"Don't think we helped much," Maxine said, taking her hand and shaking it. "Just find who did this. Find them and punish them. That's all I ask."

"We'll do our best."

David followed Susan back over the guardrail. As soon as they were far enough away from Maxine, he let out the breath he was holding. "Thank you for not saying anything about me being at Mr. James's house. I don't think she can handle all of this as it is."

"Why didn't you tell me your sister was a nurse at Phelps?"

"It never came up. I would've mentioned it."

"You should have. It's important."

"I'm sorry. I was just answering the questions you were asking. I wasn't thinking in terms of backstory. It just didn't come up until just now."

Susan looked at David, long and hard, trying to determine if this was a man she could trust or if he knew more than he was letting on. She raised her finger and pointed it at him. "You better not be playing me."

"Why would I be playing you? I was trying to find my sister and prove to all of you that she didn't kill that trooper. And now we've done both."

TRANSCRIPT

I couldn't believe what I was seeing. I simply couldn't believe it. She was lying on her bed, a pillow over her face, her blonde hair sticking out from beneath the pillow, her arms hanging over the edge of the mattress.

Sonia Garland was dead.

Noreen was sitting at the foot of the bed, crying silently, her tears dripping from the bottom of a chin that I'd kissed a hundred times. The house was empty but for the three of us. Jackson was still at work, and her other daughter wouldn't be home from school for another hour. I stood in the doorway, half in the hall and half in Sonia's room, just staring, mouth wide open, not trusting what I was seeing.

"Noreen, what's going on?" I asked. "What happened?"

"I had to," Noreen replied without looking up. Her tears dripped from her chin to the carpet. "She knew. My baby girl is smart like me, and she has this need to find out the truth about things."

"What things? What are you talking about?"

"She didn't like the fact that people were starting to give up on finding Tiffany. She kept saying it's only been a few months and that we had to keep looking. She started digging around on her own, trying to find whatever she could about Tiffany's disappearance. Said she wanted to help the police because it felt like the grown-ups were throwing in the towel."

"My god."

"At first I let her have her fun. I didn't think she'd come up with anything. I tried pushing her off the scent to get her to focus on school or sports or even boys. But she's so relentless. I love that about her. Her tenacity is a gift."

I walked into the room, my eyes fixed on the body on the bed. Tiffany had been missing for a few months at this point, and the investigation was in the final stages. We were almost in the clear.

"She found things," Noreen continued. "I don't know how, but she found your time sheet from that day. She knew you were still in the building when Tiffany disappeared, and she knew Tiffany stayed after school that day to decorate her friend's locker for her birthday."

"That doesn't prove anything," I replied. "The police know all that too. I was never a suspect."

"She had pictures. She took them with my Polaroid. They were of you and your house and your car and your license plate. For some reason, she was onto you, which meant it was only a matter of time before she'd be onto us. Maybe she already knew. I couldn't take the chance."

I stood in front of Noreen and took her by the shoulders. "What did you do?"

Noreen shrugged and looked up at me. Her eyes were vacant, flooded with tears. "I spiked her juice with some of my sleeping pills, and when she fell asleep, I saved us."

A wave of fear and anger and confusion spilled over me. I began shaking her, looking at Sonia's body on the bed. That poor girl.

"You didn't have to do that!" I screamed. "Why? Why would you do that?"

"She knew too much!"

"She didn't know anything!"

Noreen started crying harder. "Why didn't you just check if the door was shut in your classroom? Why didn't you check? If you just checked, none of this would be happening, and I'd still have my little girl!"

The words hurt, each one of them stabbing at me with their truth. If I'd just checked the goddamned door to make sure it was locked.

133

I let go of her, and she fell on top of her daughter. "Why didn't you check the lock?" she sobbed, hugging her dead child. "Why didn't you check it?"

"What do you want me to do?" I asked, pacing the room. "What do you want from me?"

"Take her where you took Tiffany," Noreen replied. "Take her away, and she'll be another missing victim. I'll get rid of the things she found out about you, and we'll let the police investigate. They'll think they have a serial kidnapper or something, and we'll play along."

"No," I snapped. "We can't keep doing this! This is crazy! You just killed your own daughter."

"For you! I did it for you! To protect you."

"From what? I didn't kill Tiffany. You did."

The room fell silent, and Noreen suddenly leaped off the bed and slapped me hard across the face. Her vacant eyes came alive with a fury I'd never seen before. "We're in this together," she hissed. "You put her in your car and buried her. You let her parents wonder what happened to their daughter. You're keeping secrets just like I am. And now this. You made me kill my own child to protect us. Can you imagine a mother killing her baby?" She slapped me again. "I did it for us. And now we have to make things right again."

"We can't," I said quietly. "This has to stop. We need to go to the police and tell them what we've done. It's the only way."

"No," Noreen replied before I'd even stopped talking. She was focused now. Determined. "If you go to the police, I'll lose you forever. I can't have that. I need you. I love you. I did this for us. So we can be together. Sonia's disappearance will be the crack in my marriage that I'll need to leave Jackson. Then we'll finally be able to live the rest of our lives together. Please. Do this one last thing. For us. We can be a family."

I can't explain why, but I found myself nodding, ensorcelled by her words and the thought of us finally being together. I loved her so much.

And, truth be told, I knew I was just as guilty as she was, and she was right: all of this had been my fault. If I'd just locked the classroom door.

"Take her," she said, pointing at Sonia's lifeless body. "I'll say that she never made it home."

"The bus driver will know he let her off."

"Then I'll say she didn't make it to the house. Somewhere between the bus stop and here, she disappeared. That'll be my story. Take her and bury her, and we'll move on. It's the only way out."

I found myself nodding again. God help me, I did what I was told.

32

It was dark now. The moon sat halfway up the night sky, full and bright. Cindy was sitting at the desk in the dining room, surfing the internet on Trevor's laptop for news about the trooper's death and the investigation. All she'd ever wanted was to know what happened to her sister. Now everything was speeding so far past the point of no return. She didn't know what to do, and she was scared. Two people were dead, and she knew James would be the third. Hagen had made that clear. But he'd also offered her an opportunity to learn the truth she'd sought since she was a little girl. How could she say no? She couldn't've anticipated the plan going so far off the rails. She wondered if there would be more death to come—namely hers.

The basement door opened, and she heard Trevor approaching.

"How is he?"

"Got him changed into his pajamas. He's fine." He walked into the dining room. "Any updates?"

Cindy spun around in her seat. "You could say that. The police found the car in the lake."

The sentence hung between them.

Trevor took a jagged breath and pushed his hair out of his face. "How?"

"We ditched it in a shallow part. Some guy in a boat ran it over."

"Jesus."

"I thought you said you knew the lake."

"I do. I didn't have depth charts, for Christ's sake. It was dark. I figured the cliff would work, and the bottom would be deep enough for the car to sink."

Cindy looked toward the floor. "They found the body in the trunk."

Trevor sat down at the dining room table and put his head in his hands. "None of this was supposed to happen."

"I know."

"We didn't do a good enough job wiping the car down because we didn't think it would ever be found."

"Hopefully the water will take away anything that was left behind."

He slammed his hands against the table. "Things are falling apart, and my wife and son are in danger! How do we fix this?"

"We just have to stay on plan," Cindy replied. She tried to be encouraging, but she knew he was right. Too many things had already gone wrong. The knot in her stomach told her she should get out of the house and run as far as she could, but she couldn't leave without confronting the monster she'd been seeking almost as long as she'd been alive. She was in too deep now. They all were.

"Why did you ever call me to take part in this?" Trevor asked. His voice was trembling. "I just wanted to be left alone to live my life. Why did you have to rope me in?"

"I didn't," she said. "Hagen made me."

He chuckled. "Hagen. We have no idea who this person even is. How is he connected to the old man? He wants him dead, sure, but how are they *connected*? Hagen suddenly lands in our lives out of nowhere, blackmails us into doing things we would *never* even *think* of doing, and now we're kidnappers and murderers, and none of us have the expertise to get out of this without being killed or arrested."

"I know."

"He abducts my family while I'm meeting with you. He hangs Mrs. Hill's liver transplant over Rebecca to get her to cooperate. He's bargaining with people's lives." He stopped and looked at her. "Did you know they were going to take my wife and son when you were meeting with me? Tell me the truth."

"Of course not," Cindy snapped. "I would never be part of something like that. Never."

Trevor looked her up and down. "Funny how everyone's being held for ransom except you. Hagen just gives you what you've always wanted. Doesn't take a thing. Doesn't ask for anything. How fortunate."

Cindy got up from her seat and walked across the dining room to say something, but the back door opened. As soon as she heard it, tears welled in her eyes. David Hill appeared in the entranceway, a backpack slung over one shoulder. The three of them stared at each other.

"Why are you crying?" David asked.

The distraction of the car in the lake, the question of Hagen's identity, all of that quickly faded. For a moment, Cindy's conviction—that the only thing that mattered was forcing a confession from her sister's killer—wavered. She took a deep breath, then said, "It's Rebecca. Something's happened."

33

Susan shut the door to Crosby's office and sat down. Outside in the barracks, the shift supervisor was taking roll call during changeover and going through the usual assignments for the night tour. The troopers were gathered in a semicircle around their sergeant, listening intently, no one other than the man in charge making a sound.

Crosby was behind his desk typing something on his computer. "Did you get anything to go on from the ME?"

"Blood type we found on the wall in the old man's bedroom matches Rebecca's. And Emily said the body has wounds consistent with the blood on the wall. COD looks to be strangulation, though. We're waiting to see if the tooth found at Darville's house is from the same mouth as the tooth found in Rebecca Hill's hand, but we know neither of them belongs to Rebecca. She has all her teeth intact. They could be Darville's."

"What about the nurse's car?"

"Brookfield PD released it to us, and we got it towed back to the garage at the lab, so forensics is working on that. The locket I found at Darville's house got dusted, but Emily said finding a print we can use is unlikely."

Crosby stopped typing and folded his hands on his desk. "Does it strike you as weird that no one's come around asking about Darville except his physical therapist, who called it in? I get that he has no family, but what about friends? I thought he was supposed to get help overnight from one of the neighbors."

"He does," Susan replied. "Mel followed up on that and found the neighbor." She flipped through her notes. "Glen Dawkins. He's lived next to Darville for six years. Mr. Dawkins just flew to Texas to see his daughter and grandkids for two weeks. Mel talked to him on the phone, and Mr. Dawkins said he worked it out with Rebecca. The nurse was going to stay with him full-time until he got back. I checked with the staffing agency, and they had no record of Rebecca's plans and said she'd need to put in for initial approval since it would be overtime."

Crosby nodded. "This is definitely sounding like an inside job. They knew exactly when the neighbor wouldn't be there and when the nurse would. Rebecca let them in and got double-crossed."

"I agree. But I also think killing her might've been a spontaneous, last-minute thing. The way her body was stuffed in the trunk of her car, it seemed forced, panicked. If I knew I was going to kill someone ahead of time and had to transport a body, I think I would've planned better. Maybe not leave such a mess and maybe get a bigger car. I could be off, but it just seems like killing Rebecca was not part of the original plan. So many cleaner ways to do it if you had time to map it out."

"Anything else?"

Susan flipped to another page in her notebook. "Should be getting the video-surveillance footage from the marina and dock tomorrow. Hopefully we can get a lead from when the nurse's car was dropped. I also had a few units ask about neighbors' cameras during their door-to-doors in Verplanck, but no one had any, so we have no footage of the actual night Darville was taken."

Roll call was wrapping up, and Susan could hear the stampede of troopers heading out toward the parking lot. The evening shift was officially on.

"I'm waiting on the judge to sign off on warrants to get Darville's medical records as well as Rebecca Hill's employment records. She worked at Phelps as a per diem nurse, and Darville was her patient. As soon as he needed long-term care, she cut her hours at the hospital and got a job with the staffing agency and specifically requested Darville. That seems odd to me."

"Okay, stay on it."

Susan folded her notepad closed. "That's all I got for now. Everything's a possibility, and this guy is still missing."

"You're heading to Philly tomorrow, right?"

"Yeah. I'll be back by dinner."

Crosby got up from his seat. "Have your cell on you. If anything comes up, we'll contact you."

"Yes, sir."

"You okay?"

"Absolutely."

"Would you tell me if you weren't?"

"Probably not."

Crosby smiled. "Fair enough. I want to make sure you take care of your family. That comes before all of this. But I also want to make sure you're taking care of you. What happened with your partner affects you as much as Beatrice and the kids. You can't help them if you're not helping you."

"I'm good," Susan said. "Seriously. And thanks for the concern."

"I'll see you when you get back from Philly."

"Yes, sir. And in the meantime, I'm a phone call away. If anything breaks, I want to know about it."

"Don't worry," Crosby said. "You will."

34

The door swung open, and footsteps came down into the basement faster than James could react. He was sitting in front of the three windows that lined the top of the wall. By the time his mind registered that someone was approaching, the man was already on him, spinning his wheelchair around so they were face to face.

"What did you do?" the man growled. He was angry. Enraged.

James didn't recognize this man. He tried to think of what he might've done or who he could be, but nothing came. The man jerked the chair back and forth as he spoke.

"What did you do?"

"I don't know!" James yelled in response. He swallowed the lump in his throat, his eyes buried in the man's.

"You killed her!"

"I don't know what you're talking about."

"You killed her, you son of a bitch!"

The man punched him. James heard the slap of knuckles against bone before he felt any pain, but when the pain did come, it consumed the entire left side of his face. He began to shake from both fear and the adrenaline that was kicking in. His being in the wheelchair made him vulnerable.

"Leave me alone!" James shouted, louder this time. He could hear the panic in his voice. "I didn't do anything!"

"You did! You killed her!"

Another punch. Same spot. James saw stars, then felt his eye beginning to swell shut. His vision blurred.

Somewhere in the background, another set of footsteps.

"Stop it!"

It was the woman.

"I'll kill him!"

The man grabbed James by the throat and started squeezing.

"Let go of him!"

"Shut up."

"Let him go!"

"He killed her, so I'm going to kill him. Eye for an eye. Stay out of my way, or you get some too."

"What about Hagen? What about your mom?"

James couldn't breathe. The pressure on his throat was making him light headed. His peripheral vision was starting to crystalize like ice on a windshield. He could hear the man and the woman arguing, but their voices were suddenly muffled, as if he had his hands over his ears.

You're dying. He's killing you.

"Get off of him! This isn't how it's supposed to go!"

"I don't care how it's supposed to go. Things have changed, and he needs to pay."

"You don't make the rules here! This isn't how it's supposed to go down!"

Blackness was seeping in from the top of his sight line. James tried to pull the man's hands away from his throat, but he wasn't strong enough. He was passing out.

"I don't care about Hagen's rules! This son of a bitch killed my sister, and now he pays!"

Footsteps again. Coming? Going? He couldn't tell. James fought to stay conscious. He looked to his right and could see the ghosts standing in the shadows, all of them, hand in hand, staring at him, waiting for him to die. He would die, and they would devour him. It was just a matter of time now. Just a matter of his heart stopping. Then the fun would begin.

James closed his eyes and fell into the blackness. Somewhere in the void of his new world, he heard a shotgun cock.

"Get off of him or I'll kill you right here."

He somehow knew it was the man who helped him into bed at night. Trevor. His mind's eye painted a picture of the scene: Trevor standing at the bottom of the stairs holding a double-barrel Winchester against his shoulder, aiming it at the other man's back. The pressure released from his throat, and James took a deep, raspy breath that hurt.

"You're going to shoot me?"

"You don't get to hurt him and jeopardize my family's safety. As long as my wife and son are in danger, we play by the rules."

"But he killed—"

"I don't care what he did. This isn't about you."

"It is now."

"No, it's not. It's about all of us. My family. Your mom. Her truth. You follow the rules or I end you. Right here."

There was a long pause while James fought to open his eyes. He was coughing and spitting up onto his chest, but he was alive. As his vision refocused, he could see Trevor standing at the bottom of the stairs with a Remington twelve gauge tucked against his shoulder. He was aiming it at the man he didn't know, who was still standing over him but slowly retreating. The woman was between them both, watching everything unfold.

"Last chance," Trevor said as his grip on the shotgun tightened. "Get out or die right here."

The other man turned back and looked at James. In a flash of movement, he lunged at him and punched him one final time, then walked up the stairs and out of the house. James fell unconscious as soon as he heard the front door slam shut and the woman ask him if he was okay.

35

Susan had become familiar with the psychiatric unit of Jefferson Hospital over the course of the last year. The sounds. The smells. The noises and erratic movements made by some of the other patients in the waiting area. She'd become used to the more extreme cases who came to see their doctors from neighboring institutions in Philadelphia and its suburbs. At first she'd felt a maternal instinct to protect her kids from the other patients, but as time rolled on, her visceral reaction waned until a visit there was no more monumental than a visit to the dentist. She longed for the day when they wouldn't need this place or their psychiatrist, when things would go back to the way they were before. Until then, this was their routine, and she tried to make it seem as normal as possible.

Susan sat with Casey on a love seat overlooking Sansom Street. She ignored the magazine that was spread on her lap and stroked her daughter's hair while Casey played a puzzle game. It had begun to rain around exit 6 on the New Jersey Turnpike and hadn't stopped since. The streets of Philadelphia glistened as the gray sky cast a gloom over the entire city. The streetlights were on even though it wasn't even lunchtime yet. The clouds were too thick for the daylight to make a difference.

They came to see Dr. Radcliffe every two weeks and had a short conference call with him on the weeks they didn't make the drive. Tim had been making great strides in terms of his interactions with his friends and classmates and had been improving his communications with others. It was only recently, with the incident at the park, that he seemed to have relapsed. She knew Tim was being triggered as they approached the one-year anniversary of the night the bad man came. She hoped Dr. Radcliffe could figure out how to make the day pass with as little pain as possible.

"Mommy, is Tim almost done?"

Susan looked down to see that Casey had flipped from the puzzle game on her iPad to one of their Disney Channel shows. "Yes, honey. Shouldn't be much longer now."

"And then we have lunch?"

"Yup."

"And see Liam?"

"Yup."

"Good."

Casey popped her earbuds in and watched her show. Susan continued stroking her hair while her thoughts drifted from her son to Rebecca Hill, the fallen trooper, and the still-missing James Darville.

The double doors to the back offices opened, and Susan turned to see Tim skipping across the waiting area. She opened her arms, and he fell into them, a smile on his face that seemed more obligatory than natural.

"Hey, bud. How'd it go?"

"Good."

Casey didn't look up from her show but took one earbud out. "How's your brain?"

Tim didn't bat an eye. "Okay."

Dr. Radcliffe followed Tim into the waiting area. He was young, maybe midthirties, with a face that made him look like he was still in high school. Susan figured that was one of the reasons why Tim felt comfortable with him. His doctors in New York had been older and were a bit more intimidating. Dr. Radcliffe's rail-thin body, wide toothy smile, freckled face, and midlength black hair made him seem more like a peer than an authority figure. That had been the first breakthrough.

The second had been the natural charm and ease with which the psychiatrist spoke to children.

"We're all set," the doctor said, clapping his hands and smiling at the three of them.

Casey popped her second earbud out and waved. "Hi, Dr. Radcliffe!"

"Hi, Casey. How are you doing today?"

"I'm good. We're going to lunch now. You wanna come?"

"I'd love to, but I have more patients to see. How about a rain check?"

Casey pointed at the window. "It's raining. There, I checked!"

He laughed and turned his attention to Susan. "She's too young to be that sharp."

"You call it sharp. I call it adolescent sarcasm."

"Brought on by an acute immersion of adult sarcasm in the house?"

"Diagnosis confirmed."

Susan got up from the love seat. Tim slid in and took her place next to his sister, the two of them sharing the iPad and one earbud each.

"You ready?" Dr. Radcliffe asked.

Susan nodded. "Lead the way."

———

Other than the framed degrees that hung on the wall behind his desk, Dr. Radcliffe's office was anything but stereotypical. The wallpaper was illustrations of the four major sports from floor to ceiling: football, baseball, basketball, and hockey. The rug was bright green with white lines and numbers painted on it to look like you were sitting on the fifty-yard line. Two giant bookcases took up the entire back wall with toys, dolls, video games, and a huge flat-screen TV. Beanbag chairs lined another wall, each one a different fluorescent color. Model airplanes and spaceships hung from the ceiling, spinning in the hot breeze blowing from the vents.

Susan sat in the same seat she'd been sitting in since the day she finally met a doctor who could help her son. Dr. Radcliffe took his spot behind his LEGO desk and opened Tim's file. The twins remained in the hall, the receptionist keeping an eye on them.

"I think we had a great conversation today," he began. "And I think Tim continues to make progress."

"Did he tell you about the fight he had on the playground?"

"He did."

"What do you think about that?"

"I think it was a visceral reaction to him thinking he was seeing his sister being chased. He defended her. The adrenaline coursing through him at the time was likely driven by a combination of his fight-or-flight response as well as the trauma he suffered. The combination was too powerful for such a young person to know how to control, so animal instincts took over. It's all completely normal."

Susan thought for a moment. "I'm not sure if that makes me feel better or worse. What I'm hearing is he flew into an uncontrollable rage and lashed out. I can't have that. He needs to control himself."

"He will. And he knows that. This was a lesson. A teaching moment for him. He doesn't like what he did and feels remorse. He apologized to the child, and the child forgave him. This is something Tim will put in the back of his mind, and if a similar situation comes up again, we hope he uses this lesson and reacts differently. I'm confident he will."

"He seems sadder lately. We're getting close to the anniversary of when everything happened. We don't talk about it, but he knows. We were making such good progress."

Dr. Radcliffe closed his file. "We *are* making good progress."

"He still goes out of his way to avoid the spot in our foyer. Every time I watch him, I hold my breath, thinking he'll forget and walk through it and that'll be our breakthrough. But he goes to the other room to avoid it every time."

"All part of his healing." Dr. Radcliffe snatched a red stress ball from his desk and squeezed it as he spoke. "And what you're seeing in Tim is correct. He is feeling down lately, and he does know the anniversary is approaching."

"How?"

"He said when it got colder after Halloween it started reminding him of how it was cold when the bad man came to the house. Then he remembered how there were Christmas decorations up at the time. Your mother helped them decorate."

"That's right."

"So, as we're getting closer to Thanksgiving, he knows Christmas is next, which triggers the memories, and the emotions they prompt."

Susan fell back in her seat and closed her eyes. She could see the scene in the foyer as if it had happened only hours earlier. The crying. The pleas for help. The screaming. The gunfire.

"What Tim's going through is normal," Dr. Radcliffe continued. "He needs to get through this first anniversary and come out on the other side. Then, I believe, we'll see real progress."

"Eric thinks I should sell the house," Susan said. "He thinks it's a constant reminder to Tim about what happened and that he's not going to get better until he's removed from it forever."

Dr. Radcliffe's expression remained neutral. "What do you think?"

"On the one hand, I think kids are resilient and he'd get over it eventually. On the other hand, I have to ask myself what kind of a mother am I to make my kid live in that house every day and be reminded of what happened?"

"Do you want to sell and move?"

"It's not about me."

"It is. It's about you and Casey as much as it is about Tim. Have you asked Tim about it?"

"Not really. I don't want to push him either way."

Dr. Radcliffe dropped the stress ball and watched it roll toward his computer screen. "Tim's going to be fine, whatever you decide. Kids *are* resilient. He'll get past this, and over time the spot won't mean anything anymore. If you leave, it could speed up his recovery. But it might not. The real question here is, What do you think? Do you think moving would help your son or disrupt your family's lives?"

Susan shook her head. "I don't know."

Dr. Radcliffe smiled his toothy grin. "You figure that out, and you'll have your answer."

36

Philadelphia had some of the best restaurants and cafés in the Northeast, and since they'd been coming down every other week, Susan and the twins had tried most of them. There had been the fancy places by the water and the upscale-but-casual eateries in Center City. They tried Pat's and Geno's in South Philly, and she'd even caved on McDonald's on more than one occasion. But nothing seemed to hit the spot like a slice of Marco's Pizza. It was simple and always fresh, and had the exact right ratio of cheese to their incredible homemade sauce. It wasn't as good as Zavaglia's back home, but it was a close second, to say the least, and the twins couldn't get enough.

Marco's Pizza Restaurant sat on the corner of 12th Street and Spruce. It was quaint with only a handful of tables in the back, each one covered in the cliché red-and-white-checkered tablecloth, an array of garlic powder, parmesan cheese, oregano, and pepper flanking the napkin dispenser. Marco and his son, Dominic, worked the counter as their customers came in for a quick slice or to pick up a pie and go. Susan and the kids had the sitting area to themselves.

Throughout the first month of Tim's sessions with Dr. Radcliffe, Susan had run into Liam Dwyer three times. In the beginning, Tim was seeing the doctor weekly, so the trips to Philadelphia were more frequent, and her son's appointments always seemed to coincide with either the beginning or end of Liam's. Initially, there was only small talk and superficial conversation about the job, but after one rather brutal session with Tim, where Susan had had to recount, in detail, what had happened at her house, she'd emerged shaken and upset. Liam, an ex-forensics specialist with the Philadelphia Police Department, had just been getting out of his own appointment with his doctor, and he'd stayed with her in that waiting room for another hour, talking through what happened. It was then that Liam spoke about his own experience with betrayal. He'd been on the job when he was accused of something monstrous and had almost died fighting to clear his name. Even now he knew there were people within the department who questioned his innocence and his true relationship with his family. He'd been wronged like she had. Maybe even worse. And that was the moment their casual greetings became a friendship. Numbers were exchanged, and their own unique support group was formed.

The bell above the door rang, and the twins spun around. Susan smiled when she saw Liam walking swiftly with his cane, shaking the rain from his jacket.

"Liam!" Tim cried, his face lighting up.

Casey waved. "We're over here!"

"Hey, guys!"

He was great with the kids, a true natural. His kindness was effortless, and the ease at which he put Tim was always something Susan was a little jealous of. She watched as he made his way past the counter and around the maze of empty tables. He looked good. Jeans, a wool sweater, a raincoat covering his thin but somewhat athletic frame. He'd let his hair grow out a bit, and she liked the way it was bushier and covered his ears. His eyes were fixed on hers as he approached.

"Good afternoon, Investigator Adler," he said, plopping down in a seat next to her and leaning his cane against the table.

Susan raised her glass of water. "Mr. Dwyer."

The twins hopped off their chairs and hugged Liam, a kid on each side of him.

"I see you rascals are full of energy as usual."

"Tim did good at the doctor's today," Casey reported. "His brain is getting better."

"Is that right?"

Tim nodded. "Yup. I answered all of his questions, and we talked and played games, and we colored and made pictures. It was fun!"

"Excellent."

Susan sipped her water and broke off a little piece of crust from her slice. She could actually see Tim's little shoulders relax and his smile become something made of real joy. It made her tear up every time she witnessed it. Her son. Happy. Who would've thought?

The twins got back to their chairs and continued devouring their slices. They'd already gone through a small stack of napkins, and Susan reached over and grabbed a full dispenser from the table next to theirs.

"So it went well?" Liam asked, helping himself to a slice.

"Yes and no," Susan whispered. "The session went okay, but he's having some trouble at home. The anniversary of what happened is coming up, and he's thinking about it more. Fighting with kids, not sleeping, not talking as much."

"Did Dr. Radcliffe tell you Tim's thinking about it, or did Tim?"

"Radcliffe. Tim told him while they were in session. But I could sense it too."

"Well, at least the little guy's talking it out. He's doing great. Just gotta hang in there."

"As long as it takes."

Susan popped the piece of crust into her mouth and refilled the twins' waters. Out of the corner of her eye she could see Liam watching her as he took a bite of his pizza.

"You're getting around pretty good on that thing," she said, nodding toward the cane.

Liam chuckled. "The PT is working wonders. Won't need it much longer. I'm all healed up and walking better each day."

"You look like you got a little toned there too."

"You checking me out?"

"You wish."

They both laughed, and it felt good, even for that brief moment. The kids were eating, she was smiling, and the conversation was real.

"You heading back to the job when you get your clean bill of health?"

Liam shook his head, and his smile faded. "I don't think I can take all the people I came up with staring at me and whispering about me every time I walk by. It'd be too much. I know they'd welcome me back, but it wouldn't be the same. For me or for them." He grabbed his glass and filled it with water from the pitcher. "But I'm too young to retire, don't have the savings, and don't have any other skills, so I'll have to catch on somewhere. Maybe state police like you. Or New Jersey. Hell, I'd even take a look at Maryland if the pay was good enough."

"Or New York," Susan said a little too quickly. She took a bite of her pizza and felt her cheeks get hot. "I could put a word in."

"I don't know," Liam said playfully. "I hate the Giants, hate the Rangers, can't stomach the Yankees, and the Mets are a joke. I'm a Philly boy through and through. New York has always been our biggest rival in every sport. Not sure if I could do it."

"You would let a sports team determine where you live?"

"Absolutely."

"A man of true wisdom."

They laughed again. It was always like this when they got together, but Susan was afraid to seek anything more than whatever it was she and Liam already had. She was attracted to him, yes, but often wondered whether his attractiveness stemmed from the way he was with her kids or an actual physical longing. It was too complicated with his backstory and hers, and with them being three hours apart, it seemed better to let sleeping dogs lie. She would never forgive herself if she pushed things and destroyed what they already had. But still, when they were together, it just felt natural.

"I need to ask you something," Susan said, turning serious for a moment. "It's fine if you're not up for it, but I could use a little help on my case. Help that would be, let's say, off the books."

Liam took a bite of his pizza. "Keep talking."

"This case I'm working on, it involves one of our troopers being killed at a traffic stop. We caught the suspects on the dashcam but have no idea who they are. Couldn't get a clean look. There's an old man, James Darville, who's missing and is somehow a part of all of it. Just can't figure out exactly how yet. I thought if I can start digging into this guy's background, I might come across something that points me to the people who killed the trooper."

"Sounds like a good plan."

She opened her phone and scrolled through her email, clicking on one that came in from the barracks. "I got Darville's background check last night. He was born and raised in Circleville, Ohio, just south of Columbus. No siblings. Parents are both deceased. No record of extended family. Graduated Ohio State in 1975 and worked as an English teacher in schools around Ohio and western Pennsylvania. Never married. No kids. Bought the house in New York where he was currently living ten years ago. No criminal record of any kind. Clean."

"So what's the off-the-books help you're looking for?"

"It seems like he moved around a bit. Spent some time in West Finley and Beaverdale. Both Pennsylvania towns. I called in to the feds to get an extensive background done, but they're all tied up, and my request just ended up in their queue. I was thinking maybe you could make a couple calls to the contacts you have in Pennsylvania. See if we can get something from the state database?"

"I can certainly try," Liam replied. "I know West Finley is south of Pittsburgh, almost on the Ohio border. I worked with a guy who grew up in the same county. Never heard of Beaverdale, though."

"It's kind of in the middle of nowhere. Center of the state."

"I can't guarantee anything, obviously, but it won't hurt to ask around."

"I appreciate it."

"Why is this off the books?"

"I don't really know what road I'm going down yet, so I'd rather not put in official requests across state lines. Like I said, I'm just hoping if I find out enough about this James Darville, I might stumble upon the man and woman involved in the trooper's death."

"Got it."

"So you're in?"

Liam smiled again. "I wouldn't miss an opportunity to be your partner on a case. Not a chance."

37

Cindy had been out for a walk to clear her head and try to come up with a strategy that would get James talking. Hagen would be there soon, and if he arrived before James had told her what he'd done to her sister and the other children, it would be too late. He'd kill the old man, and his truth would die with him. She knew time was running out, but she couldn't force a failing brain to remember what she wanted, and when. She wasn't sure what her next step should be. She was beginning to think the entire thing was hopeless.

She opened the front door and immediately heard yelling. Cindy hurried down the hall and found Trevor bent over the coffee table in the living room, pounding the wooden surface with his fist, the veins in his forehead, purple and swollen, protruding up toward his hairline.

"You leave them alone, you son of a bitch! I'll kill you! I swear to God, I'll kill you! Give me my family back!"

"What's going on?" she asked, her voice drowning in his.

"If you hurt them, I'll hunt you down and skin you alive! We're doing everything you asked. Everything! I've killed for you! Leave my family alone!"

"What's happening?"

"I want—" He pulled the phone away from his ear, and she could see the screen. It was blank. The call had been cut off.

"Trevor, talk to me. What happened?"

Trevor spun around, his eyes wide with his anger and madness. Yes, that's what she could see. The madness. It was all catching up to him, and he was losing it. They all were.

"You," he barked through clenched teeth. "Did you do this? Have you been working with Hagen this whole time? Do you know who this guy is?"

Cindy took a step back. "Of course not! What happened?"

He held up his phone. "He called me."

"Hagen called you? He never calls."

"He's angry. He knows the cops found the car, and he's still pissed about the trooper we killed. He knows about the evidence we left behind at the old man's house. We screwed it all up. It's all coming undone."

"What did he say?"

"He said we needed to pay for our mistakes. He said he can get Mrs. Hill her liver but that maybe the blood type won't match, and she'll die when her body can't process the new organ."

"Oh my god."

"Then he said I might have to choose between my wife and my son. He said maybe the best way to make things right since I killed the trooper would be to take the life of someone I care for. He said maybe I'll only get one of them back, and he wants me to choose or he'll choose for me." Trevor began to sob, deep harsh breaths filled with panic and sorrow. "Why did you get me involved in this? Why?"

Cindy rushed over and hugged him. "I'm sorry. I am. I wish you weren't involved. I really do."

"I can't choose. I love them both. I have to find them."

"We will. But right now we have to stick to the plan. Maybe if we do things right the rest of the way, he'll forgive us."

She let him cry it out before he was able to get himself under control. He wiped his eyes and sat down on the couch, coughing and clearing his throat.

"You're right," he said. "We have to see this through. Maybe he will forgive us."

"If he contacts me, I'll beg him for all of us."

"Where's David?"

"He left. He had to get back to his mother."

Trevor looked at her, his eyes both cold and resigned. "You ever notice whenever Hagen contacts us, David's not around?"

"What are you saying?"

"What do you think I'm saying?"

"You think David is Hagen?"

He shrugged. "Why not? Any one of us could be."

38

By the time Susan and the kids got back to the house, Beatrice had dinner waiting. It was a late dinner due to the traffic they ran into on the New Jersey Turnpike, but it was better than the fast food Casey and Tim had begged for. The kids burst through the door with full bladders and empty stomachs. The familiar sounds of a house in perpetual chaos returned, and life was as it should be. They were home.

With dinner done, baths taken, the dishwasher loaded, and the twins in bed, Beatrice sat on the couch with her feet up on the coffee table and a pillow tucked into the small of her back. She sipped a cup of coffee while watching a rerun of *Law & Order*, careful to keep the sound low and her attention focused while Susan worked next to her on the love seat, her papers spread out on the cushions, a glass of merlot on the side table, well within reach.

The living room was silent but for Jack McCoy and Lennie Briscoe trading theories about the motive for the homicide they were investigating. Susan was trying to do the same thing, but in real life there weren't always clues to point you in the right direction or witnesses who popped up at the right place and the right time. There were no commercial breaks to rest during and no linchpins to tie everything together with five minutes left before the end of the show. Real police work involved procedure, interviews, a little bit of gut, and a whole lot of hard work. Rabbit holes were easy to fall down and difficult to climb out of, and even when you got the story that made sense, you had the burden of proof to present, or the DA wouldn't bring charges. That's the way it was in real life. That was the law, and even within the law, the bad guys got away on occasion and the wrong guys went to prison. But not for Jack and Lennie. Jack and Lennie had it made. They always found their man just in the nick of time.

Susan closed her file and grabbed the wine from the table. She took a sip and sighed.

Beatrice looked at her. "I can go in my room and watch this there if it's distracting you."

"No, you're fine. The show isn't the distraction. It's this case."

"Tough one?"

"Kind of. I'll get it."

Beatrice waited a few beats, then asked quietly, "How's Liam?"

"He's fine."

"Mm-hmm."

"I can't argue about Liam right now, Mom."

"I'm not arguing about anything."

"I know you don't like him. We're just friends. There's nothing to worry about."

"Who's worrying?" Beatrice asked. "Have your friend. And I never said I didn't like him. I just don't want a man who has so much baggage spending all that time with my grandchildren. Not until we know he's okay. You did meet him at a psych hospital. Let's not forget that."

"Yeah, the same psych hospital that's helping the grandchild you're so worried about. Do you want Tim to have that same stigma when someone's talking about him?"

"That's not the point. I'm just saying be careful. Baby steps. See what he's made of."

"I'm on it."

A pause. "I know there's a lot happening in your life right now," Beatrice said. "Just know that God only gives us what we can handle."

Susan waved her hand over her paperwork and chuckled. "I think God is overestimating my capabilities."

"Well, I'm not. You got this."

With the remnants of her injuries still plaguing her, it took Beatrice a few minutes to get up off the couch. She took her mug and made her way toward her bedroom. "I'm heading in. I'll see you in the morning."

"Okay. I love you."

"Love you too, sweetie. Good night."

Susan listened as her mother's bedroom door closed. They'd argued about Liam before, and it always ended the same way. Beatrice would implore her to be careful, and Susan would assure her mother she knew exactly what she was doing. The truth was, she didn't know *exactly* what she was doing—if she was even doing anything at all. But her gut told her Liam was one of the good guys. He had to be. She couldn't be that wrong for a second straight time. She couldn't.

Susan pushed thoughts of the twins and Liam and Philadelphia out of her head and tried to concentrate. She picked up the copies of Rebecca Hill's address book and began skimming the names and addresses, hoping something would click. She scanned name after name, placing each page down on the cushions and moving on to the next.

She stopped on the fourth page and stared at the name she'd read before. For whatever reason it stood out to her now, in the silence of her house, when her mind had a chance to stretch.

Look for the others.

She flipped the pages back to the Fs, and he wasn't there. She flipped ahead to the Ps, and she wasn't there. Finally, she flipped to the Rs, and even *she* wasn't there. This was clearly a personal address book, void of anything related to Rebecca's job, her patients, or the facilities in which she worked.

So why was *he* there?

Susan had searched for James Darville's doctors, and none of them were in the book. Dr. Phines, his neurologist, wasn't there. Dr. Trammel, his physical therapist, wasn't there. Even Rebecca's boss at the staffing agency, Beth Ruelle, wasn't there. Susan turned back to the Cs and looked at the name.

Phillip Calib.

James Darville's primary doctor.

Rebecca didn't even have the word *Doctor* in front of his name. Just Phillip Calib. Why was he the only person associated with James Darville in Rebecca Hill's personal address book?

39

The storm that had brought gray skies and rain to Philadelphia the day before had worked its way north and moved into the Hudson Valley overnight. Susan listened to the sound of her wipers sliding across the windshield as she pulled into the back entrance of the doctor's office, her mind still running through the case since last night. After discovering Dr. Calib's number in Rebecca's address book, she'd spent the next several hours scouring her interview notes and examining the crime scene reports from Rebecca's car and Darville's house. She was confident they hadn't missed anything—at least until the lab reports came back and the extended background checks were finished.

Even at nine in the morning on a cold and dreary day, the line at the coffee shop across the street stretched out the door. Dr. Calib had been right. Double the line on a weekday. Susan scurried from her car and into the office lobby, yanking her hood over her head as she ran. The directory stated that Dr. Calib's practice was on the second floor. She took the stairs.

The doctor's office was typical. Faux-leather chairs lined two of the pristine white walls. A glass partition marked the third wall, separating the patients from the nurses and the receptionist, who worked at small desks answering phones and filling out paperwork. The fourth wall had an access door to the examination rooms as well as a magazine rack that was bolted in place. Periodicals and newspapers hung over the edges, the entire case overstuffed and on the verge of collapse.

An elderly couple sat together in the waiting area. The man was reading a magazine while the woman clutched a handful of tissues against her chest. Neither of them spoke to the other. It was a comfortable silence, Susan thought. A silence that came with years of practice and mutual respect.

The receptionist looked up just as Susan pulled her shield from her jacket.

"I need to see Dr. Calib."

The receptionist smiled as she'd clearly been trained to do. "He's with a patient right now."

"I'll wait in his office."

"You'll have a seat and wait in the waiting room, thank you."

Now it was Susan's turn to smile. "It's important that I speak with Dr. Calib as soon as he's done with his current patient. You can show me to his office, since I'm sure you don't want your other patients seeing a homicide investigator waiting to interview their physician."

The elderly couple both looked up.

"Please don't make me do this the hard way," Susan continued, her smile still plastered on her face.

The receptionist nodded slowly. "I'll buzz you in."

———

Dr. Calib's private office was simple: a metal desk with an oak top, a computer, a bookcase full of patient binders, and a corkboard that filled the wall behind the desk. Papers and graphs and articles and pictures were pinned onto the board. A small collection of dumbbells was stacked like a pyramid in the corner against the same wall. Susan sat down in one of the two chairs in front of the desk and waited. She scanned the pictures on the corkboard, searching for a photograph of Darville or Rebecca, but she couldn't see any from where she sat.

She reached into her pocket for her phone, then checked her voice mail and email to ensure neither the barracks nor the family needed her. She flipped through her social media feeds and scrolled through picture-perfect lives she knew were mostly fantasy. People posted the good and hid the bad. She knew this, but there she was, scrolling and liking, scrolling and liking. It passed the time.

The noise from the examination area suddenly grew louder, and Susan turned in her seat to find Dr. Calib walking through his office door. He was carrying a file and made his way to the cabinets, where he opened the middle drawer and slid it inside.

"Sorry to bust in like this, unannounced," Susan began. "I just need a few minutes."

Dr. Calib nodded. "Yes, well, we wouldn't want to have to do this the *hard* way, right?"

"That's right."

"Any news on James?"

"We're working on it. I'd like to ask you some follow-up questions about Mr. Darville's nurse, Rebecca Hill."

He took a seat behind his desk. "I saw what happened on the news. So tragic. I'm praying that James is okay, although if Rebecca's dead . . ." He looked up at her. "I'm not sure how I can be of help."

"I understand you were personal friends with Rebecca."

She'd decided to take an assumed-fact position to see how he reacted. Sometimes stating something in a tone that was factual disarmed a subject and made them feel more comfortable sharing information they might've otherwise kept to themselves. She watched as he briefly looked away.

"If I recall, I told you I only met her a couple of times when she came in with James. That hardly constitutes being personal friends."

"Did you ever see Rebecca outside of Mr. Darville's appointments?"

"No, I didn't."

"Ever talk on the phone?"

"Maybe. I can't remember." He paused, then snapped his fingers. "Wait, I do remember something. She called me once when James slipped and fell in the bathroom. It was a short conversation. She told me what happened, and I told her to call 911."

"You guys ever talk personally? Just to chat?"

"No. Where are you getting this?"

Susan took out the copies of Rebecca's address book. The page with Dr. Calib's number was on top, highlighted in yellow. She pushed the sheet of paper across the desk.

"This is a page from Rebecca Hill's personal address book. You're the only doctor in it. Not Mr. Darville's physical therapist. Not his neurologist. Just you. And you're listed as Phillip Calib, not Dr. Calib. Sounds personal to me."

Dr. Calib took the sheet. While he was studying it, Susan was studying him. His chest began to rise slightly. His cheeks and neck turned a very light shade of red. His right hand squeezed a pen he was holding.

"I have no idea why my number's in her address book," he replied, handing the page back. His voice was steady. Smooth. "I guess after calling me, she kept it on record. I was his primary physician, after all."

"But this is your personal cell number. Not the office line."

"Correct."

"Seems strange that Rebecca never had Dr. Solanso's number in her book. She was dealing with him long before you."

"Maybe she never needed him after hours, and after we spoke, she kept mine. I don't know what to tell you."

"If that was the case, wouldn't it make more sense to keep your number on her phone instead of in the book?"

"Sure. Did you check her phone? Is it on there?"

"We're waiting on records and access." Susan leaned forward in her seat and lowered her voice for effect. "Look, I don't want to mislead you. You're not in trouble. If you knew Rebecca, I don't care. I just want to know if you can help with other information that can point us toward finding Mr. Darville. He's my priority right now. Maybe she told you something that could end up breaking the case. Whether you knew Rebecca Hill personally or not is no concern of mine."

"I'm glad you don't care," Dr. Calib said. "But I'm telling you the truth. I didn't know Rebecca Hill outside of this facility and in the capacity of meeting her a couple of times with our mutual patient. Don't you think if I could help you find James, I would tell you everything?"

"I would certainly hope so." Susan returned the copied pages back to her bag and stood from her seat. She made her way toward the door and stopped. "Do me a favor. Stand up and walk in front of your desk."

"Why?"

"I need to see something."

Dr. Calib got up from his seat and stood in front of the two chairs that faced his desk. Susan studied his height and overall frame. It was hard to tell if he matched the man she'd seen on the trooper's dashcam. Possibly too short. She couldn't be 100 percent sure.

"Last chance," she said. "For the record. Did you know Rebecca Hill outside of this office?"

Dr. Calib shook his head. "No."

"Did you ever speak to her on the phone in a personal matter not regarding Mr. Darville?"

"No."

"Then we're good. Thank you for your time."

She turned and left without another word. There was one thing she was now certain of in this case full of uncertainty.

For whatever reason, Phillip Calib was lying.

40

Cindy came up from the basement and found Trevor sitting at the desk in the dining room. She watched as he placed a red folder in the bottom drawer of the desk and locked it. She knocked on the wall just as he was slipping the key into his pocket.

"Still no progress," she said. "I can't get him to remember anything. No matter how many times I show him the pictures of the kids, there's no spark. He just stares at them like he's seeing them for the first time."

"Keep trying."

"I will, but I'm starting to think this is hopeless." She nodded toward the drawer she'd just seen him lock. "What're you up to?"

"I'm doing some research," he replied, his back to her. "On David. I need to know who I'm dealing with from here on out. I need to know who I can trust."

"Have you looked me up already?"

"Your story checks out. So far."

She walked farther into the dining room. "What'd you find?"

Trevor turned around in his seat. "Did you know David is a writer?"

Cindy shook her head. "I don't know anything about any of you."

"He writes for a couple of tech websites. Reviews for software and new products. He's also been trying to get a book published for a while now. He has a website and a few social media profiles that talk about his writing. Thrillers and true crime. And every once in a while, he posts short stories or excerpts of books he's working on. His last short story was posted on his website over the summer, but he took it down about a month ago. I found it through a link from a fan who'd retweeted it. You know what it was about?"

Cindy swallowed the lump in her throat. The house was suddenly so very quiet. "What?"

"It's about a group of people being forced to carry out a kidnapping and murder in exchange for members of their families, who'd been abducted and tortured, being freed. You know what it was called?"

Cindy's stomach turned.

"'The Spider and the Flies.'"

"David's the spider?" Cindy asked.

Trevor nodded. "And I'm pretty sure we're the flies."

41

When Susan walked onto the investigators' floor, Sergeant Triston was sitting at her partner's old desk, waiting for her. Most of the troopers were out on patrol. Investigator Christopher Ringer and his partner, Bill Bailey, sat on the opposite side of the floor working intently, heads down, silent. They looked up when she walked in, each nodding a hello.

"Hey, guys," she said. "Things look serious over there."

"Drive-by earlier this morning on the border of Pleasantville and Chappaqua," Ringer replied. He was in his early forties, kind of a plump build, big but not all that muscular. He'd played lacrosse in college and was recruited to the state police right after graduation, but the years on the job were catching up with him, and he had the gut and gray hair to show for it. He was married with three kids. An excellent cop.

Susan dropped her bag in her desk. "A drive-by? Wow. Never thought I'd see that in those neighborhoods."

Bill shook his head. He was a few years younger, late thirties, a wife but no kids. He'd recently been promoted to investigator and came up from Manhattan. He still had the youthful exuberance in his eyes that all new investigators had on their first assignment. Susan knew that would fade over time, and his dark-black hair would soon start to disappear or turn a lighter shade. It happened to them all. "Went down right off the exit ramp of the Saw Mill," he said. "We've been up since four."

"Any suspects?"

"No suspects. No witnesses," Ringer replied. "Flying blind."

Susan chuckled. "Welcome to the club."

She sat at her desk, and before she could say anything to Triston, he was standing with a large file in his hand.

"We got some results back," he said. "Forensics was able to get some hair fibers from Rebecca Hill's car. They matched some of it to Darville and some to Rebecca."

"That makes sense. We already know Rebecca Hill was at Darville's house as his nurse, and he was in her car for his doctor appointments. There would be transference. We need to know if we get any matches that aren't from either of them."

"They did. In the driver's seat. They're running analysis on those. Hopefully our lady driver has a record, and we can match something up."

"What else?"

"Emily already told you she couldn't pull a clean print from that locket you found. Forensics couldn't get anything from the car either. We're still a few days away from DNA coming back from the two teeth. Judge finally signed off on all the warrants. We got one for Darville's medical records, one for his phone records, one for Rebecca Hill's phone records, and one for her employment records from Phelps and the staffing place. They've all been served, so we should start receiving the information soon."

"Good. Maybe I can find something in there to figure out why his primary doctor is lying to me."

"What do you mean?"

"I saw him this morning. Dr. Calib. I found his name in Rebecca's personal address book, and when I asked him about it, he denied knowing her outside the office, but I could tell he was lying."

"He's a white male. Height and weight?"

"Fits, but I can't be absolutely sure."

"I'll put in a formal request with Crosby to see if we can get a unit on him for a little while. Few days, maybe. See if that'll take us anywhere."

"And I'll run a background check on him."

"Sounds good." Triston tapped her laptop. "Check your email. Surveillance footage from the lake is in."

Susan pulled her chair closer to her desk and found the email. She clicked on the link to where the footage had been uploaded and sat back.

The time stamp on the video read 3:13 in the morning. It was footage from the marina's parking lot. The area was completely deserted from the angle the camera showed, but the lights in the lot were functional, which made it easy to pick out details in the feed.

As the digital stamp moved to 3:14, Rebecca's car—the Honda Civic—came into the frame, driving slowly, circling once, then maneuvering up to the highest point of the lot, by a thicket of trees that ended at the edge of a small cliff. The Civic's headlights went out, and the car sat idling. When the digital clock on the feed moved to 3:18, another car came into view, and Susan pulled her laptop closer to get a better look.

The car appeared to be a Jeep Grand Cherokee, but she couldn't tell what color, only that it was dark. Could've been black or blue. Maybe a deep red. Possibly a dark gray. It pulled in behind the parked Civic, and as soon as it came to a stop, the Civic's driver's-side door opened, and the woman from the dashcam video stepped out and ran toward the Jeep. She was wearing a sweatshirt, and this time her hood was up, covering her face, but Susan knew it was the same woman.

The Jeep's driver got out, dressed in a similar outfit, face hidden, hood up. He, too, appeared to be one of the people from the dashcam, judging from height, weight, and the way he moved. They both got behind the Civic and began pushing it toward the edge of the cliff until the car tipped and splashed down into the water below. They watched for a moment; then they ran back to the Jeep and drove away.

Susan restarted the footage and concentrated on the Jeep's driver, but again, the high angle of the camera only provided small bits of the driver's face. She could see that the person was Caucasian, but there were no other discernable features. She was witnessing the body dump but was no further along in solving the crime than if the footage didn't exist at all. She restarted it a third time and kept studying.

"This proves they didn't dump the old man in the lake," Susan said. "They just ditch the car and go."

Triston nodded. "Which means he could still be alive."

She paused the video and pointed to the screen. "They put tape over the license plate on the Jeep in case there were cameras."

"Smart."

"We get any surveillance from the dock or the restaurant?"

"Still working through some video from the restaurant," Triston replied. "The dock didn't have anything that showed our guys."

Susan shut off the video and rose from her chair. "Let's go talk to LT about getting that tail on Dr. Calib."

"Let me find out what kind of car he drives first."

Susan's cell phone rang, and she fished it out of her pocket while Triston broke away and began to head back toward his desk. "This is Susan Adler."

"Hey, it's Emily Nestor."

"Hey. You got something for me?"

"Yeah, the autopsy's done, but I'm still working on the report."

"Find anything important I should know about up front?"

"Oh yeah. That's why I'm calling."

"What'd you get?"

"The woman you found in the trunk of that Civic is not Rebecca Hill. And at this point, I don't know who the hell she is."

42

James opened his eyes and saw the woman standing over him. She was smiling, and for a moment he didn't know where he was. He scanned the room and found the faint familiarity of the basement return. His bed. The television that always played the same movie. The sofa he never sat on because he was trapped in his god-awful wheelchair. The hallway with the one step that led to the hurricane doors. The three windows he couldn't see out of. The shadows the ghosts lived in.

"Cindy," he muttered, his voice rough and phlegmy.

"That's right. What's your name?"

"James. My name is James Darville."

"Very good. I'm glad to see you're with us again."

James tried to sit up in his wheelchair. His lower back ached, and his neck was stiff. His head throbbed. "What happened?" he asked.

"You had a spell, but I think the fog has cleared some."

"My body hurts. And my head."

"You took a tumble and hit your face on the floor. But you're okay now."

James reached up and touched his face. He could feel that the area around his eye and left cheek was swollen. Pain shot through him when he pushed against the swelling.

"You don't remember falling?" Cindy asked, watching him.

James shook his head.

"You'll be fine."

"If you say so."

Cindy was holding something in her hand.

"What's that?" James asked.

She walked closer and showed him. It was a ticket stub, yellowed and aged. "I got this from the photo album. It's a ticket from a school play you directed. *Our Town*. You did it with the students from the drama club you taught back in Beaverdale. Do you remember where that is?"

James closed his eyes and tried to remember. Nothing came.

"It's in Pennsylvania. You taught English there. Forest Hills Middle School. And you volunteered to lead their first drama club. You helped produce and direct *Our Town*."

"Were you there?"

"Everyone was so excited. It was the first time the kids had a drama club at the middle school level. You were insistent on it, and the principal finally relented. A bunch of the students signed up right away, and you had actors and stagehands and lighting people and even a small special effects group. The kids just wanted to be part of it because it was new. And you were the head of it all."

"Was it any good? Did we pull it off?"

"You pulled it off," Cindy replied. "And it was good. It was the talk of the school. You got your picture in the local newspaper and everything. As soon as the weekend was over, the kids started brainstorming about what they wanted to put on next. You changed lives. All the time."

James knew he was supposed to feel melancholy or pride or happiness or triumph. Instead, all he could feel was bitterness. Anger. "You take these little memories and try and join them together to build a legacy. They're supposed to tell you what kind of a person you are and what kind of a life you built, but I can't remember any of it. You tell me what happened, but you might as well be reading me a story out of a book. It's like I don't exist except for right in this moment, and then this moment becomes the past, and I can't remember it. Why is this happening to me?"

"You've built a legacy, James," Cindy replied. "You've changed lives. More than you can ever know." She took his hand and placed the ticket in his palm. "If you try hard enough, I believe you can remember the kind of man you were. You can remember the things you've done and the lives you've come in contact with. You just have to will it to be. Close your eyes. Smell the ticket. Feel its edges. Bring yourself back there. Open your mind."

He closed his eyes and brought the ticket stub up to his nose, inhaling deeply, smelling the paper and the ink and the dust, waiting for a memory to surface. Something. Anything.

"Annie Tolas played the lead," Cindy whispered.

He was a teacher. He put on the production.

"Do you remember Annie?"

Beaverdale. Pennsylvania. Forest Hills.

"Annie Tolas. The kids. Your kids. Your students."

Blackness. Just pure blackness.

"Remember."

"I can't."

"You can."

He opened his eyes and put the ticket back in Cindy's hand. "There's nothing. I'm sorry."

Footsteps climbed down the basement stairs, and they both turned to find the man hopping onto the bottom landing. "Bedtime," he said.

James nodded and looked at Cindy, who was looking at him. "I know you want to make me remember. I don't think I'm capable."

"But you have to. You have to remember."

"Why?"

"You need to know who you were in this life. It's important."

"Why is it important?"

"It just is. It's everything."

The man came up behind him and grabbed the handles of the wheelchair. "Say good night, Cindy."

Cindy's entire body sagged. "Good night."

They watched as she walked back up the stairs. When she was out of sight, the man wheeled him toward the bed.

"You okay?" he asked, his voice lowering to a whisper.

177

James shrugged. "As good as I can be."

The man unstrapped the belts around his legs and lifted him into the bed. He helped him change into his pajamas and helped him with his bedpan.

"How's your face?"

"It hurts."

"What'd she tell you happened?"

"She said I fell and hit my head on the floor."

The man took the bedpan and placed it on the floor. He leaned over and adjusted the blanket. "That's not what happened."

"Then how did I hurt my face?"

"You didn't. David hit you."

James looked at the man, his mind swirling in the darkness of his memories. "Who's David?"

The man stood up and placed his hands on his hips. "Look, I'm probably the only friend you have here, so pay attention. I'm trying to help you. You're in the middle of something very serious, and you need to remember those names Cindy keeps asking you about. She needs some closure before all of this ends. She's owed that much."

James tried to follow the conversation. "I have to remember."

"Yes. Your memories are in there somewhere, so figure out how to tap into them and tell her what she needs to know."

"Why did David hit me?"

The man ignored the question and turned out the light on the nightstand. When the basement was dark, he placed a piece of paper in James's hand, then made his way to the stairs.

"Good night, James."

James waited until he heard the door shut above him, then reached up and turned the lamp back on. With fumbling fingers he unfolded the paper and read it carefully, feeling both confusion and fear.

THEY'RE NOT WHO YOU THINK THEY ARE

43

The house was quiet. Cindy sat on the couch in the living room. Trevor sat on one of the overstuffed armchairs across from her. She noticed a few framed pictures of his wife and his son and wondered where they were at that very moment. She hoped they were okay and prayed they could all get out of this alive.

"I've been trying to figure out who Hagen is since this whole thing started," Trevor said, leaning up, his elbows resting on his knees. "At first I figured it was someone who has contacts in the medical field, because how else would he be able to promise an organ transplant to Rebecca's mother? I also thought medical field because Rebecca was the first person he contacted, and she was always in and out of the hospital with James."

"Trevor—"

"But that's where I went wrong. Think about it. What's the motive for one of his doctors to want James to confess to what he did? There is none. If they found out about his crimes, they'd just report him to the police and move on to their next patient. It's not like James would be the first criminal these doctors ever had to deal with. There's no incentive for them to keep his secret. There's no point."

"So, you don't think it's a doctor?"

"Who has the most to gain by playing this ridiculous game? It's David. He had access to the old man through his sister. Rebecca could've passed him medical files or session notes from any one of his doctors because she was required to be up on everything that was going on. She was James's full-time nurse, which meant she had total access to his house and everything in it. We already know she went through his personal stuff when he was sleeping. That's how she found the compartment in the floor, which led to her finding the photo album and scrapbook, which led to Sonia, which led to you. But what if this all started years ago, and it took this long to get everything they needed in order to pull this off? Could be how they found out about me. No one else knows about me and James. They had to have found something at his house."

Cindy nodded as she began putting the pieces of the puzzle together. He was making sense. "But that would mean the promise of the organ transplant for David's mother is a lie."

"Yeah, I think it is. I think it's a lie to get us on his side so it seems like we're all in this together. Then he can get to what he really wants, which is the story. That's why he's giving you time to get the truth from James. He needs that for his book."

"Okay, but why? Why does he care about James's story? He has no ties to James like we do, so why is he kidnapping your family and trapping us here? Why go through all this?"

"For the drama of it all." Trevor stood up and began pacing the room. "It makes for one hell of a drama, right? The kind of true crime story that could launch a writing career and put a lot of money in his pocket. Might even sell the movie rights to something like this. I think he wants to write about what happened, what's happening, and, like I said, he needs James's confession. He needed me for location. He knew you were obsessed. He could hear it in your podcasts and blogs about your sister. He knew you'd already done a lot of research on your sister, but you never had the actual guy. Well, he handed you the man, and now he has proof about the other kids too. Once you were presented with the identity of your sister's killer, your obsession to learn the truth would only get stronger. So he chose the one person you'd believe was legit to deliver that identity to you."

"Rebecca."

"Exactly. He knew if he got the old man in front of you, you wouldn't stop until you got his confession. I think Rebecca agreed to be part of this so she could make sure we were taking care of James and that he remained healthy. But things started backfiring from day one. And now David's scrambling. He's panicking. I think he knows the cops are going to figure it all out, and he needs the full story before they close in. Once he gets that, we all go down. Me. You. My family. Everyone."

Cindy began shaking. She hugged her arms and tried to process what Trevor was telling her. "So what do we do?"

"David's coming here later. You keep him busy. Tell him I went to bed early. I'm going to go to his house and poke around. See what I can find. The more we know, the more we can control things on our side."

"You can't leave. What if someone spots you and calls the police?"

"I have to take that chance. It's the only way to try and learn something. If David is Hagen, we need to know."

He was right. And wasn't it in their interest to take back some control of this situation from Hagen if they could? After all, she and Trevor were the ones who were on the hook for three deaths—three deaths she'd never imagined. They had to protect themselves.

"All I ever wanted my entire life was to give my sister some kind of closure. I just wanted to know that she hadn't simply vanished into thin air. That's all. I didn't want this. I didn't ask for it."

"Too late. You're in it."

She stared at Trevor for a long while before speaking. "You know Hagen wanted you for more than just your location. This," she said, gesturing around the room, "isn't worth kidnapping your family for. If Hagen is really David, your relationship with James was much more important. Makes a nice little twist in his book."

Trevor fell back in his seat and folded his hands in front of him. "There is no relationship between me and James, and if David thinks he can play with my emotions because the old man is my father, he's mistaken. The person in that basement is a stranger, as far as I'm concerned. He can live or die, and it won't make a difference. Getting my real family back—my wife and son—is my only priority."

44

Susan burst through the double doors of the autopsy room to find Emily Nestor standing over the body of a woman the entire department had thought was Rebecca Hill.

"I got here as fast as I could," she panted, trying to steady her breathing.

"I could've conferenced you in from the barracks."

"No. I need to see this for myself."

Susan walked around the table and looked at the woman for a second time. The large lumps on her forehead and just below the left cheek from where she'd been beaten gave the shape of the face a kind of deformity. One eye remained closed, and her lips were still double the size they should've been. She took out her phone and pulled up the picture of Rebecca Hill from her driver's license, holding it next to the victim's face. Between Rebecca being about ten years younger in the picture and the swelling in the victim's face, there was no way to positively identify the person. Everyone had assumed it was her since the height, weight, general build, and skin color matched, and the body had been found in Rebecca's car with Rebecca's purse. That assumption had turned out to be a catastrophic mistake.

"Talk to me," Susan said, putting her phone away. "How did you find out this wasn't Rebecca Hill?"

"The prints didn't match," Dr. Nestor replied. She snatched a file from her desk and handed it over. "Plus, we got Ms. Hill's medical files sent to us earlier. Still waiting on Darville's. Turns out Rebecca Hill broke her ankle when she was in her twenties. ER report said she broke it after hopping off the back of a motorcycle while it was still going. I checked the body for the fracture. Wasn't there."

"So who is this?"

"I don't know. As soon as we found out this wasn't who we thought it was, I took this person's prints and fed them back into the database. No hits in the county, so I'm running it through NCIC. Still waiting on those results."

Susan paged through the file and looked at the prints taken from the person they'd fished out of Rebecca's car and compared them to the next page, which had Rebecca's prints taken from her employment records and the ones they'd lifted from her apartment. Dr. Nestor was right. They weren't close. Even with Susan's untrained eye she could see that the loops and arches weren't the same.

"Did you find anything else we should be aware of?" Susan asked, closing the file.

Dr. Nestor shook her head. "No. My initial inclination that she was strangled and dead before she went into the trunk was confirmed through the autopsy. The hyoid bone in her neck was indeed broken, and there was no water in her lungs. She was dead before she hit the lake."

"But we don't know who she is."

"Not at this point. Hopefully, we'll get a hit on her prints. Maybe you guys will hear something about her being missing, but there was nothing on her person that you hadn't already bagged, and according to the report, it all belonged to Rebecca Hill. There were no unique features on the body. No weird piercings or tattoos or birthmarks. Nothing like that."

"Of course not."

"Whoever she is, she was used to make us think she was Rebecca."

"But why?" Susan asked. She began to walk around the body as she talked. "Whoever was trying to pass her off as Rebecca would know we'd eventually find out it wasn't her, right? It's not like we'd turn the body back over to the family, and they would be tricked into burying her as Rebecca. Eventually the truth would come out just like it did."

"Yeah, but we were never meant to find the body and make the mistake in the first place," Dr. Nestor replied. "If the car had been dumped in a deeper section of the lake, this would all be moot. Rebecca would still be missing. Darville would be missing. So would her car."

"Okay. And this person matches Rebecca's height, build, skin color, and weight. She was pretending to be Rebecca."

"And now she's dead."

The two women looked at each other, the fluorescent lighting making both of them appear pale and sickly.

"Darville is suffering from late-stage Alzheimer's," Susan said. "Is it possible that this woman could've been playing the role of Rebecca for an extended period of time without him realizing it?"

"Sure. If enough time passed or the disease was acute enough, he'd have a hard time remembering specific features anyway. It wouldn't take much to pull that off."

"So she let the perps in, they find whatever it was they were looking for in the floor, they kidnap Darville, and when they didn't need this girl anymore, they kill her and cover up the fact that she'd been playing the role of Rebecca by dumping everything associated with the ruse in the lake."

"Sounds like it could be right."

"Then where's the real Rebecca?"

Dr. Nestor smiled. "I was just going to ask you the same thing."

Susan handed the file back and began to run out of the examination room.

"Where are you going?"

"Timelines," Susan shouted over her shoulder. "I need new timelines."

Susan dialed David Hill's cell phone as she walked to her car.

"Hello?"

"David, this is Investigator Adler."

"Oh. Hi."

"When was the last time you and your mother saw Rebecca?"

"What?"

"The exact last time you and your mother saw Rebecca. For dinner or whatever. When? Think."

He paused for a moment. "About three or four weeks ago?"

"Which is it? Three or four?"

"I'd have to check my phone."

"Okay, do it. I'll hold."

She waited and could hear him fumbling with his phone.

"We saw her for church on October tenth. So, about a month."

"No calls since?"

"Sure. Texts and calls. We went over that already."

"What was the last communication you got from her?"

"I spoke to her on Wednesday. When my mom got out of the hospital."

"And, according to your mom, she heard from Rebecca two days prior to the incident with the trooper."

"If you say so. What's going on?"

Susan climbed into her car and shut the door. She jammed the key into the ignition and started the engine. "I'm not sure yet, but the one thing I can tell you is that the woman we pulled out of your sister's trunk isn't Rebecca. I don't know where your sister is, but she's not in the morgue."

She could hear David take a quick, unsteady breath. "Is my sister alive?"

"I don't know. But I'm sure as hell going to find out."

TRANSCRIPT

The years passed, and the frenzy of two missing girls in a small town soon gave way to the general theory that they were both dead and would never be found. Before long, the residents of West Finley moved on with their lives, and the stories of Tiffany Greene and Sonia Garland became nothing more than warnings to the other children about talking to strangers or accepting rides from people you didn't know. Parents used phrases like "You don't want to end up like Sonia or Tiffany" to drive home points about being responsible and always knowing your surroundings. Their tragic tales became folklore, a secret every small town seemed to have, a story told around campfires at night.

The police had given up within months of the girls disappearing. Local authorities had called in the state police, and when Sonia's disappearance looked like it could be something serial, the state police called the FBI to come take a look at their case. None of them stayed long. There was no evidence to track. No suspects to look into. Noreen and I had made sure of that.

Noreen and Jackson gave their statements, just like Tiffany's folks had done some months earlier. Noreen had tried to hold it together, but the cracks in her facade were beginning to show, and the change in the woman I'd fallen in love with had become palpable. The people in town chalked it up to a despondent mother unwilling to accept what had happened to her daughter, but I knew there was something more. There was a period when Noreen stopped doing the normal things a person does. She stopped bathing and eating and would go days without leaving her bedroom. When we spoke on the phone, it was as if I were talking in a different language. She couldn't keep up with the simplest of conversations. I could see her sanity fraying as the reality of what she'd done began to overtake her. It was all she thought about and all she talked about whenever I could get her out of the house. Over the course of the next three years, her condition remained the same, and the time we spent together was more therapy session than the stolen moments of passion we used to share so intimately. I was starting to grow concerned that her flailing grip on reality would force her to confess, which would implicate me as well. I'd learned to live with my sins, as disgusting as they were. I did this by completely shutting out the images of what we'd done and replacing them with the same fantasy we'd fed the town. The girls went missing, and it was a tragedy. Sometimes it worked. Not always. But Noreen had become a true liability, and I was scared. Yet even in that fear, I never imagined I'd witness what happened next. It never even crossed my mind.

In the spring of 1980, when my relationship with Noreen was just getting off the ground, I'd come upon an old hunting cabin in the woods in Cross Creek County Park up in West Middletown while hiking one afternoon. It wasn't very big, maybe seven hundred square feet, one room, no bathroom, but to me, it was perfect. From the decaying walls and crumbling roof, I could tell the structure hadn't been used in some time, so I claimed it as mine and took Noreen there to make love on a blanket on the floor with nothing but the solitude of nature surrounding us. That became our spot, one where we knew no one would ever find us and we could be together the way we wanted. It was as close to perfect as we could get.

Over time, the cabin became a sanctuary. We went as often as we could after Tiffany and Sonia, talking things through and me letting Noreen cry it out without the need to look over her shoulder to make sure we remained alone. As her condition worsened, we would sit for full afternoons in complete silence, tears constantly streaming down her face. I wondered if she would ever get better, and I found my answer when she called me and asked me to meet her at the cabin in the summer of 1985.

Like I mentioned before, the cabin was just one big room. A dilapidated kitchen area was on the far left, and a bedroom section was on the right. The front of the cabin was where a living room would normally be, but there was no furniture to fill up the space, and we never really needed anything other than a blanket. I had a clean line of sight to the bedroom area and could see Noreen on an old cot and soiled mattress that had been left behind. She was sitting up, her back against the wall, her legs lying straight out. A child rested in her lap, unmoving.

"Noreen," I whispered as I walked farther into the cabin. "What's going on?"

She looked up at me and smiled. But her eyes were vacant, lifeless. Her cheekbones poked through her skin from all the weight she'd lost. "I wanted to spend some time with her."

I took a step closer. "Who is that?"

Her smile broadened. "Sonia, silly."

As I approached, I could see she was holding a young boy. He was African American, maybe ten, twelve years old. She'd put a blond wig on him, and the wig had red ribbons in it. Noreen was dressing him up to look like Sonia. I thought I was going to be sick.

"What did you do?" I asked.

"I saw her when I was coming home from my route. I was feeling so sad and missing her so much. There were days visiting stores when I didn't think I was going to be able to pull it off. Trying to act normal when life isn't normal is harder than you'd think. Laughing when you want to cry. Making small talk with your customers when you really just want to lock yourself in your hotel room and make the world disappear. I knew I needed to play the role of the catalog saleswoman, so

I did the best I could. But today was tough. God, I missed her terribly today. I don't know why. And then, like a miracle, I saw her, and my day brightened. I knew I could spend a little time with her to make me feel better before we had to put her back."

The boy was unmoving. Pale. Lifeless. Dead.

"You killed him?"

"Who?"

"This boy!"

Noreen laughed, and it sent shivers down my spine. "What boy? This is Sonia. Can't you see that? I saw her, and I knew I needed to spend some time with her. Just Mommy and her little baby. I missed her so much."

Noreen's bottle of sleeping pills was on the floor next to the cot, and I figured she'd drugged the boy like she'd done to Sonia at her house three years earlier. I'd later find out that she got him into her car by hitting him over the head with the baseball bat Jackson made her carry in the car when she was traveling alone. She knocked him out and stuffed him in the trunk. Then she put him to sleep and smothered him. Just like Sonia.

"Why are you doing this?" I asked, kneeling next to the cot and taking her hand in mine.

"I needed to see her."

"This isn't Sonia!"

She looked up at me. "Why didn't you lock the door?"

She hadn't asked me that in years. The guilt ran through me like a fever.

"Lives would've been saved if you'd just locked that classroom door."

"I—"

"I'd have my little girl. Tiffany's parents would have a family. Everyone would be happy."

I pulled at my hair, tugging it. "I can't do this!"

"Everything would be as it should be if you'd just locked that door."

She slipped out from under the boy and placed him down on the cot, faceup. He looked peaceful.

"I need you to put her back," Noreen said, her voice trailing off like she was dreaming. "Put her back so she can rest."

"No. I won't."

She pushed me up against the wall and curled her hands around the lapels of my jacket. We were so close I could smell her stale breath. It smelled like death. "Bury my daughter."

She let go, and I slid down onto the floor, the scene before me blurring with my tears. I wanted to refuse. To stand my ground. I know I could have stopped her. I could have hit her or tackled her or overpowered her and gone to the police, but I was too scared to move. I didn't know this woman. She was so completely mad. It shook me to my core.

And I had been the cause of it all.

45

He could hear them breathing. Raspy. Painful. Choked. He knew it was dark, and in the darkness, he knew he was vulnerable. He was sleeping on his back, his face outside the covers, exposed. He wanted to scream for help but was somehow aware that if he were to scream, those small, clawed hands would reach into his open mouth and rip out his tongue. There was nowhere he could go. No way to get help. He was trapped.

James opened his eyes, and with the help of the streetlights coming in through the three windows, he saw the outlines of them. The four children stood on either side of him with their pale skin and decomposing faces, two on each side.

"Go away," James whispered through clenched teeth. "Leave me alone."

They stared at him with dead eyes, their gazes cold, fixed only on him. He knew they wanted to hurt him, but he didn't know why.

"Leave me alone!"

He could see them in the semilit room. One of the girls wore pigtails, her blonde hair dirty and matted from being buried in the earth, her lips dry and cracked.

The boy smiled when they made eye contact. It was a lifeless smile like one a doll would give if you pulled a string in its back. Mud oozed from his lips and ran down the front of what had once been a white dress shirt.

The other girl had an eye missing. In its place, a black marble that shone in the glow of the streetlights outside. The marble was too small for its socket and moved from side to side whenever the girl turned her head. It was the most horrific thing he'd ever seen.

I'm going to scream. God help me, I'm going to scream, and they're going to rip my heart out when I do. No one will save me in time. I'm going to scream, and they're going to end me.

The girl with the ponytails moved to the end of the bed. He could see her skin was soiled with dried blood and dirt. Her nails had been snapped off each finger, leaving jagged edges. She slowly lifted her arm and pointed at him. When she did, the others followed. They were all pointing at him.

"You," the girl with the ponytails growled.

James felt his heart pounding in his chest. "Go away!"

He shut his eyes again and pulled the covers over his head.

I'm going to scream! And if I scream, they'll take my tongue, and they'll reach down my throat with their muddy hands and broken fingernails and they'll cut me from the inside, and they'll rip my heart out of me. I can't scream!

The covers began closing in on him. He could see tiny imprints of hands pushing down from the outside.

"Go away!"

They were getting closer. Closer to his chest. To his throat. To his mouth. It was getting harder to breathe. The covers were going to suffocate him.

"Go away!"

They pushed down on his body. Eight hands. Forty fingers. Four dead children seeking vengeance for reasons he didn't know. He could smell the old blanket, taste it as tiny fingers pushed the fabric into his mouth. He screamed now, no longer caring what might happen. But his screams were muffled and silent. More of the blanket was pushed down his throat, and he started choking. His chest burned and his eyes bulged. They were so strong.

Pushing down the blanket.

Suffocating him.

Killing him.

The odor of wet earth and rot filled the room. He was a dead man. It was only a matter of time.

The light came on from upstairs.

The children were gone.

James sat up and threw the blanket off of him, coughing and wheezing, inhaling heavy breaths as if he'd just surfaced from drowning. He looked toward the stairs and saw the woman standing at the bottom landing tying her robe around her waist.

"You!" he cried. "Oh, thank you for saving me. Oh my!"

"What's going on?"

"Thank you for saving me. Thank you! That was close. Too close."

She walked into the bedroom area and bent down. "You were having a nightmare. I could hear you yelling up in my room. What were you dreaming about?"

A man came down after the woman, not the man who was usually there, James thought. He remained at the bottom landing, watching.

"The children," James said, the words tumbling from his mouth without any thought or reason. He didn't know what he was saying. His mind was racing as his eyes darted around the room looking for remnants of the creatures that had tried to take him away. "The ghosts. The dead children."

"They came back?"

"All of them. Bonnie and Marcus and Tiffany and Sonia. All of them!"

Cindy sat down on the edge of the bed. Her demeanor changed instantly. She grew serious. "You saw the children?"

"Yes! They came to take me away. They tried to kill me, and you saved me. Oh, I love you for saving me. Thank you! I owe you my life!"

"He's remembering," the man on the stairs said.

James took her hand and kissed it. She pulled away before he could kiss it for a second time. Without words, she rose from the bed and ran into the living room area, grabbed the photo album, and returned quickly.

"Was she there?" Cindy asked, flipping to the first page and pointing to a photo.

"Yes. Tiffany."

Flipping. "And him?"

"Marcus."

"Keep going," the man on the stairs commanded.

"Her?"

"Bonnie." James scanned the room as he spoke, suddenly unsure of where he was.

Flipping. Pointing. "How about her?"

"That's . . ." He stopped and stared at the picture as he ran his fingers across the glossy photograph. "That's . . . Sonia," he muttered under his breath. "She was there. She's the one who told the others to kill me."

Cindy gently closed the album. "You remember."

James craned his neck to see past the woman sitting at his bed. It looked like he was underground. In a basement.

"Tell her their names again," the man on the stairs said.

James looked at him. "Who?"

"The children. The ghosts. Tell her their names."

James thought for a moment, looking down at his legs. Why were they in braces? Why was he in bed?

"James," the woman pressed. "You remembered. That's a great thing. Tell me their names again."

"What names?"

"He's gone," the man on the stairs said. "Just like that."

The woman smiled as tears glassed her eyes. "Tell me their names. Please."

"Who?"

"Tell me!"

James shook his head. "I need to get some sleep. I have class first thing in the morning. We're starting *Romeo and Juliet*, and I have to have my wits about me if I'm going to explain Shakespearean prose."

The woman got up from the bed and started spinning in circles. "This can't be happening. This can't be happening! You remembered!"

"Please. I need my rest. The students can be so tiresome sometimes."

The man on the stairs sighed and climbed back up, disappearing from the basement.

The woman looked at James, panicked. "What's my name?"

"I have no idea."

"What's your name?"

He paused, thinking.

"NO!"

The woman rushed to his bedside, grabbed him by the collar of his pajamas, and began shaking him.

"You son of a bitch! Tell me their names. You just said them! Tell me about the children you killed! Tell me their names!"

"Stop it!"

The last thing he saw was the leather-bound photo album swinging down toward his face.

He heard the woman scream.

Then blackness.

46

"I can't do this. Do you hear me? I can't do this anymore! He won't remember!"

"You told us you could get him to talk," David said calmly. She could hear the anger in his voice, but it was subdued. "You told us you could do it before Hagen came."

"Well, I guess I can't!"

"Then why are we here? Hagen could've just killed Darville at his house, and we all go home. He's giving you what you asked for, and that affects all of us now. Do you think my sister and I would've taken part in this madness if we thought things would fall apart like this? You told us you could get him to talk, and we keep waiting around while people are dying. My sister is—"

"I'm doing the best I can!"

"It's not good enough!"

David stormed down the hall and into the living room, stopping in front of a set of windows that looked out onto the front of the house. "How are we even supposed to get out of this? Everything's so far gone."

Cindy leaned against the wall, exhausted. "I don't know."

"I get that you're trying, but maybe he's a lost cause. Maybe you'll never get your truth. Maybe it's just better to let Hagen come up here and end it. We give him Darville, and he gives my mom her liver and gives Trevor back his family. You lose, but you were never really sacrificing anything in the first place."

"Screw you," Cindy blurted through her tears. "My sister sacrificed her life, my mother sacrificed her happiness, and I've sacrificed my childhood trying to find out what happened to Sonia. You don't get to tell me what I've given to Hagen and this plan. You think Hagen's just going to come up here, kill James, and let us go back to our lives after everything that's happened? We can't cover this up. Not after everything we've done. We're liabilities at this point. Don't you get that?"

David shook his head, his back still turned. "We'll get our lives back. We have to. He promised."

Cindy walked across the room and joined David at the windows. It was pitch black outside, and all she could see was the reflection of a tired and frightened woman staring back at her. "Their crime scene people will find some kind of trace of something in that car, and we'll be caught. They already have the dashcam footage, and they've already been through James's house. All they need to do is find something that links one of us, and we all go down. Hagen knows this. We're sitting ducks up here."

"We have to stick to the plan. You can keep trying to get answers from him about your sister and the other kids, and me and Trevor will keep babysitting until Hagen gets here. We'll give him the old man, and then you go home, my mom gets her new liver, and Trevor gets his family back. Hagen will forgive us. He has to."

Cindy turned away from the window and looked at David, trying to get a sense of whether Trevor might be right about David being Hagen. The story he wrote. The motive of using a new book to get rich and famous. His mood swings from panicked to calm. It was unnerving.

"How can you be so sure Hagen will forgive us?" she asked.

"I just am," David replied. "You have to have faith. Trust me."

47

Susan woke to the first snowfall of the season. It wasn't anything significant, and the ground was still too warm to worry about accumulation, but as she climbed from her bed and looked out her window, she couldn't help but feel a mix of awe and dread. The snowflakes cascading onto the neighborhood looked so picturesque and peaceful. Yet, at the same time, she feared the snow would further remind her son of what had happened a year earlier and send him spiraling even deeper into anxiety. The holidays were coming, and with them, her family's haunted anniversary.

Despite everyone's alarms going off at the same time, Susan could already hear Beatrice and the twins in the kitchen. Their conversation was quiet, mixed with yawns and stretching and the clattering of plates being passed around. Susan turned from the window, grabbed her robe from the hook on the back of her door, and made her way downstairs.

"Hey, guys," she said as she walked into the kitchen.

Casey pointed out the window. "Mommy, it's snowing!"

"I know. I see."

"Can we play in it after school?"

Susan took a mug from the dishwasher and poured herself a cup of coffee that was still brewing. "Honey, I don't think it's going to stick much."

"But can we play anyway?"

"Maybe. We'll figure it out when you get home."

Susan kissed her mother on the back of the head. "Good morning, Mother."

Beatrice smiled as she cracked egg after egg onto her skillet. "Hello, Daughter."

"Sorry I missed you all last night. Got home later than I was planning."

"Break in the case?"

"More questions, actually." She looked over her mother's shoulder. "Looks like you got a good haul this morning."

"I did. Maybe the chickens felt the weather turning or something. Got out there, and the nest boxes were as full as I've seen them in a while. Was planning to make cereal for Casey and Tim, but I can't let all these go to waste."

Susan sipped her coffee and made her way over to the sliding door that opened onto the deck and backyard. The chicken coop Eric had bought right before she'd caught him cheating on her was empty. The chickens were walking around the yard, pecking at things she couldn't see, their feet leaving unique tracks in the snow that stuck to the grass. Two of them were up on the deck, looking in at her.

"You better be careful opening these doors," Susan said. "They come up on the deck a lot now. I can't have chickens running around inside the house."

Casey nodded. "We'll be careful, Mommy."

Susan sat down at the table, gently taking Tim's little hand in hers. "How about you, bud? You want to play in the snow with your sister after school?"

Tim shrugged and stared down at his empty plate. "I guess."

"I can pull you around the yard in the sled?"

"Okay."

She knew that was all she was going to get out of him and didn't push. There was no point. She drank her coffee and waited while Beatrice made omelets, the smell of onion and bacon wafting through the entire house. Her cell phone rang from the living room, where she kept it plugged in overnight. She slipped out of her seat and ran down the hall, catching it before it had a chance to ring a third time.

"This is Susan Adler."

"Hey, I hope this isn't too early."

She relaxed when she heard Liam's voice. "No, we're up. Eating breakfast and getting the kids ready for school."

"I called a couple of guys I know and had them do a little digging on your missing teacher to get ahead of the background check you ordered. I know you said he spent time in West Finley and Beaverdale, so I had them start there. Figured I'd catch you before you clocked in."

She walked back into the hall and reached into her pocketbook, which was hanging on the coatrack, then pulled out her notepad and pen and sat on the landing of the stairs. "That's great," she said. "I really appreciate it."

"My pleasure."

"What'd you find?"

Liam cleared his throat. "James Darville was a substitute teacher in West Finley after leaving a private school in Ohio in 1979. Place was called the Lynch Academy. According to the records at West Finley, he worked at Lynch for three years, left before he was able to obtain any kind of tenure, and came to West Finley Middle School as a sub. He taught English to all grade levels for five years, never rising above substitute, and left in the summer of '84. That's the last time anyone heard from him there."

"Short stays at both schools."

"He got his footing when he moved to Beaverdale. The district there hired him as a middle school English teacher, and he floated between the middle school and the high school over the next twenty years. After the 2005 school year, he announced he was leaving. Since he was too young to retire with a pension or social security, folks figured he'd found another opportunity at another school, but he drops off the map until he comes up on your case fifteen years later. He lived in all the towns he taught in. Apartments in Ohio and West Finley. Bought a house in Beaverdale. My contact at the state police made a call into Ohio for me to look for any next of kin or distant relatives. Looks like your guy was the last leaf on his family tree. That's all they could find with the systems they were using. The feds would have the rest."

Susan stopped writing and closed the notepad. "Thanks, Liam. I'm really grateful for you doing this."

"Anytime. Kind of made me feel like a cop again."

"Grab that feeling and get back on the horse. That's an order."

"Yes, ma'am. Now go have breakfast with your family and tell everyone I said hi."

"Will do."

"See you soon."

She hung up, and before she could place the phone in her pocket, it rang again. It was Crosby.

"Hey, boss."

"You on your way in?"

"Just about."

"We got the DNA results back from the two teeth you found. Took a little work, since DNA only started being used in criminal investigations in the late eighties."

"They're that old?"

"Yup. Luckily, the Pennsylvania State Police kept pieces of clothing and other items from the victims, so we were able to match the DNA with today's technology."

"Hold on," Susan replied. "Pennsylvania State Police? *Victims*, plural? What did we stumble onto here?"

"The tooth you found in James Darville's house belonged to a young girl named Bonnie Bernstein. Bonnie was fifteen years old when she went missing on her way home from school in Shintown, Pennsylvania, back in 1989. Never found. Case has been cold since '91. No trace evidence up to now. You just found their very first clue."

Susan could feel her stomach tighten as she squeezed the phone. She flipped back into her notepad, ripping through the pages as she went. She stopped when she found what she was looking for. "When I was interviewing Darville's neurologist, Dr. Phines, she gave an example of one of his episodes, and it involved him talking about two kids, Bonnie and Sonia. I don't know who Sonia is, but we got Bonnie right here. Darville has something to do with the missing girl."

"Wouldn't think he'd have her tooth otherwise," Crosby replied.

"There's more. The tooth you found on our Jane Doe in the trunk of the nurse's car belonged to someone else. A young man, Marcus Ruley. Went missing when he was twelve on his way home from basketball practice in Hawley, Pennsylvania, in 1985. Never found. No traces."

And just like that, clarity.

"Darville's a serial abductor," Susan muttered. "Maybe a serial killer. Someone found out, and after all these years, they came calling."

"We got a victim and a suspect in two cold cases entangled in our active case," Crosby said. "Get here as soon as you can."

48

"It's him," Trevor whispered, taking Cindy's hand and pulling her into the dining room. "David is Hagen. I have the proof."

Cindy followed Trevor, and they stopped when he reached his desk. Trevor opened a small backpack that was sitting in the chair.

"I got into his house and started digging around. David's got a spare bedroom that he converted into an office with a bunch of file cabinets." Trevor pulled a sheet of paper from the backpack and handed it over. "This is a pitch letter to his agent. It doesn't specify James or the missing kids, but it pitches a true crime story that solves a series of kidnappings in Pennsylvania that have been unsolved for decades. I found a bunch of research about the abductions in the file cabinet too. He created a timeline, and his notes were in the process of linking James to two of the child disappearances. In the letter, he promises a big story that would garner national attention."

Cindy read the letter. "Oh my god. You were right. He's in this to sell his story. All the stuff about his mother and her liver was just nonsense. This giant mess for a book. He needed me to put the rest of his story together, to get a confession from James. That's why I'm here." She looked at Trevor. "And you're the plot twist. The son James never knew he had."

"I'm going to kill him," Trevor muttered. "I'm going to give him an opportunity to tell me where my wife and son are, and then I'm going to kill him and get the hell out of here. The police can find the rest."

"If he doesn't tell you where your family is, you have to keep him alive," Cindy whispered, craning her neck to make sure they were alone. "We need to play dumb for now to protect ourselves. As long as he's here, we can keep tabs on him, and he can't do anything to harm us or your family."

"I'll beat it out of him. Whatever it takes."

"No." She grabbed him by the shoulders. "As long as he thinks he's still in control, we'll have the upper hand. We have to keep acting like the plan is in motion. Keep doing what we're doing."

He finally relented. "Okay. For now."

Cindy let go of his shoulders and stumbled backward, clinging to one of the dining room chairs to stay upright. The room was spinning, and she thought she might be sick. "David's been Hagen this entire time. I can't believe it."

"There's more." Trevor dug into his bag and came away with a set of papers. "I printed these from his computer. He's got detailed information about James's physical therapy sessions and his appointments with his neurologist. Rebecca wouldn't have access to these. She just gets general notes about progress and meds. This is patient-confidentiality stuff."

Cindy skimmed the reports. "So maybe one of James's doctors is involved after all."

Trevor took the pages and stuffed them into his backpack. "That's what I'm thinking. And whoever David's partner is at the hospital, there's a good chance that person has my family."

49

Crosby had the files waiting for Susan when she arrived. She sat at her desk and laid them out in front of her, grabbing Bonnie Bernstein's case file first. The pages were half handwritten and half typed with an old-school typewriter. She could see the coffee stains and tears in the papers that had been photocopied along with the information. Bonnie was fifteen when she went missing in 1989. Shintown, Pennsylvania, was drive-through country, small and safe. She left her middle school at the end of soccer practice in late September and never arrived home. The local police began the search, which was soon escalated to the Pennsylvania State Police, but after two years of chasing leads, the case was marked unsolved and put away. Her parents, Rob and Elizabeth Bernstein, were still living in Shintown as of the last note in 1991. They had a younger son who was seven at the time, as well as an older daughter who was in high school when Bonnie disappeared.

The second file contained information on the disappearance of Marcus Ruley. Marcus went missing in 1985 on his way home from basketball practice in Hawley, Pennsylvania. Susan circled the fact that both victims had been coming home from an after-school sports practice and made notes on the side of the file.

Abductor was waiting after school. Knew there would be kids practicing sports.

Not as many kids around vs. a general dismissal. Easier to take?

Like Bonnie's abduction, Marcus's case began locally with the Wayne County Sheriff's Department, then got handed over to the state police. And, like Bonnie's, Marcus's investigation ran for two years and was then filed unsolved. Marcus's parents, Chip and Marie Ruley, were also still living in Hawley. Marcus had been their only child. He was twelve when he went missing.

She made more notes.

James was a teacher. He'd know about the after-school activities. Has to be involved. Has teeth in his house.

He abducted them alone? With someone? Killed them? Are they alive? Does he know where they are?

Someone knows James's secret and took him like he took the kids. Relatives of the missing kids? Friends? The people on the dashcam.

Where's Rebecca?

Who's Jane Doe? How does she fit in this?

Susan leaned back and closed her eyes. At the time of both abductions, James was working at Forest Hills Middle School outside of Beaverdale, where he lived. From Beaverdale, Hawley was a four-hour drive, one way, and two and a half hours, one way, to Shintown. Both long, but doable. She'd have to call the Forest Hills school district and ask about employee and attendance records. Perhaps they'd catch a break if it was documented that James had called out sick or taken vacation around the times Bonnie and Marcus went missing. But that still wouldn't answer the question of where the old man was.

According to the files, Bonnie's parents would be in their late sixties now, and Marcus's parents would be in their midseventies. Not the young man and woman she'd seen on the trooper's dashcam, but Bonnie's brother and sister would be a more likely scenario. The son would be in his late thirties. The sister would be in her midforties. Darville would be easy pickings for someone like them, and they fit the general profile of the people on the video.

Susan pulled up Google Maps to find the distance between her house and the towns where the two kids were taken. Hawley was only an hour and a half away, and Shintown was another three hours past

Hawley. It was a trek, but something that needed to be done if she was going to figure out how all these pieces fit together. She took her phone from her pocket and dialed.

"Hey there," the voice on the other end said.

Susan sighed and ran her free hand through her hair. "Hey, Liam. How are you?"

"I'm good. Just watching some TV. What's up?"

"I'm going to ask you a potentially crazy question, and if you can't do it, it's totally fine. I don't want you to feel pressured to say yes. This is just me taking a shot in the dark."

"Okay. I'm officially intrigued."

"Promise you won't feel pressured to say yes?"

"Yes. I mean, I'm not pressured. I mean, yes, I promise."

Susan shook her head. "This is a dumb idea."

"Just ask me."

"I need to take a road trip into Pennsylvania tomorrow. Probably going to take two days. I got a lead on my missing persons case, and I need to shoot over to Hawley and then to Shintown. I still don't know if I have enough to engage the state police there or the FBI, so I want to check it out myself first. Any chance you'd want to keep me company and act as my Pennsylvania ambassador in case I need one?"

She crumpled onto her desk after her question was finished, feeling like a bumbling eighteen-year-old girl asking a boy to prom.

There was a long pause on the other end.

"You can say no," Susan said, desperate to fill the quiet.

"Hold on," Liam replied.

She could hear typing.

"Hawley is like two hours and change for me—"

"If it's too far, I get it. No problem."

Liam laughed. "Take a breath. I was just going to suggest I drive to Hawley, meet you at the police station up there, we'll talk to the sheriff so he knows we're in town, then we'll take one car to the first address you need to go to. From there we can head to Shintown. When we're done, we backtrack, and you drop me at my car in Hawley. Sound good?"

Susan got up from her seat and began pacing around the unit. "It's so last minute. I don't want to put you out."

"You're not putting me out. I'd love to be your Pennsylvania ambassador. And, like I said before, it'll help get my juices flowing again. I need a little police work in my life."

"You're sure?"

"Positive. I have no plans for the next few days. It's all good. Email me the details, and I'll meet you there."

Susan stopped pacing and smiled. "I appreciate your help."

"And I appreciate yours. I'll see you tomorrow."

She hung up and sat on the edge of her desk. Her hands were still shaking from the adrenaline, although she didn't know exactly why. She knew she should have a little backup and also knew Crosby wouldn't let Triston leave his shift for two full days. The other investigators had their own cases, and although she probably could've borrowed a trooper or another investigator from the Hawthorne barracks or Manhattan, she preferred the company of someone she already knew and was fairly certain she could trust.

But that was all it was. Nothing more. Backup. A temporary partner. Someone to bounce theories off of. A professional.

So why was she still shaking?

Susan sent the details to Liam, setting a time for nine in the morning to meet at the Wayne County Sheriff's Department on Main Avenue. When she was done, she made her way into Crosby's office to fill him in on her plans. With any luck, she'd be leaving Pennsylvania with a few more answers than she was starting out with.

50

Hawley, Pennsylvania, was a quintessential blue-collar town that had thrived in decades past but was now crumbling under the weight of progress. It was built in the same vein that all the old industrial towns in the Northeast were built. This one happened to be founded around coal, but with its single main street, which stretched between three- and four-story brick buildings that had shops on the first floor and offices or apartments on the upper floors, and its single traffic light in the center of town, Hawley was identical to most of the other towns built during the Industrial Revolution.

Just as Google Maps had predicted, it had taken Susan a little under two hours to arrive at the Wayne County Sheriff's Department. Liam was waiting in his car when she arrived. He'd stopped off and gotten them each a coffee and a bagel in case she was hungry and tired from the ride. She sat with him in the car, finishing the bagel while they talked through their plan. She took her coffee, and they went inside the station house to see the sheriff together.

Sheriff Brody sat behind his desk and stared at his new guests. He was a stout man, late thirties or early forties, his tired eyes making him seem older. The top two buttons on his uniform shirt were undone, allowing his neck some room to move. His breathing was loud and labored. The cigarette burning in the ashtray didn't help.

"So you want to see the Ruleys," he began. The skepticism in his voice was unmistakable.

Susan nodded. "As I explained on the way up, I'm investigating a double homicide and missing persons case back in New York, and I think part of my investigation has intersected with what might've happened with their son."

"How certain are you?"

"Not certain enough to make anything official, but certain enough to take this drive in the hopes that they can help further connect some dots."

"From what I'm told, that was a dark time," Sheriff Brody said, snatching his cigarette from the ashtray and taking a drag. "I was a boy back when it happened, but I lived west of here in Avella, over on the other side of the state. Got to Hawley about ten years ago. Anyway, the story goes, the entire town shut down. Neighbors were looking at neighbors with suspicion. No one trusted anyone else. Marcus was black, so a lot of folks thought race had something to do with it. No one likes talking about that time. Luckily, most of the kids who grew up back then have moved away, and the old-timers know enough not to speak of it. I'm worried about you coming in here and dredging up old wounds."

"I understand your concern," Susan replied. "And I promise to be tactful. No one other than you and the Ruleys even needs to know we're here. In and out. Gone by lunch."

The sheriff took another drag of his cigarette and snuffed it out. "Gone by lunch?"

"Yes, sir."

"Don't make them remember too much, and don't lead them on. They're old, and I don't want to give them any false hope. In and out."

"You can join us if you'd like."

"Yes," the sheriff replied. "I think I will."

They shook on their new pact, and Brody called Chip Ruley to explain that they would be stopping by with a few questions. Chip agreed to see them, and after one last cigarette, they were off.

210

51

The drive to the Ruley house couldn't have been more than three miles from Main Avenue. Susan followed the sheriff, turning down two streets and briefly paralleling the Lackawaxen River. They ended up on a small dead-end road that was built up against acres of untamed woods.

The house was a two-story bungalow, green with white trim, the structure itself dying a slow death. The porch was decaying, the wood pillars splintering and coming apart with the help of the carpenter ants that had been feeding on them for decades. The floor sagged when they walked on it, and the screen door was missing its screen. Brody stepped back and allowed Susan to knock. The doorbell didn't work. They waited, Susan's shield hanging around her neck.

"I'm going to need you to wait out here," Susan said, looking at Liam. "You're technically on leave and out of your jurisdiction. If something comes of this, you being present could put a wrench in the report and open the door to a future defense case."

Liam nodded. "Yeah, that makes sense."

"I'm sorry you had to come all the way here just to wait outside. I should've told you yesterday on the phone, but it didn't occur to me until just now."

"It's no problem. This is your case, not mine. I'm just an ambassador. Here when you need me."

Chip and Marie Ruley answered the door together. Chip was bald but for a sliver of thin white hair. He wore glasses that magnified his eyes and hearing aids in both ears. His skinny frame was covered with an oversized wool sweater and corduroy pants. Marie's eyes were dark and vacant. She, too, wore a large sweater that hung to her knees. Her hair was white and cut short. Even in their seventies they shouldn't have *looked* that old, but the loss of their son had aged them.

"Investigator Adler," Chip murmured as he opened the front door. "Please, come in."

Susan stepped inside and shook their hands while Liam sat down on the porch steps.

"Sheriff."

"Hey, Chip. Thanks for seeing us."

"Come into the living room," Marie said. "I made tea."

Susan and Brody followed the couple into the living room. Everything inside the house was old, but not as dilapidated as the outside was. The interior was clean, dusted, things put in their places. The beige-and-maroon-checkered wallpaper was a bit dated, as was the overstuffed recliner and the denim couch, but it could've been worse.

A huge family picture hung over their brass-and-brick fireplace. Both parents, young and full of success and possibility, were standing behind a preteen Marcus, who was seated in front of them. Everyone was smiling.

"We took that for Christmas in '83," Marie said. "It was supposed to be the start of a family tradition for each Christmas thereafter, but we got too busy the next year, and just a month after the holidays, Marcus disappeared. We left that one up so I could see my whole family every day and remember the good times we had. I won't take another family photo like that without my son in it. I just won't."

"I understand," Susan replied, sitting on the couch. Brody stood off by the doorway to the kitchen. "I think I'd have a hard time doing that too."

"Are you a mother?"

"Twins."

"Then you know." Marie smiled, but her eyes were full of sadness. "You know."

There was a brief moment of silence before Chip took the teacups and passed them around. He poured each of them a cup from a white porcelain pot and sat back in his recliner, legs crossed, staring at the strangers in his house.

"So," he began. "I understand we need to answer some questions and cooperate. I certainly intend to do that, but may I ask you what this is about, specifically?"

"To be honest," Susan replied, pulling out her notepad, "I'm not entirely sure. We're investigating a homicide and the disappearance of a man in New York, and we may have stumbled onto something that links to his past in Pennsylvania. It's too early to tell what we have, so I was thinking we could discuss what happened with your son and go from there."

"Okay."

"Tell me about that day. The day Marcus disappeared."

Chip stared out into space, swallowing once as the images came back to him. He took a sip of his tea and cleared his throat. "I'm sure you know what we told the police at the time. Can't add much to it, I'm afraid. Marcus had basketball practice that afternoon, and sometime between walking from the gym and coming through the side door like he did every day, he disappeared. Never came home."

"Where was the rest of your family that day?"

"Marie was home. I was at work at the local bank on Main. Used to be called American Federal Savings. It's a Chase now. Anyway, I didn't get home until around five, and Marcus usually came home about an hour after me, and we'd all eat together. He just never came home. Ever."

Susan looked at Marie. "And you were at the house the entire time?"

"Yes. Earlier that morning I ran a few errands in town, but I was home by eleven that morning and never left again."

"Did Marcus call the house or leave any kind of message with you?"

"No," Marie replied. "Last time I talked to him was when he was leaving for school that morning."

"Did he mention any new friends or coaches or strangers that he was talking to? Anyone new in his life?"

Both Chip and Marie shook their heads.

"Do you know if there were new teachers on staff that year?"

"The state police looked into that at the time," Chip replied. "Other than my boy disappearing, it was a normal day in Hawley. Nothing, and I mean nothing, was abnormal, as far as I remember. He just vanished."

Susan reached into her purse and came away with three pictures of James Darville she'd found online. Two were old yearbook photos from Forest Hills Middle School in 1988 and 1989. It was the closest she could find to the year Marcus disappeared. The third was a candid shot of James marching in a town parade in West Finley in 1981.

"This is the man we're looking for. He's much older now, but this is what he looked like in the eighties. Does he look familiar to you?"

Chip took the photographs and studied them, his gaze intense, focused. After a few minutes he shook his head and handed them to his wife. It didn't take Marie quite as long to hand them back.

"No," she said softly. "Never seen him before."

"Who is he?" Chip asked. "Is he the guy you think took Marcus?"

"His name is James Darville," Susan said. "Does that name ring a bell? He was an English teacher at Forest Hills Middle School outside of Beaverdale."

"Beaverdale isn't anywhere near here."

"I know. Just adding context in case it jogged a memory."

It didn't.

"He's elderly and under the care of a nurse back in New York," Susan continued. "Both he and the nurse disappeared from his home almost a week ago. Like I said, he was a teacher in Beaverdale. West

Finley too. It looks like he traveled through the state a lot. We thought there could be a connection."

Chip leaned up in his seat and rested his tea on his skinny thighs. "But what did you find that brought you here, specifically, to our house, talking about our son?"

"I can't tell you that right now. I'm sorry. I know you want to know, and as soon as I can disclose that, I will. I just needed to know if Mr. Darville looked familiar to you. That's all I can offer at this point in the investigation."

Chip pointed to the pictures in Susan's hand. "If this man knows where my boy is, find him. I realize Marcus is probably dead. We both do. But I'd like to give my boy a proper burial before someone has to put *me* in the ground. That's all I ask. Find this man and find my son."

"Chip, I don't want you worrying about a single thing," Sheriff Brody said, stepping closer. "If there's anything new to find out about what happened to your boy, you can count on me getting that information over to you. That, I can promise."

Susan stood up from the couch. "We'll do our best to find out how Marcus plays a role in all of this, Mr. Ruley. As soon as I know something concrete, you're my first call."

52

James opened his eyes and immediately smelled urine. He tried to move, but his lower back was stiff and screamed in agony when he rocked to one side. He'd pissed himself. The smell was pungent, and his legs were wet and cold. He pulled the covers back and could see the puddle that had formed on the sheet and most likely seeped into the mattress. What a mess.

"You know the bedpan's right next to you," a voice said from the bottom of the stairs. "All you had to do was grab it and slide it under you."

James craned his neck and watched as the man approached.

"I know where the bedpan is."

The man made his way over to his bedside. "Do you? Maybe this is your way of getting back at us for neglecting you. Could that be it?"

"Of course not. I wouldn't do this to myself just to get back at *you*."

"It's okay if you did. I mean, I'd get it. I'd probably do the same thing." He bent closer. "We're not taking very good care of you."

"I'm looked after fine."

"Yeah? When was the last time anyone fed you?"

As soon as the man finished his sentence, James could feel his stomach growl, and he suddenly realized he was hungry. Starving, in fact.

"You haven't eaten in a long time."

The man yanked him up and quickly took off his shirt. He spun James to the edge of the mattress and worked his pants off over his leg braces and did the same with his underwear.

James was suddenly naked and shivering. "I'm cold," he said. "My legs and feet are freezing."

The man threw an old wool blanket over his shoulders and helped him into his wheelchair, then stripped the bed and tossed the sheets and blankets into a pile at the foot of the stairs.

"Can I have something to eat?"

"We need to get you cleaned up first. I'll roll you to the shower and help you wash. Then we'll have some lunch."

"Lunch? What about breakfast? What time is it? What day is it?"

"Does any of that really matter? If I told you it was eleven o'clock on a Wednesday, what difference would that make? There's no clock down here, and you can't see out those windows. There's no calendar. Why should you care if it's morning or night or if you're eating breakfast or lunch or dinner?"

"I do care."

"Why? Those are simple questions that have no relevance to your day-to-day life. You need to start asking better questions. Deeper ones. You need to think about your situation and start figuring out what's really going on here. You remember what I told you about the names of those children? You need to remember them."

James looked at him, his mind blank.

"Do you remember what I wrote on that piece of paper?"

Again, nothing.

The man leaned in and lowered his voice. "These people are here to hurt you. Cindy is here to hurt you. They're not taking care of you. You can't trust them."

"Why do they want to hurt me?"

"Because of what happened with Sonia and the others. But I'm going to help you. You don't deserve this."

James knew the name Sonia should mean something, but he couldn't quite grasp the connection. "What are you talking about?" he asked. "Who's Sonia?"

"Do you remember making the tapes?"

"The tapes?"

"About what happened with Noreen and Sonia and the rest of the kids?"

"No, I don't remember."

"Forget it." The man walked behind James and pushed him toward the bathroom. "There's no use talking about it now. We don't have time. But you need to start asking better questions. That was my point."

"What kind of questions?"

"Ones that matter to you surviving this." He stopped pushing when they arrived at the bathroom. "Do you remember Cindy telling you that you were paralyzed, and that's why you couldn't walk and you had these braces on your legs?"

James nodded. "Yes. I *do* remember that. A car accident."

"Do you remember any piece of that accident? Anything at all?"

He tried to recall something about what happened, but there was nothing. "No. Just that I was in an accident. I'm paralyzed from the waist down."

The man stepped into the shower and started the water, then took the wool blanket from him and rolled him inside the bathroom.

"You just told me before that your legs were freezing. Do you remember that?"

"Of course. They still are. The urine dried on my legs and is chilling my skin. I'm naked and wet, for god's sake."

"So, here's the kind of questions you should be asking: If you're paralyzed from the waist down, how can you know your legs are freezing? How can you *feel* the cold or the wetness or anything?"

James looked at the man, processing what he'd just said. "I guess sometimes you can be paralyzed and still feel things," he said.

"You're right," the man replied. "Sometimes the nerves aren't totally cut off, and a person can still feel some sensation, but it's usually dulled." The man bent down and slapped him hard on the knee. "Did that hurt?"

"Yes!"

"Did it feel like your nerves were dulled?"

"No."

"Then what's the question you need to ask?"

James paused. "If I'm paralyzed, how is it possible that I felt pain so acutely just then?"

The man smiled. "Acutely. I like that teacher vocabulary you have there. Very good."

Before James could say anything further, the man rolled him into the shower and washed him in silence.

53

They ate lunch in the car while Liam drove and Susan called ahead to Shintown, making arrangements with the desk sergeant on duty, who, in turn, contacted both the chief and the mayor to let them know they were getting a visit from an investigator from the New York State Police. Unlike Sheriff Brody, the chief didn't feel the need to escort them to the Bernsteins' house. He and the mayor were accommodating, but there was definitely a sense of trepidation. No one liked reliving nightmares.

Shintown was, by far, the smallest town she'd ever been to. There was hardly a main street or center plaza. Instead, she saw a tiny cluster of mom-and-pop shops for about a block and a half before the downtown area gave way to a single neighborhood that spread out for about six blocks in each direction. The houses were small, old. This had been a blue-collar, nose-to-the-grindstone neighborhood once and was now a relic of a time when people could earn a decent living working in rural parts of the state without the need to be married to Philadelphia or Pittsburgh to make ends meet. Now the town was a museum of how things used to be. The folks still living in those parts would undoubtedly die there. That's just the way it was.

The Bernstein house was a single-level ranch with dirty white asbestos siding and an asphalt roof that was covered in moss and stained with soot from the chimney. There was no porch or walkway other than a dirt path with some gravel laid down for drainage. The snow that had already fallen had been shoveled to the side to allow access to the front door. Rob Bernstein was waiting in the doorway, hands on his hips, watching Susan climb out of the car while Liam stayed put. He looked younger than Chip Ruley, and he had a belly three times the size. A thick gray beard covered his face but couldn't hide the anguish in his eyes. He was still hurting after thirty years. It was as plain as the scar atop his bald head.

Rob nodded his hellos and waved her inside. Susan followed him into the house. Elizabeth Bernstein was sitting in a worn-out green wingback chair that had faded from the sun. She had on sweatpants and a matching sweatshirt. No makeup. Her stringy silver hair was tied in a single ponytail. She smiled when she saw Susan but said nothing.

Susan stopped when she reached the center of the living room. They hadn't offered her a seat, so she remained standing. "Thank you for meeting with me. I'm Investigator Adler from the New York State Police."

Rob plopped down in the wingback opposite his wife. "You have news about Bonnie?" he asked immediately, not bothering to introduce his wife.

"Not really," Susan replied. She sat on a yellow-and-brown couch after Rob finally motioned for her to do so. "We're investigating a man who went missing back in New York. James Darville?"

"Never heard of him."

"We have reason to believe he might have come into this area at some point in the eighties and want to quickly retrace what happened with your daughter's disappearance. That's all I can really say at this point."

"That's a hell of a drive to take for a simple question like that," he said. "Could've called. No reason to come all the way out here."

"I'm planning to drive around a little. Get a feel for things."

"Waste of time, if you ask me, but if it'll help find this guy and get some information on my daughter, then by all means. Ask me all the questions you got."

"Can you take me through the day Bonnie disappeared?"

Rob shrugged his big shoulders. "Can't tell you much more than what's already on record. She was supposed to come home after her soccer practice. Never did. We looked everywhere for her, and she just disappeared. Wasn't like the movies, where they find a piece of clothing or something and the bloodhounds catch a scent and we eventually track them down. This was years of searching with no results. Not a stitch of anything. One minute she was saying goodbye to her friends at the field at school, and the next she was gone."

"Did she always walk home alone?"

"Yup. We lived too close for busing. She walked to school and home since she was in the third grade."

"So people knew she walked by herself."

"Sure, I guess. But the police have interviewed the people of this town two and three times over. It wasn't one of us. We would've known by now if it was."

"Where were you and your wife the day Bonnie went missing?" Susan asked.

"Liz was working at the supermarket. She was a cashier. And I was working at the railroad over in Renovo. We're both retired now."

"Your chief tells me you have two other kids," Susan said, pretending she hadn't already done her homework on the family.

"That's right. Jake and Maggie."

"Where were they the afternoon Bonnie went missing?"

Rob thought for a moment. "Jake always went to his friend Joe's house after school when Liz was working. Joe Tock was the friend. They moved away about twenty years back, but Joe and Jake were best buds up until they left. Liz picked Jake up from Joe's house that day on her way home from work, and Maggie babysat after school for a family in Drury Run. She never got home until after seven."

"Where are they now? I'd love to talk with them."

Rob laughed. "Can't drive to them, that's for sure. Gotta be a phone call. Maggie got married, and her husband works for the oil and gas folks. They live in Houston. Jake is in Afghanistan. Marines. Makes his dad proud every day. I'll get you Maggie's number if you want. I don't have a number for Jake. He calls us."

"Understood." Susan mentally scratched the Bernstein kids from her suspects list and reached into her bag. She came away with the same pictures of Darville that she'd showed the Ruleys and handed them to Rob. "This is the man I mentioned. James Darville."

"You think he took my daughter?"

"Not really sure about anything at this point. Does he look familiar to you? These pictures were taken in the eighties, so that would be how he looked around the time Bonnie went missing."

Rob shook his head and handed the pictures to his wife. "Don't look familiar to me."

Elizabeth took the photos and flipped through them. When she got to the last one, her eyes grew wide. "Oh my," she said. Her voice was hoarse and strained.

Susan sat up. "Do you know this man?"

Elizabeth nodded. "Sure. I mean, I didn't know his name, but I certainly know the face. He used to come to town with the woman who stacked the Sears catalogs in the grocery store I worked at. She loaded up the pharmacy too. Oh, what was her name?"

The living room was silent with anticipation as Elizabeth racked her brain, trying to remember.

"Talk through it," Susan whispered. "How often did she come?"

"Twice a year. Every time a new catalog came out. We got to chatting a few times, and she said how she was in charge of distribution for the entire state. The company gave her a car and everything. I used to fantasize about her life, how she was always on the road seeing all the different places, the big cities and other towns. Sears would mail the catalog to everyone's house, and her job was to stack extra copies in markets and such."

"And James Darville was with her?"

"Yes. Maybe not every time, but enough times that I remember his face. God, that was over thirty years ago. I know he was with her, but I can't remember her name. Maybe you should ask the chief. He was around back then. He might remember or have some record or something. Oh, and ask in the pharmacy too. Ben Pillsman was the owner back then. He still lives here. His son, Jerry, runs it now. They might know, since he was one of her regular stops. I guess she quit or got laid off because one day a new guy started coming, and I never saw her again. I wish I could help more."

"You have helped," Susan said, taking the pictures back. She dug into her pocket and came away with her card. "If you remember anything else, please call me. Day or night."

"I will."

She left the house quickly. Liam was waiting in the driver's seat when she climbed in. The first thing she did was dial the Shintown police station. She needed to speak to the chief and whoever else might've been around in the late eighties who could recall the Sears catalog lady. She wasn't sure where things were leading, but it finally felt like they might be getting somewhere.

Her phone rang once before the call was picked up.

"Adler."

"Susan, it's John Chu. I got an update for you."

Chu was the head of the forensics unit and had been assigned her case. He'd been on the force for almost ten years and was good at what he did. "Hey, John, what's up?"

"We got the analysis from the dirt and mud that was in the nurse's car. Some of it was from the lake, but some matched the soil samples we found in the carpet at James Darville's house. It was Honeoye soil."

"Okay. What does that mean?"

"Honeoye soils are fertile. They have a high base saturation, and they're slightly acid at the surface but neutral in the subsoil. This type of soil is very deep and well drained. It was formed in glacial till and is distinct because it has limestone and calcareous shale in it."

Susan rubbed her eyes. "John, I'm too tired for the science. Sum this up for me."

"Honeoye soils are used for corn, soybeans, wheat, oats, alfalfa, grass pasture, and hay. They're present on about five hundred thousand acres in New York State. But we also found trace amounts of cow feces and corn, which boils those half-million acres down substantially. We're looking for someone who works on a farm in New York. Do you have anyone like that?"

Susan looked out the window as they drove down another dilapidated road. "No, but we're in Pennsylvania farm country now. Would that work?"

"Maybe in some parts. I'd have to check."

"Okay, do that, because this entire region is nothing but farms and woods."

TRANSCRIPT

I'd buried the boy at Pifer Mountain, just as I'd done with Tiffany Greene and Sonia Garland. And, like the others, it felt like a dream. By the time I woke the next morning, I knew this madness couldn't continue. I decided I was going to tell the police everything that happened, and I'd accept whatever consequences came my way. I knew I'd most likely be locked away for the rest of my life, and I knew there was a distinct possibility that I'd even get the death penalty, but I deserved it. I'd had a hand in killing three children, and I'd helped cover up each of the crimes. My payment was due.

Noreen was standing on my porch when I came outside. It was as if she already knew my plans or sensed I was going to do something drastic. She smiled when she saw me, tilting her head back so the morning sun caught her silhouette in just the right way, and for a moment I could see a bit of the woman I'd first fallen in love with.

"I wanted to stop by and make sure everything was okay," she said. "I was thinking about you last night."

I pushed past her and walked down the steps toward my driveway. "Everything's fine."

She fell in behind me. "Where are you going?"

"To the police. I'm going to tell them everything. I can't keep this secret anymore. We've disrupted too many lives. It has to end." It felt good just to say the words out loud. "Don't worry—I won't implicate you in anything. I'll say it was all me, and I'll take whatever's coming. I deserve it."

I expected Noreen to plead with me to reconsider or beg me to stop being so foolish. I assumed tears would follow, an entire hysterical scene that would play out for my neighbors to watch. But I was wrong. Noreen calmly caught up with me and slipped between me and my car before I could get in. In those few moments, a darkness had come over her, and the woman I'd caught a glimpse of when she smiled in the morning sunlight was gone, replaced by someone I didn't recognize and didn't want to know.

"You can't go to the police," she said. Her eyes were cold, staring into mine.

"I have to. This can't continue."

"I need you. When I see Sonia, I need you to put her back."

I grabbed her by the wrists and squeezed. "Sonia is dead. You can't see her, and a wig isn't going to change that. She's gone."

"She's gone because you didn't lock the door."

I nodded. "That's right. I didn't lock the door, which makes this my fault. And now it's time to confess. Everything."

I let go of her wrists and tried to push her out of the way, but she stood her ground. "She's yours," Noreen said.

"Get away from the car."

"She's yours, and if you do this, you'll never see her again. I'll make sure of it."

"What are you talking about?"

Noreen looked at me. Through me. "Cynthia is your daughter. I never told you because I didn't want to burden you with the truth. Jackson thinks she's his, and my girls had each other, so I kept up with the charade. One big, happy family. But that's all gone now. Because of you. Because you didn't lock the door. So now you need to know the truth before you do something stupid."

It took me a moment for the words to register. I looked at her. "Cynthia is my daughter?"

"Yes."

"You're lying."

"I'm not."

I knew she wasn't lying. I can't tell you how, but I knew. I felt it in my heart the moment she said it.

"If you go to the police, I'm going to kill her."

The words hung in the air. I remember a delivery truck rumbling down my street, and that was the only sound on the entire block. Even the birds had stopped singing.

"I'll kill her, and I'll kill myself. That will be two more deaths on your hands. Another child you couldn't save."

I retreated a step as if she'd just pushed me back. "You're insane."

"No," Noreen quickly replied. "I'm protecting you from yourself. You can't go to the police. I won't let you. I need you. So, if you go, you'll be punished worse than any prison could punish you. I'll kill your daughter slowly, and it won't be like the others. She'll feel pain. She'll be awake the entire time. I'll take pictures, and I'll send them to you in jail. You'll be helpless to stop it behind bars. I'll drag her death out over days. Maybe weeks. And I'll make sure she knows it's your fault."

"She's your daughter. Your child."

"I've already killed one daughter. You think I can't do it again?" Noreen held out her hand. "Give me your keys."

"No, I—"

"Give me your keys!"

Her burst of anger tore down any defense I thought I had. I placed my car keys in her hand and watched her, fearing what else might come out of that wretched mouth.

Noreen closed her fist around them, and her mood lightened. "I'll give these back when we're done with my route through Pittsburgh. You're coming with me, so pack enough for three days. I need to keep an eye on you. Go inside and think about what I just told you. You have an opportunity to get to know your daughter, or you can become complicit in her torture and death. The choice is yours. I know you'll make the right one."

"Why are you doing this?"

She smiled, and this time there was nothing but lunacy behind her grin. "I'll pick you up at seven tomorrow morning. Don't sleep in. I need to keep my schedule. I have four stores to hit."

"Why are you doing this?" I repeated.

Still smiling as she turned to leave: "Because I need you around. I'm not done making you pay for your sins just yet."

54

Her name was Noreen Garland. The chief hadn't remembered her, but the old pharmacy owner, Ben Pillsman, did. Noreen had visited him twice a year, whenever the Sears catalogs came out for the fall/winter and spring/summer seasons, and they were known to have had lunch together on more than one occasion.

As was protocol, Noreen would contact Ben about six weeks before the new catalogs were issued. She would give him her scheduled delivery dates via telegraph or letter. No phone calls. The corporate offices at Sears needed the paper trail. She was in charge of the entire state of Pennsylvania, stocking the catalog in supermarkets, doctor's offices, post offices, retail stores, delis, and pharmacies. According to Ben, she'd been a regular up until one day some new driver, Skip Tooro, started making the deliveries. Skip became the new rep until the magazine ceased to exist in 1993.

Liam drove while Susan called her house. She said her hellos, got the rundown from her mother (all was fine), and talked to the twins about their day at school. Casey apparently got a gold star for cleaning up after art without anyone having to ask her, and Tim's team won their dodgeball game at recess. Both kids sounded happy and didn't seem bothered that they wouldn't see her until the following day. Spending weekends with Eric had gotten them used to nights without Mommy, and that was a good thing. But she couldn't kid herself. It tugged at her heart to know they were more than fine without her.

Susan disconnected the call and placed her phone in one of the empty cup holders. The radio was off, with only the steady hum of the engine filling the car.

"Sounded like everything was good at home," Liam said, breaking the quiet.

"Yeah. Both kids had good days at school, and they were getting ready for peanut butter squares."

"What's that?"

"It's their favorite snack. It's just a peanut butter sandwich cut in fours. They like the little pieces."

"No candy bars or chips or gummy bears or something junky like that?"

"I don't know what to tell you. We go with what works."

Liam laughed and switched on the radio, turning it low. "You give any more thought to moving?"

"Yes and no." Susan looked out the window, watching the landscape pass by in a blur. "When this case is over, I'm going to find a real estate agent and get some figures. Then I'll have to sit everyone down and talk through it. Eric too. I'm just not sure what I want to do. I keep telling myself I can't afford to move, but the truth is, that's crap. I can afford it. I just don't want to. I brought Casey and Tim home from the hospital to that house. Eric and I fixed it up to make it ours. The good memories far outweigh the bad ones. I know I could sell it and get enough for a down payment on something else. Maybe we'd need to move a little north or head across the river into Rockland County or something, but it's not like I can't afford *anything*. I just don't want to give up the one I'm in."

"Then don't," Liam replied. "Find those good memories and talk about them with the kids. Maybe those good times will start to outweigh what happened for Casey and Tim too. You never know." He looked at her, then back to the road. "After what happened with my brother and my wife and the entire department thinking I was a murderer, I didn't think I'd ever be able to step foot in the city again or live in the same house where everything went down. I was in the same position Tim is in. Every time I'd walk into my house or come downstairs, I'd be reminded of that afternoon when I got home and found Vanessa in the dining room. I'd relive it all over again. Every time I drove into Philly, I'd be reminded of the streets I had to hide out on and the people I needed to run from in order to find the truth."

"How did you get through it?"

"Takes time. I sold the house and moved. That was my decision. I'm not saying it has to be yours. I started going into the city and walking the streets and recounting the places I went to during that time, and it ended up being very therapeutic. Kind of faced my fears, you know? After a while, I started to find the places where I had good times and good memories. It helped a lot. I eventually moved back to South Philly, and things started becoming routine. It began to feel like home. I'm not saying you guys moving will help Tim. I'm just saying I kind of went through what Tim is going through, and it'll take some time before he starts to come out on the other end. But it'll happen. Did for me. Talk about the good times you've all had at the house. Remind him of them. Relive them. That could be a huge first step."

Susan let the words sink in and choked back tears that came out of nowhere. She thought about her little boy and cursed herself for letting her work invade her private life. She'd been too trusting, and it had almost cost her everything. She promised herself she wouldn't make that same mistake again.

They drove for another hour before stopping in Milton, Pennsylvania, about halfway between Shintown and Hawley. It had been a long day, and both of them were tired from driving. Liam pulled into the parking lot of the Quickway Motor Inn and shut off the engine. They sat in silence.

"Okay," he said, playing nervously with the edge of his jacket. "Is this the part in the movie when we have to share a room, and the manager asks if we want one bed or two, and we both shout, 'Two beds!' at the same time?"

"This is official state police business," Susan replied, trying to hide a smile. "I'm sure there's enough in the budget for two separate rooms at a crappy motel. Why make things awkward when they don't have to be? Let's write our own movie."

Liam's shoulders relaxed, and he opened his door. "You're the director," he said. "I'm just a stagehand. Lead the way."

———

They got two rooms next to one another but worked in Susan's. The sun had gone down, and the neon lights from the motel's sign in the parking lot cast everything in a pink hue. Remnants of Chinese takeout were scattered across the small round table near the bathroom. The case files had been spread out on Susan's bed and on top of the dresser.

"These two kids, Marcus and Bonnie, were taken from really small towns, both at the end of an after-school sports program," Susan said, tapping Bonnie's file with the pen she was holding. "I'd say that could be a pattern. A kind of MO."

Liam nodded. "Agreed. Taking the kids from a small town was both clever and risky. Risky because towns that small know when a stranger rolls in, so they would be easy to identify after the fact. All the local folks would point to the person who didn't belong, and that would be the primary suspect. But it was also clever because towns as small as Hawley and Shintown don't have the manpower or infrastructure from a law enforcement standpoint to carry out an investigation like that. By the time they realized the kids weren't lost or didn't run away or weren't at a friend's house, the kidnapper would be long gone."

"And back in the eighties, law enforcement didn't have the kind of computer systems that could match an abduction with a similar one across the state or detect some kind of a pattern. Different departments had no idea who was working on what. They were all concentrating on their own jurisdictions."

"Exactly." Liam got up from the bed and paged through Marcus's file, which was on the dresser. "And as far as the after-school activities, that might've just been an easier opportunity. James was a teacher. He knew the deal. He knew they'd be walking home from school hours after most of the kids had been dismissed, which would make it easier for him to grab them and run. Less of a crowd milling around the streets."

Susan stuck the pen in her mouth and paced the small room as she spoke. "But other than the after-school thing, these two abductions don't really fit a pattern. One's a boy, and one's a girl. Marcus was twelve, and Bonnie was fifteen. Bonnie was Caucasian with red hair. Marcus was African American with black hair. Nothing matches. Seems totally random except for the fact that they were both coming home from an after-school practice. We know it's not random because James Darville has their teeth. And he knew Noreen Garland, who had a job crossing the state twice a year. We know James traveled with her sometimes because Elizabeth Bernstein recognized him as the man being with her."

"Yeah, but the Ruleys didn't recognize him. Neither did Ben Pillsman. He just knew Noreen."

"Maybe James was out scouting for victims while Noreen was having lunch with her clientele."

Liam stared at the picture of each kid, flipping between them. "They both have brown eyes. That could be something."

"Maybe."

Liam closed the files. "Noreen running interference for Darville could be why he was able to get away with abductions in a small town. Noreen wasn't a stranger, as far as those folks were concerned. They knew her, and if James went with her often enough, they knew him too. No one would suspect either of them. They come and go twice a year with their catalogs and get to talking to townspeople and grab some lunch or dinner or whatever. They were part of each town they visited. Hiding in plain sight."

Susan grabbed her phone from the nightstand. "If they traveled together, there's no way Noreen could be in the dark about the abductions. You can't hide a kid in the trunk of a car you're sharing and dispose of the body without the person you're riding with knowing. Wouldn't make sense. She was part of it."

"Like a Bonnie and Clyde type. Roll into a town and roll out with a victim."

"But why?"

"No idea."

She began dialing. "I'm wondering how many times they've done this. We happened to find two teeth, and they both connect to unsolved missing persons cases. How many unsolved abductions are still out there that we didn't find? What else was in that floor that we didn't get to see?"

"Who you calling?" Liam asked.

"The barracks back home. Got some assignments for them. Before we left, I called the three schools James Darville taught at to try and get his employment records. They all told me I'd need a warrant, so that's what I'm going to get. If we can match vacation days or sick time with the schedule Noreen kept for her catalog deliveries, we might really have something. And I'm going to need old records from Sears too. Plus, we need to find out where Noreen Garland is living these days. If she's part of this, the people who took Darville might be after her too. We need to find her. And fast."

55

James woke up and looked around the empty basement, unsure of where he was until tiny slivers of memory began to break through the fog. He was in his wheelchair, sitting in front of the television with *The Birds* on again. The television remote was on his lap. He turned the movie off and wheeled himself to the bottom of the stairs, stopping to listen for anyone walking around upstairs. He hadn't seen the woman in a while, or perhaps he had and just couldn't remember. The humming of silence filled his ears. No murmured voices or muffled conversations. It appeared as if he was alone, yet at the same time, he couldn't help but feel as if someone was watching.

An empty plate of crumbs sat on the coffee table next to an empty mug of coffee, and a memory came. The man had fed him after his shower. He'd pissed himself. He'd woken up in a pool of his own urine, and the man had come down to help him out of the bed and into the shower. James checked his pajamas and saw that they were the same ones he always wore, so the man must've washed them. He held his arm up and smelled the fabric. Yes, it smelled like fresh linen. The man had washed his clothes.

And the sheets. What about the sheets?

James wheeled himself into the bedroom area. The bedpan was on the bed where it always was, clean and ready. The sheets and comforter were pulled up, and the bed had been made. He reached out and pulled a fistful of blanket toward him, sticking it up to his face and inhaling as deeply as his lungs would allow. The fresh scent of cotton and cleanliness filled his senses. He did the same thing with the sheets. The man had washed everything.

A small piece of paper slipped from behind his pillow when he pulled on the comforter. He watched it as it rocked gently to the floor, landing next to his wheelchair. It might as well have been ten miles away. There was no way he could reach it from the chair. He couldn't bend that far with the way his legs were extended out in front of him.

The paper landed facedown. He couldn't see what was written on it. It could've been junk or a tag or a piece of doodle he didn't remember drawing, but something told him it was important. Important enough to keep under his pillow, apparently. He wondered if the man had seen what he'd written, and if that was a good thing or not.

James looked around the room, searching for something he could reach the paper with. A pile of cleaning materials sat in the far corner by the electrical panel. He could see a bucket, a mop, a stack of rags, a dustpan and brush, and a broom. The broom would work.

He wheeled himself toward the supplies, turning and snatching the broom all in one motion, aware that the light wasn't as strong in the back corner and the ghosts were always waiting in the shadows. He laid the broom across his lap and closed his eyes into slits until he was back in the bedroom area and under the safety of the wall sconces.

The top edge of the paper was curled up a bit. James took a steady breath and eased the broom handle beneath it. He flicked his wrist, and the paper flew up for a moment, then came to rest again, facedown.

"Damn."

He tried it again, and this time he flicked the broom handle a little harder. The paper shot into the air, toppling end over end several times before coming to rest on the floor again next to the wheelchair.

James bent over the chair and looked. The paper had fallen message up. As he read the words, he could remember what the man had instructed him to do. He needed to challenge things. Ask the right questions. He needed to find the truth. And some of that truth had been written on the paper that was lying on the floor.

James read the message over and over again. He knew what it meant. There was no sense of confusion this time. He knew. It told him what to do. What he *could* do. It was the truth among so many lies he couldn't remember them telling him.

WALK

56

Susan made her way onto the investigators' floor just as Crosby was exiting his office. She yawned and waved, fighting the urge to stretch her sore back. "I was just coming to see you," she said. "I was hoping you were still here."

"Wasn't going home before you and I debriefed. We got some information today while you were gone. Come in and talk."

She followed him into his office, her stomach rumbling with hunger. They'd left Pennsylvania just after lunch, and she'd come straight to the barracks. It wasn't quite dinnertime yet, but she hadn't eaten anything other than a blueberry muffin and a coffee. She popped a handful of Tic Tacs she kept in her bag to keep her satisfied for the time being.

Crosby sat down behind his desk and pulled a large binder from atop his printer. "So I'm told we're looking for a Noreen Garland now?"

"That's right," Susan replied. "I got an updated warrant list to the DA's office that added James Darville's employment files from the schools he was teaching at back in West Finley and Beaverdale. I also have some of our guys talking to the Sears headquarters in Illinois to see if they could come up with some old schedules Noreen might've kept from her distribution routes. It's a long shot, but I have two witnesses that put Noreen in their town, and one witness who puts James Darville with Noreen. Elizabeth Bernstein ID'd James and Noreen. A pharmacist Noreen used to deliver to back in Shintown also confirmed her ID but didn't know James. I checked back with the mayor in Hawley, and he dug through some old records and confirmed the town was on the Sears distribution route. He couldn't find anything to confirm whether it was Noreen who was making the deliveries, though. I need to put these loose ends together."

"Sounds like the trip was worth it."

"I'm hoping to look at Darville's work records to track the vacation days or sick time he took from his school and match them with the schedule Noreen kept for her catalog deliveries. If we have matches, we can start to tell a story about his past, and if we can do that, maybe we can connect the past and present and find both Darville and the people who killed the trooper. In the meantime, we need to locate Noreen so we can start working from the other end too."

Crosby waited for her to sit. "Start a search in areas surrounding West Finley. If Noreen Garland knew Darville, she probably lived somewhere nearby. We checked, and there's a bunch of Noreen Garlands on social media, but none currently in West Finley. Same with a Google search. Too many to count, but none in West Finley. We can't check for warrants or outstanding tickets or IRS tax filings or social security payments until we know which Noreen Garland we're looking for."

"Darville could even be with her right now."

"Okay, stay on it." Crosby opened the binder. "In the meantime, I have an update for you. We ID'd the Jane Doe from the nurse's trunk. Her name was Kimberly Stokes, but everyone knew her on the street as Kim Kitten. She was a prostitute from the Bronx. Worked Saint Anne's Avenue between 143rd Street and 149th, just outside Saint Mary's Park. Got her file from the NYPD after she showed up during our NCIC search. Arrested a bunch of times for soliciting and petty theft, but nothing major. I want you to go down there and ask around. See what you can find out about her. Try and figure out what she was doing up in Verplanck that got her in the trunk of that nurse's car."

Susan took the file, then paged through it, skimming the information. "Yes, sir."

"We also got Rebecca Hill's cell phone records back."

"Anything stick out?"

"Maybe. There's a number that comes up a bunch of times in the last eight weeks. Pennsylvania area code."

Susan's eyes widened. "Noreen Garland?"

"No idea," Crosby replied. "We called it, and it rolled to a voice mail that has a standard message, and the voice mail is full. Forensics tried tracing the signal, but couldn't get anything. The phone is either off or in a place where there are no cell towers in the vicinity. We're backtracking the number to get to the owner. Just a matter of working with a new warrant and the cell phone company."

"That could be the break we need."

"Let's hope so." He handed her the cell records.

"Anything else?" Susan asked, putting the records with Kim Kitten's file.

Crosby shook his head. "That's it for now. Go home. See your kids. I want you in the Bronx with Triston. I already gave him the heads-up. See what you can find on Ms. Kitten. Hopefully that'll bear some fruit."

Susan got up from her seat. "We're on it."

"How was your trip otherwise?"

"Long."

"And your boyfriend?"

"I'm not even going there."

"Boy toy?"

"Good night, LT."

He was still chuckling to himself when she walked out of his office. She couldn't help but smile herself. There weren't a lot of men who could bust her chops like Crosby could, and even fewer she'd allow to get away with it, but he was like a father to her, and their relationship was so much deeper than supervisor and subordinate. She trusted him and he trusted her, implicitly. It was the kind of bond that made her want to do right by him and his department each and every time she could. If she made one promise to herself, it would be to serve that man to her fullest capacity.

That meant solving her case and clearing it.

57

Susan went home and caught the twins right before they were turning in for the night. A silent house was suddenly filled with running and jumping and laughter and excited little kid conversation. Casey and Tim showered their mother with butterfly kisses, and Susan returned the love with giant hugs and tickles all around. It felt good to be home, but she knew the stay would be short lived. If the twins hadn't been expecting her and calling every half hour for an update on when she'd be arriving, she would've slept at the barracks and saved the commute back and forth for what was going to be a short turnaround. Susan read the kids a book, tucked them in, took a shower, and caught a quick few hours of sleep before she was back up and on the road. You didn't get to talk to ladies of the street during everyone else's regular working hours. If you wanted information from real sources, you needed to be up and out and among those real sources. That was the deal. There was no other way around it.

Triston was in the passenger's seat, half-asleep, his head leaning on the side window. She'd picked him up at the barracks at two thirty in the morning, and they'd taken the Taconic Parkway to the Sprain Parkway, then Interstate 87 into the Bronx. At that hour, traffic was light. They were rolling toward Saint Mary's Park by three.

"I shouldn't be up this early," Triston moaned, his eyes more closed than open. "I've worked hard over the years. I've earned seniority so I don't have to be driving around the boroughs at three o'clock in the morning."

"Pretend you're going fishing," Susan replied. "You need to get up early for that, right?"

"You need a partner."

She smiled in the darkness and patted him on the thigh. "You are my partner."

"I mean a real partner. Someone who can keep these crazy hours with you while you're on a case. I'm an old man. A sergeant whose job it is to oversee my troopers and delegate assignments. Maybe sometimes I get pulled to a scene, but not at this hour. I work the day shift. That's my gig. *This* is temporary. One and done. Understand?"

"I'm going to put in a commendation for you when this is closed out. And I'm going to talk to Crosby about promoting you to investigator so you can be my partner full-time."

Triston huffed. "I got two more years hanging out with you knuckleheads, and then it's sunny Florida for me. I just want to ride out my time and stay out of trouble. After this, you leave me alone."

Susan pulled off of Saint Anne's Avenue and onto 143rd Street. Saint Mary's Park was on her right. As soon as she turned, her headlights caught a small group of women huddled against the perimeter fence of the park. They looked young, but it was hard to tell their exact ages with all the makeup caked on their faces and the bulky fake furs that kept them warm. They started to walk out toward her, then saw the car was a Ford Taurus—synonymous with unmarked police cruisers—and immediately split in different directions.

"Damn, I should've taken my mom's car," Susan mumbled as she focused on one girl and hit the accelerator. "Might as well have bar lights and decals. I'm not fooling anybody in this thing."

Triston sat up and pointed. "Climb the curb and cut her off up ahead. She'll have nowhere to go if you pin her in the corner."

Susan hit the gas and sped past the girl, who was trying to make it to the entrance of the park, hobbling on heels that were too high for her.

Susan turned the car right and hopped the curb just before the entrance, instantly blocking the entire sidewalk.

Triston was out of the car before she could react. He waited until the girl's momentum carried her past him, and then he stepped in behind her, his gun still in its holster, his hand on its butt.

The girl was trapped between the car and the sergeant.

"Leave me alone!"

The girl was, indeed, young, skinny, her face dirty under the extra lipstick, blush, and eyeliner she tried to cover it up with. Her skin was olive, her eyes and long curly hair brown. Under her gray fur that flapped open when she walked, she was wearing a pink miniskirt with fishnet stockings and black heels. A tiny pink leather coat covered her upper half.

Susan hopped out of the car and held up her hands as if she were the one surrendering.

"I'm not NYPD, and I'm not here for you or your friends. My name is Susan, and I work for the state police. I just need to ask you about another girl who works out here. I'm hoping you know her."

"I don't know anything," the girl spat. "And I ain't no snitch, so I'm not telling you shit."

"This isn't about being a snitch. I'm working a homicide."

It took a minute for the girl to understand what Susan meant. Her face suddenly softened, and her shoulders sagged. "I still don't know nothin'. You're wasting your time with me."

"Can we just talk for a sec?"

The girl shook her head.

"How about your name? Can you at least tell me your name?"

"No."

"Okay then." Susan looked her up and down as she slowly approached, hands out, unarmed. "I'm going to call you Pinky. For your outfit. If you get tired of that nickname, you tell me what you want me to call you."

"I want you to leave me alone. I ain't telling you anything, and we're not going to have no conversation."

"Let's start with my victim's name. Can I tell you her name?"

"I don't want to know."

"It was Kim. Kim Kitten. She's dead."

Pinky stumbled backward when she heard the name. She stopped just before falling into Triston, tears immediately welling in her eyes. "You're lying."

"I'm not."

"Kitty's dead?"

"Yes. I'm sorry."

Her head fell. "Damn, I thought she got scooped by a Streeter."

"A what?"

"A Streeter. That's what we call them rich guys who take you for a couple of days. Wall Street types. I knew she got picked up a while back, but I never thought something bad happened."

"What's a while back? How many days ago?"

"Like, four days? Maybe five?"

"So you knew her."

Pinky wiped her eyes and shrugged. "Yeah, I knew her. She was the best. Kind. Took care of her johns. Taught us new girls how to roll. How things worked. How the four of us had to stay on this side of the block and never go around no corners. Stuff like that."

Susan put her hands down and stood next to the young girl. "Were you working the night she got picked up?"

"Yeah, but I already got me a john. By the time I got back, she was gone."

"And all these days she was gone, it never occurred to you that she might be in trouble?"

Pinky cocked her head and waved her hand. "I told you, I thought a Streeter picked her up. That's like winning the lotto. You milk that for every day they wanna keep you. The more you do for him and his friends, the more they might keep you around. I figured she was doing her thing, you know?"

Susan looked up past Triston and could see another girl emerging from the park. As soon as she saw them, she disappeared again.

"Anyone else working that night who might've seen who Kim went with?"

"I have no idea. I mean, there're four of us who work this side of the park, and if I was out and Kitty's the one who got picked up, I guess that leaves two, but I wasn't there, so I don't know."

"Who are the other two? What're their names?"

"I told you," Pinky sneered. "I ain't no snitch."

"Fair enough." Susan took out a business card and gave it to the girl. "Do me a favor. Don't throw this out. Tell your friends about what happened to Kim and ask them if they saw something. If they did, have them call or email me. They can keep it anonymous. I'm not interested in busting prostitutes. I need to find a few missing people and solve two murders. If your friends do right by me, I'll let the NYPD know how helpful you all were. Maybe they'll cut you some slack for whatever you get yourselves into next time."

Pinky took the card without saying anything. She slipped it into her pink pocketbook and pushed past Triston toward where she'd been standing with the others when Susan first turned onto 143rd Street. Susan watched her go.

"We need to see if this park has any security cameras set up on this side."

Triston nodded. "And we should go door-to-door once these businesses open and see if they have any cameras that point to the street. Maybe we get lucky."

"Maybe." Susan turned and walked back toward the idling Taurus. "In the meantime, let's find a diner. Breakfast is on me."

"Well, that's nice of you, considering you pulled me out of bed at this hour."

Susan opened the driver's-side door. "Anything for my partner."

TRANSCRIPT

The message on my machine wasn't long: "Come home. I'm with Sonia, and I need you to put her back for me."

It had been four years since I buried the boy, and I was beginning to think the madness had ended and Noreen's pressuring me not to go to the police that day had somehow saved us both. I still felt the guilt of what I'd done—there was no question about that. But moving from West Finley to Beaverdale had changed my surroundings, which changed my perspective on things, and suddenly I didn't have to think about what I'd done every day. My new job as a middle school English teacher helped too. Being part of a new community. Having a new life. It was all so cathartic. I'd volunteered for everything the town offered as some kind of way to pay penance for what I'd done. Trash pickup, Big Brothers, homeless supply drive, food kitchen. Whatever they had, I took part in, and it felt good. Giving back was helping.

I hadn't heard from Noreen since her last trip with the catalogs for the fall/winter season. As her mental state started to decline, I joined her on her trips for as long as I could to make sure she could keep it together. She thought she was keeping an eye on me, but it was really the other way around.

The last trip had been good, and it seemed as though we were both getting past everything. As time went by and I took root in my new life, I found myself fighting the urge to call her and check up on things. A part of me wanted to let sleeping dogs lie, but another part of me wanted to see if there was an opening for me to get to know my daughter. I'd mentioned it a few times on our trips, but Noreen would dismiss me or change the subject, so I didn't press. After enough time passed, I came to the realization that us not interacting was probably for the best. But all those good feelings of optimism and hope disintegrated the second I heard her voice on my answering machine. "Come home," she'd said. She didn't mean West Finley. She wanted me to come to the cabin.

Four more years of seasons had pushed the cabin further toward the point of collapse. Large holes in the roof had allowed the rain and snow to fall into the structure, which warped the wooden support beams and bent the drywall into different shapes. Black mold had grown halfway up the walls, and the kitchen counter was full of mouse droppings and nests rodents tried to make in the corners. The blue braided rug I'd dragged up so many years ago was now brown with filth and muck. And the cot remained in the bedroom area, its frame rusted, the mattress torn and dirty. Noreen was sitting on the mattress and looked up when I came in. She smiled, and my stomach turned. In her lap was a girl, older than the rest of them, the blond wig secured on her head, the red ribbons still intact.

"I thought we were done with this," I choked. I remember my mouth was so dry I could hardly speak.

Noreen nodded. "I had nothing to do with this," she said, her voice holding that familiar distant, dreamy tone. "I was minding my own business, driving home from one of the shops in Shintown, and I saw her. She was perfect. I thought Sonia was gone forever, but there she was, walking alone on a side road. She looked over at me, and I knew it was her. I just wanted to spend some time with my baby girl, that's all. I hadn't seen her in a while. But I need you to put her back for me."

I crossed the room and looked down at the girl. She was sleeping, but still alive. Her porcelain face was full of tiny freckles, and I could see a birthmark on her chin. Tiny strands of red hair slipped out from beneath the blond wig. "Why her?"

"It's Sonia."

"It's not Sonia," I growled. "This is an innocent girl, and I'm not going to let you kill her. It's over, Noreen. Sonia is dead. You smothered her, and I buried her seven years ago. We committed the worst sin you can imagine, and you can either live with it and try to move on, or we can turn ourselves in, but this insanity has to stop."

"I just wanted to spend some time with my little—"

I slapped her across the face as hard as I could. She looked at me with a combination of rage and madness, but her grip on the girl didn't waver, and she wouldn't budge from her spot on the rusted bed.

"Give me the girl," I commanded. "This is not going to happen."

"No."

"You're not going to hurt her."

"I love her. I would never hurt her."

"Give her to me!"

Noreen pushed back against the wall. "Leave us alone!"

"Give me the girl!"

"Get out of here! I changed my mind. I don't want you here! You're spoiling everything!"

I took the girl's arm and started to pull her off Noreen's lap. Noreen began screaming, yanking her back on her lap. It was a tug-of-war that neither of us was willing to lose.

"Hello?"

The voice registered in my mind, but I was so busy concentrating on getting this poor girl away from Noreen that I didn't give it the attention it deserved. It wasn't until Noreen's grip loosened and I saw her gaze shift to something behind me that I turned and saw the boy standing in the doorway, watching us.

He was wearing a white sweater, a beige nylon vest, jeans, and hiking boots that were caked with mud. Acne dotted his face. He kept looking at us as we were looking at him, the cabin silent, the girl on Noreen's lap hanging half off the cot.

"I heard yelling," the boy finally mumbled. "Is everything okay? Does she need help?"

I remember my chest rising and falling as I tried to catch my breath, imagining what this scene would look like to someone walking into it. I put on a smile that felt so utterly fake and crossed the room toward him.

"Everything's fine," I said. My voice was cracking, still dry with fear. "What are you doing all the way out here?"

"Hiking," the boy replied. "I need to log a ten-mile hike for my Boy Scout badge."

"You're by yourself?"

"Yes, sir. I have a map and compass, though. I know where I'm going." He looked past me and pointed. "Are you sure she's okay? I have a first aid kit in my backpack, if you need help."

I turned around, readying myself with an excuse and an assurance that she was fine, but stopped cold when I saw only the girl lying on the cot. I heard a loud thump and spun back in time to see the boy falling to the floor. Noreen stood over him, gripping a log from a pile of firewood we'd stacked next to the kitchen. We looked at each other, and we knew without saying a word.

Things were spinning out of control.

I rushed over to the boy and knelt beside him. The front of his head was bleeding, and a large lump was already forming just above his right ear. He was breathing, but he'd been knocked unconscious.

I was about to stand when I sensed Noreen behind me. Before I could react, I felt a blow to the base of my skull, and everything dimmed. I tried to stand, but she kicked at the back of my knees, and I fell to the floor. She hit me again, and this time there was only blackness.

(Eleven-second pause in tape.)

That was good, but I want you to try that last part again. You need to make it—

58

Susan and Triston returned to the park two hours after leaving Pinky. A middle-aged man was unloading a bread truck that was double-parked in front of the bakery across from the park's side entrance. They pulled onto the curb and got out.

Susan held out her shield. "You the owner?" she asked.

The man hardly looked at them and didn't stop working. "Yeah, I know," he said. "I'll move it in five minutes. You swallow your ticket, and I'll hook you up with some of the freshest bread you ever tasted."

"Oh, now you're bribing us?"

"Come on! I'll move it in a minute. I'm almost done!"

Only in New York, Susan thought. She stepped closer and met the man as he climbed down from the back of the truck. "I don't care that you're double-parked. I'm state police. All I want to know is whether you have a security camera that looks out onto the street."

The man walked past her, his arms full of loaves. "Yeah, I got one in the corner." He motioned toward where a gutter pipe ran from the second floor of his shop to the street. Nestled against the gutter and the brick was a tiny camera no bigger than a Snapple bottle top.

"How far out does it capture?"

"It's a fish eye, so it ain't the most accurate picture, but it gets a wider view. Takes the front of the store, both neighbors on each side, and across the street to the park. Got it at Best Buy for like a hundred bucks. Nice and easy. Hooks up to my phone. With all the overnight crap that goes on in the park, I gotta make sure my store is safe. And if

I catch any of them hookers turning a trick in my alley, there's gonna be problems."

Susan and Triston followed him into the store. The smell of fresh baked goods almost knocked her off her feet.

"How long does the camera archive for?"

The man laughed and dropped the loaves on the back counter. "Everything's in the cloud now, lady. I don't think it has a limit, far as I know."

"Good," Susan replied. "Then I suggest you finish up with the truck and get back here quick. Me and your phone are going to be spending the morning together."

———

Morning dragged into early afternoon. The owner put Susan and Triston in a back office where they could work in private. She spread out a picture of Kim Kitten on the owner's desk, and they took turns watching the videos, fast-forwarding through the days and nights, searching for a woman they couldn't quite see, not knowing what night she'd actually been picked up. It was a shot in the dark, but it was all they had for now.

Triston suddenly sat up as his pudgy fingers stabbed at the screen to pause the video. "I think I got something."

Susan put down her coffee and climbed from her chair. "What?"

"That's her, right?"

She took the phone and held it closer so she could see. "Yeah, that's her."

"Hit play."

Susan tapped the screen and watched as the prostitute turned the corner onto 143rd Street, walking slowly, purposefully, as if on display. She stopped when a silver Honda Civic pulled up alongside her.

"That's Rebecca Hill's car."

Triston nodded. "Exactly what I was thinking."

They continued watching as the driver, who was hidden in the shadows, talked to Kim, who bent toward the passenger's-side window. Kim talked and laughed, throwing her head back so her coat would open, engaging the driver. After a few more moments, Kim nodded and opened the passenger's door. When she did, the Civic's dome light came on.

"Stop!" Triston shouted.

"Oh my god," Susan whispered. "Is that—"

"Yes, it is. Plain as day."

She pulled out her phone and dialed the barracks. "We need to get back up to HQ now," she said to Triston. "I'll have Crosby get a team assembled."

Triston nodded. He was focused, looking at the screen. "Ten-four."

The driver was David Hill.

Rebecca's brother.

59

Cindy and David were in the kitchen preparing lunch in relative silence. David was mixing two cans of tuna in a bowl while Cindy set the table. She watched him out of the corner of her eye, trying to determine if he really could be the one behind all of this. There was no way to tell. She could be Hagen as easily as he could. Too many questions. No answers.

At first it had sounded like a perfect plan. Kidnap the old man and finally get the truth that she'd been longing to hear for three decades. She knew Hagen was planning on killing Darville when he arrived, but no one else was supposed to get hurt. When Rebecca was telling her about the plan, Cindy had no idea families were going to be kidnapped or organs were going to be withheld from recipients in exchange for their help. All she was focused on was learning the story behind what happened to her sister so she could finally let Sonia and her mother rest in peace. The burden of being the last Garland left weighed heavily on her. She had to hear the story from the old man, but she knew she was running out of time. Hagen was coming. Or maybe he was already there, making tuna sandwiches with her in the kitchen.

"How did Hagen contact you?" Cindy asked, piercing the silence.

David didn't look up. "I already told you."

"Tell me again."

"He got in touch with Rebecca. That's all I know. He told her he knew she was James's nurse and that he had proof James was the man responsible for killing a bunch of kids back in the day. Over a period of like six weeks, he would send her newspaper articles and timelines of where James was when one of the kids was abducted. Some of the names matched names she'd heard James talk about when he was confused. He convinced her, and at that point he told her he could get my mom to the top of the donors list for her liver if we could recruit you and then follow through with a plan he would tell us about later on."

Cindy was familiar with the proof Hagen had sent Rebecca. Rebecca had shown her the same things, but even that hadn't been enough at the time. Cindy needed to hear the old man's confession from his own lips.

"So, you weren't supposed to be part of this?"

"No, but I was the first person Rebecca came to. When she told Hagen about me, he agreed I could help, but I think at that point he figured it was easier to keep tabs on me if I was part of this. I don't think my involvement ever sat well with him." He put the bowl down and grabbed a loaf of bread. "Rebecca knew all along that Hagen was going to kill James, but she justified being part of this with the fact that he had abducted those kids and killed them. She figured if a serial abductor's death could give my mother a new shot at life, she was willing to go for it. I agreed. I guess she never realized how close she'd actually gotten to the old man. She had real feelings for him. It's not her fault that she couldn't go through with it. She tried to help him, and that son of a bitch killed her."

Cindy watched him as he scooped the tuna and spread it on the bread. She felt like she needed to talk about what had happened to Rebecca but knew that was something she'd have to reckon with later. She couldn't let herself think about it now. "Hagen never talked to you directly? Not once?"

"No. Everything was a text. Just like you guys."

"You know Trevor talked to him the other day."

David looked up. "Really? I didn't know that."

Cindy nodded. "I think because of his wife and son. Trevor was screaming at him and pleading for Hagen to give them back. He was losing it. Maybe Hagen needed to reassure him his family is okay."

"Or maybe Trevor is Hagen."

Cindy opened the cabinet above the toaster and pulled out three mugs. She'd been thinking the same thing, but she didn't want to show her hand.

"How could Trevor be Hagen?" she said. "He didn't even know about James being his father until I told him."

"We only know what we've told each other." David put a second slice of bread on top of the tuna and transferred each sandwich to a plate. "None of us know the real truth. You realize that all of our interactions with Hagen are one-offs. We never hear from him as a group. We were all contacted by each other except for my sister, and she's dead. I mean, let's think about it. You could be Hagen. I could be Hagen. Trevor could be Hagen. Or Hagen really could be some guy on the outside. No one knows anything for sure. That's the messed-up part in all this."

Cindy listened to what he said, watching to see if she could find any tells that would betray him. There was nothing she could see, so she decided to push.

"How's your book coming along?" she asked.

David pushed a plate toward Cindy and took a bite of his sandwich. "Everything's on hold until this is over. This is my priority right now. Has to be."

"True crime, right?"

"How do you know?"

"Google said you dabble in fiction and some true crime." She continued to watch him. "This here is one hell of a true crime story, huh?"

"It sure is."

"Could make some big money from it if it's told right."

He dropped his sandwich and stared at her. "I'm not writing about this. Ever. This needs to be a secret we all keep with us for the rest of our lives. Understand? If my mother knew what happened to Rebecca? The liver transplant wouldn't matter. That would kill her."

He looked serious, almost angry. Cindy nodded and grabbed her plate, sliding it toward her.

"How do we get out of this?" she asked. "I mean, what's the end game? Do you think we live, or do we all die with James?"

"I don't know." David turned away and looked out the window above the sink. "I keep getting the feeling that we were never meant to get out of this alive in the first place. All those promises Hagen made might be bullshit. I'm starting to think everyone dies at the end."

60

Susan stood in front of the Special Operations Response Team that had assembled two blocks from David Hill's home in Tarrytown. The team's massive black Humvee idled behind them, growling like a lion eager to hunt. The two teams of four men huddled around her, waiting for her final instructions, their matte-black tactical gear matching the vehicle they rode in, their bodies as armored as the truck itself. Bulletproof vests, helmets, goggles, gloves and kneepads, steel-toed boots, automatic weapons. They were ready for anything.

Triston was back at the barracks preparing his troopers for the day shift in his regular role as sergeant. He'd offered to come and assist, but Susan had refused. He was already doing more than he should to help her. He didn't need to be part of a raid that was solely her responsibility.

Susan had worked with the SORT team before. They were usually reserved for things like counterterrorism operations, hostage rescue, barricaded suspects, and high-risk dignitary protection, but they were also known for their skills in potentially violent felony arrests, expertise that very well might be needed here. She had no idea what was going to happen once they came calling on David Hill and was very aware of how sideways these types of things could go. She'd have to be careful. For the twins as much as for herself.

"Okay," she began as she held up pictures of David and his two-story colonial, which sat on the corner of Lincoln Avenue and Embree Street. "Our suspect lives alone. No spouse. No kids. We're not sure about a girlfriend. I'm going to need two men with me when I knock, and we'll go in teams of two on the other three sides of the house. Radio communication at all times. Do not open fire unless he presents a danger. We have two missing people, and I need our guy alive so we can interview him. Preferably at the barracks and not in a hospital bed after surgery. I'll knock and announce. If we get no response in five seconds, we'll come in the front, and the team in the rear will go through the back door. At that point, we'll have four of you inside with me, and the remaining four will each take one side of the house in case he tries to escape and run. According to his property map, he has no garage and no shed, so the property outside the house should be clear. Any questions?"

The men shook their heads. They'd already been briefed back at HQ. There were no questions.

"Okay. Let's move out."

Susan got into her car as the men climbed in and onto the Humvee. She drove behind the truck as they made their way toward the house at a slow fifteen miles per hour. The men hanging on the outside of the vehicle began fixing their goggles and tightening their helmets. It was showtime.

The Humvee rolled to a stop, and the men hopped off and out, each team scurrying to their assigned positions. Susan hurried out of her car and ran to catch up to the two SORT officers who were already climbing the steps to the front door. The morning was still and cold. She could see her breath popping from her lips as she ran across the front yard, slipping on frozen dew. It was as if the neighborhood was waiting for them to make the first move. No one dared exit their homes until it was over, whatever it might've been. But they were all watching. Out their windows, through their curtains, and around their doors, all eyes were on her and the team. She could feel it.

She pushed in front of the two officers who had already flanked the door on each side. One man held his M16 to his chest, calm, ready. The other had his gun hung over his shoulder as he held the iron battering ram with both hands. The intensity between the three of them was real.

She could feel sweat dripping down her back despite the cold air. She carefully lifted her Beretta from its holster and held it at her side, pulling on the bottom of her bulletproof vest, taking one last breath.

The trooper with the ram nodded. He was ready.

The trooper with the M16 on the opposite side of the door also nodded. He was ready.

Susan rapped her fist on the front door.

"David Hill! New York State Police. Come out with your hands up! Now!"

She silently counted.

One . . . two . . .

The trooper with the battering ram spread his legs and got into better position.

three . . .

The street was completely quiet.

four . . .

The trooper on the other side pushed off the wall and got into a low shooting position. Susan backed away.

FIVE!

The trooper with the ram swung around. In one motion, he faced the door and brought the massive piece of iron down hard on the brass knob, shattering it and most of the locking mechanism along with it. Splintered wood, slivers of brass, and tiny bits of screws exploded up and out onto the porch. He dropped the ram and slid his weapon off his shoulder, and the two men slipped inside.

"State police!"

"David Hill! Come out with your hands up!"

Susan fell in behind them. As she crossed into the living room, she heard the back door explode as more voices filled the air.

"David Hill! Come out with your hands up!"

"State police! Come out slow!"

She swept around the living room while the other two made their way into the dining room. The men who'd come through the back cleared the kitchen, walked down a short hallway, and headed upstairs in single file.

"Clear!" she heard one of the troopers say as he rounded the corner, working from the dining room to the kitchen.

"Checking the basement!"

"Living room clear! Kitchen clear! Dining room clear!"

She walked down the hall and could see another one of the men outside the window, stationed in the driveway, his head on a swivel.

"Clear!"

"Clear!"

"Basement's clear!"

"Second floor clear!"

She holstered her weapon and could hear the lead trooper who had been with her at the front door call the men in from the outside. The raid was over. David Hill wasn't there.

———

The house was crawling with troopers, forensics technicians, and a few lingering members of the SORT team, who were in the kitchen sketching the layout inside the house for their report. It was relatively quiet, considering the number of people milling about, but everyone had a job to do, and they were all focused on doing it.

Susan had sent out a BOLO as soon as they left the bakery, when she and Triston were still in the Bronx. There had been no updates or sightings in the hours that followed. It seemed as though David Hill had vanished into thin air. Just like his sister. Just like Darville.

John Chu made his way over to her, snapping off his gloves. He looked to be in his early thirties and was handsome in a boyish kind of way. "I think we're about done here."

"Anything?"

"Nothing from the search. No bloody knife in the closet or gun under the toilet. The house is a house. We took carpet and fabric samples, vacuumed for fibers and hair, dusted for prints. We'll have the analysis back to you shortly."

"Make it a priority. Now I have *three* missing people, and I need something, John. Anything."

"I'm on it."

She watched him walk away, and her phone rang. She snatched it out of her pocket and looked at the screen. It was Triston calling from the barracks.

Susan put a hand over her other ear and walked out of the house onto the porch. "Mel, what's up?"

"Guess who we just caught breaking in and snooping around Rebecca Hill's apartment?"

"You found David?"

"No. It was Phillip Calib."

It took a moment to remember who that was. Then it clicked. "Darville's primary doc?"

"Yup. One of my men was on him, per your instructions. The guy drives to Rebecca Hill's building, heads up to her apartment, breaks in, and starts rummaging through the place. My guy calls the White Plains PD because of jurisdiction, and the uniforms nab him in the middle of tearing through her closet. They got him down at their main headquarters on Lexington."

"Yeah, I know it."

"I told them you'd be down to have a chat with our doctor."

Susan hopped off the porch and made her way toward her car. "Thanks. I'm on my way."

"I know you are," Triston replied. "Go get 'em."

61

The interrogation room at the White Plains Police Department was three times the size of their room at the Cortlandt barracks. This room looked similar to the ones portrayed in movies and television shows. It had the large steel table, two chairs on each side, the two-way mirror stretching across one wall, with video cameras mounted in the corners to record both sides of the table simultaneously. Susan looked at Dr. Phillip Calib through the glass. He was sitting at the table with his lawyer, his arms folded against his chest, calm but for his left knee bouncing ever so slightly. He'd been in the room for about forty minutes, waiting for her to arrive from the scene at David Hill's house. From what the officers told her, he'd simply offered his hands for cuffs at Rebecca's apartment, walked quietly to the patrol car waiting downstairs in the parking lot, and was silent through the prints and pics. He hadn't asked for anything other than his lawyer.

One of the arresting officers came into the observation room.

"We're ready when you are," he said.

Susan nodded. "Video and audio?"

"As soon as you open the door, we'll start recording both."

"Okay, let's do it."

She walked out into the hall, gripped the knob on the interrogation room door, and turned. One deep breath, and she walked inside.

Both men looked up when she came in. Dr. Calib's eyes glazed over, and she knew he recognized her.

"Good morning, gentlemen. My name is Investigator Susan Adler of the New York State Police, Troop K. Before we get started, I'm required to inform you that we are being recorded through audio and video. Please acknowledge that I've made you aware of these recordings and that we can proceed."

The attorney, an older pudgy man in what looked to be a pretty decent suit, brushed his curly gray hair back and cleared his throat. "My name is Randolph Brewer, and I represent Dr. Calib. I acknowledge the recording of audio and video."

He nudged Dr. Calib.

"My name is Dr. Phillip Calib, and I acknowledge the recording."

Susan sat down and placed a file in front of her. "For the record, this is file number seven-nine-three-C. Both parties understand and have agreed that this is on the record and being recorded. I'm here at the White Plains Police Department representing an open case for the New York State Police involving the shooting death of New York State Trooper Patrick Kincaid; the murder of Kimberly Stokes, a.k.a. Kim Kitten; the disappearance of Rebecca Hill; and the disappearance of James Darville. Dr. Calib was arrested for entering a crime scene, which was Rebecca Hill's apartment in White Plains, New York."

She took an exaggerated breath.

"Whew. Okay, now that that's all done. Let's get started with the good stuff."

Dr. Calib raised his hand and looked at her. "I can clear this up. It's just a massive misunderstanding."

Brewer put a hand on his client's forearm to shut him up.

"What my client is saying is that we can explain his presence in Ms. Hill's apartment, and you'll see that although it may look suspicious on the surface, his explanation will allow you to see things as they truly are."

Susan opened her file and picked up her pen. "I'm all ears."

"We would like some assurances first."

"Such as?"

Brewer cleared his throat and lowered his voice. "The reason my client was in that apartment in the first place is rather sensitive. We'd like to keep the episode from becoming public record. We also see no reason for charges to be filed. Let us just clear this up, and we can all be on our way."

Susan chuckled. "I'm not sure what to tell you. As you know, I have no control over what charges are filed. That's the DA's job."

"But you do have control over what charges are brought in the first place. I'd like to change the tenor of this interview from an arrested suspect to a cooperating subject and have the record of Dr. Calib's arrest and processing expunged from all documents and files pertaining to your case."

"Mr. Brewer," Susan replied carefully, "whether this ends up being a misunderstanding or not, your client broke into an apartment that wasn't his and rummaged through an area that had been marked as a crime scene. He broke through the police-barrier tape and damaged the apartment door lock to gain entry."

"I had a key," Dr. Calib blurted. "She must've changed the locks since the last time I was there. I didn't think I'd have to break the door."

Susan continued, focusing on the lawyer and ignoring the doctor. "Charges will be filed one way or the other. Whether it's a felony or misdemeanor depends on his story and whether or not I believe him. I'm not agreeing to anything until I hear what happened."

There was silence in the room, each person looking at the other, waiting for someone to speak. Finally, Brewer fell back in his seat and nodded for his client to begin. Dr. Calib nodded in return and wiped away the hair that had fallen into his eyes.

"Rebecca and I were having an affair," he began. "Off and on for about a year now. At first it was nothing. I mean, she's not the first nurse to bring a patient in for an exam. But there was something about her. She was smart and pretty, but I think most of all it was how caring she was. She didn't treat James like he was a patient. She treated him like he was her father or uncle. There was something extraordinary about the way she looked after him, always making sure he was comfortable and knew what was happening. Even during his episodes when the dementia really kicked in, she was so understanding. I never saw her get frustrated. That was what was most attractive about her. We started flirting a little and then met for drinks one night. And then another night. And then it was dinner. And eventually I ended up at her place. Couple times I even made my way over to James's house when she was there overnight."

"So you know where she lives and where James Darville lives, and now both of them are missing."

"I had nothing to do with that. I'm married with two young daughters. I know what I did was wrong, but I can't jeopardize my marriage over a dumb mistake. I love my wife. This was a moment of weakness on my part."

"Sounds like more than one moment."

"You know what I mean. When she first went missing, I didn't know what to think. It was crazy. I started driving to all the places we used to go to, but there was no sign of her. I called and texted but never heard anything back. When you came to see me with that copy of her address book, I started to worry about what else you might find out about our affair. I had to wait until the activity around her place died down a bit; then I went to her apartment to get rid of anything that might've given you a clue about us. I had nothing to do with why she's missing, I swear. I just wanted to keep our affair a secret. My wife can't know. She simply can't."

Susan watched as tears welled in the doctor's eyes, the same way David had shed tears in the back of the cruiser the night he was caught breaking into Darville's house. David's reason for being there had turned out to be a lie. How could she not suspect there was something more here?

"What's your cell phone number?" Susan asked.

Dr. Calib recited it, and Susan wrote it on the inside of the file. When she was done, she traced her finger along the numbers listed on Rebecca's phone records. Dr. Calib's cell phone number was there sporadically, both incoming and outgoing.

"You and Rebecca texted?" she asked.

"Yes."

"And if I were to look at your phone, I'd see those texts, and the nature of those texts would confirm your story about an affair?"

"Absolutely. She sent me flirty texts and naughty texts. Sometimes she sent me pictures of . . . you know . . . she was naked and whatnot. We were in a relationship, so to speak. That's what people in relationships do." He leaned forward. "But I deleted them right away. I couldn't let my wife find them, and Rebecca knew not to contact me after six. That was the deal."

"So then you have no record. This is just another story you're telling me."

"No! I mean, I can't provide the proof from my phone, but if you contact the phone company and get records or whatever it is you do, you'll find them. I'll sign a waiver if you want."

Susan closed the file and shook her head in disgust. "I came into your office and asked you three times if you knew Rebecca outside of work," she sneered. "You told me no, all three times. I even asked a final time, for the record. You still said no. I knew you were lying."

"I froze," Dr. Calib replied. "I didn't want anyone to know about the affair. I screwed up."

"You impeded a police investigation by lying to me, broke into a crime scene with the intent of removing evidence that would shed light on your affair with one of the missing people in question, and you think your cooperation now, at this point, is going to prevent you from being charged with a crime? That's pretty funny."

"I think we can work something out," Brewer said. His voice was calm, steady. "We've brought you up to speed now. There are no more secrets."

"So you say."

"So I say."

Susan looked at her suspect. "You know, you fit the description of one of the suspects we have on tape murdering Trooper Kincaid."

"I had nothing to do with that!" Dr. Calib cried. "I'm serious. I was home each night the week Rebecca disappeared. I had a few school things for my kids, and we hosted a dinner with friends one night. You can check with the school. We had to sign in. I had a parent-teacher conference, and my youngest had a clarinet recital. And I'll give you a list of attendees who came to our dinner, as long as you keep my relationship with Rebecca out of your inquiry."

Susan got up from her seat and gathered her file. "Stay here," she said. "I'll be back soon."

"Where are you going?" Brewer asked.

"Across the street to the DA's office. I need to see which crimes he wants to charge you with."

62

The DA decided to charge Dr. Calib with obstructing a police investigation, breaking and entering, and attempted larceny. He was charged, booked, and sent to a cell to wait until they could confirm his whereabouts the week Darville went missing and the night Trooper Kincaid was killed. If he was cleared, the judge would then determine if he would be released on bail or held. But there was no way to keep his affair with Rebecca a secret any longer. One bad decision, coupled with the randomness of his lover's disappearance, and the life Phillip Calib knew was over. Regardless of whether his wife could forgive him, their marriage would always be scarred by his infidelity and bruised by the pain of betrayal. Susan knew both the scar and the bruise all too well.

She turned up the radio and cracked the windows as she drove from White Plains to the Cortlandt barracks. The cold air felt good and helped her stay alert. It wasn't even noon, and she'd already been awake for nine hours. She felt like she'd put in a full day, while most of the East Coast still wasn't ready for lunch. Perhaps she could catch a few minutes of sleep when she got back to the barracks. Nothing too long. Maybe just a half hour in one of the interview rooms to recharge.

Her cell phone, connected to the car's USB port, began to ring through the speakers. It was loud and piercing. Susan glanced at the screen and saw it was Liam.

"Hey," she said, rolling up the windows so she could hear better. "What's up?"

"I found her," Liam replied, his voice crackling. "Noreen Garland. The Sears catalog lady. Called in a second favor, and the boys let me come in and do some digging on their computer. Found a property record for her husband, Jackson Garland, in West Finley and then found tax-filing information and went from there. We got some general DMV data and her social security number."

"We were doing the same thing here," Susan replied. "Looks like you beat us to it."

"Good to get the win," Liam said. "But, unfortunately, she's dead."

"Are you serious?"

"Died in a fire in '89. Suicide. The husband worked for the post office. He died of colon cancer in '98."

"Damn."

"There's more. They had two daughters, Cynthia and Sonia." Liam paused. "Sonia went missing back in '82 on her way home from school."

Susan let the words hang in the air. "Darville's first victim," she said.

"That's what I was thinking."

"He's been at the scene of each girl who went missing, and we found the teeth from two of the missing kids at his house and in his nurse's car." She slammed the wheel with her hand. "The locket!"

"What locket?"

"We found a locket at Darville's house too. It was old. Had the initials *SG* on it."

"Sonia Garland," Liam said. "There you go."

Susan stepped on the accelerator. "Email me everything you have. I'm heading to the barracks now, and I'll break everything out when I get there."

"You got it."

"I'm going to call Crosby and brief him on what you found." She looked down at the phone as if she were looking at Liam himself. "You did great," she said. "Thank you."

"No problem."

"You need to get back in the field. You were made for this."

"I'm a crime scene tech. We're not in the field."

"You know what I mean."

"Yeah, I'm working on it."

"Okay, I'll talk to you later."

"Wait," Liam said before she could end the call. "One more thing."

"Shoot."

"I just keep thinking." Liam's voice grew soft. "You found two teeth and a locket at the scene. I'm guessing they were left there by accident. Probably part of whatever was in that hole in the floor you were telling me about."

"Yeah, probably."

"So if you found three random things that belonged to three missing kids, the real question is, How many things did you *not* find? How many missing kids was this guy responsible for? How many souvenirs are there?"

TRANSCRIPT

I woke up, and the first thing I felt was a throbbing in my head, the pain matching the rhythm of my beating heart. I was on the floor, and as my vision came into focus, I could see that Noreen had bound my arms and legs with pieces of an old extension cord. My hands were fastened behind my back, and my legs were tied together at the ankles. I tugged at the cord, and although most of the rubber casing had disintegrated or broken off over time, the wires were still strong and held firm. I pulled with my hands and moved my ankles. There was give in the knots, but not enough to break free right away.

The girl on the cot was dead. From my angle, I could see the unnatural way her arm hung across her body, and I could also see the filthy pillow covering her face. Noreen had killed her while I was knocked out.

There was heavy panting coming from behind me. It sounded like an animal growling and whimpering at the same time. I rolled onto my side to find the boy who'd been hiking tied to one of the exposed pipes that ran along the baseboard to the kitchen sink. Like me, his hands were bound with an old extension cord, but not his legs. The side of his head was swollen. Blood matted his hair and stained his cheek. Dirty tears ran down his face.

Noreen was on the cot, bent over the girl she'd just killed, stroking the blond wig, whispering something I couldn't hear. She slowly sat up, removed the pillow, then took the wig off the girl.

"Noreen, let me go," I said. "Untie me."

She ignored me as she got up from the cot, walking slowly into the kitchen area as if she was in a trance. Her gaze was distant, her eyes unfocused. A tiny smile curved the edges of her lips.

The boy began to thrash about, crying and screaming as she approached him, kicking and pushing himself away, but she straddled him, pinning his legs under her weight so he couldn't move.

"Shhhh," she said as she reached up and slid the wig over the boy's head. "I need to see."

"Leave him alone!" I barked. The cords around my wrists were starting to give a bit, and I continued pulling and yanking them.

Noreen sat back on the boy's thighs and studied him.

Silence between them.

No one moved.

I held my breath until she snatched the wig off his head.

"It's wrong," she said. "You're not Sonia. Your eyes are blue."

"Let him go," I said. I could feel the cord coming undone on my wrists. I was almost free.

"He can't go," Noreen replied. "He's seen us."

"He doesn't know what he's seen. Let him go, and this ends. Today. We end this. We have to."

Noreen was staring at the boy, lost in her own world. She didn't see me pull my hands free, nor did she hear the extension cord drop to the floor. I watched her as I worked the cord on my ankles, but she never turned around. I carefully got to my feet, snatched the log she'd left on the floor, and swung as hard as I could. She was unconscious before her body hit the floor.

I knelt down next to the boy and untied his hands from the pipe. We stood up together, and I took him by the shoulders, shaking him so he'd focus on me.

"Leave here," I said. "Run. Get home, and don't ever come back. I'll make sure she doesn't bother you again, but you can't speak about this, ever."

I reached into his pockets and came away with a handful of things: a compass, a pack of gum, a folded-up baseball card of Lenny Dykstra, and a small Velcro wallet. I opened the wallet, took the boy's scout membership card, and held it up in front of his face so he could see it.

"If you tell anyone about what you saw, I'll come get you. I know your name, and I know where you live. I've memorized it. But if you keep this secret, you'll never hear from me again. Do you understand?"

The boy nodded through his tears, and I gave him back his stuff. "Go."

He ran from the cabin, and I listened to his feet against the dead leaves until they vanished with distance. He was gone. I'd saved him. Now it was time to save me.

I turned to Noreen and straddled her body, placing my cold, trembling hands around her neck. I was crying and praying and telling her how much I loved her as I squeezed with all the strength that was left in my body. I kept squeezing and sobbing and apologizing, not only to Noreen but to the children I helped bury and the families whose lives I irrevocably changed. I squeezed until I could no longer feel my hands, and then it was over. Just like that. It was done.

Noreen was dead.

63

James had managed to sweep the note from the floor onto the second step, where he could lean from his wheelchair to snag it. He'd slept with the note crumpled into a ball in his clenched fist. When he woke, he read it again, afraid that he might've forgotten where he'd found it or what it was telling him, but he remembered everything from the night before.

WALK

When the woman brought down his breakfast, he'd hidden the note in his pants, and as soon as she went back upstairs, he took it out and held it. Then when she returned to change him into his day clothes, he'd hidden the note in his cheek like a tiny wad of chewing tobacco, folded so many times it resembled a Chiclet. When she left, he took it out of his mouth, unfolded it, read the message over again, and then returned it to the palm of his hand.

WALK

It seemed impossible. He looked down at his legs, sticking out in front of him, each encased in a brace with hard plastic sides and strong leather belts fastening it from thigh to ankle. They'd told him he'd been in a car accident and was paralyzed. He could remember the woman telling him that. But he could also recall the man, who'd asked a very important question.

"If you're paralyzed from the waist down, how can you know your legs are freezing? How can you feel the cold or the wetness or anything?"

He bent forward and knocked on his thigh with his fist. He could feel the thumping of his knuckles, and when he hit them harder, he could feel the pain intensify.

WALK

He could walk. And if he could walk, that meant he could make his own breakfast and change his clothes and climb out of the basement they kept him in and go to the bathroom without help or the need of that goddamned bedpan. He could confront the man and the woman and find out why they were lying. He could take his own walks outside. And he could get up and change the channel when he didn't want to watch the Hitchcock movie anymore.

WALK

James wheeled himself back toward his bed. He didn't know what time it was, but he figured the woman would be down soon to check on him. He positioned the wheelchair next to the bed, parallel so he could use the mattress as something to steady himself on as he tried to stand. And if he fell, hopefully he would be able to fall onto the soft mattress and not hurt himself. That was the plan, anyway.

He folded the note back into its Chiclet square and placed it in his cheek again. He'd need both hands if this was going to work. His fingers were old and arthritic. He would take it slow and concentrate on each strap, but at the same time, he would try to hurry before anyone came down.

WALK

James reached over and, with fumbling hands, grabbed onto the strap that secured the thigh of his left leg. He carefully brought the belt through the loop, pulled back to release the metal clip, then pushed the belt through the second hole and watched as both ends of the strap fell away, displaying a small slit of an opening. He did the same on his right leg, then moved to the strap above his knee on his left leg.

Perspiration was beginning to form on his forehead as he worked silently, moving his fingers as quickly and as steadily as he could. The clock in his mind told him he had to hurry. When the strap above his knee fell away, he leaned back in his chair, gripped the armrests, and carefully bent his leg up, watching in amazement as he moved his leg on his own.

The muscles in his thigh ached and the tendons around his knee were taut, but he could move it. Up and down, stretching and bending, all of his own doing. Not paralyzed. Not bound to the wheelchair. This was proof. This was what he needed to find the answers he sought.

James worked on the strap above his right knee, then did the same exercise, stretching and bending, teaching his muscles how to work again. With both knees being able to bend, reaching for the straps around his shins and ankles was no problem. He worked the straps until the last ones around his ankles fell away and crashed to the floor, making a noise much louder than they should have in the silent space. James held his breath, waiting to hear footsteps above or the basement door open, but after a few minutes he knew no one was coming. He was alone.

The clock in his head continued counting the seconds. He had no strength in his lower body. His legs hadn't been used in some time, so he had to lift each one off the wheelchair footrests and place them on the floor. He put the brake on the wheelchair, then gripped the armrests again and readied himself, the message on the paper screaming its encouragement.

WALK

He pushed up as hard as he could, the tendons and ligaments and muscles and fibers crying and stretching from hip to ankle as he fought himself into a standing position. He spit the piece of paper out of his mouth and bit the bottom of his lip to keep from screaming. He could hear bones and joints popping into place. The bottoms of his feet were pins and needles as blood rushed back into them. The pain. The sounds. The funny sensations.

But he was standing. By himself. On his own.

James let go of the wheelchair and shuffled his feet a few inches in front of him. He kept his balance. The pain was beginning to subside a bit. He lifted his right foot off the ground and placed it back down, then did the same with the left. He began marching in place, lifting his feet only centimeters from the floor to try and get the blood circulating and his muscles used to carrying his weight again. The popping of his joints continued, as did the crackling around both of his knees, but eventually he was able to lift his feet a bit higher off the ground, and still higher after that.

WALK

He took a step, steadied himself, then took another. When he took his third step alongside the bed, his right knee gave out, and he lost his balance. He reached out in front of him as he began to fall sideways, realizing almost immediately that he was too far from the bed and was going to fall to the floor. At the last second, he caught the edge of the mattress with both hands and ended up on his knees. The mattress slid off the box spring, but he was unharmed. He waited to see if he could feel any sharp pain in his legs, knees, or hip, but other than a little pain in his knees from hitting the hard tiles, he was fine. He stood back up, then sat on the bed to catch his breath.

He'd done it. He'd stood. He'd walked. He wasn't paralyzed. They were lying to him. But why?

A piece of paper that was stuck between the mattress and the box spring caught James's eye. He reached down and pulled it out. It was folded in half but looked like the same kind of paper he'd had in his mouth. He unfolded it and read words he knew he'd read before.

DON'T EVER FORGET

He flipped the paper over.

TIFFANY GREENE

SONIA GARLAND

MARCUS RULEY

BONNIE BERNSTEIN

James stood back up, using the wheelchair to balance himself. He could see the corner of another sheet of paper sticking out from between the mattress and box spring. He bent down and pushed the mattress as hard as he could, sending it off the bed and onto the floor on the opposite side. As he did, several sheets of paper flew up and rocked back down to the box spring, settling on top of one another. Some were folded. Most were open so he could read the words the man had written for him to help him remember. His eyes widened, and a chill ran down his spine as he read them.

THEY WANT TO HURT YOU

YOU'RE IN DANGER

THEY'RE NOT WHO YOU THINK THEY ARE

THEY'RE GOING TO KILL YOU

It took a minute for James's overworked mind to process what he was seeing. The notes lying in a pile under his mattress the entire time. The man had been warning him day after day, but he could never remember.

James could hear the noise from the street outside the three windows and was reminded that he was in the city. All he had to do was get outside and grab the first person walking by. He would ask them to call the police, and he would put his faith in the authorities to make things right. The police would rescue him from the people who had lied about his life and kept him hidden from the world.

He just had to get outside.

The fog was thin enough for him to know that he couldn't risk climbing up to the main floor. The man and the woman could be around, lurking in the house or just outside on the street. In a crowded city it would be easy for them to subdue him before he could cry out for help. They'd undoubtedly be ignored by people who were focused only on themselves. They'd have no time to help a hysterical old man. The only other option was the hurricane doors down the dark corridor where the ghosts lived. He knew they were waiting. For him. But it was the only way.

He looked at the notes again.

THEY WANT TO HURT YOU

YOU'RE IN DANGER

THEY'RE NOT WHO YOU THINK THEY ARE

THEY'RE GOING TO KILL YOU

He had to go. His life depended on it.

64

Cindy stood in front of the desk in the dining room, chewing on her bottom lip, staring at the drawer she'd seen Trevor put a folder in a few days earlier. She remembered he'd locked that drawer and put the tiny key in his pants pocket. Never really wondered about it until now. Her conversation with David replayed in her mind, and it wasn't lost on her that each of them was trying to get her to buy into the fact that the other could be Hagen. There was too much uncertainty to take a side. Yes, either of them could be Hagen. Or neither of them. That's what made things dangerous. There was no one she could trust with 100 percent certainty. And as the plans they'd made with such precision and care crumbled at their feet, she needed to find out everything she could about the men she was living with. And that meant she needed to know what was in that drawer.

She knelt in front of the desk and gripped the chrome letter opener she'd taken from the mail basket in the hallway. The desk was made mostly of balsa wood and hard plastic, so she didn't think the locking mechanism would be too tough to overcome. Of course, just asking Trevor what was in the drawer would have been the easiest way to go about this, but whatever his answer was, she knew she wouldn't believe him without seeing for herself. The truth was the one thing that she could no longer compromise.

Cindy pushed the tip of the letter opener into the keyhole and tried turning. It was always done with such ease in the movies. A bobby pin, a twist, a turn, an opened door. In reality, this was not the case.

The lock didn't budge, so she applied more pressure, leaning in, using her upper body for leverage as she pushed even harder, trying to turn the letter opener at the same time.

Come on.

The lock suddenly gave without warning, shattering into pieces, the wood around it splintering and falling to the floor. Cindy held her breath as tiny metal parts bounced across the hardwood. When everything finally settled, she slid the drawer open and peeked inside.

The red folder—the one she'd seen him put in the drawer the other day—was on top. Cindy took it out and sat on the floor, opening it across her lap. It was a mail-order paternity test from one of those trace-your-family-tree websites. After her father died, leaving her the last surviving member of their family, she'd contemplated taking a DNA test to see if there were others out there who she could reach out to, but ultimately decided against it. Her family had too much baggage as it was, and finding out she was a descendant of one of the largest slave-owning bloodlines in the country or discovering that a distant great uncle was a spy for the Germans during World War II would be too much. Better to let sleeping dogs lie.

She scanned the results page, and her breath caught in her throat. According to the report, twenty-two genetic markers had been tested, and the results concluded that the father was a 99.99 percent match to the child, making paternity a certainty.

Her world began to spin, the ceiling dipping to her left while the floor came up on her right. She could feel her heart beating in her chest and sweat forming under her arms. Her breathing became shallow and labored. She thought she might be having a heart attack.

How can this be?

How is this possible?

There was a handwritten note next to the subject line marked *Child*. It was her name.

Cynthia Garland.

The note next to the subject line marked *Parent/Father* was a name she thought she couldn't possibly be seeing.

James Darville.

According to the test she was looking at, James Darville was her father.

"What are you doing?"

She looked up and saw Trevor standing in the doorway, although his outline was skewed by the tears in her eyes and the throbbing in her head. Under normal circumstances, she'd be trying to fumble for an excuse as to why she was breaking into his desk and rummaging through his things, but the weight of this news was so heavy and confusing that she forgot about manners or the fact that she'd done anything wrong or the fact that she'd thought she was alone in the house. Instead, she simply held up the results report as she began to cry.

"What is this?"

He rushed into the dining room and snatched the folder from her. "You weren't supposed to see that."

"Why do you have that? How could you have that? What's going on?"

"Nothing."

"Tell me."

"Forget it. It's nothing."

"Tell me!" she screamed as loud as she could. "Tell me right now! What is this?"

The room fell silent.

"I needed to know the truth," he finally said.

She pointed and laughed as if he were mad. "That is not the truth!"

Trevor shook his head. "I'm sorry. It is." He took a moment, and she could tell he was trying to figure out what he was going to say. "That jewelry box of souvenirs wasn't the only thing I found in the hole at James's house. I found cassette tapes too. Four of them. They were tucked in a plastic bag under the part of the floor that didn't pop out, behind where the jewelry box was. You had to really stick your hand in there, or else there's no way you would've seen them. Anyway, my flashlight happened to catch the reflection of the bag, so I grabbed it to see what it was. Before I could tell you guys what I found, David tripped and spilled everything out of the box. We were scrambling to pick it all up and get the hell out of there. I mean, we were making way too much noise, and we had James in one car and a dead woman in the other. It was crazy. When we got back to the house, I figured I would listen to see what was on there before I said anything about them."

Cindy's eyes were wide. She was hyperventilating. "I don't care what was on those tapes. That man is not my father. You're not my brother."

"James said on the tape that he met your mother when he was still teaching at the Lynch Academy in Ohio. She's the reason he moved to West Finley. She'd just started her job delivering her catalogs and had a little piece of Ohio as part of her route. They met at a coffee shop, and that chance encounter started everything."

"No, no, no, no, no, no."

"It's all there," he replied, pointing to the drawer. "Look for yourself."

Cindy reached in and pulled out a small plastic bag. She opened it and grabbed one of the cassettes. Old-school blank tapes. The kind she used to record her favorite songs on right from the radio, always catching the DJ at the beginning or end of a song. She never could get that quite right.

"I wasn't sure if he was lying or confused, so I had to find out for myself. I waited until he was asleep and swabbed his mouth with one of the Q-tip things they give you in the test kit. Did the same to you when you were passed out from all the wine you drank after you were watching the news coverage of that trooper's funeral."

"You bastard."

"I needed to know. I took the samples and mailed them in. Came back two days later, just like the package said. He was telling the truth."

Trevor held up the results page. "Ninety-nine point ninety-nine percent match. He's your father. And I'm your half brother."

Cindy couldn't believe what she was hearing. She *refused* to believe what she was hearing. "That report doesn't have our names on it. You wrote our names on there. That could be anyone's report and you're lying."

"Why would I lie?"

"I don't know! To hurt me or make me feel vulnerable. To knock me down so you can use me."

"Use you for what? All I'm trying to do is get my family back and not get me or them hurt in the process. Hagen, and whoever else is working for him, is going to be coming for James soon. There's a good chance he's going to want to kill us once he's done with the old man. We're all loose ends here. Think about it. I need you lucid and with me. Why would I try and manipulate you with lies about James being your father? You're not making any sense."

"None of this makes sense!" Cindy cried, her tears still blurring her vision, the room still tilting up and away. "That man is not my father."

He held up his hands. "Okay. If that's what you want to believe. That's fine with me. I wasn't going to tell you anyway. You're the one who broke into my desk."

Cindy turned around and reached into the bag, pulling the remaining three tapes out. "I want to listen."

"I'm not sure you do."

"If the man in the basement really is my father, that means he had an affair with my mother, killed my sister, and killed the other children too. I want to hear what's on those tapes. If you say it's the truth, I want to know. That's all I've been after for three decades. I want the truth."

Trevor bent down next to her and gently grabbed her shoulders. She'd done the same to him only days earlier. His eyes were compassionate, and that scared her the most.

"We've been through a lot these past few days," he said. "You and I have done things we never would've dreamed a month ago. People died because of us. I'm not sure you can take what's on those tapes. It's too much. You shouldn't listen."

She blinked a new set of tears from her eyes and slowly lifted the tip of the letter opener up to the bottom of his chin. "Don't worry about me," she said through clenched teeth. "I can handle it. Let me listen."

He exhaled through his nose. Resignation. "Okay, but just remember—you asked for this. For the record, I think it's a very bad idea."

65

James shuffled past the wheelchair, using the bed to steady himself. His legs ached from being immobile for so long; his head swam from being in an upright position. When he reached the end of the bed, he focused on the dark corridor across the way, immersed in the shadows. The ghosts were waiting for him there. He couldn't see them or hear them, but he knew they were there, with their decaying skin and horrific eyes and toothless grins. They were waiting to tear him apart. But that was the only way out.

James pushed himself off the end of the bed and took his first few, unsteady steps without the assistance of anything to help his balance. He kept his arms out to his sides as if he were on a tightrope, swaying from right to left as he went, making slow progress across the tiled floor. The open mouth of the shadows came closer, his eyes fixed on the hallway that would lead to the hurricane doors, his mind concentrating on each step.

Left . . . stop.

Right . . . stop.

Left . . . stop.

His legs burned, and his breath came quick, more from fear than exhaustion. If the ghosts wanted him, he'd be vulnerable. They could come from the shadows and take him while he was busy concentrating on walking. He'd never see them approaching. He'd just feel their small, dirty fingers curl around his skin, and that would be it.

The concrete step seemed larger now that he knew he had to get up on it. He held his breath and bent one knee, pushing himself up and forward while balancing a hand on the wall. He fought to keep steady and brought his other leg behind him, then balanced himself again as he slid his hand farther down the wall. He'd made it.

James took a step, and his leg suddenly gave out. He landed hard on his right hip and rolled onto his back. His head bounced off the floor, and he saw stars for a moment. The fog was coming. He could feel it. His body wanted to stay there and rest, to sleep the remainder of the day away and not worry about escaping the people who were trying to hurt him. Just a few minutes of rest.

No!

He clawed his way through the fog and pushed himself up off the floor. He got into a kneeling position, then used the wall to steady himself as he stood. A thin trail of blood trickled down the side of his face.

The hall ended with a single door. James opened it and walked through to another corridor that turned left. He could see the outline of the hurricane doors at the end of this new hallway. The daylight outlined the seams in the frame.

As he walked, he noticed something else in front of him, off to the side, against the wall. He couldn't make out what it was in the dark and thought it could be one of the ghosts, but he had to keep moving. He was in their world now. The shadow world. If they were going to take him, so be it. He would focus on the doors and not stop moving.

Each step was painful. At first just a dull thud in his hip and knee, but it quickly became more excruciating. Perhaps he'd broken something when he fell. But he couldn't stop. He had to keep moving. He was close now. Almost there.

The object against the wall was long and white. James kept his focus on the daylight outlining the hurricane doors, swallowing the pain, which was getting worse. As he got closer to the object, he could see that it wasn't white after all. It was plastic. Clear plastic. He stopped when he reached it and looked down. Fear enveloped him. What was this thing he was about to pass?

His subconscious registered what he was looking at before his mind allowed him to see it for what it was. Clear plastic. Long. Rolled like a carpet. Kept against the wall. He bent closer and could see something through the rolled layers. It was as if he were looking at it through a thick patch of ice.

It was a body.

The light from the seams in the door helped him make out the blurred features of the face. Although it was faint, he could smell the stench of rotting skin even through the tight wrapping. He got down on his knees, wincing at the pain, and bent even closer. A small fragment of recollection came to him. The hair. The dark skin. The scrubs she was dressed in. Those purple scrubs with the small embroidered cartoon cats. She'd loved that top.

It was Rebecca.

"No!"

His voice echoed in the quiet space as he clawed at the plastic. It couldn't be Rebecca. It couldn't! But he knew it was. She was dead, and somehow, he knew he was to blame. But the fog kept the details from him, hiding the actions that had led the poor, kind nurse to where she was, wrapped up and discarded like a bag of trash.

The plastic was too thick and his hands and fingers too weak to break through. He wiped the tears from his eyes and stood back up on shaky legs. He had to get out of there. Had to get help. People needed to know what was happening in that basement. Even if the fog kept him from the ultimate truths, others would figure it out.

James pushed himself through the last few painful steps until he was leaning against the hurricane doors, panting and crying. He unlocked the bolt and turned the knob, opening the doors onto the Manhattan streets that would bring him the help he so desperately needed.

Only the streets of the city weren't there. No cars. No pedestrians walking. No taxis honking or busses revving their engines. No police sirens or ambulances working their way through backed-up traffic. There was none of that. There was, in fact, no city at all.

James stepped out from the basement and surveyed the acres and acres of land that were laid out in front of him. All he could see were dead cornstalks, cut off or bent in the center, in a field so dense it blocked everything else but the tip of a silo off in the distance. Snow covered the ground here, and he looked down at his feet, realizing for the first time that he was only wearing socks. He'd never considered the weather when planning his escape. He'd never considered anything but the crowds of people who were supposed to be there to help him when he got out. But this. What was this? *Where* was this?

The notes hidden in his mattress flashed through his mind again as the fog tried to roll in.

THEY WANT TO HURT YOU

YOU'RE IN DANGER

THEY'RE NOT WHO YOU THINK THEY ARE

THEY'RE GOING TO KILL YOU

James tucked his hands into his armpits to protect them from the cold and started walking. The pain in his hip and knee was worse now, but there was nothing more he could do but try and find a way out. But a way out from where? That was the real question.

66

Triston was waiting in the parking lot when Susan pulled up to the barracks.

"Still no sign of David Hill," he said as she climbed out of her car. "We went to his work, and they said he took a couple of days off. They figured it had to do with his mother's condition, but we went by her place, and she claims she hasn't seen him."

"Did you try tracking his phone?"

"Phone's turned off. No signal. Last trace it pinged at was his house two days ago. He's off the grid for now. We have a BOLO out for New York, New Jersey, and Connecticut. We'll find him."

Susan opened the steel door that led directly onto the investigators' unit. As soon as she did, Crosby stood from his desk and motioned for her to come into his office.

The unit was quiet, which was unusual for that time of day. Susan walked into Crosby's office and shut the door. "Where is everyone?"

"Out looking for David Hill."

"Triston told me about the BOLO."

"Not much we can do now but wait until he makes a mistake and someone picks him up." He handed her a file. "We got the trace back from the Pennsylvania phone number that kept showing up on Rebecca Hill's cell phone records. Number belongs to Cynthia Garland."

Susan smacked the file as she opened it and began reading. "Sonia's sister. I knew it. Cynthia and Rebecca have been calling each other for the last six months." She looked up at her boss. "This whole thing was planned, and that trooper got in the way. We got Rebecca caring for a man who was friends with Cynthia's mother back in the day. Cynthia's older sister, Sonia, went missing in '82, and all of a sudden Darville's nurse becomes cell phone buddies with the last surviving Garland?"

"I think you finally found your connection." Crosby pulled up an old newspaper article on his computer. "Sonia Garland went missing in the spring, about a month before the school year ended. According to what the papers had back then, she was an average student, no extracurricular activities except cheerleading in the fall. She went home on the bus from school on Tuesday, and no one saw her after that. Bus driver claimed he let her off at the corner of her street like he did every day. Student witnesses support his version of events. No suspects or charges were ever formally brought. They did the whole search party thing and interviews of townspeople. Even the FBI took a look, but no one turned up anything. West Finley isn't big. Everyone knew everyone, and everyone knew the Garlands."

"That's Darville's MO. He only took kids from small towns who were walking home alone from school. This one was a little close to her house, though. Risky."

"This was '82, so it could've been his first one," Crosby replied. "Darville was close to the family. In the same town. If it wasn't his first, it was one of the first. He was still learning how to do this. He hadn't created his full MO yet."

"Maybe."

Crosby continued reading. "The Garlands held a memorial service on the five-year anniversary of Sonia's disappearance. That's the last time anyone wrote anything about it."

"And now we have Cynthia Garland appearing out of nowhere."

"Not completely out of nowhere. She hosts a rather successful podcast about true crime and unsolved cases. She's done a lot of episodes on her sister. People know who she is."

"Is her phone still off?"

He nodded. "And voice mail is still full."

Susan closed the file. "Okay, so where are they? Rebecca calls Cynthia Garland, tells her what she knows about Darville. Rebecca lets the woman into Darville's house, which is why we see no B and E. Cynthia and David Hill take the old man, and Rebecca goes with them, willingly or unwillingly. But where? And we also have David picking up the prostitute because she was a look-alike for his sister, but why?"

"We're checking second homes and alternate locations for everyone in the picture," Crosby said. "We'll find them." He pointed to her desk. "Your job is to go deeper and find out everything we can about Cynthia Garland. We find her, chances are we find everyone else. Go."

TRANSCRIPT

The boy was gone. The girl was in the trunk of my car. I placed Noreen on the cot and just stared at her for what seemed like forever. I know this sounds strange, but even after all of that, I still loved her. I told myself that if things had been different, I would've gladly spent the rest of my life with her. But the truth of that matter was, I couldn't be a part of her insanity any longer. I wanted my life back. I wanted to be free of the guilt and sorrow I'd felt every day since that moment in my classroom. I wanted to be able to get on with my life—whatever kind of life that might be—without the constant fear of getting a phone call from Noreen, telling me she'd found Sonia and that I'd have to put her back. I would end this, move on with my new life in Beaverdale, and work each day to repent for the sins I'd committed. It was the only path I could see to take.

I used the kerosene that I'd stored under the sink a few winters before, when we'd sneaked a portable heater up to keep warm. We figured it would attract less attention than a campfire, and we'd be able to put it out quicker if we heard someone coming. I never thought I'd be dumping it around the interior of the cabin, up onto the cot, and over Noreen herself. I walked the kerosene back out of the structure and then tossed the can into the corner of the living room before leaving.

Noreen was dead. It was over. I had created a monster that needed to be put down, and I'd done just that. As I lit the match and watched it drop from my fingers onto the dilapidated porch and heard the roar of a fire coming to life, I knew this would be the end. It had to be. No more.

In the days, weeks, and months that followed, it was determined that Noreen, so distraught over her daughter's disappearance, decided to take her own life in an abandoned cabin in Cross Creek County Park, up in West Middletown, about an hour north of where she lived. Her husband said she'd often talked about her fondness for Cross Creek Park, although he'd been unaware that she'd ever visited and had no idea whose cabin that had been. I wanted to assure everyone that Noreen hadn't felt a thing, but I knew I couldn't. I moved on like I said I would, knowing that the many lives that had changed—and ended—over the course of those eight years had been my fault. If only I'd locked that classroom door. I'd have to carry that with me forever, or at least until this sickness takes the memories from me. Noreen Garland was dead. The killing was finally over.

She left me with one final task to complete before I could move on with my new life. That task was wrapped in a dirty sheet in the trunk of my car.

I had one more body to bury.

I had to put Sonia back one last time.

67

It was midafternoon, almost three. Susan was exhausted. She was on her fifth cup of coffee, struggling to read the reports on her computer, her eyes sliding in and out of focus, heavy with fatigue. The background check on Cynthia Garland was typical. She was single, lived alone in a house in King of Prussia, Pennsylvania, west of Philadelphia. Aside from hosting and producing her somewhat popular podcast, she worked as a customer service rep for a dog food manufacturer in Wayne County and had been there since moving to the area fourteen years prior. She had no arrests, no parking tickets, and no traffic violations. She paid her taxes on time and volunteered at a homeless shelter in West Philadelphia. Cynthia Garland appeared to be the quintessential law-abiding citizen, conscious of those around her who were less fortunate, and always there to provide help.

The Upper Merion Police Department checked on her house as well as her place of employment. The house had been empty, and her work said that she'd gone on short-term leave for a family emergency about a month ago. Considering she had no living family, Susan knew this had to have been the beginning of the execution of her plan with Rebecca, but the details of the plan and the location of where the rest of that plan was being carried out remained a mystery. Her podcast was still uploading new episodes, and the tech team out of Manhattan HQ was trying to trace where that connection was coming from. That could be the key they were missing.

The BOLOs issued for Cynthia, David Hill, Rebecca Hill, and James Darville had been updated to include New Jersey, Pennsylvania, and Ohio. Almost the entire Northeast was looking for the old man and the crew who took him. Now it was a matter of waiting to see what someone might find.

Susan yawned as she scrolled through Rebecca Hill's phone records again, this time looking at each occurrence of Cynthia Garland's number. The call frequency diminished the closer it got to the date of Cynthia's leave from work; it looked like once the plan had really gotten rolling, they'd moved to disposable cell phones. They'd had no reason to think they would ever get caught, but everything began to unravel when they killed the trooper. No one could have foreseen that.

The phone rang at her desk, and she picked it up with one hand while printing some records from the screen. "Adler."

"Hey, it's John Chu."

"What's up?"

"We finally got the extensive check back on James Darville."

"Talk to me."

"We had to cross-reference like six different databases, courthouse records, and medical files and trace his life through his social security number. We found a bunch of documents, and in one set we found court papers from a Madeline Foster seeking to change her son's birth certificate to her maiden name instead of the father's."

Susan gripped the phone. "Darville has a son."

"Yup. Lives upstate on a farm in Gloversville. Name's Trevor Foster. Born August 1985 to a Madeline Foster. James was listed as the father on Trevor's original birth certificate, but the mother got approval to change it. Remember the dirt we found in the Civic and the house?"

"Yeah."

"It's consistent with the soil composition of a farm in upstate New York."

Susan laughed out loud as she shot out of her seat. "John, have I told you how much I love you?"

"No, but I could use all the love I can get."

"I do. I love you very much."

She hung up and ran into the lieutenant's office; he was finishing up a call of his own.

"Boss! I know where they are. Darville had a son. Trevor Foster. He owns a farm up in Gloversville. I think we got 'em."

Crosby, still holding his phone, began dialing. "I'm rolling units from Troop T up that way, and I'll have them call in to the Gloversville PD for assistance. I'll instruct them to hold a perimeter until you arrive. Get going now. And take Mel with you. Lights and siren the entire way. Be careful."

68

Her fumbling hands struggled to find the right button to stop the tape. Sniffles and heavy, labored breathing filled the dining room. Cindy stared at the cassette player, James Darville's voice still resonating in the chambers of her mind. She felt no more panic or tantrums, no outbursts or screaming. Shock had taken over with each part of the story James had told on the tapes. She was calm now.

Trevor sat across from her, watching, waiting for some kind of reaction. She looked at him and wiped tears from her eyes with clenched fists. "These are lies," she said, trying to convince herself more than him. "He's lying."

"Yes, he could be," Trevor replied. "We won't know unless we get him to remember, and you're the only one who can do that. You know how to get him to talk. I've seen it. That's why you're here, right? To get closure? It's what you've been searching for since 1982." He stood from the table. "Or he could be telling the truth. It could've been your mom who killed your sister."

"It wasn't."

"But you have to leave open the possibility that it could have been. And if it was, this could also be an opportunity to get to know your real father before it's too late." He offered his hand. "Let's go find out if the stories on those tapes are true. James won't know to lie now. Not with his mind failing him. This is the time to get the real story about your family. And at the very least, you got a half brother out of the deal."

Cindy took his hand and got up from her seat. She followed him out of the dining room, and they walked down the hall toward the front door.

Trevor stopped. "Someone's here," he said, craning his neck to listen.

"Who?" Cindy pushed past him and looked out the window in the top of the door. A black BMW was pulling up the long driveway, headlights on in the dusk.

"Who is that?" she asked.

The car came to a stop in front of the house. The headlights shut off, and the driver's-side door opened. When she glanced back at Trevor, he'd gone pale.

"It's time," he whispered. There was panic in his voice. "Hagen's here."

"I thought you said Hagen was David."

"I guess I was wrong."

Cindy heard him run back down the hall behind her. She remained glued to the window. A figure climbed out of the car and looked up at the house. The porch light cast strange shadows, but there was no mistaking it was a woman.

"Who is that?"

Footsteps returned. Cindy spun around in time for Trevor to thrust a shotgun in her hands. She caught it against her chest as he looked out the window.

"That's Sara Phines," he said. "James's neurologist. She's Hagen. Or she's working with David, or he's working with her. She's David and Rebecca's connection at the hospital." His eyes were wide with panic. "We're all here now. It's time. She's going to kill us, and then she's going to kill my family."

"You don't know that."

"They didn't do anything wrong. They don't deserve this. We don't deserve this!"

"You talked to Hagen on the phone. You said it was a man."

"It was. At least I thought it was. The voice had that distortion to disguise it. I figured it was David, but it could've been a female. There was no way to know!"

"Okay, we need to calm down," Cindy said. "If she's Hagen, then she's just here for Darville. That was the plan all along. We knew Hagen was coming up here for him."

"No, things have changed. I know it. We've screwed up too much, and we're all loose ends now." He grabbed Cindy by the shoulders. "I don't want to die. I just wanted to be left alone. Why did you guys have to find me? Why is this happening?"

Dr. Phines was getting closer, the tall woman walking with her head down, balancing as she navigated the gravel driveway in her heels. Cindy held up her shotgun. "Is this loaded?"

He nodded. "Just pull the trigger. Pull the trigger and end this!"

"I'm not shooting anyone! We'll hold her until we figure out what's happening and use her as our hostage to protect ourselves from David, if he really is Hagen." She ran to the window in the kitchen and looked out from the back of the house. "Is David still with James?"

Cindy returned to the front door. Dr. Phines was walking up the steps to the porch. Cindy could hear her heels clicking on the wood.

"She's g-going to kill us," Trevor stammered. Panic had completely overtaken him. "My beautiful family. Oh my god, she's going to kill us all."

Before Dr. Phines could knock, Cindy opened the door and let it swing back on its hinges. She retreated a few steps down the hallway until she was between the front door and the dining room. A small table next to her held the mail basket, a mug that contained a set of keys, and two framed pictures of the family Trevor was so desperately trying to save. She held the shotgun up and aimed it at the doctor.

"Get in here and shut the door. Slowly."

Dr. Phines looked shocked, her eyes wide, her mouth hanging open. She raised her hands. "What's going on?"

Trevor was cowered around the corner, crying and breaking down. "Ask her where my family is. Ask her if they're okay."

Dr. Phines closed the door with her foot and stood still, hands in the air, her pocketbook strung across her chest.

"Are you Hagen?" Cindy asked. The gun was heavy in her hand.

"Who?"

"Hagen! Are you Hagen?"

"Please. I have no idea what you're talking about. I'm here for Trevor."

He squealed when he heard his name. "Oh my god, oh my god, oh my god. She's going to kill me. She's here to kill me. You have to shoot her."

Cindy tried to hold the shotgun steady. "What do you want with Trevor?"

"I have to see him."

"Why?"

"He knows why. Please. I don't want any trouble. Is Trevor okay?"

"Shoot her. Shoot her. Shoot her. Shoot her."

Cindy tried to concentrate, but a voice kept whispering in her mind.

Why is Trevor so panicked?

This is not the same man who killed the trooper and dumped the car.

It's his family. He's scared for his family.

He doesn't want to die. Not like this. None of us do.

We have to save ourselves.

"I want you to tell me who Hagen is right now!" Cindy yelled.

Dr. Phines was beginning to cry. "I don't know anything about a Hagen. I came here to see Trevor. Look."

She put her hands down and grabbed her pocketbook, reaching inside.

"She's got a gun!" Trevor screamed. "Shoot her now! Shoot her!"

Trevor ran from the corner he was hiding behind and pushed Cindy toward Dr. Phines, screaming in her ear to shoot her and save them. The sudden impact and the screaming startled her, and she felt Trevor's hand close over hers, another finger poking through the trigger guard and squeezing. The house exploded with a single shot, rocking Cindy and Trevor backward. Trevor let go and fell to the side while Cindy crashed into the small table that held the mail and the keys.

She'd been too close to miss. Dr. Phines flew against the door, the pellets from the shotgun shell ripping through her chest and stomach. She landed faceup, staring at the ceiling, the side of her body against the front door. Smoke filled the space.

In a matter of seconds, everything was still. Cindy's ears were ringing as she sat up. The only sounds she could hear were the two or three ragged breaths Dr. Phines took before dying.

Trevor scurried past her and knelt down next to Dr. Phines. He checked her pulse while Cindy tried to push herself to her feet. As she climbed to her knees, she noticed the framed picture of Trevor's family that had fallen off the table and shattered. She picked up the frame by its corner, and the photograph fell out.

The picture wasn't a picture. She could see the watermark from the stock photo website; the photo had been printed and placed in the frame. The thin matting around the scene of the pretty blonde woman and young boy had covered the advertisement and logo from the site. Now that she thought about it, Trevor hadn't been in any of the pictures that were displayed around the house. Not one. It hadn't registered until just then.

Cindy held her breath and looked over at him. He was whispering something into Dr. Phines's ear; then she watched as he kissed her gently on the lips. When he looked up at her, she could see a bit of Dr. Phines's blood on his chin. He smiled, and this time his eyes narrowed and the edges of his lips curled up higher than they normally did. He looked so completely different.

"Hagen," she murmured.

"Hello, Cynthia."

Cindy immediately raised the shotgun and pulled the trigger, but nothing happened.

Trevor shook his head. "Just one shell for just one purpose." He rose to his feet and wiped the blood from his hands with the bottom of his shirt. "You did good. I'm proud of you. It's nice to see something finally go right." He walked toward her, and she cowered against the wall. "I'm not going to hurt you, but we need to find the others. It's time to end this. We've waited long enough."

69

The ground was cold, wet, the snow about two inches deep. Within a few steps, his socks were soaked and his feet frozen. James staggered through the dead stalks, pushing them aside as he tried to run with no real destination in mind. Where was he going? What was his plan? His head was still spinning, confused at the reality of being in a cornfield instead of on the streets of Manhattan, where help from a stranger was supposed to be right there.

The sky was turning deep shades of pink and purple as the sun slid toward the horizon. He realized this was the first time he'd seen the sky or been outside that he could remember. The air felt good in his lungs and on his face, but with each passing moment he knew his body temperature was dropping. His sweatpants and sweatshirt wouldn't keep him warm for long. The wind and the cold would have him before the night was through.

He ran toward the silo, which was the only visible structure. The field he was in must have been hundreds of acres, if not thousands. The silo stretched into the purple sky like a lighthouse on a rocky shore. It was his only option.

James staggered forward, his feet so cold they hurt. His hip and knee barked with every step, but he pushed himself, seeing only the silo. Seeing his salvation.

There was movement behind him.

More movement off to his left.

Then his right.

James stopped and listened. The snow crunched lightly all around him, and he turned in time to see one of the ghosts—the girl—slipping in and out of the cornstalks. He looked to his left and could see the boy standing still, staring at him with those dead eyes that no longer held life or color. The boy smiled, and James saw his black gums and rotting teeth, one tooth missing. The sun was going down. They were coming for him. He had to keep moving.

"Get away from me!" he cried as he started walking again, stumbling through the snow, his feet hurting so much he could feel them burning.

The silo was still about two hundred yards away. There was no way he was going to make it. He began to lose his balance. Between his feet freezing underneath him and the fact that his legs had been immobilized for so long, his muscles didn't have the stamina to keep him upright and active. He knew if he fell, he would die where he landed. The cold would take him. Or perhaps the ghosts would get him first. Either way he'd be nothing more than a corpse by morning. He never should've left the basement.

The boy and girl were flanking him about two rows away on each side. He could see them on his periphery, their dirty and tattered clothes streaming behind them like tails on a kite. The wind blew, and the girl's hair pulled away from her pale gray face. The rot along her hairline was starting to pull her skin from her skull. And she laughed. The entire time she chased him, she laughed and skipped along.

The boy was quiet, concentrating on keeping pace. He ducked and dodged around the cornstalks, his brittle dead fingers pushing them out of the way as he went. His eyes were focused on James. No more smiles. No more games. They wanted him, and they knew they were close. The other two girls appeared a row behind the boy. They were all there now, tracking him, closing in.

James stepped and hit a patch of ice. His left leg slid out from under him, and he lost his balance, falling into the snow. He pushed himself up on his elbow and lifted his head. The sky was getting darker. From where he lay, he could no longer see the silo, but his feet wouldn't allow him to stand. He rolled into a sitting position and gently touched his toes. Pain shot through him. His feet were frozen. His hands weren't far behind.

The children were coming. They would take him, piece by piece, leaving nothing but ashes to be spread across the cornfield by the winter wind. James closed his eyes and waited for them. He didn't want to watch as they took their first bite, to feel the pain as they tore him limb from limb. He wanted to sleep. Just . . . sleep.

———

"Get up!"

James felt someone poking him, and he tried to open his eyes.

"Get on your feet."

So dark. Everything. No stars in the sky or lights anywhere he could see. His eyes *were* open, but it didn't matter. It made no difference.

"Get up now, or I'm going to hurt you."

Hands slipped behind his back and roughly pushed him into a sitting position. He looked around and tried to figure out where he was. All he could make out was the shadowy figure in front of him and the outlines of cornstalks as far as he could see. It was the black man who he'd seen a few times before. Or maybe more than that. He couldn't remember.

"Where am I?" he asked.

"Are you serious? You're in the fields. Could've died out here. No shoes. No coat. We probably should've let you."

"How did you find me?"

"Followed the tracks in the snow." The man grabbed him by his arms. "Get up."

James got himself into a standing position. Pain shot through his feet and legs.

"I can't walk. My feet."

"I don't care."

"I can't walk."

"You probably got frostbite or something, but you have to walk. I'm not carrying you. Let's go."

James felt the end of a blade press against his cheek.

"They stopped me before, but no one's here now. Just you and me. You killed my sister."

"No. I didn't kill anyone."

"I could pull this knife across your throat and tell them you tried to attack me and there was a struggle. Something like that. They'd buy it. I can be convincing. They'd buy it, and I'd deal with Hagen and the rest of them, and your body could rot out here."

"Please," James muttered. His teeth were chattering. "Don't kill me."

"As long as you keep walking, you don't have to worry about me killing you. Yet." He pushed him hard. "Walk."

"Where?"

"Back to the house. We're not done with you."

70

James felt the heat coming from the basement as soon as he stumbled in past the hurricane doors. His extremities began to thaw almost immediately, his skin burning as he got warmer. The pain in his hip and knee was a constant now. His body was failing him.

The familiar sounds of the city filled the room again, and James knew, at that moment, the honks and footsteps and calls for taxis and sirens were all just recordings, pumped through speakers he couldn't see. He looked toward the three windows, knowing now that there was nothing beyond them. He'd been trapped all along.

"We didn't want you to feel like you were alone out here," the man explained, following James's gaze toward the windows. "We knew you liked to visit Manhattan, so we found a soundtrack to make you feel more at ease."

"Who are you?" James asked.

"You don't remember me?" the man asked. He held up one of his fists, the knife occupying the other. "You remember this?"

"No."

"I'm Rebecca's brother. David."

James had to think. The fog was rolling in and out, and it was difficult to hold on to a single thought for any length of time. "I think I know the name."

"We've met a bunch of times, but whatever." David leaned in and whispered, "I'm going to get you for what you did to her."

"I didn't do anything. I love Rebecca."

David grabbed the back of James's shirt and pushed him into the wheelchair. Before James could wiggle away, David pressed his weight against him and pinned down each hand, then pulled zip ties from his pocket and fastened his wrists to each armrest. He did the same with his ankles, tying them to the footrests that were still raised from when he'd had the braces on.

The woman and the other man who'd helped him at night came down the stairs. The woman looked like she was crying. The man had a shotgun resting casually against one shoulder and an ornate wooden jewelry box under his other arm. Something in the back of James's mind clicked. He recognized the box. How did they know about the jewelry box?

The man nodded toward the upended mattress and the papers that had been scattered about. "What happened?"

David secured the last zip tie, stood up, and shrugged. "I have no idea. When I came in, I saw on the monitor that the room was empty. I came down to check it out, and I found everything like this, with the doors in the back open." He reached down and grabbed a few of the notes. "What are these?" he asked, reading them as he flipped through. *"They want to hurt you. You're in danger. They're not who you think they are."* He looked at the man and woman. "Which one of you did this?"

"I did," the man on the stairs said. "I tried to show him that he had someone looking out for him, but he kept forgetting what I was telling him, so I wrote these little messages to help him remember. Never worked."

David let the notes fall. "What are you talking about?"

"He's Hagen!" the woman cried. "All this time, it was Trevor. Trevor's Hagen!"

Trevor nudged the woman down the rest of the stairs and set the jewelry box on the landing. Before David could react, Trevor pulled the shotgun from his shoulder and aimed it at him. "Everybody calm down."

David could only stare, his hand clenching the hunting knife. "Is that true? You're Hagen?"

"It's true."

"Why?"

"I realize in the grand scheme of all this, it's going to sound stupid," Trevor began. "The bottom line was, I wanted a family. I wanted to start fresh with my dad, but between the dementia and him confessing to being an accomplice to murder, it didn't seem like that would be possible unless I silenced everyone who knew his secret. I needed to get you all up here so I could put an end to it. All of it. All of you."

James watched the scene play out before him as if he were watching a movie. None of it seemed real. The fog was in and out, confusing him at times, then clarity seconds later.

"When my father was first diagnosed with Alzheimer's, the hospital found me from some of his old medical files that linked him to my mother and me. They wanted to add me as a next of kin, make me responsible for him. I told them no. We were father and son in blood, but that was it. I never even knew the man, and at that time, I didn't want to."

The room was silent.

"They dropped it, but there was a note about me in the file that was given to Sara Phines when she became his new neurologist. She called a couple of times to update me about his treatments, and I started to warm to the possibility of having a second chance with my biological father. My mom was gone, and my grandparents had died years ago. I never got married. Had no kids. I was lonely, and this was a chance to have a family again. This was my chance to start new. I knew it would be short lived. The Alzheimer's was getting worse, and it would only be a matter of time before it took him away, too, so I decided to let him into my life. I decided I wanted a father."

The woman was still crying, standing alone, head down.

"I started digging into James's past and visiting him on the weekends, when I knew Rebecca wasn't around. He'd tell me stories when he could remember, and I'd tell him about my life growing up on this farm with my mom and my grandparents. It was good; things wouldn't always stick. One second he'd be telling me a story, and the next he was asking me to drive him to his class. One day he was having an episode and told me about killing Sonia Garland. He told me about what he did with Cindy's mother and how he still carries all that death and remorse around with him. After a few more visits of me trying to push him to remember, he showed me the hole in the floor and the jewelry box of things he kept down there to remind himself about what he'd been a part of. I couldn't believe it."

James tried to move, but his hands were fastened too tight. All he could do was sit and watch and listen to them talk about things he'd done but that he didn't remember. The other man and the woman were focused on Trevor, hanging on his every word.

"Then he told me about Cindy being his daughter, and just like that, our family grew. I had a sister. And she was someone who could be part of my life even after James passed. I was going to reach out to her, but then he started getting worse and couldn't control his thoughts or what came out of his mouth anymore. I think because I was making him tell me about what had happened, it was fresh in his mind, and he started blurting out details of the abductions and the murders. All of a sudden people knew his secret. Sara Phines knew. Rebecca knew. I figured it wouldn't be long before one of them told the police, so I decided to do something to help him. I mean, he was my dad, and I wanted to try and have a relationship with him before it was too late."

"You're crazy," David mumbled. "All this to reconnect with your *father*? All these lives changed or ended because you were trying to build this sick relationship?"

"No," Trevor said. "Lives were changed and ended because people got nosy and greedy and became liabilities. That was their own fault. I just wanted to protect my dad from himself. That's all."

Fear gripped James as Trevor looked at him and continued talking.

"I decided the best way to find out what everyone knew was to get close with Dr. Phines. I romanced her. Took her places. Did things to her and with her that hooked her for real. Once I had her trust, I made her promise she wouldn't go to the police, and she agreed. She told me how Rebecca had said James kept talking about kids he'd kidnapped and killed, and for whatever reason, playing *The Birds* seemed to trigger it. Sara also told me Rebecca had told her brother, which made sense, since she knew he was trying to come up with an idea for a book. I couldn't have that—right, David?"

David was silent, his eyes focused only on Trevor, his knuckles white around the handle of the hunting knife.

"And my dad just kept getting worse. So I set up cameras in the house to keep tabs on things. I watched Rebecca come in every day and put the movie on to try and coax a confession, while David sat around taking notes. Total exploitation. It was tough to watch, but at the same time, it helped me come up with this plan. I knew I had to get you all together in one place so I could stem the flow of information that was in danger of getting out and wrecking my new family. So I dangled a few carrots. I created Hagen and texted Rebecca from a burner phone, telling her I knew all about what James had done, and in exchange for helping me kidnap him, I promised a liver for their mother. Once she was on board, I knew she'd tell David and that he would be too. Then I had her contact Cindy with an opportunity I knew she couldn't refuse. I offered her the chance to finally learn the truth she'd been obsessed with finding for decades. All she'd ever wanted was to hear the real story about what happened to her sister, and I was the only person who could provide that. After she agreed, I had her contact me, and I played the victim, panicked after Hagen kidnapped my fake family. I had to show you all that I was in this with the rest of you, and you all bought it. It was easier than you might think."

Trevor took a few more steps into the basement.

"I thought if I could give Cindy the truth about Sonia, she'd forgive me for lying to her about being Hagen, and we could start fresh as brother and sister with our father. My new family. The plan really had a chance to work, but then Rebecca panicked and backed out because she'd grown too attached to James. That left us with the hooker. Then the hooker freaked out after we abducted my dad, and she became a very dangerous loose end. I had to take care of her. I had to kill the trooper after Cindy got pulled over, and when the police found Rebecca's car, I knew everything had gone to shit. At that point, it became time to just clean up the mess and go. No more games. No more screwing around. I would've done it sooner, but I had to wait until I could get Sara up here. She couldn't leave while she was a resource in an open investigation. It would've drawn too much attention to her."

David pushed tears out of his eyes. "Did you kill my sister?" he asked. His voice was a growl. He was so angry. "Just tell me. Was it you or James?"

Trevor ignored the question. "We never thought Rebecca's car would be found, so we didn't wipe anything down. They're going to find something that traces back to me, but by the time they do, everyone will be dead, and my dad and I will be north, living out the rest of his days together, at peace." He looked at James. "That's all I want for you, Dad. Just peace."

"Did you kill my sister?" David screamed, shaking the quiet room.

"I did," Trevor replied. "It wasn't James. It was me."

David suddenly ran toward him, arms flailing, knife in hand.

James watched as Trevor focused and calmly pulled the trigger of his shotgun. David instinctively threw his hands up to protect himself, but there was nothing he could do. The shot discharged, and his chest exploded, sending him sprawling against the back of the couch and onto the floor. Blood began to spurt from the wound, driven by his beating heart, his eyes widening in both panic and horror. Trevor stood over him as David looked up, coughing and struggling to breathe. He tried to cover the wound with his hand, but the blood seeped through his fingers and ran down his chest.

Cindy screamed.

"You sealed your fate the moment your sister told you what my father was confessing," Trevor said. "I told Rebecca the same thing. It's not your fault. You learned something you shouldn't have known, and this is how it has to end. I'm sorry."

David tried to speak, but only a gargling sound emerged from his blood-soaked mouth. The basement was silent as they waited for him to die. It didn't take long. The young man grunted once more, closed his eyes, and was gone.

"No, no, no," Cindy whispered, her eyes pooling with tears. "This isn't happening."

Trevor turned to look at James. "In case you haven't caught on yet," he said, "you're my father. You can never seem to remember lately. My mom was Maddie Foster. No way you remember her. You guys were just a fling. Met in Austin during some—"

"Teacher's convention," James replied without thinking. "Mideighties."

Trevor smiled. "That's right."

"She never told me."

"She lived here in New York, and you were in Ohio. She didn't want to mess your life up having to take care of us. It's all good, though. She moved me here to this farm, and her parents helped raise me right. No harm, no foul, as far as I'm concerned. She finally told me about you when she knew she wouldn't survive the cancer, but I never had any desire to meet you until the hospital called. Now I wish I had more time with you. Funny how life works like that."

He turned his attention away from James and walked toward Cindy.

"What do you think?" he asked. "You wanna be part of this family? Come up to Canada with us? You can't go back home. If the police don't already know about you, they will soon enough. Come with us, and we'll start fresh. You know the truth now. Your mother killed your sister. You can learn to let go of the hate you thought you had for this man and get to know him before he dies. I'll take care of you. I promise."

Cindy collapsed next to David's body and wiped her eyes, nodding slowly. "Okay," she whispered. "I'll come. What other choice do I have?"

Trevor smiled. "That's my girl."

James watched as Trevor turned to go back up the stairs. As he did, Cindy pulled the knife out of David's hand and lunged at her half brother, trying to stab him in the back. Trevor spun around at the last moment and grabbed Cindy's wrist, kicking her legs out from underneath her and landing on top of her at the bottom of the stairs.

"Get off of me!" Cindy screamed. "Get off!"

Trevor squeezed her wrist until her grip on the knife waned. The weapon fell to the tiled floor, useless.

"I'll kill you!"

Trevor shook his head. "Why?" he asked as he wrapped his hands around Cindy's throat. "You were the only one who got what Hagen promised. What I promised. You got the truth, and now you have an opportunity to start a new life with your new family. Why isn't that enough? Why can't you love us?"

71

By the time Susan and Triston had gotten up to Gloversville, Crosby had made the necessary arrangements, and she had a small army of police personnel waiting. Six troopers and a SORT team from Troop T joined four officers and a sergeant from the Gloversville Police Department. They all met about two miles south of Trevor Foster's farm, assembling in the parking lot of a used car dealership and reenacting the scene she'd had with the other SORT team at David Hill's house in Tarrytown. The officers formed a semicircle around her as she went over final instructions.

"We have reason to believe that Trevor Foster is holding James Darville at his farm," she explained as Triston passed out ID sheets with each person's name and photo on them. "Trevor matches the person we see on the dashcam video, so be careful. I'm also expecting to encounter his nurse, Rebecca Hill, but I'm not sure if she's a suspect or a hostage at this time. Treat her like a suspect. Rebecca's brother, David Hill, could be there too. Finally, we have Cynthia Garland, who we believe is the woman in the dashcam video."

The officers took the sheets and studied them.

"We have to go in fast. According to the property map, there's a long driveway that leads from the street to the house, and it'll be easy for Foster to see us coming. We need to get up that road and into the house before he, or anyone else in there, has time to react. I want teams of two men on each side of the house, a team of four men in the rear, and the rest of us through the front. Front and rear breach at the same time. We sweep, take down everyone we see, cuff them, and clear. Any questions?"

The men shook their heads.

"Anything we should know from the local guys that I missed?"

The officers from Gloversville also shook their heads. Everyone was good to go.

"Okay," Susan said as she made her way to her car. Triston was right behind her. "Let's do this. Fast and easy. No one gets hurt."

Each team hustled to their vehicles and climbed in. The two Gloversville cruisers led the way, followed by the SORT truck and then Susan. They left the parking lot in a rush, spilling onto the road, leaving clouds of dust and gravel in their wake.

The snow had already begun to accumulate up here and was piled along the curbs, dirty and brown even though it couldn't have been more than a few weeks old. The roads themselves had been plowed and salted and were in good condition.

Trevor Foster's farm was the third swath of land they came upon and a few miles away from downtown. As Susan crested a hill, she could see a few structures—a barn, a cowshed, a silo—and as they got closer to the main entrance, she spotted the farmhouse and iron gate welcoming them to Foster's Farm.

They flew up the long driveway and skidded to a stop in front of what looked to be a stereotypical farmhouse with an oversized wrap-around porch, peaked roof, and old shutters made out of wood. Officers and troopers spilled from their vehicles, footsteps crunching gravel and snow as they took their preassigned positions at the sides and rear of the main structure. Susan and Triston ran up the front stairs with the SORT team and stopped. This time there was no courtesy knock or five-second count. As soon as everyone was in position, they crashed through the door with the ram and immediately found the body of a woman lying in the hallway.

"We got a body!" Susan shouted. "Clear the house!"

The team began their sweep.

"State police! Come out now!"

"Gloversville Police Department! Come out with your hands up!"

Footsteps stampeded from room to room. Boots marched through the rear. Susan bent down and checked the pulse on the woman. Dead. She stood back up and watched as several officers made their way up to the second floor, weapons drawn and aimed ahead of them. She saw a pair of SORT members descend to the basement.

"State police!"

"This is the Gloversville PD. We are armed, and you're surrounded. Show yourself with your hands in the air!"

"I think we're too late," she said to Triston as he came up beside her. She could see beads of sweat forming on his head. "Whatever happened, it looks like they cleared out."

"You ID this one?" Triston asked.

"Yeah. Dr. Sara Phines. She was Darville's neurologist out of Phelps."

"How was she involved?"

"No idea."

A member of the SORT team approached. "We've got Cynthia Garland's car in the driveway. Same make and model. Trevor Foster's truck is there, and David Hill's SUV too."

"They have to be here somewhere," Triston said as he bent down to peer out the living room windows.

The calls began, one after the other.

"Clear!"

"All clear!"

"Top floor clear!"

"Basement's clear!"

319

"Dammit," Susan muttered. She walked down the hall to the middle of the kitchen and stood up on a chair so the men could see her. "Listen up! This farm is hundreds of acres. I want teams of two each taking a north, south, east, and west direction. Most of the fields are cut down from the harvest, so you should be able to see what's up ahead. Look for any structures where these people could be hiding. We already know there's a barn and a silo. Could also be sheds and other structures. All of the suspects' vehicles are here, so they have to be somewhere on the property. If anyone gets a hit, call it in. I also want units on the roads that surround the farm. No one gets out. If you need backup, call it in."

The team agreed and split up into pairs, tromping through the fields and onto paths that led in different directions. Susan stayed on the porch and watched them go. When they were gone, she pulled Triston by the arm.

"Let's move."

Triston tipped his cap. "After you, my lady."

They made their way up an uneven path toward the oversized barn near the main house. It looked to be in good shape, well built, sturdy. Inside, the barn was split into two areas. The left side was a staging area for the cows to be tended to. There were empty stalls and equipment Susan wasn't familiar with, but it looked as if maybe that was where the local veterinarian worked with the herd or where they were milked. She had no idea. The right side held most of the farm equipment: tractor, backhoe, loader, corn harvester. Next to the equipment was a large workbench full of tools and supplies. She and Triston checked the entire barn. It was empty.

"Let's keep going."

They walked off toward the silo, which was a shadowy obelisk in the middle of a cornfield now that the sun had gone down. Triston shined his flashlight as they worked their way in a southeastern direction. Susan was at his side, her Beretta ready. The only sounds were the other men on the grounds, searching for their suspects.

As she walked, Susan began to think about James Darville, confused and panicked about what was happening to him. She knew there was a good chance that he could already be dead, but her gut told her he was still alive. Her gut also told her she was running out of time.

Triston stopped when they reached the silo. "Look at that," he said, pointing his flashlight at a ten-yard swath of snow that had been disturbed. "You got footprints coming out of the cornfields where this snow is all messed up, but nothing past this point. Doesn't look like anyone went in the silo."

Susan surveyed the tracks. "I agree. But let's give the silo a quick once-over, and then we'll follow the tracks."

They walked as quietly as they could toward the silo's door. Triston pulled it open, and they both slipped inside. It was a grain silo, four stories tall. An iron spiral staircase was the first thing they came upon. They climbed the stairs quickly, Triston's light bouncing as he went. The interior was quiet but for their footsteps on the metal treads.

The stairs led to a small catwalk only wide enough for one person. Susan followed Triston about twenty feet out until they were standing over the grain that was packed below them.

"Nobody," Triston said. "Nowhere to hide."

"Come on. We'll follow the prints in the snow."

They made their way back down the stairs and out into the cornfields. Triston picked up the tracks with his flashlight, and they kept moving. The air was cold with the sun gone. The wind scratched at Susan's face and hands.

The footprints looked as if more than one person had been walking along this route. Susan stood on her toes to try and see beyond the tops of the trimmed cornstalks. She caught sight of a small house in the middle of the field, about two hundred yards away. If there hadn't been lights on in a few of the windows, she never would've seen it. But there it was. And she knew.

"We have a small outbuilding up ahead about two hundred yards. Call it in. They have to be there."

Triston nodded, shut off his flashlight, and whispered into his radio, stating their location and requesting backup.

Susan kept moving toward the house, stopping every few feet to look up past the stalks to make sure she was moving in the right direction. Her gun was drawn in front of her, and she could hear Crosby's voice in her head.

You need a partner on this one.

We all know what happened, and I've been trying to give you space, but on things like this, you need backup.

Damn him for being right.

72

"Let her go!" James cried, helplessly yanking on the zip ties that pinned his wrists to the wheelchair. "Please! I don't want to see anyone else get hurt!"

Trevor ignored him, instead squeezing his hands tighter around Cindy's throat. He was killing her, and there was nothing James could do to stop him.

Cindy's face had turned purple. Her eyes bulged from their sockets as her grip on Trevor's forearms began to loosen. She was about to lose consciousness.

"I wanted you with us," Trevor growled through clenched teeth. "I wanted you in my life. I wanted to love my sister and share things with her. But you don't want that. You don't want us."

James was about to scream again for Trevor to stop when the front door above them burst open. Even in the basement they could hear it crash against the wall. Trevor froze, loosening his grip. Cindy gasped for air, choking and coughing.

Someone was in the house.

Footsteps stomped above them. It was hard to determine how many people there were. More than one, for sure.

"Help!" James began shouting as he tugged on his zip ties. "We're in the basement! He has us both! Help us!"

The footsteps galloped toward the basement door. The man—he'd forgotten his name—looked at James, his lips curling back, showing his crooked teeth like fangs. "Why are you doing this?"

"Because it has to end."

"I'm trying to help you. I'm trying to save us."

"I don't want to be saved. Not anymore."

The man jumped to his feet and raised the shotgun. "There was no point in any of this," he said. "I should just kill you right now."

James nodded. "I'm ready."

The man stood there for a moment longer, the shotgun aimed at James's face. He closed his eyes and waited to die, but the man suddenly ran past him and disappeared into the darkness down the corridor. The hurricane doors opened just as the basement door above did the same.

"New York State Police!" a woman shouted.

"Down here!" Cindy coughed, sitting up and massaging her throat. "He went out through the storm door. It's Trevor Foster. He's getting away."

James watched as an older man in uniform descended the basement stairs and surveyed the scene. He pulled the radio from the clip on his belt.

"We got multiple suspects at the grain house. I got a man down. Looks to be David Hill. James Darville is alive. I'm placing Cynthia Garland in custody. Trevor Foster is still on the grounds and fleeing. Do you copy?"

James could hear the calls coming back from voices on the man's radio. They all confirmed the transmission and copied.

The uniformed man placed his radio back on his belt and made his way to James. "Are you all right?" he asked.

James nodded. "Yes, but you need to check the fish," he said. "They've been in the oven for too long. I think they're burning."

73

Susan scurried back out of the house and jumped off the porch, running around to the side where she knew the hurricane doors would be. When she got there, the doors were open, and she could see a fresh set of prints in the snow trailing away from the house and into the cornfields, toward the direction of the silo. For a second she thought about grabbing Triston to help her, but she heard the call over the radio. He had a scene to secure, and backup was coming. She couldn't pull him from that, and she couldn't wait for the others. Trevor was getting away, and he knew his own land better than anyone. She had to get moving.

It was hard to follow the tracks in the snow without the aid of Triston's flashlight. Susan moved as quickly and as quietly as she could. Muffled shouting came from all directions as the other officers and SORT team members closed in on the grain house. She moved on, alone.

You need a partner on this one.

She took a few steps and stopped, trying to listen past the voices that were approaching the house in order to hear movement in her immediate vicinity. She picked up the faint sound of snow crunching underfoot off to her right and up ahead just a bit. She burst into a sprint, then stopped to listen, then ran again. It didn't take long to track the footprints back to the silo. The door was ajar. Was that something she and Triston had done? Was Trevor Foster inside?

Or was it all a trap?

Susan took a breath and broke free from the cover of the dead cornstalks. She pressed her back against the curved side of the structure and looked out into the darkness, trying to see if anyone was there, beyond the first line of cornstalks. She stood up on her toes again and noticed several beams of light bouncing toward the grain house. She grabbed her radio from her pocket, and something banged against metal in the silo.

Trevor.

"This is Adler," she whispered. "I'm at the silo. Need backup. Going silent."

Before anyone could respond, she turned the radio off to keep it from giving away her location and slipped through the door, quickly ascending the spiral staircase as carefully as she could. Her breath came in short clips as she climbed, her thighs aching from moving so fast. She reached the top landing and immediately crouched into a shooting position. A silhouette stood in the middle of the catwalk, trapped, with nowhere else to go.

"Stay right there," Susan said, her voice echoing off the metal walls. "State police. You're under arrest. Put your hands in the air, spread your fingers, and get down on your knees."

"No."

She couldn't see if he was armed, so she stayed hidden at the top of the stairs.

"There's nowhere for you to go, Trevor. The farm is surrounded, and the only way out of the silo is down these stairs. If you rush me, I'll shoot you, and that'll be the end of it. But if you comply, you'll leave here alive, and then we can all figure out what happened."

"James Darville is my father."

"We already know that."

Silence.

"I have a gun." Trevor's voice sounded hoarse. He was still breathing heavily from running through the cornfield and climbing the stairs. "I could shoot you and take my chances in the fields. I could get off this farm without your guys finding me. I have the cover of night, and I know this place better than anyone. I grew up here. I know every inch of land, every rock and cave and hay bale I can hide behind. I know which trails lead where, and by the time the sun comes up, I could be a state away. All I have to do is pull my trigger and take my chances."

You need a partner on this one.

"If you shoot me and run, who'll take care of your father?"

"If I stay and surrender, who'll take care of my father?"

"I can help you."

"James made his choice back in that basement, and apparently it doesn't include me. He's on his own now. Just like I am."

Susan tightened her grip on the Beretta.

Trevor's silhouette moved.

"Stay where you are!"

Trevor hopped over the catwalk and in one motion was gone. Susan stood from her position and heard him hit the grain at the bottom of the bin. Her eyes had adjusted to the darkness, and she could faintly make him out, scampering toward the back wall.

"Stop!"

He ignored her and kept moving. The sound of screeching metal filled the space, reverberating in the cavernous silo. Susan tucked her Beretta back in its holster and jumped off the catwalk before she could talk herself out of it. It felt like she was falling forever; then she hit the grain hard and rolled against the wall, slamming the side of her head against the metal. It took a moment to realize she hadn't broken anything, and she scrambled to her feet, working her way toward where she'd heard the sound coming from.

It was an escape flap. She'd read that, after numerous cases of people being buried and suffocating in grain bins across the country, a lot of silos were required to have escape flaps installed in case someone got trapped down there. The flaps could be used for rescue from the outside or, as in Trevor's case, for someone from the inside to get out. Susan poked her head through and saw nothing but the darkness of the cornfield ahead of her. She removed her weapon from its holster, slipped out of the escape flap, found a new set of prints in the snow, and began tracking.

She no longer cared about sneaking through the fields or not being heard. She had to get to Trevor before he had a chance to escape to a section of the farm that she was unfamiliar with and had no backup stationed at.

She jumped as she ran, trying to see what was up ahead. When she saw the farmhouse in the distance, she knew. Trevor was either heading for the house or his car. She broke away from the tracks she was following and ran as fast as she could in a straight line toward the house, cutting down the distance and time it would take to follow the prints in the snow. The cold air burned her lungs as she pushed herself forward, the dead cornstalks and brittle leaves scratching her skin as she broke through them. When she got to the edge of the cornfield, she stopped and waited. She had a clear line of sight to Trevor's Jeep and the front door to the house. No way he could make it without her seeing him. Now it was just a matter of waiting.

"You make too much noise running like that."

She froze when she heard him behind her.

You need a partner on this one.

"When I stopped to see if you were following me, all I could hear was you crashing through the corn," Trevor said. He was panting, but calm. "Not the best hunter. I just circled back around and started following you."

She felt the barrel of the shotgun press against the base of her neck.

"I'm sorry," he said. "I have to do this in order to escape. It's the only way."

"Wait," Susan said, trying to buy some time. "You can't kill another cop. This has already gone too far."

"I'll do whatever I have to in order to get out of here."

Susan folded her arms against her chest and looked straight ahead. "You're making a mistake," she said.

"I'm not."

"You are. You never told me to get my hands up."

Before Trevor could react, Susan fired the Beretta that had been tucked under her armpit, pointing behind her. As soon as the first shot was fired, the barrel of the shotgun fell away from her neck. She spun around and fired a second shot, watching as Trevor Foster tumbled backward into the cornstalks and fell to the ground. Susan kicked the shotgun away, then stood over him with her weapon aimed until she heard the shouts of her backup finally arriving.

"Shot fired!" someone screamed in the darkness.

"It's okay," Susan called. "I'm okay. Suspect down."

It was over.

74

Saint Peter's Hospital was about an hour away from Gloversville, but it had the best facilities to treat a patient who'd had some physical injuries and who was also suffering from late-stage dementia. The EMTs on scene at the farm had sedated James, and the decision was made to transport him with a police escort to the Albany hospital. He'd been in and out of consciousness since he'd arrived.

James was treated for a mild concussion and a broken nose. The doctors also looked at his hip, and it seemed okay. His feet and fingers had a bit of frostbite, but that would heal. Had it been a month later and twenty degrees colder, it would've been a different story. In the limited amount of time they'd had with him, the police had tried to get his version of what had happened, but the old man's Alzheimer's made any kind of detailed interview impossible. They'd try again when he was more stable, but Susan had her doubts about whether they'd ever get more than what was already on the tapes.

Cindy Garland survived, with no injuries, and had been taken into custody at the grain house. She confessed to being the driver of the Honda Civic involved in the state trooper's death, and she confirmed Trevor had been the person who'd attacked the trooper and killed him. She was cooperating and had an audience from three departments collecting every detail of what had happened over the last few months. It was now her turn to offer the truth, and she felt she had no choice but to do so.

Susan walked down the hospital corridor with a coffee in one hand and her phone in the other. She smiled at the guard who'd been stationed outside Darville's hospital room door, and she was about to enter when she heard the nurse's voice from inside.

"Can I help you?"

"Just had to see this for myself," a man's voice said. "I can't believe we finally have him."

"And you are?"

Susan slowly opened the door to find a round man shuffling his feet, hands in his jacket pockets. She recognized him instantly. "Sheriff Brody. Wayne County Sheriff's Department."

Brody looked past the nurse and nodded toward Susan. "Hello."

"What're you doing here?"

"When you called me to let me know what happened, I had to come to make sure I wasn't dreaming. We've been looking for this guy since 1985."

"Quite a drive."

"Had to be done. Had to see it for myself."

The nurse finished her charting and logged off the computer. "Not too long," she called over her shoulder as she left. "He needs to rest."

She slipped out the door, and the room was quiet except for the muted beeping from Darville's monitors. Brody walked over to the edge of the bed.

"We got him," Susan whispered. "All this time. All those innocent kids. We got him."

James was asleep. Brody gripped the safety bar and squeezed it, his knuckles turning white.

Susan walked farther into the room and put her coffee down. "You okay?"

Brody shrugged. The weariness she'd seen in his eyes in Hawley was still there, but he looked younger, less burdened. Like a weight had been lifted. Yet at the same time, she could also see fear. "I don't know. All those years, hiding what I'd seen. What I'd been through. Those nights waiting up to see if this madman would come to my house and kill me or kill my parents or my sister."

"What are you talking about?" Susan asked.

Brody was staring at James again. "I lost years of my childhood worrying if he was coming for me. He had my name and address. He knew who I was, but I had no idea who *he* was. I never knew if he was coming for me."

Brody reached into his pocket and came away with a small piece of paper that looked like a business card. He dropped it onto James's chest.

It was a Boy Scout membership card.

Susan took a quick breath. "You're the Boy Scout at Cross Creek County Park."

"You listened to the tapes."

"I did. But how do you know about the tapes?"

Brody offered a small grin. "It's already been leaked to the press. I told one of the commanders that I was the one who got away, and they let me listen."

"You were so brave," Susan said. "I couldn't imagine going through that. I mean, Noreen tried to *kill* you."

"The tapes are lies," Brody replied, shaking his head. "Just a performance. If you listen closely, you can hear someone directing him. Noreen didn't do what James said she did. It was him. All of it."

"What do you mean?"

"When I ran into that cabin to help whoever was screaming, I saw James trying to kill that girl. It was Noreen who was begging him not to. Next thing I know, I was knocked out. I woke up tied to the pipe in the kitchen, and James was in the process of pulling out one of my teeth. Noreen was crying and pleading for him to let me go. Begging him to stop all the killing. He'd cut a piece of an old extension cord to tie my hands around that pipe and left the pair of scissors lying next to me.

While I was thrashing around from the pain of having my tooth pulled out of my head, the cord came loose, and I was able to free myself. The first thing I did was pick up the scissors and stab him in the shoulder. He fell, and I scrambled to my feet and ran. I was gone before he could gather himself, and I knew those woods better than anyone. I hid until dark, then made my way home and told my parents I got turned around on the hike. I told them I fell into a ravine and lost a tooth when I hit my head on a rock. I guess James panicked and tried to clean up his mess. He killed Noreen and burned the cabin to the ground. He killed her because he knew I was out there. I'd left my backpack behind, so I knew he'd have my name and address. My mom put my info on everything back then. But he never came after me." He shook his head. "It was all him, though. Noreen was the one trying to stop him."

Susan walked over to the opposite side of the bed and gently pulled James's hospital gown down from his neck. A small scar on his left shoulder was old but still looked raw. It had never properly healed.

"I'm the one who put that there," Brody said, pointing at the scar.

Susan watched James, still sleeping soundly with the help of the drugs pumping through his IV. He looked so peaceful and still, and for a moment, she had a hard time envisioning the monster hiding within his old and failing body. Sometimes you could look at a person and just never know. A wolf in sheep's clothing if there ever was one.

"You think we'll ever get the complete truth from him?" Brody asked.

Susan looked up at the sheriff. "We'll try."

"That would be a dream come true. After all this time. The absolute truth."

He started to cry, and Susan walked around the bed to hold him as his sobs grew louder in the quiet room. After almost forty years, the case had been solved, and the ghosts of the children could finally rest now.

In peace.

Forever.

75

Susan walked into the house, locked the door behind her, and leaned against it, eyes closed, pure exhaustion overtaking her. She'd been on the go for days now, and her body was starting to shut down. There was no more fighting it. It felt good to be home, and it would feel even better after a shower and some sleep. But first, she needed to see her mother and the twins.

"I'm home!"

Susan pushed herself off the door and made her way into the living room.

"Hello?"

Her phone rang, and she pulled it out of her pocket, smiling when she saw it was Liam.

"Hey," she said.

"I heard you solved the case. Congratulations."

"Yes, we did. Just got back."

"I knew you'd do it."

"Had a little help, you know. When you found Noreen Garland, which led to Cindy, all the dominos started falling. That was the string I'd been looking for to pull on."

"What can I say? I have friends in high places. A few favors called in, and we had our suspects."

"Well, tell them I said thank you."

"I will."

Susan could hear the back door open and close. "So my boss keeps telling me I need a partner, and now that you've demonstrated that you can do some real police work, I wanted to let you know that he thinks you'd be good to have around on a consultative basis."

"Are you serious?"

"I am. But just until you're able to find something more permanent. It'd be a good way for you to get yourself back in the game, and he liked the way you were able to contribute. He thought we made a good team. And I may or may not have slipped him a list of your credentials."

Liam laughed. "Like I said. Friends in high places."

"So you're in?"

"Can't hurt to talk to your boss, right?"

"Right."

"Mommy!"

"Hi, Mommy!"

The twins tackled her with hugs on the couch, almost knocking the phone out of her hand. She kissed each of them as they burrowed into her, showering her with kisses of their own.

"Sounds like the reunion is complete," Liam said. "I'll let you go."

"Okay. I'll see you next week when we come down, and we can talk about the consultant gig a little more. Good?"

"Count on it."

She hung up and tossed the phone onto the table so she had both arms for hugs. Beatrice came into the living room and sat in the chair opposite the couch.

"We didn't hear you come in. We were feeding the chickens."

"I'm home. Case closed."

Beatrice clapped her hands. "That's great news!"

"Get in here," Susan said as she waved her mother over. "I got room for one more. I need all the love I can get. I've earned it."

They huddled in their hugs, laughing and talking all at the same time, Susan taking it in and realizing how much she'd missed it. She was about to suggest they all go out to dinner after she had a chance to take a nap when movement caught the corner of her eye. As soon as she saw it, she heard her mother.

"Oh my!"

The twins turned and looked.

"Mommy!" Casey shouted. "One of the chickens got in the house!"

"They must've climbed up onto the deck again!"

"Who left the door open?"

They all piled off her as she got up from the couch. The chicken was trying to fly but kept bumping and crashing into things. It made its way across the floor and flew into the hallway.

"How are we supposed to catch it?" Tim asked.

"I have no idea," Susan replied. "Get a blanket, and we can throw it over him and bring him back outside."

Casey screamed with laughter. "Here comes another one!"

A second chicken walked into the hall.

"Someone close the back door!"

"He's trying to go upstairs!"

"Get him!"

Beatrice grabbed a blanket from the couch and handed it to Susan before scurrying into the kitchen to shut the sliding door. Susan took the blanket and spun around as the twins broke from her side and began chasing after the chickens, which had begun to climb the stairs. Time slowed as she watched Tim cross from the living room and run into the hallway, right over the spot he'd been avoiding for the past year. He ran across it without a second thought, focused only on the two crazy chickens that were heading up to the second floor.

"Come on, Mommy!" he shouted.

Casey was still laughing. "They're getting away!"

Susan chased after them up the stairs, laughing and crying and screaming, finally knowing without a doubt that everything was going to turn out okay.

ACKNOWLEDGMENTS

Writing a book is such a solitary thing, but so many people contribute to the finished product, and I'm grateful for each and every one of them.

To my agent, Curtis Russell of PS Literary Agency. Thank you for continuing to be my biggest advocate out there in the publishing world. You always shoot me straight and guide me as we build this brand together. You're always the first person to see my work, and your feedback continues to be incredibly important. I appreciate everything you do for me.

To my editors, Megha Parekh and Caitlin Alexander. This one was a bit of a struggle, and your feedback and suggestions were instrumental in getting me to shape this book the right way and to finally find the heartbeat of the story I was looking for. I think readers will really love what we've created here. Thank you.

To Sarah Shaw, Ashley Vanicek, and the rest of the Thomas & Mercer team. Your enthusiasm for my work means so much. Thank you for everything you do out in the marketplace to make sure my books get into the hands of the readers.

Special shout-out to the line editors and copyeditors who keep things in order so the story is one cohesive (and readable) thing. What you do is special, and I'm truly thankful for your help and suggestions.

To Crystal Patriarche and the BookSparks team. Thank you for helping spread the word about my books to the farthest reaches of the book-reading community. I love all the new and creative ideas you've come up with to let readers know about me and my work. Couldn't do this without you guys.

To Investigator Brian Martin of the New York State Police, Manhattan. This is the second book you've helped me on. Thank you for your insight on the inner workings of the state police and for responding to strange texts that come out of nowhere about murder, protocols, and random procedural questions. If I got anything wrong, that's on me.

To my family and friends, who continue to support me. I love you all and thank you from the bottom of my heart.

To my wife, Cathy. This wild journey keeps chugging along, and I'm so glad you're by my side to share it with me. I love you.

To my two daughters, Mackenzie and Jillian. As I stated in my previous book, you two are the inspiration behind everything that's good, pure, loving, and strong about Susan Adler. When I tell her story, I see you two in my mind. I love you.

Finally, a *huge* thank-you to my readers. Your ongoing support and willingness to spread the word about my books is so inspiring. I'm forever grateful that out of all the novels you can buy and read, you choose mine. I hope you continue to enjoy my stories and share your reading experiences with me. I write for you, and as I always say, thank you for reading.

ABOUT THE AUTHOR

Photo © 2019 Mima Photography

Matthew Farrell lives in the Hudson Valley, just outside of New York City, with his wife and two daughters. Get caught up on the progress of his next thriller along with his general musings by following him on Twitter @mfarrellwriter or Instagram at mfarrellwriterbooks or by liking him on Facebook: www.facebook.com/mfarrellwriter2.